PRAISE FOR
JOEL C. ROSENBERG

"His penetrating knowledge of all things Mideastern—coupled with his intuitive knack for high-stakes intrigue—demand attention."

PORTER GOSS
Former director of the Central Intelligence Agency

"If there were a *Forbes* 400 list of great current novelists, Joel Rosenberg would be among the top ten. . . . One of the most entertaining and intriguing authors of international political thrillers in the country. . . . His novels are un-put-downable."

STEVE FORBES
Editor in chief, *Forbes* magazine

"One of my favorite things: An incredible thriller—it's called *The Third Target* by Joel C. Rosenberg. . . . He's amazing. . . . He writes the greatest thrillers set in the Middle East, with so much knowledge of that part of the world. . . . Fabulous! I've read every book he's ever written!"

KATHIE LEE GIFFORD
NBC's *Today Show*

"Fascinating and compelling . . . way too close to reality for a novel."

MIKE HUCKABEE
Former Arkansas governor

"[Joel Rosenberg] understands the grave dangers posed by Iran and Syria, and he's been a bold and courageous voice for true peace and security in the Middle East."

DANNY AYALON
Israeli deputy foreign minister

"Joel has a particularly clear understanding of what is going on in today's Iran and Syria and the grave threat these two countries pose to the rest of the world."

REZA KAHLILI
Former CIA operative in Iran and bestselling author of *A Time to Betray: The Astonishing Double Life of a CIA Agent Inside the Revolutionary Guards of Iran*

"Joel Rosenberg is unsurpassed as the writer of fiction thrillers! Sometimes I have to remind myself to breathe as I read one of his novels because I find myself holding my breath in suspense as I turn the pages."

ANNE GRAHAM LOTZ
Author and speaker

"Joel paints an eerie, terrifying, page-turning picture of a worst-case scenario coming to pass. You have to read [*Damascus Countdown*], and then pray it never happens."

RICK SANTORUM
Former U.S. senator

THE
FIRST
HOSTAGE

A J.B. COLLINS NOVEL

JOEL C.
ROSENBERG

TYNDALE HOUSE PUBLISHERS, INC., CAROL STREAM, ILLINOIS

Visit Tyndale online at www.tyndale.com.

Visit Joel C. Rosenberg's website at www.joelrosenberg.com.

TYNDALE and Tyndale's quill logo are registered trademarks of Tyndale House Publishers, Inc.

The First Hostage: A J. B. Collins Novel

Copyright © 2015 by Joel C. Rosenberg. All rights reserved.

Cover photograph of seal copyright © Ironman Stabler Imagery/ Getty Images. All rights reserved.

Author photograph taken by Stephen Vosloo. Copyright © 2014 by Tyndale House Publishers, Inc. All rights reserved.

Designed by Dean H. Renninger

Scripture quotations are taken from the New American Standard Bible,® copyright © 1960, 1962, 1963, 1968, 1971, 1972, 1973, 1975, 1977, 1995 by The Lockman Foundation. Used by permission.

The First Hostage is a work of fiction. Where real people, events, establishments, organizations, or locales appear, they are used fictitiously. All other elements of the novel are drawn from the author's imagination.

For information about special discounts for bulk purchases, please contact Tyndale House Publishers at csresponse@tyndale.com, or call 1-800-323-9400.

ISBN 978-1-4964-0628-6 (International Trade Paper Edition)
ISBN 978-1-4964-2328-3 (mass paper)

Printed in the United States of America

23   22   21   20   19   18   17
7   6   5   4   3   2   1

To our son Jacob, a brave and steady

soul in dark and troubled times.

"Blessed is the man who fears the Lord,

who greatly delights in His commandments. . . .

He will not fear evil tidings; his heart is steadfast."

PSALM 112:1, 7

CAST OF CHARACTERS

★ ★ ★

JOURNALISTS

J. B. Collins—foreign correspondent for the *New York Times*

Allen MacDonald—foreign editor for the *New York Times*

AMERICANS

Harrison Taylor—president of the United States

Martin Holbrooke—vice president of the United States

Marco Ramirez—lieutenant general, commander of Delta Force

Jack Vaughn—director of the Central Intelligence Agency

Robert Khachigian—former director of the CIA

Arthur Harris—special agent with the Federal Bureau of Investigation

Matthew Collins—J. B.'s older brother

JORDANIANS

King Abdullah II—the monarch of the Hashemite Kingdom of Jordan

Prince Marwan Talal—uncle of the king of Jordan and a senior advisor

Prince Feisal bin al-Hussein—brother of the king of Jordan and deputy supreme commander of the Jordanian armed forces

Abdul Jum'a—lieutenant general, head of the army

Ibrahim al-Mufti—major general, head of the air force

Yusef Sharif—colonel and senior advisor to and chief spokesman for the king

Mohammed Hammami—the king's personal physician

Ali Sa'id—chief of security for the Royal Court

TERRORISTS

Abu Khalif—leader of the Islamic State in Iraq and al-Sham (ISIS)

Jamal Ramzy—commander of ISIS rebel forces in Syria and cousin of Abu Khalif

ISRAELIS

Daniel Lavi—Israeli prime minister

Ari Shalit—deputy director of the Mossad

Yael Katzir—Mossad agent

PALESTINIANS

Salim Mansour—president of the Palestinian Authority

Youssef Kuttab—senior aide to President Mansour

EGYPTIANS

Amr El-Badawy—general, commander of Egyptian special forces

PREFACE

★ ★ ★

from *The Third Target*

AL-HUMMAR PALACE, AMMAN, JORDAN

Two Jordanian F-16s caught my eye.

They were flying combat air patrol, keeping any stray aircraft—Jordanian or otherwise—out of this corridor, away from the palace and away from the peace summit. Both were quite a ways off in the distance, but what seemed odd was that while they had been flying from left to right across the horizon, heading from south to north, one of them was now turning right and banking toward the palace. Was that normal? It didn't seem so. Several pairs of fighter jets had been crisscrossing the skies over Amman for the last half hour or so in the same predictable manner. So why the deviation?

The jet was still several miles away, but there was no question it was headed in our direction. I turned and whispered to Ali Sa'id, chief of security for the Royal Court.

"What's going on with that F-16?" I asked. "He's broken off from his wingman."

Sa'id had been scanning the crowd, not the

skies, so he didn't immediately respond. But a moment later, he said something in Arabic over his wrist-mounted radio. Then he whispered back, "Stay calm, but come with me, both of you."

Startled, I had a hard time taking my eyes off the plane, but when I saw Sa'id get up and walk toward the doorway from which we had come, I followed his lead. Yael Katzir was right behind me. The band was playing again.

"Where are we going?" I asked Sa'id.

"The command center."

"Why? What do you think's going on?"

"I'm not sure," he conceded. "But I'm not bringing His Majesty out here until I know."

As he said this, I turned and took one last look at the F-16 before going inside. And at that very moment I saw a flash of light and a contrail. The pilot had just fired a missile.

A moment later we felt the explosion.

Inside the palace's security command center, I turned to check on Yael.

The Mossad agent had a large gash on her forehead and was bleeding profusely. I called for a first aid kit, and one of the watch commanders rushed to my side with one. As I bandaged her up, though, Yael gasped. At first I thought I had hurt her further. But when I saw her eyes grow wide, I turned to see what she was looking at.

On the video monitors in the command post, I could now see dump trucks and cement trucks loaded with explosives making speed dashes for the outer gates of the royal compound. I watched as soldiers fired automatic weapons at them, but one by one the trucks were hitting their targets and erupting in massive explosions. Huge gaps appeared in the perimeter fences, and hundreds of fighters in black hoods and ski masks rushed through to engage in brutal gun battles with Jordanian soldiers fighting desperately to save themselves and their beloved king.

Just then the vault door opened behind us. Suddenly King Abdullah was coming out of the safe room and directly toward us.

"Ali," he said, "we need to go now."

★ ★ ★

Outside the palace, I could hear bullets whizzing over my head.

I could hear them smashing into the side of the armor-plated trucks. I could see round after round hitting the bulletproof windows, though fortunately they refused to shatter. But as I came around the far side of one of the U.S. president's Suburbans, I froze in my tracks. Prime Minister Lavi and President Mansour were lying side by side, surrounded by several more dead agents.

The king was crouched over them. I couldn't see what he was doing. Was he trying in vain to revive them or just mourning over them? Either way, it was no use. They were gone. Nothing was going to bring them back. We had to go. We couldn't stay out in the open like this.

At that moment, I went numb. I could feel myself beginning to slip into shock, and I couldn't help it, couldn't stop it. And then, as if through a tunnel, I thought I heard the sound of someone calling my name.

"Collins, they're alive!" the king yelled. *"They're unconscious, but they're still breathing. They both have a pulse. But we need to get them into the Suburban. Cover us!"*

I couldn't believe it. They weren't dead? They looked dead. They weren't moving. But at the very thought, I snapped to.

Sa'id opened the back of the truck and put down the rear seat to make space while Yael covered his right flank. Then Sa'id helped the king lift the Israeli prime minister and gently set him inside the SUV.

Reengaged, I pivoted hard to my left and followed my orders. Firing the MP5 in short bursts in multiple directions, I had no illusions I was going to kill many rebels. But I was determined not to let them get to the king or his family or these other leaders. All I had to do was buy time. The question was whether it would possibly be enough.

As the king and Sa'id put the Palestinian leader in the back, I continued firing. Then I heard one of the other SUVs roar to life. For a moment I stopped shooting. I looked to my right and saw a Suburban peeling off without us with two American agents in the front seat.

The Secret Service wasn't waiting. They'd gotten their man into a bulletproof vehicle and now they were getting him to the airport. We had to move too, and fast.

The king directed me onto Route 40—the Al Kodos Highway—and soon we were heading southwest out of Amman. We were now going nearly a hundred miles an hour, and we had a new problem. The king was on the satphone with his brother, who informed us that there was a police checkpoint at the upcoming interchange with Route 35, the Queen Alia Highway. The checkpoint itself wasn't the issue. The problem, the king said, was that it had apparently been overrun by ISIS rebels, and they were waiting for us with RPGs and .50-caliber machine guns.

"How long to the interchange?" I asked.

"At this rate, two minutes, no more," the king replied.

"What do you recommend, Your Majesty?" I asked, not sure if I should try to go any faster or slow down.

"Do you believe in prayer, Collins?" he said. "Because now would be a good time to start."

"I'm out of ammunition," Yael said. "Does anyone have more?"

"There's a full mag in my weapon," I replied.

"Where's that?" she asked.

"Here," the crown prince said from the backseat. He picked up my machine gun from the floor, removed the magazine, and handed it to Yael.

In the distance, I could see the interchange

approaching. Were we going to try to blow through this checkpoint? That, it seemed, was a suicide mission. And I wasn't ready to die.

A second later the issue was moot. Rising over a ridge off to our right were two Apache helicopter gunships coming low and fast. Yael noticed them first and pointed them out to the rest of us. Now we were all riveted on them, and one question loomed over everything, though no one spoke it aloud: which side were they on?

The checkpoint was fast approaching. So were the Apaches.

And then in my mirror I saw the 30mm open up.

"They're shooting at us!" I shouted.

I saw a flash. I knew what it was. I'd seen it a hundred times or more, from Fallujah to Kabul. Someone had just fired an RPG. I could see the contrail streaking down the highway behind us. The queen screamed. I hit the gas and swerved to the right just in time. The RPG knocked off my side mirror and sliced past. It hadn't killed us.

But the next one might.

I saw another flash, this one from the lead Apache. He too had just fired, and this wasn't a mere RPG. This was a heat-seeking Hellfire missile. There was no swerving or avoiding it. It was coming straight for us, and there was nothing we could do about it. We were about to die in a ball of fire. It was all over.

But to my relief, the missile didn't slam into us. Instead, we watched it strike one of the Humvees at the checkpoint ahead. In the blink of an eye, the entire checkpoint was obliterated in a giant explosion. Stunned—mesmerized by the fireball in front of me—I forgot to exit. I just kept driving. Then we were crashing through the burning remains of the checkpoint, racing through the interchange, and getting on Route 35, bound for the airport.

None of us cheered. We were relieved beyond words, but we all knew this was not of our doing. Forces beyond us were keeping us alive and clearing the way for us.

Soon we saw one squadron after another of Jordanian F-16s and F-15s streaking across the sky. I had to believe they were headed to Amman to bomb the palace and crush the rebellion. I couldn't imagine how difficult a decision that must have been for the king, but I also knew he had no choice. He was the last of the Hashemite monarchs, and he seemed determined not to go down like those before him.

As we sped along Highway 35, against all odds, strangely enough I actually began to feel a sense of hope again. We were still alive. We were safe for now. And I had the strongest sense that the king was going to prevail. He had been blindsided, to be sure. But he had enormous personal courage. He had an army ready to fight back, and he had the Americans and the Israelis ready to fight with him. But when we arrived at the airport, those feelings instantly evaporated.

As I surveyed the devastation around us, all hope disappeared.

The gorgeous new multimillion-dollar terminal

was a smoking crater. The roads and runways were pockmarked with the remains of mortars and artillery shells that apparently had been fired not long before we arrived. Jumbo jets were on fire. Dead and dying bodies lay everywhere. Fuel depots were ablaze. The stench of burning jet fuel was overwhelming.

And Air Force One was gone.

PART
ONE

"Virtuous motives—trammeled by inertia and timidity—are no match for armed and resolute wickedness."

WINSTON CHURCHILL
IN *THE GATHERING STORM*

1

* * *

"The president of the United States . . . is missing."

Even as the words came out of my mouth, I could hardly believe what I was saying. Neither could my editor.

There was a long pause.

"What do you mean, *missing*?" said the crackling, garbled voice on the other end of the line, on the other side of the world.

Allen MacDonald had worked at the *New York Times* for the better part of forty years. He'd been the foreign editor since I was in high school. For as long as I had been with the *Times*—which was now well over a decade—we'd worked together on all kinds of stories, from assassinations to terror attacks to full-blown wars. I was sure he had heard it all in this business . . . until now.

"I mean missing, Allen. Gone. Lost. No one knows where he is, and all hell is breaking loose here," I said as I looked out over the devastation.

Amman's gorgeous new international airport was ablaze. Thick, black smoke darkened the

3

midday sun. Bodies were everywhere. Soldiers. Policemen. Ground crew. And an untold number of jihadists in their signature black hoods, their cold, stiff hands still gripping Russian-made AK-47s. Anyone not already dead, myself included, was wearing a protective chem-bio suit, breathing through a gas mask, and praying the worst of the sarin gas attacks were over.

"But I–I don't understand," Allen stammered. "CNN is reporting Air Force One is safe. That it's already cleared Jordanian airspace. That it has a fighter escort."

"It's all true," I replied. "But the president isn't on it."

"You're sure?"

"Absolutely."

"There's no chance that you misheard."

"No."

"Misunderstood?"

"No."

"Fog of war?" he pressed.

"Forget it."

"Maybe somebody said it as a tactical diversion, to throw off ISIS or other enemies."

"No, Allen, listen to me—the president is not on that plane. I'm telling you he's missing, and people need to know."

"Collins, if I go with this story and you're wrong . . ."

Allen didn't finish the sentence. But he didn't have to. I understood the consequences.

"I'm not wrong, Allen," I said. "This is solid."

There was another pause. Then he said, "Do you realize what this means?"

"No," I shot back. "I don't know what this means. And neither do you. I don't even know for sure if he's been captured or injured or . . ." Now my voice trailed off.

"Or killed?" Allen asked.

"I'm not saying that."

"What, then? Missing and presumed dead?"

"No, no—listen to me. I'm giving you precisely what I know. Nothing more. Nothing less."

"So where do you think he is?"

"I have no idea, Allen. No one does. But my sources were explicit. Air Force One took off without the president."

"Okay, wait," Allen said. "I'm putting you on speaker. I'm going to record you. And Janie is here. She's going to type up everything you tell us."

I could hear some commotion as he set up a digital recorder, cleared space on his desk, and shouted for Mary Jane, his executive assistant, to bring her laptop into his office immediately. A moment later they were ready.

I took a deep breath, did my best to wipe some of the soot from my gas mask, and checked my grandfather's pocket watch. It was now 3:19 p.m. local time on Sunday, December 5.

"Okay, take this down," I began. "The president of the United States is missing. Stop. Air Force One took off from the Amman airport under a U.S. fighter jet escort shortly after 2:30 p.m. Stop. But President Harrison Taylor was not on the plane. Stop. U.S. and Jordanian security forces are presently engaged in a massive search-and-rescue effort in Jordan to find the president. Stop. But at the moment the president's whereabouts and safety are unknown. Stop."

My hands were trembling. My throat was dry. And my left arm was killing me. I'd been shot—grazed, really—above the elbow in a firefight back at the Al-Hummar Palace during the ISIS attack. It had been bleeding something fierce until Yael Katzir, the beautiful and mysterious Mossad agent who had assisted me in getting King Abdullah and his family to safety, had tied a tourniquet on it. That was just after we arrived at the airport, just before she boarded the chopper that was taking Prime Minister Daniel Lavi back to Israel for emergency medical treatment. I was going to need something for the pain, and soon, but I knew Allen required more details, so I kept going.

"The devastating chain of events began unfolding early Sunday afternoon in the northeast suburbs of Amman. Stop. Forces of the Islamic State launched a multiprong terrorist attack on the Israeli–Palestinian peace summit being held at Al-Hummar Palace. Stop. Just before the ceremony to sign a comprehensive peace treaty began, a Jordanian F-16 flying a combat air patrol fired an air-to-ground missile at the crowds gathered for the summit. Stop. The pilot of the F-16 then flew a suicide mission into the palace. Stop. Simultaneously, thousands of heavily armed Islamic State terrorists penetrated the grounds of the palace. Stop. Under heavy fire, security forces evacuated President Taylor, Jordan's King Abdullah II, Israeli prime minister Daniel Lavi, and Palestinian president Salim Mansour from the palace grounds. Stop. Lavi and Mansour were severely wounded and are being airlifted to Jerusalem and Ramallah, respectively. Stop. Witnesses saw a black, bulletproof Chevy Suburban driven by U.S. Secret Service agents whisking President Taylor away from the scene of the attacks. Stop. But that vehicle never reached the airport. Stop. Sources tell the *Times* the president learned the airport was under attack by ISIS terrorists and called the commander of Air Force One and ordered him to take off immediately to protect the plane and crew. Stop. The president reportedly told the pilots he would recall them once Jordanian military forces regained control of the airport grounds. Stop. However, at this moment, senior U.S. government officials say they do not know where the president is, nor can they confirm his safety. Stop. Neither the president nor his Secret Service detail is responding to calls. Stop."

I paused, in part to allow Janie to get it all down, but she was a pro and had had no trouble keeping pace.

"I'm with you," she said. "Keep going."

"I think that's it for now," I said. "We need to get that out there. I can call back and dictate more details of the attack in a few minutes."

"That's fine, but who are your sources, J. B.?" Allen asked.

"I can't say."

"J. B., you have to."

"Allen, I can't—not on an open line."

"J. B., this isn't a request. It's an order."

"I have to protect my sources. You know that."

"Obviously. I'm not saying we're going to include them in the story, but I have to know that the sources are solid and so is the story."

"Allen, come on; you're wasting time. You need to get this out immediately."

"J. B., listen to me."

"No, Allen, I—"

"James!" he suddenly shouted. I'd never heard him do it before. "I can't just go on your word. Not on this. The stakes are too high. A story like this puts lives in danger. And getting it wrong is only half the issue. I'm not saying you're wrong. I can hear in your voice that you believe it's true. And I'm inclined to believe you. But I have to answer to New York. And they're going to have the White House and Pentagon and Secret Service going crazy if we publish this story. So tell me what you know, or the story doesn't run."

2

★ ★ ★

Allen was right, of course.

The stakes couldn't be higher. But still I hesitated. I couldn't tell him *how* I knew. I could only tell him *what* I knew and that the story—however horrible, whatever the repercussions—was solid.

The monarch of the Hashemite Kingdom of Jordan—King Abdullah II himself—had just hung up from a secure call with the Pentagon. He'd spoken with the chairman of the Joint Chiefs of Staff. And he'd just relayed to me the essential details of the conversation. Did that count as one source or two?

I realized it could be argued that it was only one. After all, I hadn't spoken with the chairman myself. But under the circumstances I was counting the intel as reliable. The king had told me nearly verbatim what the man had said. There was no reason for him to lie to me. I could see in his eyes he was telling me the truth, especially after all we had just been through. And what he told me rang true with everything that was playing out around me. I could see for myself that Air

Force One was gone. I could see that the Chevy Suburban that had carried the president from the palace was not here on the airport grounds and was nowhere to be found. I had heard with my own ears when the king called his brother, Prince Feisal, the deputy supreme commander of the Jordanian armed forces, and ordered a massive search of Route 35, the Queen Alia Highway, the very road we'd just taken to the airport and the last known location of the president.

I knew the facts. But I also knew I couldn't directly betray the king's confidence. I couldn't run the risk that if I told Allen these details, some of them might wind up in the final story. I trusted Allen, but I wasn't sure I trusted his bosses in New York. What's more, I couldn't chance any errors. Allen had mentioned the fog of war, and I'd experienced the phenomenon myself countless times before. I knew mistakes could happen. I'd made my share over the years. I didn't intend to make one now.

I looked out on the burning wreckage of two jumbo jets as His Majesty strode across the tarmac. He was about to board a Black Hawk helicopter that had just landed and was kicking up a huge cloud of dust. Before stepping aboard, the king turned and frantically waved me over. He wasn't going to wait for me. If I was going to stay with this story, I had to go and go now.

It was suddenly clear to me that I was about to make a career-altering decision. The king hadn't specifically authorized me to tell the world what he'd just told me. But he hadn't expressly forbidden it either. He knew full well I was a foreign correspondent for the *New York Times*. He had to know I was going to call the information back to Washington. He could hardly expect me to keep this a secret. Still, it was a judgment call. He might have just been telling me as a friend, as someone who had saved his life. Maybe at that moment he didn't see me as a journalist but as an ally. Or maybe he wasn't thinking clearly.

I didn't want to burn a source. I certainly couldn't burn a king. But in my mind there simply was no choice. Americans had to know their commander in chief was missing. After all, weren't there serious national security implications at play here? Weren't there grave constitutional implications as well? Was Harrison Taylor still technically the president? Or in his absence had power shifted to the vice president, even temporarily? For that matter, where *was* the VP at the moment? Was he safe? Had he been briefed? Was he ready for what was coming? Was anyone in Washington ready for this? Then again, what was "this" exactly?

I had no idea. We were in uncharted waters. All I knew for certain at that moment was that the American people needed to know what I knew. They needed to know the facts. They needed to be asking the same questions I was asking. And people at the highest levels of the American government needed to be providing answers.

It was true, of course, that informing the American people that the leader of the free world was missing meant simultaneously informing the enemy. What would ISIS do with such information? Would it give them a tactical advantage in the current crisis? It would almost certainly give them a propaganda victory of enormous proportions unless the president resurfaced quickly, safely, and in full command. But none of that was my concern. My job was to report what I was seeing and hearing, regardless of the consequences to me or anyone else. I just had to make sure I didn't expose my sources.

Running now for the waiting chopper and fearing His Majesty might lift off without me, I shouted into the phone. *"Allen, I'm sorry. I hear what you're saying, but I can't do it. Are you going to run the story or not?"*

There was a long pause. For a moment I thought I'd lost the connection, but as I approached the Black Hawk, I could see that—incredibly—I still had four out of five bars of service and an open line to Washington.

"Are you going to run the story or not?" I shouted again over the roar of the rotors.

Allen's answer knocked the wind out of me.

"No, J. B., I'm not," he shouted back. *"Not until you give me your sources. I'm not a federal grand jury. I'm your editor, and I have a right to know."*

3

★ ★ ★

Hanging up, I jumped into the waiting chopper.

A soldier slammed the door behind me, and seconds later we were off the ground. To my astonishment, King Abdullah was at the controls. He still had his chem-bio suit on, as did we all, but he had taken full command of the situation. We shot hard and fast over the desert floor, then gained some altitude and banked east.

"Where are we going?" I asked the Royal Jordanian Air Force captain who had clearly been asked to relinquish the controls and was now sitting beside me, along with a half-dozen heavily armed special forces operators scanning both the skies and the ground for trouble.

"I can't say," the captain replied.

"Classified?" I asked.

"No," he said into my ear. "I just have no idea."

The king—a highly experienced helicopter pilot, not to mention the supreme commander of Jordan's military—was keeping his cards close to his vest, and given the circumstances, he was probably right to do so. He was in the midst of a coup d'état. Much of his government had just been killed by forces loyal to the Islamic State. His palace, his friends, and the region's hopes for peace had been destroyed by a traitorous member of his own air force. He clearly wasn't taking any chances with who was going to fly his chopper, and he was certainly not going to confide his immediate plans to anyone he didn't implicitly trust, which at the moment had to be almost no one.

Wincing in pain and feeling blood trickling down my left arm, I buckled up and looked out at the billows of smoke rising over Amman. Wherever we were going, I could only hope I could get some medical care when we arrived. I hadn't had time to examine the wound, and Yael hadn't had time to clean it, much less dress it. She'd simply taken the queen's scarf and tied it tightly around the wound before helping the queen and the crown prince into their chopper, bound for some secure, undisclosed location.

I closed my eyes for a moment and tried not to think of the excruciating burning sensation shooting up and down my arm. Instead I tried to turn my thoughts to Yael. Was she okay? She'd been twice punched hard in the face during a struggle with one of the hooded jihadists that had stormed the palace grounds—a struggle that had nearly taken both our lives. She'd also sustained a terrible gash to her forehead while we were escaping from the compound in the king's Suburban. But she'd never complained for a moment. She'd done everything she could to save the lives of her own prime minister and of the Palestinian president, even while protecting the royal family and me. Was she safe now? Were she and her team already on the ground in Jerusalem? Was Prime Minster Lavi going to make it? Was President Mansour?

Opening my eyes, I turned to the window and winced at my reflection. Aside from the cuts and scrapes and bruises on my cheeks and forehead— not to mention across my entire body—the face of an increasingly weathered and tired old man was staring back at me. I was barely into my forties, but a line from a Harrison Ford film echoed in my brain. *"It's not the years, honey; it's the mileage."* That was exactly how I felt. I was a foreign correspondent, a war correspondent, part of "the tribe" of reporters who cheated death and covered the news from the front lines of the most terrifying events on the planet. But death was catching up fast. I was an adrenaline junkie who had always loved jetting around the globe, living out of a suitcase, pushing the envelope in every area of life. But now I was also divorced, a recovering alcoholic, exhausted, and alone. My friends were dead or dying. My family was half a world away, and I barely saw them. I hadn't had a date in years. And no matter how hip and expensive my black, semi-rimless designer glasses were, they couldn't hide my bloodshot eyes. No matter how many years ago I'd shaved my increasingly gray head bald, I was still sporting a salt-and-pepper mustache and goatee. They no longer looked cool, I decided. They just made me look like a guy trying too hard to hold on to his youth.

Unable to take any more of myself, I shifted

focus and tried to make sense of the surreal scene out my window. From our vantage point, south-southeast of the capital, I could see squadrons of F-15s and F-16s streaking across the skies of Amman, dropping their ordnance on the ISIS forces below. I watched the spectacular explosions that ensued and could even feel the impact ripple through my body. I quickly snapped some photos on my iPhone and then took a shot of the king flying the Black Hawk before anyone could tell me not to.

My thoughts shifted back to the president. Where was he? Were he and his security detail under fire? Were they in immediate and over-whelming danger? Or was the Secret Service just lying low, keeping their charge out of sight and off the air until they had more confidence they could truly get him to safety?

Allen's refusal to run my story stunned me. The more I thought about it, the angrier I became. After all these years, after who knew how many stories—many of them exclusives—how could he not trust me now? Did he really think I would run with such a provocative story as the president of the United States being missing in the middle of a coup attempt unless I was absolutely certain? I didn't mind if he added caveats to the story, hedged the language a bit to make it clear this was a fast-developing story and the situation could change at any moment. To the contrary, that was undoubtedly the right thing to do. But he knew I was in the eye of the storm. He knew I was with the highest-ranking leaders in Jordan who were still breathing and fully conscious. Where did he think I was getting this information?

The whole thing enraged me. I felt powerless and cut off. Until I looked down at the iPhone in my hands. I realized we were flying low enough that I still had cell coverage. And just then it occurred to me that I didn't need to wait for Allen MacDonald or the brass at the Gray Lady to get this story out. I could do it myself.

A soldier offered me a bottle of water, but I waved it off. Instead, opening my Twitter app, I began typing and sending dispatches, 140 characters at a time.

> EXCLUSIVE: President of the United States missing. After ISIS attacks in Amman, Air Force One took off without POTUS on board. #AmmanCrisis

> EXCLUSIVE: Where is POTUS? I saw Secret Service whisk him away from palace, heading for Amman airport. But he never arrived. #AmmanCrisis

> EXCLUSIVE: Massive search for POTUS under way using Jordanian military, U.S. Secret Service, U.S. military assets. #AmmanCrisis

Over the next few minutes, I sent nineteen tweets. In many ways, I realized, the story read more dramatically over Twitter than it might on the *Times'* home page. This was the epitome of a breaking news story. Raw. Dramatic. Unfiltered. Fast-moving. And in this case, exclusive. If Allen and the brass in Manhattan wanted to skip the biggest story of our time, they could be my guest. But I had news, and I was going to share it with the world.

After getting out the core of the story, I then sent three more tweets using some cautionary language. I made it clear this was a fluid situation. I stressed my hope that additional reporting from other journalists—and disclosures from U.S. government officials themselves—would shed light on the situation. But in less than five minutes, the story was out there. Now all I could do was wait.

I'd never broken a story via Twitter before. It wasn't my style. In my heart, I guess I was old-school. I believed in filing dispatches and having editors clean them up and make their own decisions about what and when to publish. It wasn't just safer for readers—and for me. It wasn't just the way things had been done forever in the world of responsible journalism. I genuinely believed it was the right approach. It's certainly the way my grandfather operated, and I held him in the highest esteem.

Back in the day, back when Andrew Bradley "A. B." Collins was writing for the Associated Press in the forties, fifties, and sixties, he worked his craft by the book. He wrote up his stories on old-fashioned typewriters (hunting and pecking with just his pointer fingers as, remarkably, he never formally learned how to type). His dispatches were hand-edited by grizzled old men wearing bifocals and smoking pipes or fat Cuban cigars. His stories were rigorously fact-checked and sometimes heavily revised, sometimes even rewritten, before they were finally transmitted over the wires and printed out in the clackity-clack of cacophonous newsrooms the world over. He didn't like being questioned by his editors over his facts or sources. He didn't like being rewritten. No reporter worth his salt did. But he wasn't a rebel. He took his risks in the field, not in the newsroom.

Sure, occasionally when a story was breaking big and fast, he had no time to type it up and cable it to his editors. Sometimes he had to phone in his stories from exotic locales to the news desk in London or New York. But my grandfather would never have even imagined doing an end run around his editors. They were the gatekeepers. Everything went through them. That's just the way it was done. That was the system. And my grandfather respected the system.

I did too. Or I had until now. It had never occurred to me to "publish" my interview with Jamal Ramzy, the ISIS commander in Syria, via Twitter or Facebook or some other social media just moments after I'd finished talking to him. Nor had it occurred to me to tweet out the story of the prison break at Abu Ghraib or the grisly sarin gas tests conducted by Abu Khalif and Jamal Ramzy in Mosul. To the contrary, I knew such stories needed Allen's critical eye and the go-ahead from those above him. If I could convince them of the story's merit, and if they were satisfied with the care I'd taken to write it, then they'd publish it—and not a moment earlier.

But this was different. This story was too big to hold, too important to sit on. I couldn't reach millions of people directly, the way the front page of the *New York Times* or the home page of the official website could. But I had 183,000 followers on Twitter. People all over the country and all over the world were tracking my stories. More importantly, most of my fellow war correspondents and most of the reporters, editors, and producers in Washington and numerous foreign capitals followed me, as did political, military, and intelligence officials throughout the U.S. government, NATO, the Middle East, the Kremlin, and the Far East. I could guarantee they were all tracking their Twitter accounts right now. They were all desperate for any scrap of information from inside the battle zone.

By "publishing" this story directly, at least I could reach people who could reach others—many others—and fast.

4

★ ★ ★

The story instantly blew up the Internet.

As I scanned my notifications screen, I could watch in real time as reporters and various Middle East experts and analysts started retweeting my news flashes. Their readers then retweeted, others retweeted them again, and the story spread at an exponential rate. The feedback effect was stunning.

Preternaturally, Matt Drudge picked up the scent almost immediately. He and his colleagues quickly cobbled together my tweets into an article of sorts and made this the lead story on his site— complete with his trademark red siren—with a simple yet stunning tabloid headline: **POTUS Missing in Amman.**

Within minutes, Drudge's version of my story became the biggest trending topic on Twitter worldwide. Reporters began instant-messaging me questions, probing for more details. Rather than respond to them each directly, I started tweeting out the photos I'd just taken over Amman and providing tidbits of detail and context as best I could. I couldn't possibly report all that I'd seen and heard over the past few hours. Not 140 characters at a time. But as we shot across the eastern edges of the capital, flying low and fast, barely above the rooftops, I came to the horrifying realization that most if not all of the other reporters who had been covering the peace summit were now dead or dying. Most of the TV crews and satellite trucks providing coverage from the palace had been wiped out in the attacks. Across the world, live streams had been cut off midtransmission. Anchors back in their home studios had been left hanging, unsure at first why their feeds had been cut. What images had gotten out to the world? Any? How much on-the-ground reporting from Amman was actually taking place?

A few minutes later we were on approach to a large air force base located in Marka, a suburb northeast of Amman. I recognized the base immediately. It was named after the first King Abdullah and served as the general headquarters of the Royal Jordanian Air Force and the home base of three squadrons of attack aircraft, including advanced F-16 Fighting Falcons and older Northrop F-5s.

As we touched down outside the main air command center, I put my phone down. I could see that the base was heavily fortified by tanks, armored personnel carriers, and well-armed soldiers. I saw sharpshooters strategically positioned on numerous roofs as well. But I refrained from snapping any photos. There were lines I didn't dare cross.

When the side door opened, the special forces

operators around me jumped out and took up positions around the chopper. They knew the king was a target, and they were taking no chances.

I unfastened my seat belt and then caught a glimpse of Prince Feisal bin al-Hussein. He was flanked by an enormous security detail, and they were moving toward us rapidly. The prince was not a big man, but he was taller than I'd imagined, well built, a classic professional soldier, with closely cropped black hair graying a bit at the temples. He sported a small mustache and a somber expression and wore fatigues and combat boots, not his formal dress uniform. As deputy supreme commander of the Jordanian armed forces, he was the highest ranking officer after only His Majesty himself. He glanced at me somewhat coldly and then at his brother. It was clear he wasn't coming to bring greetings but only to get the king quickly and safely inside the command center.

Abdullah climbed out of the cockpit and removed the chem-bio suit. Following his lead, I removed mine as the king returned his brother's salute.

"Your family is safe?" the king asked.

The prince nodded, then quickly assured his brother that the queen, the crown prince, and the king's other children were safe as well.

"And the president?" His Majesty asked.

"Wait till we're inside," the prince replied, anxious to get the king safely out of any potential line of fire and apparently not prepared to discuss the president's situation in the open.

The king started moving toward the door, then

turned suddenly and said, "Feisal, where are my manners? There's someone you need to meet."

"Yes, Mr. Collins from the *Times*—the pleasure's mine," the prince replied without emotion or any apparent real interest. He clearly knew who I was and had been aware I was coming, but it was also clear in his eyes that he didn't like the notion of my presence at this place at this time one bit.

Even so, he reached out and gave me a firm handshake, but he had no intention of standing on the tarmac making small talk. Again he urged His Majesty to come inside, and the king agreed. With the security detail flanking us, we moved briskly into the lobby of the GHQ—general headquarters—which was filled with more soldiers on full alert, then headed down several flights of stairs until we passed through a vault-like door to a bunker that stank of stale cigarettes. As we entered, the head of the prince's detail prepared to close the vault behind us, but Feisal held up his hand and motioned him to wait a moment. Then he pulled his brother aside and whispered something in Arabic I couldn't hear.

"No," the king said. "Collins stays with me."

"But, Your Majesty," Feisal protested, "given the circumstances, I must insist that—"

But the king would have none of it. "He stays—now lock the doors and initiate your protocols. We are at war, gentlemen. I want a full briefing on current status."

A spark of something flashed in the prince's eyes. Anger? Resentment? I couldn't quite place it, but I was close. Nevertheless, he had just been given a direct order by his commander in chief, and like a dutiful soldier he followed it.

All nonessential personnel were quickly ushered out. I stayed.

As the vault door closed, the king briefly introduced me to the elite few who remained inside the bunker with us. Lieutenant General Abdul Jum'a, head of the army, and Major General Ibrahim al-Mufti, head of the air force, were both likely in their midfifties. Colonel Yusef Sharif, a senior advisor to and chief spokesman for the king, looked like he was about my age, maybe early or midforties. Dr. Mohammed Hammami, an older gentleman, perhaps seventy or thereabouts, served as His Majesty's personal physician. The remaining four men were a young military aide who looked to be no more than twenty-five and three armed members of the security detail. As we shook hands, the king excused himself, stepping into an adjacent washroom.

"Have a seat, Mr. Collins," Dr. Hammami said. "Let me take a look at that arm."

That caught me a bit off guard. Nothing had been said in my presence about my injuries, but the king must have radioed ahead. I did as I was told; as I sat, I noticed for the first time my blood-drenched sleeve. The doctor asked me to take off my shirt, but the pain was too much to raise my left arm over my head. Eventually, with no small amount of difficulty and discomfort, I both unbuttoned and removed the shirt only to reveal the queen's now-crimson scarf-turned-tourniquet. The doctor opened his bag, withdrew a pair of scissors, rubbing alcohol, and some gauze. He cut away the scarf and examined my injuries.

"You're a lucky man, Mr. Collins," he said after a moment. "This isn't nearly as bad as I'd been expecting."

That was comforting . . . I guess.

He asked me a few questions for his chart. "Full name?"

"James Bradley Collins."

"Date of birth?"

"May 3, 1975."

"Height and weight?"

"Six foot one, 175 pounds, give or take."

"In kilos?"

"Sorry—no idea."

"Do you know your blood type?"

"A-positive, I'm pretty sure."

"Any history of heart problems or other chronic medical issues?"

"No."

"Any allergies?"

"None."

"Are you taking any medications?"

"Not currently."

"Are you a smoker?"

"No."

"Good. Any history of alcohol or drug use?"

"How much time do you have?" I asked.

He just looked at me, didn't find me clever at all, and scribbled a few notes. "Past surgeries?"

"Broke my leg in ROTC at the end of my freshman year. They had to do three different surgeries to get it right. And that, my friend, was the end of my career in the American military."

Dr. Hammami wrote it down but didn't seem to care, particularly. Questions finished, he proceeded to clean my wound.

But Sharif, the king's advisor and spokesman, picked right up on what I had said. "You were in ROTC?" he asked.

"It was a long time ago."

"Which branch?"

"Army."

"Did you really want to serve in the U.S. military?"

"Actually, I wasn't sure. A bunch of my friends enlisted. I'd grown up hunting with my grandfather in the forests of Maine. I loved guns. I loved the outdoors. I thought maybe I'd wind up as a reporter for the *Army Times*."

"And then you broke your leg."

"And wound up in a series of hospitals for the next few months, so yeah, that was pretty much a wasted year."

I can't tell you how much at that moment I craved a drink. But I was fairly sure that in a room of reasonably devout Muslims, I wasn't going to find anything suitable, so I did my best to focus on something—anything—else.

I looked around the room. It certainly wasn't the White House Situation Room with its state-of-the-art, high-tech wizardry. Nor was this the handsomely appointed official reception room at the Al-Hummar Palace, where I first met the king. It looked more like a conference room at a Holiday

Inn or Ramada somewhere in the American Midwest: simple, spare, and without any frills. There was a large, old oak table—scuffed up a bit and covered in newspapers and used coffee mugs—in the center of the room, surrounded by twelve executive chairs that looked a little worse for wear. Overhead hung several harsh fluorescent lights. On the wall to my left was a large map of the greater Middle East and North Africa, covered in plastic and marked with notes and diagrams written with erasable pens of various colors. On the far wall was a large map of the Hashemite Kingdom of Jordan and several kilometers of each of its immediate neighbors. Directly across from it on the wall behind me was yet another large map, this one a detailed street map of the city of Amman and its surrounding suburbs, showing all major landmarks and military facilities, including the air base we were at now. These maps were also covered in plastic and even more heavily marked up, showing the current known locations of rebel forces and the movement of Jordanian military response teams. On the fourth wall, to my right, just over the door through which we had entered, were mounted five large television monitors. They were all muted but displayed live feeds from Al Jazeera, Al Arabiya, CNN, and two local Jordanian stations.

The young military aide quickly cleared away the newspapers and coffee mugs and emptied the ashtrays, then replaced them with Dell laptops and thick binders for the king, the prince, and the others. I turned my attention to the TV monitors.

For the first time I could see the images the rest of the world was seeing.

It was immediately apparent I'd been wrong. Many more images of the attacks had gotten out than I'd expected, and they were both mesmerizing and brutally hard to watch. All the networks were replaying footage of the missile strike and kamikaze attack on the palace and the ensuing scenes of horrific chaos and carnage from a variety of angles and vantage points. It was one thing to have seen black-and-white images from the security command post underneath the Al-Hummar Palace, as Yael and I had while the attacks were unfolding. But these chilling images showed far more of the magnitude of the destruction—and in living color.

The generals took seats in front of the bank of phones on the table and went right back to work, presumably getting updates from their men in the field. Out of the corner of my eye, I felt Prince Feisal's glare, though I disciplined myself not to look over at him. Not just yet. He clearly didn't want me there, and I didn't fault him. He had a rebellion to suppress. He knew full well there was a mole somewhere in the system, maybe several of them, who had known enough of the details of the summit to set into motion this devilish attack. He didn't know whom to trust any more than his older brother did. He certainly didn't want to trust a journalist, a foreigner least of all. I had to believe the very notion of having a reporter—a non-Jordanian, non-Arab, non-Muslim, non-Hashemite reporter—in his command bunker while he was orchestrating a massive counterassault against the forces of ISIS and an extensive search and rescue to find the president of the United States must have seemed nonsensical and unbearable.

It made me wonder why, in fact, the king would keep me around. I certainly didn't have the security clearance to be in the war room at such a time as this. Surely the king, who still hadn't come back into the room, was taking a moment to consider his brother's counsel. It was one thing to show me a measure of kindness and hospitality given the role I'd just played in saving his life. But now the king had serious work to do. There was no reason whatsoever to keep me around.

But if—and more likely, when—he kicked me out, what exactly would I do? Where would I go? Would I be stuck in the lobby upstairs with no sources, no access, perhaps not even any ability to communicate with the outside world, in the middle of a base in full lockdown and under imminent threat of attack by the forces of the Islamic State?

It suddenly struck me that not flying out with Yael and the prime minister might have been a serious mistake.

5

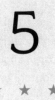

I decided I had to stay in this room, whatever it took.

It was the only way I would be able to cover the hunt for the president, a story of enormous import. But staying in this room meant finding a way to make peace with the prince. He very likely held the key to whether I stayed or was kicked out. But how was I going to win him over? Feisal and I had never met before. He didn't know me, and I knew precious little about him other than his public career.

I did know he was born in 1963 and was thus just a year younger than Abdullah. What's more, I knew the royal brothers had taken similar career paths, straight into the military. Abdullah, of course, had made the special forces his focus and had risen through the ranks to become commander of all Jordanian special forces before his father, the late King Hussein, had appointed him crown prince just days before passing away, thus leaving the kingdom to his eldest son. Feisal, by contrast, had focused on the air services. He, like his older brother, had gone to school in the U.K. and the U.S. Later he'd trained with the British Royal Air Force, completing his studies in 1985 and going on to become an accomplished pilot of fighter jets and helicopters in the Royal Jordanian Air Force. Over time, he had distinguished himself as an impressive airman and strategist. I recalled that in 2001 or 2002, Feisal had been appointed chief of the Air Staff and had been promoted to the rank of lieutenant general several years ago, later becoming deputy commander of all of Jordan's military forces. Beyond that, I knew the prince was married and had several children. But I didn't know what I could possibly say to convince him to let me stay. He was sitting on the other side of the table, working the phones but careful not to let me hear anything he was saying. I couldn't build trust if I couldn't talk to him, and I couldn't talk to him if he was on the phone. My anxiety was rising fast.

Dr. Hammami gave me a shot and then a bottle of pills to manage my pain. Just then, His Majesty reentered the bunker and we all rose. The generals saluted him. I merely stood there, waiting for the ax to fall.

The king told us to take our seats and turned to me. "Mr. Collins."

"Yes, sir."

"I understand you used our flight here to tell the world the president of the United States is missing."

My stomach tightened. "Yes, sir."

"That was a mistake."

I disagreed but held my tongue.

"I told you that in confidence. I never imagined you would tell the world."

"I didn't quote you, Your Majesty."

"You didn't have to," he replied. "The White House and Pentagon know you're with me. They know they didn't release the information. Nor would they. So that leaves me as your source."

I kept my mouth shut.

"Now ISIS knows. Iran knows. So do the Kremlin and Beijing."

No sooner had the words come out of the king's mouth than I saw a breaking news logo appear on the monitor tuned to CNN. The sound was still muted, but the network was clearly now going with the story of the potential death or capture of the American president.

I took a deep breath but maintained eye contact with the king. I wasn't sorry. I was doing my job. But I was pretty sure I was about to be kicked out of the war room, and I knew there was nothing to say that wouldn't make the situation worse.

"Your Majesty, may I make a recommendation?" Prince Feisal asked.

"No," the king said. "Mr. Collins, I need your phone."

"My phone?"

"You heard me."

"Why is that, Your Majesty?"

"Isn't it obvious?"

"Not to me, sir."

"I can't allow you to disseminate any unauthorized information, Mr. Collins. Is that clear?"

Not exactly, I thought.

"Does that mean you're going to allow me to disseminate *authorized* information?" I asked.

The king leaned forward in his seat. "Why else do you think you're here?"

"I honestly have no idea."

"The world needs to know what's happening here," he replied. "They need to hear it from a credible, independent reporter they trust. I've chosen you. You're going to be at my side during everything that happens for the next few days. However . . ."

"Sir?"

"While you're at my side throughout this crisis, Colonel Sharif here will be at your side. Nothing gets published in any way, shape, or form unless he clears it first. Do you understand?"

"That's not exactly the way the *New York Times* operates, Your Majesty."

"Do I look like I care?"

"No, sir."

"Do you want to report from the vortex of the storm or sit in the lobby?"

"I'll take the vortex."

"Very well. Now hand over your phone."

My iPhone was sitting in front of me. I slid it across the table to the king. In return, he slid back a notepad and a pen. We were in business—under military censorship, to be sure, but in business just the same.

The king then turned to his team.

"Okay, now, where are we in finding and rescuing the president?"

The prince took that one. "As you've ordered,

we have a massive aerial reconnaissance effort under way up and down Route 15, Route 35, and the adjacent roads. We're massing ground forces into the area as well. We're coordinating with the Secret Service, the Pentagon, and the American embassy downtown. But so far, nothing."

"How is that possible?"

"I don't know, Your Majesty, but we're doing everything we can."

"And you've beefed up protection around the embassy?"

"Yes, the American compound and most of the rest of the Western embassies too. But we're stretched very thin at the moment and . . ."

"And what?"

"It's a bit delicate, sir."

"You can speak freely."

"Well, sir, we're still not entirely sure whom we can trust."

"I know, but there's nothing else we can do right now. Keep giving orders and watch to see who obeys and who doesn't."

The king now turned to General al-Mufti, the air force commander. "Where are we with the palace?"

"Al-Hummar has been leveled, Your Majesty."

"There's no chance of ISIS getting control of vital papers or communications equipment?"

"No, sir—we've firebombed every square inch."

"And how many ISIS forces are we dealing with?" the king asked, turning to General Jum'a, commander of Jordan's ground forces.

"Our best guess is about fifteen thousand."

"Just ISIS?"

"No, ISIS and al-Hirak."

"The Brotherhood?"

"No—for the moment they seem to be standing down."

"How much of Amman has ISIS taken?"

"Our forces are clashing with them throughout the city. They've taken out the radio stations and captured two banks. But at this point I wouldn't say they control a single quadrant of the city."

"Do we?" asked the king.

6

"It's a very fluid situation just now, Your Majesty,"
the general said.

It was hardly a satisfactory answer. The capital
was under siege. Control of the kingdom itself was
in jeopardy.

"What about casualties so far?" the king asked,
abruptly changing topics.

"The prime minister is in critical condition,"
Prince Feisal replied. "Most of the cabinet is dead.
The mayor of Amman and most of the tribal
leaders we invited to the summit are dead too. So is
the White House chief of staff, the national security advisor, and all of the congressional delegation
that came with the president."

This was going from bad to worse so quickly I
could barely breathe.

"Where is Kamal?" the king asked, referring
to Kamal Jeddah, director of the Mukhabarat, the
Jordanian intelligence directorate.

"Kamal is dead too, Your Majesty," the prince
replied.

I couldn't believe it.

"So is Ali Sa'id."

That much I knew. Sa'id had died at my side. I'd been the one to feel for a pulse and find nothing, and hearing his name in this setting was almost more than I could bear.

"How many casualties overall?" the king asked.

The prince turned to General Jum'a.

"Your Majesty, at this point we're estimating over a thousand people dead within the palace compound—not counting the terrorists, of course," the general reported.

The king was silent. I put my hand over my mouth. I didn't know exactly how many had been in attendance at the summit, but the number of casualties struck me as upward of 90 percent.

"How many survived?" the king asked.

"Fewer than a hundred, Your Majesty," the prince said.

"How many fewer?"

"It's too soon to say."

"How many?"

"Your Majesty, please—we will get you updated figures as soon as we can. But—"

"How . . . many . . . survived?" the king said quietly.

There was another long pause.

"Some, of course, were able to escape," the general said. "And some—thanks be to Allah—were evacuated to area hospitals. The minister of justice, for example, is in critical condition, but I'm afraid he isn't expected to live through the week. I've been told that several members of the Palestinian delegation miraculously escaped, unharmed or nearly so. Youssef Kuttab, for one, and several others. But I really don't think . . ."

He stopped midsentence.

The king waited, but his patience was growing thin. He wanted numbers, and he wanted them now.

Finally the prince stepped in. "Fewer than a hundred, Your Majesty."

"I'm not going to ask again."

The prince took a deep breath. "We estimate no more than fifty survived."

The doctor gasped, as did the young aide standing in the corner.

"This number includes my family?"

"It includes everyone in the vehicle you escaped in, Your Majesty—all seven of you. Prime Minister Lavi and President Mansour too."

"For now," said General al-Mufti.

"What do you mean?"

"It doesn't look good, Your Majesty."

"What exactly do we know about their status?"

"President Mansour is at a hospital in Ramallah," al-Mufti replied. "He was shot in the back. He's just come out of surgery, but it's touch and go."

"And Daniel?"

The prince fielded that one. "The prime minister was rushed to Hadassah Medical Center near Jerusalem. He's still in surgery. I just got off the phone with Ari Shalit. He said . . ."

The prince stopped and looked at me.

"It's okay," the king said. "Mr. Collins isn't going to tell anyone. Right, Mr. Collins?"

"Yes, sir."

"I have your word."

"You do, sir."

"Very well. Proceed."

Feisal hesitated for a moment, but then did as he was asked. "It's pretty grim, Your Majesty. Ari said it's not clear the prime minister is going to make it."

"Why not?"

"Ari said the PM sustained three bullet wounds, two to the back and one to the leg. He lost an enormous amount of blood. They nearly lost him twice on the chopper flight across the river. Apparently it was that Mossad agent, the woman, who saved his life."

"Yael?" I asked. "Yael Katzir?"

"Yes, her," the prince said. "She set up a blood transfusion midflight and performed CPR on him—twice. Still might not have been enough, but . . ."

Feisal didn't finish the sentence. What more was there to say?

The room was silent. I was in shock. I don't know why. I'd known Lavi and Mansour were both in bad shape. When they'd first been shot, we'd all thought they were dead right then. It was the king who'd realized they were still breathing, still had a pulse. But somehow once they were put on the choppers and evacuated back over the Jordan River, I guess I'd just assumed everything would be okay. I couldn't bear the thought that they both might soon be gone—especially after nearly consummating a peace deal they'd worked on so hard for so long.

Suddenly one of the phones in front of Feisal rang. The prince answered it immediately, then handed the receiver to the king.

"Yes," he said without expression. "Yes, I understand. Very well. Good-bye."

I feared the worst and was absolutely stunned by what the king said next. "That was Jack at CIA. We may have found the president."

Everyone instinctively stood. Finally there was some desperately needed good news. *Thank God for Jack Vaughn,* I thought. The director of the Central Intelligence Agency and I had clashed pretty hard in recent days. But I was suddenly thrilled to hear his name mentioned. He and his team were on the case. Maybe things were going to take a turn for the better.

"An American spy satellite has just picked up the signal of the emergency beacon coming from the Secret Service vehicle the president was riding in," the king said. "Jack said it wasn't automatically activated, meaning the vehicle hasn't crashed. It was set off manually. Which is a good sign. Someone is with the vehicle—someone who knows what he's doing, knows that the beacon is in the car and how to trigger it."

"But?" I asked.

"But if it's the agents protecting the president, why aren't they on a secure satphone back to Washington, calling for help and providing a clearer sense of what's happening?"

"Where is the signal coming from?" General Jum'a asked. "I've got extraction teams on standby, ready to go."

"Where would they be deployed from?"

"Here, Your Majesty. They're on the tarmac right now."

"Good," the king said. "Can you redirect ground forces to the site as well?"

"I can, but there are risks."

"We still don't know whom we can trust?"

"I'm afraid not."

"Do you trust these extraction forces?"

"Implicitly, Your Majesty. These are my best men. Bedouins, all. Most are sons of men you trained and served with yourself."

"Can you put them on a secure channel so I can talk with them directly and no other unit can listen in?"

"Absolutely."

"Good, then put them in the air—but don't tell any other unit."

"Yes, sir."

"But, Your Majesty, doesn't Jack want to send in U.S. forces to rescue the president?" I asked, taking a risk by interrupting but trying to understand what was about to play out.

"Of course," the king said. "The Pentagon is deploying a SEAL team off one of the carriers in the Med. But we're closer, and Jack's afraid if ISIS forces have the president pinned down . . ."

He didn't have to finish. The thought was too terrible to contemplate.

"The signal location?" General al-Mufti prompted.

"Near the airport. Get your men in the air. You

and I can give them precise coordinates in a few moments."

"Of course, sir."

"Your Majesty, can I go with them?" I asked, moving toward the door.

"Absolutely not," al-Mufti said.

General Jum'a concurred and the prince was about to, but I spoke first. "Please, sir, I need to see this. You said it yourself—this is why you've got me here."

"It's out of the question, Mr. Collins," al-Mufti shot back. "His Majesty said you'd be at his side during the crisis, not out in the field."

"Please, Your Majesty, Colonel Sharif can go with me," I said. "He'll keep me out of trouble. But I need to go, sir. I need to see the rescue operation. The world needs to hear this story from me, not from a government spokesman."

When the king said nothing, the prince spoke up. "What if it goes badly, Your Majesty?"

"All the more reason," the king said. "Okay, Collins—I want you to go. But Sharif goes with you, and nothing gets published unless he or I approve it."

"Thank you, Your Majesty."

"You're welcome. And may God be with you."

7

Lieutenant General Abdul Jum'a led the way to the tarmac.

Colonel Sharif and I followed close behind and soon found ourselves climbing into the back of an MH-6 helicopter. Known as the "Little Bird," the chopper would serve as the command-and-control aircraft for the unfolding mission as the general directed the movements of six Black Hawk helicopters and the elite SF operators they were carrying. And Sharif and I would be able to see and hear everything that was happening in real time.

We were still buckling up as the two-man crew up front lifted off. Soon we were racing south by southeast to an area not far from Queen Alia International Airport, where the emergency beacon's signal was coming from.

So much was still unknown. Were the president and his security detail out in the open or in an urban area? Were they alone or under assault by ISIS forces? And what exactly was the rescue strategy?

With the president's life potentially in imminent danger, there was no time to develop a detailed and proper plan. Rather than gather all kinds of intelligence and put his men through several hours or days of training, the general was going to have to improvise, and that was going to make a risky situation all the more dangerous.

I had a hundred questions. Was there any way to approach the target by stealth? If not, what would be the best way for the general's men to get to the president and extract him? How was Jum'a going to handle the fact that it was the middle of the day and we weren't going to have the cover of darkness? What if the enemy had RPGs? Would it be possible for the approaching aircraft to be shot down? If that happened, then what? If there was no plan A, what was plan B?

These and other questions were racing through my mind, but for the moment I didn't dare ask any of them. It seemed best merely to keep quiet and observe.

The general was sitting in a row of seats ahead of the colonel and me, just behind the pilot and copilot, before a communications console he was powering up and preparing to use. I had no idea what he was thinking. But nor did I want to bother him. For whatever was unclear at the moment, two things *were* clear: this guy did not want me on his chopper, and time was of the essence.

My job, I knew, was to document everything that happened without getting in the way or complicating a tense situation more than I already was. One thought crossed my mind: I was dying to take some pictures. In times of crisis, readers wanted to see what was happening behind the scenes. They wanted to try to understand how leaders made decisions and what it was like to be "in the room" in moments of great stress and drama. My phone had been taken away, so that wasn't an option. But just then, as if he were reading my thoughts, the colonel nudged me. Without saying anything— only the pilots were talking—he handed me a small backpack he'd brought on board and motioned for me to open it. As I did, I was speechless. Inside the bag I found a nearly brand-new digital SLR camera. And this wasn't any old model. It was a six-thousand-dollar Nikon D4, professional grade, top-of-the-line. As I dug deeper, I found a high-powered Nikkor telephoto lens as well. I couldn't believe it. Sharif hadn't let me head into the field empty-handed after all.

I smiled and slapped the colonel on the back to thank him. This was far more than I needed and probably more than I knew how to handle. I was a war correspondent, after all, not a photojournalist, and this was like handing Tiger Woods's personal clubs to some kid at a miniature golf course. Nevertheless, with the colonel's gesture of permission, I took a few shots of the general at work and then quickly attached the telephoto lens.

Then Colonel Sharif nudged me again. As I turned, he handed me a pair of headphones with an attached microphone. He was already wearing a set and pantomimed that I should put mine on immediately. As I did, I could hear the general's cool, professional, unflappable voice. And he was talking to me.

"Mr. Collins, can you hear me back there?"

"Yes, General, I can."

"Good. Now listen, back at the palace, when you were preparing to evacuate the king and his family, you were one of the last people to see the president, correct?"

"Yes, sir, that's true."

"You saw him get into the Suburban next to the king's vehicle?"

I thought about that for a moment. I wanted to say yes, but it wasn't exactly true. "No, I saw the SUV pull away, but the president and his men were already in the vehicle."

"How many agents were with him?"

"Well, at least two, but maybe not more," I said, closing my eyes and trying desperately to remember every detail. "I saw the driver and another agent in the front passenger seat. But I can't say there were more. Most of them were killed in the firefight, as you know."

"The king just radioed me," the general replied. "He says he's pretty sure he saw an agent in the backseat, covering the president with his own body."

"That could be," I said. "I don't know. I was just trying to get our Suburban started."

As I said this, I noticed the chopper was now banking toward the desert, not toward Amman. And it wasn't just us. All six Black Hawks beside and behind us were changing course too. Why the new course? Why weren't we heading back to the area around the airport? Was the president on the move?

The general relayed the information I had given him to the rest of the troops. The president had at least two agents with him, possibly three. But even if there were four agents with him, which was possible but seemed unlikely, it wasn't going to be nearly enough protection if they really had been found and attacked by ISIS.

Worse, while the Chevy Suburban the president was in was solid—armor-plated with bulletproof windows like all the Suburbans used by the United States Secret Service—it wasn't nearly as secure as the fleet of presidential limousines, each of which was known by agents as "the Beast." These specially designed Cadillacs were essentially luxury battle tanks. Each door was made of reinforced steel eight inches thick, built to withstand the direct impact of an antitank missile. The trunk and gas tank were armor-plated. The windows could withstand armor-piercing bullets fired at point-blank range. Each limo had its own oxygen supply, fire-suppression system, and special steel rims supporting Kevlar-reinforced tires that could continue at high speeds for miles even after being blown out in an attack. Each model also had a supply of the president's blood type on board, the most secure satellite communications known to man, night-vision technology, and even a state-of-the-art system that would allow its driver to navigate through fire and smoke. The Suburban the president was in couldn't possibly compare. How long could he and his men hold out under a direct assault?

Suddenly the king's voice came over the radio. He explained that he and Prince Feisal had just opened up a secure conference call with the American vice president, the director of the CIA, the chairman of the Joint Chiefs, the director of the Secret Service, and the commander of CENTCOM. For the first time, King Abdullah now gave General Jum'a precise coordinates of the beacon's location and explained that momentarily they'd be sending live images of the location from two different sources, a U.S. spy satellite and a Jordanian drone.

"The signal is coming from a warehouse several kilometers north of the interchange between Routes 35 and 15," the king said. "And it's been completely overrun by the enemy."

8

One of the monitors in the communications console flickered to life.

Though my angle was partially blocked by General Jum'a, the images I could see were at once compelling and chilling. Clearly visible via a spy satellite feed was an area that was part industrial and part agricultural. I could see a compound composed of seven main buildings. Six appeared to be warehouses. The seventh looked like it housed the main offices for whatever company this was. The entire rectangular site was enclosed by a high concrete wall and surrounded on the north, east, and west sides by open fields, though there appeared to be a factory of some sort just across the field to the west. On the south side was a two-lane road, and across the street there appeared to be a nursery of some sort, as there were dozens and dozens of greenhouses covering multiple acres. Down the road a bit was a major oil depot.

We were patched in on the conference call but could hear only the king and prince, not the principals in Washington or the CENTCOM commander, who I assumed was in Tampa. The king explained that the beacon's signal was coming from the midsize building located in the center of the compound.

The general opened a laptop, connected it to the monitor, and then took a moment to highlight the specific warehouse on his screen and transmitted the image to the men on the Black Hawks around us. "What exactly is this place?" Jum'a asked as he pulled up a GPS map on a separate screen.

"The factory you see on the west side is the SADAFCO plant," Prince Feisal said. "We think the compound we're looking at was recently purchased by SADAFCO as a warehousing and shipping center. But my men are checking on that. Stand by."

I turned to the colonel. I didn't want to talk over my headset microphone as it would be heard by everyone in the chopper and by the king and prince as well. But I had no idea what SADAFCO was. The colonel saw my questioning look and quickly took out a pad and pen and scribbled me a note.

> *SADAFCO—Saudia Dairy and Foodstuff*
> *Company*
> *Largest producer of milk and dairy products*
> *in Arab world, or one of them.*
> *Also make foodstuffs—cereals, tomato paste,*
> *frozen french fries, etc.*
> *This must be their Jordanian subsidiary.*

Why in the world was the signal coming from there, of all places? That was my first thought. My second thought was whether there could be a connection between the ISIS terrorists and the Saudis.

None of that was clear. What was clear—and what made the images so terrifying—was that the place was crawling with heavily armed men. Whether they were ISIS for sure or some other group, I couldn't tell. But I counted more than sixty fighters, all wearing black hoods, and several were holding rocket-propelled grenade launchers. They had taken up positions on all sides of the compound and were using a tractor-trailer truck to block the main entrance. Snipers were clearly visible in the upper stories of the office building, and several more could be seen looking out the doorways of the warehouses. Whoever these guys were, they weren't running a food processing plant.

Another monitor on the communications console now flickered to life. I could see this one a little better, though again my view was partially blocked by the general. But it appeared to be the feed from a drone over the site providing thermal images of the building from which the signal was coming. While it looked to me like a warehouse from the outside, the images suggested it was more of a garage. I could see the outlines of numerous vehicles, including one that potentially could be the president's. I could also see the heat signatures of dozens of people in the facility. Most were grouped in what might have been an office of some kind in the back right-hand corner. Others were clumped in the remaining three corners of the building.

"General, are you seeing the feed from the drone?" the king asked.

"I am, Your Majesty," Jum'a replied. "Is that the president's Suburban on the far right in the back, near the office and all the people?"

"We believe so," the king said. "The Secret Service director says the signal is strong and authentic. It's not being jammed or manipulated. As best he can tell, that's the real thing."

"But am I seeing this right—the doors are open, and no one's in the vehicle?"

"I'm afraid that's right."

"So what do you want to do, Your Majesty?"

"Can your men take that compound?"

"Yes, sir—in less than two minutes."

"Can you get the president out safely?"

"Honestly, Your Majesty, I can't say. There are an awful lot of variables in play here. But an assault is not our only option. We could surround the place and try to negotiate his release."

"No," said the king. "The vice president has ruled that out. The U.S. won't negotiate with ISIS under any circumstances. And Jack Vaughn is worried that if they're given any more time, they will behead him."

The very notion gave me flashbacks of seeing Abu Khalif, the ISIS emir, behead the deputy director of Iraqi intelligence just outside of Baghdad. That was horrifying enough. I couldn't imagine the sight of the president of the United States being beheaded. Surely they would do it on camera. Surely they would post it on YouTube for all the world to see.

I tried to imagine what was going through the vice president's mind at the moment. Martin Holbrooke had been a senator from Ohio for more than thirty years when he'd been tapped by Harrison Taylor to be the VP nominee. He certainly had lots of Washington experience. But was he ready for this? Was anyone?

"This all presupposes the president is even in that building," the general said.

"Right."

"We still don't know that."

"No, we don't—not for certain," the king conceded.

"Can the Secret Service say for sure? Do they have a way to know, like we know where you are at all times?"

"Good question," said the king. "I'm sure they do. But wait one."

He put us on hold, and we waited. But not for long.

"Yes, they have a way to know," said the king. "The president wears a special watch, a Jorg Gray 6500 Chronograph. It was picked out by the president but specially built for the Service. It operates as a panic button and has a tracking device inside it."

"And?"

"And right now none of the American satellites, drones, or other assets are picking up the signal from the watch. They can't say why. Could be any number of reasons."

"You mean the watch could have been removed from him and destroyed."

"Yes, that's possible. But there are other possibilities as well."

"Bottom line—can they say the president is in that building?"

"No, General, at the moment they cannot. But they can't rule it out either."

"Well, it's your call, Your Majesty. What do you want us to do?"

"Give me a moment," said the king. "And make sure your men are ready to go if I give the order."

"Yes, Your Majesty. I certainly will."

Again we were put on hold. We still couldn't hear the conversation between the king and the American leaders. But it was now clear to me why our pilots weren't proceeding straight to the site but were instead circling over the desert. Until the general was sure what his orders were, he didn't want to tip the enemy off that he was coming. So we waited.

And waited. Much longer than the last pause.

Two minutes went by. Then five. Then ten.

I said nothing, only glanced at Colonel Sharif. The look on his face said it all. He was just as bewildered by the delay as I was. If the Jordanians were going to strike, they had to move hard and fast. If the president wasn't in that Suburban—and clearly no one was in any of those vehicles in that building—then his life was in grave danger. There wasn't a second to spare. He might be killed in a rescue attempt. But he was going to be killed anyway. The only hope was a forcible extraction. And it had to happen now.

Finally our headsets crackled back to life.

"Okay, General, they want you and your men to go in. God help you. The fate of us all is in your hands."

9

I opened my notebook and furiously scribbled down every word.

"The fate of us all is in your hands."

It was a sobering line, one I wanted to ask the king about when I saw him again. It suggested the monarch saw not only the president's personal fate hanging in the balance but his own, his kingdom's, his people's. In many ways, he had prepared his entire life for a moment like this. Yet he was not in the field. He was back in the bunker. He had to trust the men under his command, and if they got it wrong . . .

The general ordered the choppers to bank back toward the target and hit the deck. We were going to come in low and fast. Then he ordered his commanders on the ground to mass tanks and armored personnel carriers at two points, one kilometer east of the compound and one kilometer west, both significantly off the main road and out of sight of all civilians.

"Do you want us to cut off traffic?" one of the battalion commanders asked. "There are a lot of trucks and other vehicles passing through that area."

To my surprise, the general said no.

"We don't want to do anything to tip them off that we're coming," he explained. "Let everything proceed as normal."

But that wasn't all. Jum'a then instructed his special forces teams on the ground to commandeer buses, minivans, and SUVs and be prepared to drive up to the compound at normal speeds, like all other traffic, upon his command.

Next the general asked the prince if there were any calls being made to or from mobile phones or landlines at the target site.

Feisal said both Jordanian and U.S. intel assets were monitoring the site but that they weren't picking up anything. "It's all quiet—oddly quiet," the prince said. "We're trying to monitor Internet traffic at the site too. But so far, nothing. They seem to have shut down the Wi-Fi system."

The general thanked the prince, then gave his men their orders.

"Two minutes out," he said when he was done. "Radio silence from this point forward."

And all was quiet, save the roar of the rotors above us.

Colonel Sharif reached behind him, grabbed an MP5 machine gun, and inserted a fresh magazine. Then he reached for two flak jackets, put one on, and gave the other to me. It suddenly dawned on me that we might not be staying on the chopper. We might be getting off. I pulled out the gold pocket watch I always carried with me, the one my grandfather gave to me before his death. We had less than a minute. I could feel my heart pounding in my chest and a surge of adrenaline coursed through my system.

Suddenly the pilot pulled back sharply on the yoke. Rather than flying barely fifty feet off the ground, we climbed rapidly to two hundred feet, then three hundred, and kept climbing until we leveled out at five hundred feet.

We were less than thirty seconds out. I was pretty sure I could see the compound, but now we banked sharply to our right and began a circling pattern around the target. The Black Hawks didn't follow. Nor had they climbed as high as we had. They were still racing for the compound at an altitude I figured to be no more than a hundred feet.

Just then our helicopter was rocked by a massive explosion. One of the warehouses, in the far left corner of the compound, erupted in an enormous ball of fire. But how? Had someone inside detonated a bomb? Or had someone just fired a missile? I looked to my left and saw nothing. But when I turned and looked out the window to my right, I saw an Apache attack helicopter—and it was firing again.

Two more Hellfire missiles streaked across the afternoon sky. I followed the contrails and watched spellbound as one destroyed the main office building. An instant later, the second missile took out the 18-wheeler that had been blocking the entrance. Then a Cobra gunship swooped in below us and to our left. Its pilot opened fire on the armed rebels patrolling the grounds, then

trained his fire on the rebels stationed in the doorways of the remaining five warehouses. One by
one I watched men in black hoods shredded into
oblivion.

The Apache opened fire again. More Hellfire
missiles rocketed down into the compound. They
weren't targeted at the buildings, however. Rather,
they exploded in the open spaces, vaporizing the
remaining visible terrorists but more importantly
creating deafening booms and raging fires I had
to assume were intended to stun and disorient the
enemy combatants inside the main building.

Now the Black Hawks moved into position.
Two hovered over the warehouse where the president's Suburban was located. A moment later I
could see the king's most elite forces fast-roping
to the warehouse roof. Two other Black Hawks
broke left. The remaining two broke right. The
commandos in all four choppers were soon fast-
roping to the ground, then scrambling to secure
the perimeter. And that's when the shooting
started.

The initial explosions had done their job. They
had caught the terrorists completely unaware.
They had temporarily thrown the enemy into con-
fusion. But some of the ISIS soldiers were firing
back. Within seconds, the fighting had reached a
fever pitch. From our vantage point, watching the
drone and satellite feeds and looking out the window to our left, we could see the Jordanian commandos in the heart of the compound. They were
using Semtex to blow the doors off the warehouse
on the north and east sides. Then we watched

mesmerized as they tossed flash grenades into the main warehouse.

The thermal images on the second monitor revealed the chaos inside the facility. The king's commandos were now storming in from all directions. They were firing at anything that moved. I could see bodies dropping, including some of the king's men. But they didn't stop. They kept firing, kept pushing forward, kept advancing toward the back office, though they were encountering fierce resistance.

I was feverishly snapping photos through the windows of the Little Bird as well as at the images from the two video monitors. I was also trying to keep track of the radio chatter. But it was in Arabic and it was coming fast and furious. My Arabic wasn't horrible, but I certainly wasn't getting it all. Too much was happening to take it all in. And then, without warning, the Little Bird plummeted. I realized too late it was a planned descent as we hit the ground hard in the driveway just yards from the remains of the tractor-trailer out front, now engulfed in flames.

The moment we slammed to the deck, Colonel Sharif threw open the side door and jumped out. When he shouted at me to follow, for a moment I didn't move. Was he crazy? The situation was hardly secure. There was an intense gun battle under way. In the chopper, we'd had the perfect vantage point. Why in the world would we get out now?

I'm not saying I was scared. Okay, I was scared. He had an MP5. I had a Nikon. He was a trained soldier. I was just a journalist. Besides, I'd had enough excitement for one day. I'd already been shot at—and hit. I didn't want to go back into the fray. I wanted to stay with General Jum'a, high above the action. It wasn't just safer; it was an ideal way to track all the elements of the battle. But now the general was shouting at me to get out. The colonel was unfastening my seat belt and yelling at me to move faster. He wasn't kidding. This was really happening.

I ripped off my headset, grabbed the camera bag, and scrambled out of the chopper after him. And no sooner had my feet touched solid ground than I felt the Little Bird lift off behind me and race out of the hot zone.

"Come on, Collins, let's go," Sharif yelled over the nearly deafening roar of the helicopter blades and the multiple explosions. *"Follow me."*

10

* * *

I did as I was told, though I hadn't much choice.

To my shock, Sharif didn't head for the cover of the perimeter. I guess I'd expected him to put me *close* to the action, at the side of some of the Jordanian forces, to see and hear and smell the battle for myself. Instead, the colonel took me into the heart of darkness.

Suddenly we were racing into the compound, even as the ear-shattering explosions and blistering staccato of machine-gun fire echoed through the courtyard. Sharif didn't take us around the raging flames of the 18-wheeler. He literally jumped right through them, and I had no choice but to follow suit. He was, after all, the only one with a weapon, and I didn't dare get separated.

Inside the courtyard, Sharif was running flat out, and I struggled to keep up. He was in far better shape. I was gasping for air. Just then fresh machine-gun fire opened up from a window above us. Fortunately it wasn't aimed at us but at an armored personnel carrier that was coming in behind us. The ground reinforcements were beginning to arrive, and they were drawing intense resistance.

The colonel broke right, then dove through a gaping hole in the wall of that warehouse. Terrified, I dove too. By a minor miracle, the camera wasn't damaged, though I did drop the bag with all the attachments. I should have worn it like a backpack, but I wasn't thinking clearly. I turned and saw the bag through the smoke, about twenty yards away. I started to go back for it, but out in the court-yard bullets were now whizzing in all directions. A moment before we'd been able to race through unharmed. Now it was a kill box out there, and there was no way I could retrieve it.

Then again, how could we go forward? Gunfire suddenly erupted on the other side of the ware-house floor. I had no idea if it was from the terror-ists or friendly fire from the Jordanians. There was no way either side could see us clearly. To them we were only shadows moving through the smoke. That's certainly how they all looked to us.

Scrambling to my feet, I ducked into a row of pallets piled high with canned goods and other foodstuffs. Sharif aimed his MP5 and returned fire. Then he ducked in beside me and took cover behind the pallets.

Why we were in this particular building I had no idea. If we were going to take such risks, then I wanted to be in the main event, in the next ware-house over. That's where the president's Suburban was. That's presumably where the president him-self was. That's certainly where the biggest gun battle was taking place. We needed to be there too. Instead, we were hunkered down in a warehouse that, as far as I could tell, had no strategic significance. We couldn't go back. We couldn't press forward. And the raging fires of the main office building were rapidly spreading. The flames had reached this building and were leaping up the walls. The entire warehouse was going to be consumed in the next few minutes. We had to get out.

If that wasn't enough, we knew for sure there were terrorists above us—the ones that had been shooting from the window on the second floor seconds earlier.

Through the flames, I noticed a stairway to my right. When I pointed it out to Sharif, he quickly motioned for me to get down and stay behind him. The reason was fast becoming obvious. The terrorists were either going to be consumed by the fire racing to the second floor or get suffocated by the thick black billows of smoke that were surging into the rafters—or they were coming down those stairs any moment.

The heat was infernal. Sweat was pouring down my face and back. My shirt was already soaked. I mopped my brow, steadied my camera, and started shooting just as Sharif did. Sure enough, three masked terrorists came barreling down the staircase. They weren't expecting us. Sharif unloaded an entire clip. The men were dead before they hit the ground. I'd captured it all, but Sharif wasn't finished. He raced over to the men, checked their pulses to make sure they were really gone, then pulled off their hoods as I kept snapping pictures. Then I rifled through their pockets and came out with cell phones, maps, and other articles. I shot all of it, item by item.

As he began loading the items into his own backpack, I got curious. Looking up the stairwell into the hazy darkness, I hung the camera around my neck, pried an AK-47 from one of the terrorists' death grips, and began moving slowly up the stairs.

When the colonel realized what I was doing, he must have thought I was crazy. He yelled at me to come back. No one in his right mind would be going up those stairs at that moment. The entire building was now on fire. We had maybe a matter of minutes before the whole structure collapsed. But I kept moving, and I'm not sure I can tell you why. If I'd taken some time to think about it, I would never have done it. But I wasn't operating on rational thought at that moment. I was going by instinct, and my instincts were calling me upward.

Every step seemed an act of delayed suicide, yet I couldn't stop. More gunfire erupted behind me, but I kept moving, step by step, into the unknown. I'd thought the heat was unbearable when we'd first entered the building. But it was getting worse and worse by the second. When I reached the top of the stairs, I could barely see. The smoke was nearly impenetrable. It and the flames were sucking out what little oxygen was left in the air. I dropped to my knees, then quickly glanced back. Sharif was no longer with me. From the sound of the gunfire below, he was in full contact with the enemy. I was alone.

Crawling forward, I could barely see the window from which the terrorists had been firing, but I decided this was my destination. I scrambled ahead, stopping every few moments to check my six, terrified someone in a black hood was going to come up and shoot me in the back. Yet the farther I pressed forward, the less I could see behind me. My eyes were watering. I was choking on the smoke and fumes. The gunshot wound to my left arm was throbbing.

I was now crawling on my belly. The only air that was left was down here. The Nikon was on my back. I still held the Kalashnikov, sweeping it forward from side to side as I crawled, just in case.

Why was I doing this? It made no sense. I was moving farther away from the center of the story and putting myself in grave danger in the process. Parts of the roof were collapsing all around me. The holes created new sources of oxygen, giving new fuel to the flames now shooting twenty or thirty feet into the air. I was completely drenched with sweat. I could barely breathe or see. But as I reached the window, I found the bodies of two terrorists. I checked their pulses. They were both dead. I went through their pockets for phones or IDs or anything else useful but found nothing. Was that it? Was this why I'd come? I'd risked my life for what? For nothing?

Cursing myself, I ripped off their hoods and took a few pictures, then turned to leave. But then I began to panic. What if I couldn't make it back? What if I died here, foolishly, without cause and without any idea where I was going next? I thought about my mom. I thought about my brother, Matt, and his wife, Annie. I thought about their kids. I thought, too, about Yael. I desperately wanted to see them. I wasn't ready to die. Not yet. Not here.

As I scrambled back toward the stairs, I stumbled upon something I hadn't seen coming the other direction. It was a leg. A body. But whoever it was wasn't dead. He was groaning. He was bleeding heavily, but he was alive. And this wasn't a terrorist. He was dressed in a suit. I rolled him over and to my astonishment found it was an American. This was an agent of the United States Secret Service. He had a sharpshooter rifle at his side and a gaping wound in his chest. His breathing was shallow. His pulse was erratic.

I threw the strap of the Kalashnikov around my neck so the weapon itself was now slung over my back, side by side with the camera. Then I scrambled around the agent and began dragging him toward the stairs. There was no way I could stand up. The flames along what was left of the roof were coming down closer and closer to the floor. We had only seconds left, so I used every ounce of energy I had to drag the agent across the floor, inch by inch, begging God to allow us to make it to the stairs before it was too late.

But just then the roof above us collapsed, and part of the floor below us gave way.

11

Amid the blazing wreckage, we plummeted toward the first floor.

But we didn't fall the entire way. We dropped, instead, onto a row of pallets, then rolled off and landed with a thud on the concrete floor. My left arm was in excruciating pain. My knees had smashed on the pavement and were killing me. But as I looked up and wiped sweat and soot from my eyes, I could see the agent's suit was on fire. I summoned what little strength I had left, tossed the Kalashnikov to the side, and threw myself on him, extinguishing the flames with my own body. It had all happened so quickly I didn't think the agent had actually suffered any serious burns. But I feared the fall might have finished him off. Again I checked his pulse. It was weak, but it was there. He was still alive, though barely.

I turned to look for the colonel, to call for help, but instead found myself face-to-face with one of the terrorists. Shrouded in a black hood and covered in blood, he was pointing an AK-47 and screaming at me in Arabic.

"Get up—get up and prepare to die!"

Slowly, and with some difficulty, I rose to my feet, my hands in the air, not wanting to make any sudden movements. His eyes were locked on mine, and they were wild with a toxic mixture of rage and self-righteousness. I'd never seen anything quite like it, and I instantly lost all hope that this could turn out well.

And then something changed. I couldn't see his full expression, of course, just his eyes, but behind the rage something was different. Whatever was fueling his emotions at that split second didn't soften, nor did it weaken, but it did alter somewhat.

"You," he said, shaking the barrel of the machine gun at me. "I've seen you."

I said nothing.

"You're . . . you're the infidel . . . the one who interviewed the emir," he said, practically spewing the words out of his mouth as if they were laced with poison. "You filthy *kafir*—you will pay for what you have done!"

I was frozen—couldn't move, couldn't think, couldn't speak. I saw the man's finger preparing to pull the trigger, and I wish I could tell you that I reacted in some way—that I lunged at him or dove for cover or at least closed my eyes and prayed. But I just stood there. Eyes wide open. Waiting for death. And then a machine gun erupted to my right and the terrorist's head exploded.

Before I fully realized what was happening, Colonel Sharif was rushing to my side to see if I was all right. I wasn't, though I told him I was fine.

Smoke was curling out of the barrel of his MP5 as a squad of Jordanian commandos came rushing by.

"Clear," I heard one of them say.

"You sure you're okay?" the colonel asked.

I couldn't answer. Instead I drew Sharif's attention to the agent.

"Who is he?" Sharif asked, dropping to the man's side and checking his vitals.

"I have no idea," I replied.

"Where did you find him?"

"Upstairs, near the window."

"What was he doing up there?"

I just shook my head.

Sharif pulled out a radio and called for a medic. Moments later a team of four men rushed in. They immediately put the agent on a stretcher and raced him out to a chopper that was landing in the courtyard. At the same time, Sharif grabbed my arm and led me out of the inferno—and just in time, for we had no sooner begun to cross the courtyard than the entire building collapsed in a huge ball of sparks and smoke.

I turned and looked at the burning wreckage. I just stood there for a few moments, watching it. Then I heard Sharif telling me to follow him again. I wasn't sure that was a good idea, but it was dawning on me that the entire site was now secure. All of the terrorists must now be dead or in custody.

Soon I found myself stepping inside the next warehouse over. It was cavernous, much larger than the others, and it was swarming with Jordanian commandos. Some were tending to their wounded. Others were collecting clues or taking photos as if it were a crime scene. One soldier was videotaping the scene, presumably for the king and the prince, perhaps even to uplink to the White House Situation Room, the war room in the Pentagon, and CENTCOM. The floor was littered with shell casings, shrapnel, and shards of safety glass from the blown-out windows of one vehicle after another. The metallic, acrid smell of gunpowder hung in the air, mixed with the stench of the fires all around us.

Instinctively, I grabbed the Nikon around my neck and began snapping photos as well.

But Sharif pulled me aside. "Stop," he said.

"Why?"

"It can wait," he said quietly.

"For what?" I pressed. "This is why I'm here."

"Trust me," he replied. "It can wait."

Sharif asked me to come with him. I didn't want to miss anything. I had an unprecedented world exclusive, if only the king—and my editors back home—would let me run with the story. (That, of course, assumed I hadn't been fired yet, though I knew I'd cross that bridge later.) Reluctantly, I did let go of my camera and let it dangle around my neck as the colonel brought me to the very back of the warehouse.

There it was—the president's bullet-ridden Chevy Suburban.

I stiffened. The scene was eerie—haunting, really. The two front doors were open. So were the back doors. The bodies of three Secret Service agents lay before me. I peered into the backseat of the SUV. It was covered with blood. And on the concrete floor was a trail of blood leading away from the Suburban and out a side door.

"Tell me you found the president," I said, suddenly sure they hadn't.

"We haven't," Sharif said, confirming my suspicion.

"Please tell me he's safe."

"I can't."

"Tell me you know where he is," I pressed.

"I'm sorry, Collins; we have no idea."

PART
TWO

12

* * *

We landed back at the air base in Marka just after 8 p.m. local time.

It was now one o'clock in the afternoon in New York and Washington, and I knew Allen and his bosses had to be furious at me for not answering my phone.

As we headed into the bunker, I asked Colonel Sharif to brief me on what was happening in the outside world. He might not be authorized to give me back my iPhone, I argued, but I couldn't do my job if I had no idea what everyone else was reporting. He agreed and summarized several of the stories he was reading on his Android.

Agence France-Presse was reporting casualty figures of more than five hundred dead in the attack on the peace summit, though Sharif and I knew the real figure was, tragically, double that number.

Reuters was reporting that Palestinian president Salim Mansour was now in guarded condition at a hospital in Ramallah but was increasingly expected to make a full recovery.

Al Jazeera and the Associated Press were reporting rumors of a major military operation not far from the Amman airport. Interviews with unnamed local residents suggested a heavy concentration of Jordanian ground and air forces and large explosions in an industrial park just off the intersection of Routes 15 and 35. So far, however, Sharif noted, neither story even hinted that this operation might have anything to do with the hunt for President Taylor.

The big story, far and away, was the rumor—driven by the Drudge Report and my tweets—that the president of the United States was missing.

Sharif checked the *New York Times* home page.

"Your story is the lead," he said. "It was posted twenty-two minutes ago."

"So they went with it after all," I said, not sure if I was more surprised or angry.

"How could they not?" Sharif said. "Once Drudge moved it, every news organization in the world picked it up."

"You don't know Allen and the brass."

"What were they going to do?" Sharif asked as we showed our IDs to the MPs guarding the general headquarters building and ran our backpacks, camera gear, and other supplies through the X-ray machine, stepped through metal detectors, and were patted down for good measure. "Their top correspondent in the region broke the story. Sure, you did it on social media, but no one knows the difference anymore. Or cares. And once it was out there, of course the *Times* was going to 'own' it. You're their man, and this is a sensational story.

Terrible—don't get me wrong. But from a journalist's perspective, this is the mother of all news stories. I guarantee your editors are kicking themselves for letting Drudge get the jump on them. And look, no one but you and I and a handful of others even knew they weren't going to run it in the first place."

"I guess," I said. "What about the White House? Are they confirming the president is missing?"

"Not quite," said Sharif, quickly scanning the full story. "But they don't actually deny it either."

"What are they saying exactly?"

"The story says, 'A senior administration official, who asked that his name be withheld as he was not authorized to speak on so sensitive a matter, insisted that Air Force One has landed safely at Israel's Ben Gurion International Airport without damage and without casualties. The official went on to say that the White House is grieving the loss of several senior officials and numerous support staff but is withholding the names of those killed and wounded until their families can be properly notified.'"

"That's it?" I asked. "That's all the White House says about the whereabouts of the president?"

"That's it," Sharif said, gathering his things from the X-ray machine.

"Talk about a nondenial denial," I said. "They can't shoot my story down because they know it's true. But by not providing any other details, they're creating a global firestorm of interest. Why don't they just tell everyone the truth?"

"Who's going to say it?" asked Sharif. "The

White House press secretary is dead. So is the chief of staff. So are the secretary of state and at least a dozen senior White House officials."

"Secretary Murray is dead?"

"Sorry—I thought you'd heard."

"I hadn't."

"He and his team got to the ceremony late," Sharif explained. "Their plane landed about twenty minutes after the president's, just in from Beijing."

"I didn't even see him."

"He was meeting with a half-dozen other foreign ministers in the east wing of the palace. They were going to join up with the principals immediately after the ceremony."

A wave of nausea hit me with the news of the secretary of state's death. Though I'd never interviewed him or developed him as a source, I had met him twice—once when he'd made a surprise visit to Baghdad to hold a press conference with a new Iraqi prime minister, and once with his lovely wife, Bernadette, and their three teenage girls at a Christmas party at the American embassy in Paris. I couldn't imagine what this family was going through, and so many other families like theirs.

There was no time to grieve, however. We headed down several flights of stairs, with soldiers flanking us both ahead and behind. I appreciated the colonel's help. It occurred to me that beyond his name and rank, I really had no idea who he was. We'd had no time to get acquainted. What was his background? Where was he from? And why was he so trusted by the king? I was about to ask him to tell me a bit about himself, but he started talking first.

"You know, your name isn't the only one on the byline. There are three others."

"Really? Who?"

"Conyers from the White House, Baker at State, and Neeling at the Pentagon."

"They're all backups, second-stringers," I said. "What about Fisher, Thompson, and O'Malley?"

"Says here they were all at the summit," Sharif said. "They all died in the attacks."

"What about Alex?" I asked, referring to Alex Brunnell, the *Times'* Jerusalem bureau chief.

"I'm afraid he was killed too."

We were approaching the vault door into the bunker. But I had to stop. I needed a moment. There was too much happening, too much death. I was sure some kind of emotional circuit breakers were going to blow at any second, and I didn't want to see the king until I had gathered myself together. I stood there, just outside the bunker, eyes closed, inhaling and exhaling very deliberately. *Just breathe,* I told myself. *Just breathe, in and out, in and out, in and out.*

What made it all worse was my complete inability to do my job properly. With no phone, I had no way to check my messages, no way to respond to e-mails, no way to track information or stay in touch with my family or my team in the States. And now I had a huge story that would rock the world. The Chevy Suburban carrying the president had been found bullet-ridden and abandoned in a facility swarming with terrorists. The president's entire Secret Service detail was dead or gravely wounded. The backseat of the Suburban was covered with blood. There was a trail of blood leading to a side door. But the president was nowhere to be found. The Jordanians didn't know where he was. Neither did the entirety of the American government.

The door of the bunker opened. Sharif told me it was time to go see the king. I braced myself for the fight that was coming. I understood full well that there were national security implications here. But the American people needed to know. The world needed to know. These were no longer rumors. The president was gone, and the only logical conclusion that could be drawn from the facts at hand was that he was now in the custody of the Islamic State.

13

★ ★ ★

"You're right," said the king.

"I beg your pardon?" I said, unprepared for his response. I'd just completed an extended and somewhat-heated treatise on the importance of being able to write and transmit back to the States a detailed article on the missing president and the failed rescue attempt, but apparently for no reason.

"Why do you think I sent you out there, Collins?" the monarch asked. "Why do you think Colonel Sharif pulled you into the middle of the action rather than staying up in the helicopter? Write the story quickly. As soon as the colonel clears it, you can e-mail it to your editors. I just have two requirements."

"Requirements?" I asked, bracing myself.

"Yes."

"And they are?"

"First, I'm asking you not to speculate," he said.

"Meaning what?"

"Meaning just report the facts. Nothing more. Nothing less. We don't know where the president is. That's a fact. The rescue attempt failed. That's a fact. A massive manhunt for the president remains under way. Also a fact. But you can't say the president is in the hands of ISIS. That's speculation. I know you fear that. We all do. But that's what I mean—don't guess, don't surmise, don't provide commentary or analysis. Not now. Not in the middle of a fast-moving crisis. Let the pundits back in the States or wherever do the speculation. And obviously you can't mention any sensitive military or intelligence information, either, like where I am, what base we're at, and so forth. The colonel will make sure there's nothing classified or sensitive in your piece."

I deeply rejected the very concept of a military censor. I'd fought it all over the world—in Afghanistan, in Iraq, and wherever I went. But there was no time to fight it at the moment. And there was no point. The king understood what I was trying to do. He wasn't asking for me to paint Jordan in a good light. He was just asking me to be a reporter, not a commentator, and under the circumstances that seemed fair enough.

I nodded, then asked, "What's the second requirement?"

"Speed," the king said. "Get some version of the story out fast. To write up the whole battle story will likely take you most of the night. But the American people can't wait for the whole thing. Nor can anyone else. They need to know the most crucial facts right now. So don't write it all up at once. Do a first draft. Get the basic details out there. We'll let you transmit additional paragraphs with more details every thirty to forty-five minutes throughout the evening, if you'd like. It's a world exclusive no matter what. No one else has the story. People will be hanging on every word. The *Times* web traffic will be off the charts. But at least everyone will know the lead right away. Agreed?"

"Photos too?" I asked.

"A few at a time, sure."

"Then agreed," I said.

"Good. Can you give the colonel a first draft in fifteen minutes?"

"I can do it in ten."

"Even better."

With that I was dismissed. Sharif led me out of the bunker, through a vestibule, down the hall, and into a complex of offices where staff members were hard at work coordinating sorties of fighter jets against various ISIS targets and managing the air portion of the enormous manhunt for the president. We came to a small, unoccupied office that apparently had been set aside for the colonel and me. Everything had been cleared from the shelves. The desktop was cleared off as well. But there was a new laptop waiting for me and a laser printer, along with a Keurig machine and a supply of coffees and teas. There was also a small refrigerator, like the kind I'd had in my college dorm room a million years ago, stocked with water and soft drinks.

I soon realized the phone on the desk was disconnected, and while there was Wi-Fi, the colonel said he wasn't authorized to give me the password.

Still, it was clean and quiet and far better than what Abu Khalif had provided me. So I sat down, took some more pain medication for my arm, and got to work.

Ten minutes later, as promised, I was done with the first draft.

Four hours later, I slid the laptop across the desk.

On the screen was the final draft. The colonel, as bleary-eyed as I was, carefully reviewed my copy, struck out only four sentences, and cleared it for publication. Then he plugged in a memory stick, downloaded the file, and took it to another room to e-mail it to Allen MacDonald.

While he was gone, I pulled out my grandfather's pocket watch and wound it up. It was now just after midnight. Over the past several hours, I had spoken to Allen three times, under the colonel's supervision, on a borrowed satphone. After assuring Allen that I was physically okay, I'd explained the unique circumstances under which I was operating. I figured the king's admonition against disclosing my location probably applied to phone calls as well as news stories, so I didn't say exactly where I was. Allen didn't exactly apologize for our dustup earlier in the day, but he was clearly glad I was alive and well and able to keep writing. With the pipeline cleared between us, he began posting my new material every hour or so. Thus far I'd written—and Sharif had cleared—three updates to my original ten-minute story on the ongoing hunt for the president, complete with additional details provided by the king and the prince themselves, including the fact that Egyptian and Israeli intelligence services were now working closely with the Americans and the Jordanians in the search. I'd also written a brief first-person account of being at the palace when the kamikaze attack took place. I'd wanted to write a story about helping to evacuate the king and his family, but the colonel had rejected this concept out of hand. Instead I wrote a detailed, blow-by-blow description of the battle at the SADAFCO warehouses north of the airport.

Every muscle in my body ached. The pills the doctor had given me earlier in the day were dulling the intensity of my gunshot wound, but the pain was still there, still throbbing. My head was killing me as well. I was feeling dehydrated and chugged down two bottles of water before deciding finally to retire for the night and get some desperately needed sleep.

Sharif requested pillows, an air mattress, and a few blankets for me, and they were all graciously delivered within the next ten minutes, along with basic toiletries, including a toothbrush, toothpaste, and some mouthwash. After Sharif said goodnight, an armed MP led me to the restroom, where I washed up, then led me back to the cramped little office. As I lay down, the MP took up his position outside my door. I wasn't going anywhere tonight. Nor was anyone coming in. For now, that was all I needed to know.

I turned out the lights and lay down on the

thin mattress. I pulled the blankets over me, trying to ignore the smell of the dirty carpet and trying equally not to think about the discomfort of not being able to fully stretch out my legs.

Instead, staring up at the ceiling, I thought about my mom back in Bar Harbor, Maine. I knew she was worried sick. But I also knew she was praying for me. I wished I could have called her, but there hadn't been time, and I knew she was tracking the story on the *Times* website. She could see my dispatches. She knew I was alive and kicking. She knew I was doing my job, and I knew she was proud of me. Indeed, I was writing each of my stories with her as my audience—not Vice President Holbrooke or the secretary of defense or King Abdullah or Abu Khalif or anyone else. I was trying to explain what I was seeing and hearing to my mom, in language clear and colorful enough to bring it all alive for her. Still, I wanted to talk to her, wanted to tell her personally that I was okay, wanted to hear her voice. Had she talked to Matt? I hoped he'd called her. I hoped he'd explained why he'd left Amman and reassured her that he and Annie and the kids were safe. Where exactly had they gone? I wondered. I had begged them to leave Jordan immediately. Abu Khalif had personally threatened them and our entire family. I was glad Matt had texted me to let me know they were now someplace safe. I could only hope that was really true.

I was not, by any means, a religious man. That was Matt's thing, not mine. My older brother was the pastor and theologian in the family. I was, you might say, the family's black sheep. But I loved my brother. I truly wanted him and his wife and kids to be safe. I couldn't bear the thought of ISIS getting to any of them. So it occurred to me it might be a good idea to pray for them right then, before I fell asleep.

In the darkness, I closed my eyes and folded my hands like I'd done when I was a little kid, and rarely since.

"So, hey, God . . . how's it going?" I began, then felt foolish for sounding so ridiculous. "Look, I don't really know if you're there. But if you are, I'm asking you to please—you know—keep my mom safe. And Matt. And Annie. And the kids. I'm scared for them. They haven't done anything wrong. But I feel like I've put their lives in danger. And I'm sorry about that. And I just ask that you, well, protect them, and make sure nothing happens to them. Okay? All right, well, thanks, and good night—or amen—or whatever. Anyway, that's it. Okay. I'm done. Good-bye."

I felt like an idiot. That had to be the worst prayer in the history of prayer. If there was a God in heaven, I was sure he was laughing at me. Well, not sure. The truth was I had no idea what God might be thinking. But as intensely uncomfortable and deeply self-conscious as I felt at that moment, there was also, I had to admit—if only to myself— something vaguely comforting in having tried to have a meaningful conversation with God for once in my adult life. I couldn't explain it. I didn't even really want to think about it, much less analyze it. But it was true. And that made me curious.

14

★ ★ ★

The next thing I knew, Colonel Sharif was trying to wake me up.

"J. B.? J. B., can you hear me?"

"What time is it?" I groaned, rubbing my eyes and trying to remember where exactly I was.

"It's just after four."

"A.m. or p.m.?"

"A.m.," he said. "Very a.m."

I groaned again, rolled over, and pulled the blanket over my eyes. In this windowless room, there was no evidence it was morning, but regardless, I still needed many more hours of sleep before I could function effectively again.

"Sorry, J. B.," the colonel said, not really sounding that apologetic. "I let you sleep as long as I could. But we have breaking news. You need to come into the bunker."

He handed me a cup of freshly brewed black coffee, a peace offering of sorts. It worked. The aroma alone helped get me to my feet. Given that I was bald, I didn't need to worry about how my hair looked, though a shower and a good shave would have been nice before seeing the king and his brother again. But Sharif insisted there was no time. I needed to move quickly. So I threw on my shoes, gulped down some Sumatran Reserve Extra Bold, and followed the colonel to the war room, a fresh MP at our side.

The bunker was a beehive of activity. The king didn't look like he'd ever gone to bed, but he had changed out of the suit he'd been wearing at the summit into fatigues. He was in battle mode now, the warrior king, and he looked angry.

"Collins, take a seat," he said as he caught my eye and the vault door shut behind me. "Abu Khalif has just sent a new video to Al Jazeera. The network has been told to broadcast it precisely at 6 a.m. local time. But one of their producers contacted the colonel here and suggested we should watch it first."

"Have you seen it?" I asked.

"No, not yet," the monarch said. "None of us. Whatever it is, I thought you'd want to break the story."

"Isn't the whole world going to see it at once?" I asked.

"The video, yes," he replied. "But I want you to report my reaction and the next steps we take against ISIS."

I took a deep breath and tried in vain to steel myself for what was coming. The king ordered Sharif to play the video, and I turned so I could see the monitor. It took a moment before Sharif could get the images from the e-mail on his laptop to the main screen, but a few seconds later, the image appeared. When the video began to play, I felt I could hardly breathe.

The first shot was that of a man who had become all too familiar to me in recent days: Abu Khalif, the emir of ISIS and self-proclaimed caliph, wearing a kaffiyeh and flowing white robes. While I had met him and spoken to him and even interviewed him in person, face-to-face, this image startled me because it was the first video ISIS had ever released with its leader in the starring role. Until a few days earlier, Khalif had been locked away in a maximum-security prison in Abu Ghraib, Iraq, not far from Baghdad. But now, as the world knew because of my reporting, the forces of ISIS had attacked the prison, killed most of its leaders and guards, and freed the spiritual and political leader of the Islamic State. The photos I had taken that had accompanied my front-page story in the *Times* just a few days ago were some of the first the world had ever seen of this barbaric tyrant. Now they were going to see him on television and hear his voice, and I didn't dare imagine what he was about to say.

What struck me in particular was not the dark eyes or carefully trimmed beard of the emir but the setting he'd chosen in which to shoot this video. He was standing in the courtyard of what appeared to be an ancient, crumbling, perhaps even abandoned mosque. There were several decaying arches behind him, though one of the archways had collapsed entirely and was just a heap of stones. It wasn't obvious whether this was from recent bomb damage or from an earthquake centuries before, but it was clear that the video had been shot at night. The partially collapsed structure revealed the night sky, and stars were clearly visible, as was part of the moon. The rest of the courtyard was awash in klieg lights that created harsh and oddly formed shadows in the background.

"I am Abu Khalif, the head of the Islamic State," he began, speaking in flawless, classical Arabic and looking straight into the camera. "I greet you in the name of Allah, the most beneficent, the most merciful. All praise and thanks be to Allah, the Lord of the *'Alamin*, the only owner, the only ruling judge on the Day of Recompense, the Day of Judgment, the day of the glorious resurrection. The Day of Reckoning is coming, the Day of Decision you used to deny."

He was citing various passages from the Qur'an, pretending to be the spiritual and political leader of a billion and a half Muslims worldwide rather than the savage, soulless terrorist he was in reality.

"Truly, all praise belongs to Allah. We praise him and seek his help and his forgiveness. We seek refuge with Allah from the evils of our souls and from the consequences of our deeds. Whoever Allah guides can never be led astray, and whoever Allah leads astray can never be guided. I testify that there is no god except Allah, alone without any partners, and I testify that Muhammad—peace and blessings be upon him—is his slave and messenger. It was this messenger who instructed us in the holy Qur'an that 'he who deceives shall be faced with his deceit on the Day of Resurrection, when every human being shall be repaid in full for whatever he has done, and none shall be wronged.' Tonight judgment has begun for some of the worst deceivers on our planet. As many of you know by now, forces of the Islamic State have launched an operation inside the heart of Jordan, territory that once was held by the dark forces of the Hashemite infidels but has been liberated by our brave forces and is now part of the ever-expanding caliphate."

The image quickly changed to shots of distinctive black ISIS flags flying over various landmarks in Amman as well as over villages that could conceivably be Jordanian but weren't immediately distinguishable from villages throughout Syria or Iraq. I glanced at the king, but he was inscrutable. He was serious and intently focused on both the images and what Khalif was saying, but his expression hadn't changed at all. Colonel Sharif, on the other hand, looked like he was about to become violently ill.

"Presently the warriors of the Islamic State are embarked on a brave and glorious mission to overthrow the wicked regime in Amman, to rid the holy lands of corruption and betrayal of the Qur'an and the Prophet. Our forces are determined to restore this land and its people to the rightful rule of the caliphate and Sharia law. As I speak to you, this operation is already bearing great fruit. For tonight, by the power and greatness of Allah, I announce to you that our forces have captured the leader of the arrogant powers, the dog of Rome, the president of the United States."

An audible gasp went through the command center as the image panned from the emir to a shot of President Harrison Taylor wearing an orange jumpsuit, his hands and feet in shackles, standing in the middle of a grotesque iron cage.

15

★ ★ ★

The camera zoomed in on the president.

And then, on cue, Taylor spoke directly to the camera.

"My name is Harrison Beresford Taylor," he said slowly, methodically, wincing several times as if in pain. As he spoke, Arabic subtitles scrolled across the bottom of the screen. "I am the forty-fifth president of the United States. I was captured by the Islamic State in Amman on December 5. I am being held by the Islamic State in a location that has not been disclosed to me, but I can say . . . I can say honestly . . . I can say honestly that I am being treated well and have been given the opportunity to give *ba'yah*—that is to say, to pledge allegiance . . . to the Islamic State. I ask my fellow Americans, including all my colleagues in Washington, to listen . . . to listen carefully . . . that is, to listen carefully and respectfully to the emir, and to follow the instructions . . . he is about to set forth for my safe and expeditious return."

I could envision the experts and analysts back at Langley carefully scrutinizing the video in every possible manner. But there was no doubt. The face. The voice. The inflections. He was being forced to read a prepared text, to be sure, but there was no question it was really the president. This wasn't a look-alike. This wasn't a trick. ISIS had really captured him, and it was really, tragically, Harrison Taylor in the cage. For me, the real questions were where exactly this had been recorded and when.

When Taylor was finished, the camera panned back to Khalif.

"Allah has given this infidel into our hands," he continued, once again speaking in Arabic. "O Muslims everywhere, glad tidings to you! Raise your heads high, for today, by Allah's grace, you have a sign of his favor upon you. You also have a state and caliphate, which will return your dignity, might, rights, and leadership. It is a state where the Arab and non-Arab, the white man and black man, the Easterner and Westerner are all brothers. Their blood mixed and became one, under a single flag and goal, in one pavilion, enjoying this blessing, the blessing of faithful brotherhood. So all praise and thanks are due to Allah. Therefore, rush, O Muslims, to your state. Yes, it is your state. Rush, because Syria is not for the Syrians, and Iraq is not for the Iraqis, and Jordan is not for the Jordanians. The earth is Allah's. Indeed, the earth belongs to Allah. He causes to inherit it whomever he wills of his servants.

"We make a special call to the scholars, experts in Islamic jurisprudence, and especially judges, as well as people with military, administrative, and service expertise, and medical doctors and engineers of all different specializations and fields. We call them and remind them to fear Allah and to come to the caliphate so that they can answer the dire needs of their Muslim brothers.

"And I make a special call to you, O soldiers of the Islamic State—do not be awestruck by the great numbers of your enemy, for Allah is with you. I do not fear for you the numbers of your opponents, nor do I fear your neediness and poverty, for Allah has promised your Prophet—peace be upon him—that you will not be wiped out by famine, and your enemy will not conquer you or continue to violate and control your land. I promised you that in the name of Allah we would capture the American president, and I have kept my word. The king of Jordan will soon be in our hands. So will all the infidel leaders in this region. So will all the dogs in Rome. The ancient prophecies tell us the End of Days is upon us, and with it the judgment of all who will not bow the knee and submit to Allah and his commanders on the earth."

Khalif now turned to his right and we had a new camera angle of him, against the backdrop of a shadowy stone wall. When he resumed speaking, it was in English.

"Now I speak directly to Vice President Holbrooke, the new leader of Rome. Fearful and trembling, weak and unsteady, you and the infidels you lead have lost your way. You have three choices—convert to Islam, pay the *jizyah*, or die. You have these three choices, but you do not have time. You must choose your fate and choose it quickly. If you and your country choose to convert, you must give a speech to the world doing so under the precise language and conditions of Sharia law, and you will be blessed by Allah and have peace with the caliphate. If you choose to pay the *jizyah*, you must pay $1,000 U.S. for every man, woman, and child living in the United States of America. I have just sent to the *New York Times* the details of a certain bank account. I am certain they will forward the information to you. Upon its receipt you must immediately deposit the full amount into the account to cover the *jizyah* tax. If you do not, or if you act with aggression in any matter against me or against the caliphate, the next video you see will be your beloved president beheaded or burned alive. From the time of this broadcast, you have forty-eight hours, and not a minute more."

Khalif turned again, back to the first camera, and spoke in a close-up, once more in Arabic.

"The spark was lit in Iraq," he concluded. "It spread to Syria and now to Jordan. Its heat will continue to intensify until it burns the crusader armies in Dabiq. Let there be no doubt. Let all the world understand. Rome is falling. The Caliphate is arising. We are waiting for you in Dabiq."

16

* * *

When the video was finished, the room was deadly silent.

No one spoke for several moments. Everyone seemed to be processing both the chilling words and images. Every minute that went by, I had more questions, but I didn't feel it was my place to ask. Not yet. I wanted to see how the king and the prince and the generals would react to the tape, not to me.

Meanwhile, the young military aide who attended to the king's every need was typing furiously on a laptop. I would soon learn he had been creating a precise transcript of Abu Khalif's words in Arabic and then producing a flawless English interpretation. When he was finished, he printed out copies of both and handed them to each person in the room. I'd gotten most of what Khalif had said the first time. He had spoken slowly and deliberately, so in that sense it was easier for me to process. There was some vocabulary and several theological references that I didn't immediately understand. But reading both the Arabic and the

English versions just moments after watching the video and hearing the words spoken was enormously helpful.

I glanced at the clocks on the wall and then at my pocket watch. The video was going to air across the globe on Al Jazeera in less than twelve minutes. But the king had yet to react.

When he finally spoke, rather than revealing his own thoughts, he asked his war council for theirs. The suspense was killing me, but I held my tongue.

Lieutenant General Abdul Jum'a went first. "I don't believe he is on Jordanian soil, Your Majesty," he began.

"Why?"

"Too risky," the army commander replied. "They know our forces are fully deployed. Yes, we have lost control of some towns and parts of some cities in the north as the ISIS uprising has spread. But they know it's a matter of hours, at most a few days, until we reclaim full control over those places. I don't think Abu Khalif would risk being captured—and the president being rescued—here in Jordan. Not when he has other, better alternatives."

I could hardly process the information. This was the first I'd heard of additional ISIS offensive operations outside of Amman, and certainly no one had mentioned that any Jordanian territory had actually been seized by ISIS in the north—not in my hearing, anyway.

"So where do you think they are?" the king asked.

"I cannot say for certain, of course, but in my opinion the most logical thing to do would be to evacuate the president and take him into Syria or Iraq."

"Dabiq?"

"No, that's too far north—past Aleppo, almost to the Turkish border," Jum'a said. "They wouldn't have had time to get him up there this fast."

"What about Homs?"

"Maybe, but again, that's quite a ways north. And if they were driving, they'd have to make a wide berth around Damascus, given that Assad's forces are still in control of most of the capital."

"Then where?"

"If it were me, I'd take him to southeast Syria, to the heart of ISIS territory, somewhere along the Euphrates, someplace the Americans would never go."

"Deir ez-Zor? Mayadin?"

"Perhaps, though again, if I were Abu Khalif, I'd create my base camp someplace even smaller, a little town or village that was off the radar, discreet, unnoticed. There are a hundred of them up and down the river on both sides."

"And what if they took him to Iraq?" asked Prince Feisal, now on his feet and poring over one of the maps on the wall.

"They wouldn't," the general said.

"Why not?"

"Because you've got too many forces trying to retake northern Iraq," Jum'a explained. "You've got the Kurds, the Americans, the Shia militias, the Iraqi regular forces—they're all trying to retake the north. Why should Khalif take the risk? Why not set up his base camp in Syria? No one's trying to retake Syria except Assad, and he simply doesn't have the strength to get the job done."

"Okay, but what if they did go to Iraq?" Feisal pressed.

"Then they're crazy."

"And they're not?"

"Abu Khalif is crazy like a fox. He's not a lunatic. Take my word for it. He's not in Iraq. He's in Syria."

"But Khalif was just in Mosul," noted the prince. "He was just there with Mr. Collins. They're testing chemical weapons there. They have a warehouse full of munitions, captured from Aleppo."

"Had," the general insisted. "They *had* a base in Mosul. They *had* a warehouse full of chemical weapons. The only reason to reveal it all to Collins and the *New York Times* was if everything was being moved. I guarantee you—none of it is there today."

The prince let it drop.

The king nodded but made no comment before turning to Major General Ibrahim al-Mufti, his air force commander. "Could they have moved the president by air?"

"Not from Amman, Your Majesty," al-Mufti replied. "They would have moved him in the trunk of a car or the back of a van or truck, driven him a few kilometers, switched vehicles, and kept moving like that until they could get well outside our initial perimeter."

"But then, couldn't they have put him on a small plane or helicopter and flown him out of the country?"

"If they had help from locals, yes, I'm afraid they could have."

"Did we detect air activity heading to Syria or northern Iraq overnight?"

"I don't know, Your Majesty. I just sent an e-mail to my intel chief and told him to run the tapes on all air traffic control stations for the last twelve hours. It'll take some time, but I will let you know when I hear something."

For several moments the king said nothing. He showed no emotion. He had a pretty strong five o'clock shadow and was clearly exhausted. He had to be. Yet he struck me as remarkably calm, given that his kingdom was under attack from all sides, much of his government was dead or incapacitated, and ISIS had captured the leader of the free world on Jordanian soil.

"What do you make of the video?" he asked al-Mufti.

The general leaned back in his chair and took some time to answer. "Abdul is right," he said at last. "Khalif is crazy like a fox. He has a plan. He's trying to draw us into a much more dangerous war, a ground war, a war in Dabiq."

"You think he's in Dabiq?" the king asked.

"No, I don't," al-Mufti replied. "But I think he's trying to draw us and the Americans into a ground war there."

The room grew silent again, but I couldn't hold back any longer. "Why?" I asked. "Why Dabiq?"

"Because that's where he believes the last battle will be fought."

"The last battle?"

"The End of Days," said al-Mufti. "The Day of Judgment. It's all going to consummate in Dabiq. That's what they think."

"Who?"

"Abu Khalif, ISIS, all of them," said the general. "They believe the Prophet—peace be upon him—spoke of a final, catastrophic, apocalyptic battle between the Muslims and the forces of Rome that would unfold on the plains of northern Syria in a place called Dabiq."

"The forces of Rome? What does that mean—the Italians, the Vatican?"

"Maybe yes, maybe no," said al-Mufti. "You heard Khalif call the president 'the dog of Rome'?"

"I did, but why? What does that mean?"

"Some Sunnis believe the Americans are the new Crusaders, that Washington is the new Rome, that the president is the new Caesar. The ISIS crowd certainly believes it. No question that Khalif does. Believe me, they're never going to give up the president of the United States, even if your entire country converts or pays the tax. The president is their prize. I wouldn't be surprised if he was dead already."

17

★ ★ ★

The king became visibly angry, though he controlled his tongue.

"Don't speak like this, Ibrahim—I will not have it," he insisted. "We have to operate on the assumption that the president is still alive. We cannot give up this hope. There are forty-eight hours left. We need to use them wisely. We need to find the president and rescue him or help the Americans rescue him. The fate of the kingdom hangs in the balance. Now, Abdul, you think Abu Khalif and the president are in southeastern Syria?"

"Yes, Your Majesty, I do," Jum'a confirmed.

"Ibrahim, what about you?"

"Where do I think they are?"

"Yes."

"I'd say Abdul is probably right—Khalif is in Syria."

"And the president?"

"If he's still alive?"

At this, the king's jaws tightened. "Yes," he said carefully.

"I don't think they'd keep the two together."

"Why not?"

"Operational security," Al-Mufti said. "The entire universe is now looking for the president of the United States. It's highly unlikely anyone finds him within forty-eight hours, but if they do—if we do, if anybody does—Abu Khalif is no fool. He's not going to be in the same location."

"Would Khalif send the president into Iraq or just put him in a different safe house in Syria?"

"That I can't say, Your Majesty. But I'm happy to develop contingency plans for both scenarios."

"Yes, do that—work together, both of you," the king said to his generals. "Get your best people working on this. You've got an hour. I want a detailed intelligence analysis of everything we've got so far—the video, the radar tracking of aircraft moving across the Syrian and Iraqi borders, the interrogations your men are doing with ISIS forces captured at the palace and at the SADAFCO plant, signals intelligence, paid informants we've got on the ground in Syria and Iraq—everything. And where are we with Jamal Ramzy's cell phone, the one Collins here pulled off his body at the palace? It turned out to be encrypted, did it not?"

"It was, Your Majesty," Prince Feisal said.

"Have we cracked it yet?"

"They're still working on it."

"Tell them time is running out," the king insisted. "I want to know everything about that phone—what calls were made on it, what calls were received, all of it, when we meet in an hour. Am I clear?"

"Yes, Your Majesty."

"Good. Now get to work."

The king stood, and the rest of us did as well. The generals saluted and then bolted out of the bunker. The prince was about to begin working the phones again, but the king pulled him aside. Colonel Sharif, meanwhile, suggested he and I head back to my temporary office to write up the story of the video.

But as we left, I heard the king ask his brother in a somewhat-hushed tone, "Now, listen—where are we with this mole hunt?"

Back in the office, Colonel Sharif opened a safe and pulled out my iPhone.

He let me put in my password, but since I was not allowed to send any messages without his permission, he kept control of the phone. As the phone reconnected to the data service, hundreds of messages began to pour in. But we were looking for just one—an e-mail from Abu Khalif with the details of a bank account to which the U.S. government was supposed to wire more than $320 billion.

"Got it," Sharif said at last.

"Is it from Khalif directly?" I asked, immensely curious.

"It doesn't say," Sharif replied. "It's an anonymous Gmail account."

"No note?"

"No, just the account number and SWIFT code."

The colonel quickly forwarded the e-mail to the king and the prince with a note asking for instructions on whom in the American government to forward it on to. The prince wrote back almost immediately, saying he would take care of it personally.

I spent the next half hour writing up the story of the video. Sharif wouldn't allow me to go back in the bunker to interview the king. But he did step out for a few minutes, and when I was nearly finished, he returned and handed me a typed statement from His Majesty.

This video is further evidence of Abu Khalif's descent into evil. It is proof of his apostasy, his wickedness and barbarism. The forces of ISIS have abandoned all pretense of being Muslims. Such *takfiris* are not practicing true Islam. They have perverted the religion of my fathers and forefathers beyond recognition. The kingdom of Jordan stands against such evildoers. We stand for peace and moderation.

On behalf of all the peace-loving people of my kingdom, I pledge to do everything in my power to assist the United States, our great ally, in safely recovering President Taylor and returning him to his family and his nation.

At the same time, I pledge to bring Abu Khalif and his men to justice. They

are guilty not only of terrorism but
of treason and a host of other crimes
punishable by death. And I will not rest
until they have been captured, tried,
convicted, and eradicated from the earth.

This last part intrigued me. The king was vow-
ing to execute Abu Khalif and the leaders of ISIS.
I asked the colonel to clarify this, given that I was
quite sure Jordan's government hadn't executed
any criminals in years. Sharif confirmed it but
noted that death penalty laws were still on the
books for a variety of heinous crimes from rape,
murder, and drug trafficking to weapons smuggling, espionage, and treason.

I dropped in the king's entire statement, verbatim, toward the end of the article. Normally I'd
include only a line or two, but I figured in this case
it was safer to let the Jordanians see I was transmitting everything they gave me and leave it to Allen
and the brass back in the States to edit it down as
they felt appropriate.

As this was a straight news piece, I led, of course,
with Abu Khalif's demand for the vice president
of the United States to lead his country in conver-
sion to Islam or else pay an ancient tax described
in the Qur'an. The only alternative was to see their
president executed in the most despicable manner possible. I emphasized the forty-eight-hour
deadline and noted that "unnamed intelligence
officials believe the president has most likely been
moved out of Jordan and is probably in Syria or

Iraq, though this could not be confirmed." At first Sharif was bothered by that line, saying it was the very type of speculation the king objected to. But I pushed back, noting that it was the king's own speculation and that of his top military leaders, not my own. In the end, I prevailed and the colonel transmitted the story as written.

By the time Sharif was finished e-mailing the story to Allen and I'd had a few minutes to wash up and get another cup of coffee, we had only about ten or twelve minutes before we had to be back in the bunker to meet with His Majesty and hear the briefings by the generals. I asked the colonel if he'd be willing to scroll through my e-mails and text messages and print out anything from my family, anything from Allen, or anything that seemed either personal or particularly urgent. He graciously agreed and left the room to take care of it. I used the time to lie down on the air mattress for a moment to close my eyes and catch a few z's. But exhausted as I was, I could not sleep.

I found my thoughts turning to the king's question to his brother.

"Where are we with this mole hunt?"

It was an important and frightening question, and with all that had been happening over the past eighteen hours or so, I'd completely lost track of the fact that there was almost certainly a mole within the Jordanian government. The ISIS attack on the Al-Hummar Palace had been exquisitely planned and executed. Surely it had required someone on the inside—more likely several people. The name of the Jordanian F-16 pilot who had fired on the summit assembly and then flown a suicide mission into the palace had not yet been released, but I had no doubt the royal family was doing a full investigation into the man's background, family, associates, and possible connections to ISIS. But the full-blown coup d'état scenario—in which more than fifteen thousand ISIS jihadists had participated—could not have been the work of just a single rogue pilot. Someone else—someone with access, with detailed knowledge of the plans for the summit—had to have tipped off Abu Khalif and his men to the peace summit's location, timing, and other details. But who?

There was a fairly limited list of possible suspects, and most of those people were now dead. The question was who on the list was still alive, still in a position to bring down the king and prevent any possible rescue of the president from being successful?

At that moment it occurred to me that everyone in the bunker—short of the king himself—was a suspect.

18

★ ★ ★

It was just before seven o'clock when there was a knock on my office door.

The colonel entered, but he was not alone. Prince Feisal was with him, along with one of the MPs who had been assigned to me and a half-dozen other elite soldiers guarding the prince.

"Mr. Collins, would you take a walk with me?" the prince asked as we stepped out into the hallway. "There is a matter of great importance I'd like to discuss with you."

"Hasn't His Majesty asked us to gather in the bunker?" I asked.

"That meeting is already under way," Feisal replied. "I'll join them in a little while. But this matter cannot wait."

"Well, sure, okay; if you insist," I said.

"I do."

We headed up the stairs, trailed by the security detail. When we reached the vestibule, however, we didn't stop. Rather, the prince led me outside and across the tarmac. It was the first time I'd been outside in nearly twelve hours, and it was good to feel the rising sun on my face and a brisk December breeze as well. There were scattered clouds overhead and actual patches of blue between them. Yet to the north, dark thunderheads were rolling in. Another storm was coming.

We paused at the flight line as a squadron of F-15s took off toward the west, headed, no doubt, back to Amman with a fresh payload of missiles and bombs. To our left, two Cobra helicopter gunships were on approach to land, while two more were powering up to lift off and take their place in the fight to reclaim the kingdom. As the last of the Strike Eagles roared past and climbed rapidly into the morning sky, the prince beckoned me to continue walking with him across the tarmac.

"Have you had the opportunity to talk to your mother yet or to your brother?" he asked as we headed toward a series of hangars and administrative buildings on the other side of the base.

"No, not yet, with the time difference and all," I said. "The colonel let me send an e-mail to both of them, though, letting them know I'm okay."

"But not where you are, of course."

"Of course."

"And I understand your brother—Matthew, is it?"

"Yes."

"I understand he and his wife and children left Amman in quite a hurry two nights ago."

"They did."

"Almost like they knew what was coming," the prince said as we passed through a security checkpoint and entered an unmarked three-story office building.

"What are you implying?" I asked, suddenly caught off guard by his tone.

"I'm not implying anything," said the prince, boarding an elevator with me and three of the six members of the security detail right behind him. "I'm simply noting that they just up and left the country—leaving all of their possessions behind— just hours before the worst terrorist attacks in the history of our country."

"And?"

"And how did they know?"

"I warned them to leave."

"Why would you do that?"

"You know why."

"I'm afraid I don't," the prince said. "Enlighten me." He pushed the button for the third floor and the door closed behind us.

This was no longer a friendly conversation. I wasn't about to get an exclusive interview with the second-highest-ranking military officer in the kingdom. This was an interrogation.

I took a deep breath and tried to maintain my composure. There was no point in getting angry—not visibly, anyway. It would only make me look guilty. But angry I was. I could feel my face starting to get red and the back of my neck getting hot.

"Your Royal Highness, you know very well why I encouraged my brother and his family to leave," I said as calmly as I could. "Abu Khalif threatened them by name. He indicated to me that he knew exactly where they lived in Amman. I didn't feel they were safe any longer. And it turns out I was right."

"Khalif threatened your mother as well, did he not?"

"He did."

"Has she suddenly evacuated her home in Bar Harbor?"

"No."

"Did you advise her to leave?"

"No."

"Just your brother. Why?"

The bell rang. The elevator stopped. The door opened on the third floor, and the other three security guards were somehow already waiting for us.

The prince now led us down a long hallway, past one cubicle after another packed with air force officers of various ranks, all hard at work, talking quietly and moving quickly. We were walking briskly, but I could see lots of maps and satellite photos on the walls. I wondered at first if this was a flight-planning and meteorological center, but when we reached the end of the hall, the prince ushered me into a spacious corner office guarded by two MPs. Four of the six security men entered the office with us, while two stayed outside with the guards, and the door was locked behind us.

To my right were a desk and chair and credenza and a Jordanian flag on a stand. Straight ahead was a long set of bookshelves, and to my left were a round wooden conference table and four chairs and a large window looking out over the airfield. The prince led me over to the table and asked me to take a seat. As I did, I glanced at the titles of the books, and it became instantly clear the work being done here was neither aeronautic nor weather-related. This building was part of the Jordanian intelligence directorate, and I was under suspicion.

"Would you like some coffee?" the prince asked, pouring some for himself from a freshly brewed pot on a side table.

"No thank you."

"A soft drink?"

"No."

"Water?" he asked.

"I'm fine."

"Nevertheless . . . ," he said and poured me a plastic cup of water from a pitcher beside the coffeepot and set it down in front of me.

I nodded my thanks and braced myself for what was coming next.

"So," the prince continued when he had taken a seat, "your brother."

"What would you like to know?"

"I'd like an honest answer as to why you told him to leave his home in such a rush, but not your mother."

"Isn't it obvious?" I asked. "Matt was closer to Abu Khalif. He and Annie and the kids were in far greater danger. My mother lives half a world away."

"And you didn't think she was in imminent danger from ISIS?"

"Of course not."

"But you thought it was obvious Amman was going to be attacked."

"Yes."

"And your brother believed you?"

"I'm glad he did," I said. "As it turns out, I was right."

"So you were."

"Matt wasn't the only one I told, Your Highness," I noted. "I told the king I was afraid ISIS would attack the peace summit. He didn't believe me."

"Perhaps he didn't realize you weren't speculating."

"Meaning what?"

"Meaning perhaps you knew for a fact the attack was coming."

"If I'd known for a fact, I would have said so. But I warned the king as clearly and urgently as I could. I warned the president as well."

"When?"

"On Marine One, en route to the palace."

"Did the president believe you?"

"No."

"Did he take you seriously?"

"No."

"Because he thought you were speculating, correct?"

"Apparently."

"He didn't think you knew exactly what was going to happen."

"I didn't know exactly."

"So you say."

"Let's just be clear, Your Highness—are you actually accusing *me* of being the mole?"

19

* * *

The prince glared at me.

"You have to admit, Mr. Collins, the evidence is rather compelling, is it not?"

"How so?" I asked, incredulous but determined to maintain control.

"You really need me to explain it to you?"

"Uh, yeah, I'm afraid I do."

"Very well," the prince said. "As you know, the list of suspects—the people who knew the summit was going to be held in Amman, at the Al-Hummar Palace, who knew the exact time, the precise details—is a very short list indeed. What's more, as you also know, most of the people on that list are dead, strongly suggesting that none of them were the culprits. But you, Mr. Collins—of all the names that remain on that list, you're rather unique."

"How so?" I asked again, not sure what else to say.

"Well, of course, you are the only one who has ever met Abu Khalif face-to-face. You're the only one to have spent time with him. Significant time. And not just with the emir of ISIS but with his senior commander in Syria, Jamal Ramzy. You know them both. You've spoken with them both, at length. You've been to their lairs. You've met their advisors. They've told you their plans. They've instructed you to tell the world certain things, and you've done exactly what they asked of you."

"That's my job, Your Highness."

"Some are beginning to wonder what that job actually is."

"Are you actually accusing me of being an agent of ISIS? Don't you see how ridiculous that sounds?"

"I'm not accusing you of anything, Mr. Collins. I just thought it was only fair to let you know what some are saying about you, so you can, shall we say, disabuse them of their concerns."

"I don't believe this."

"Why not? Being a foreign correspondent for the *New York Times* would be the perfect cover for a mole." The prince stood and began to walk about the room as he explained the emerging theory of my crimes. "Who else has spent time with the leaders of ISIS and repeatedly lived to tell about it?"

"If I was plotting to kill the four leaders at the summit, why in the world would I have warned two of them in advance about such an attack?"

"There could be any number of reasons."

"Pick one."

"Very well," the prince said. "To create plausible deniability. You certainly don't have an alibi. You're consistently in the wrong place at the wrong time, yet you keep surviving while everyone around you keeps dying. By telling His Majesty and the president that ISIS was about to attack—yet providing no proof whatsoever—you could make it look like you were only trying to help."

"That's ridiculous."

"Is it?"

"And the wrong place at the wrong time? I myself was nearly killed each time."

"Of course—but you weren't. You survived."

"Yeah, but—"

"Take Istanbul, for example."

"What about Istanbul?"

"A car bomb goes off in the heart of an Islamic capital," the prince said, still pacing. "A Jordanian national is killed, allegedly a good friend and coworker of yours, but somehow you survive. The prime suspect in the bombing is a mysterious woman you were having drinks with, yet you refuse to give the authorities her name or any details about her."

He paused, but I said nothing. I was in shock.

"Or take Union Station," he continued. "A terrorist group—apparently an ISIS sleeper cell—opens fire in the middle of the train station in Washington, D.C. The shooters target everyone on the top floor of the restaurant—the, uh, the . . . What was it called again?"

"Center Café," I said numbly.

"Right, the Center Café. The shooters kill every patron on the top floor of the restaurant—every FBI agent and a former director of the CIA—and you're the only one who survives. Doesn't that strike you as just a little odd?"

"Are you forgetting that I actually shot and killed one of the terrorists?"

"Oh, you're ready to admit that, are you? I've seen the surveillance tapes. The FBI has seen them too, and from the various angles of the cameras and the lighting and the shadows, it's impossible to tell who actually shot the female terrorist on the ground floor. Very convenient, isn't it? Yet, remarkably, a few moments later, you go running through the crime scene, uninjured, unharmed. The FBI is still wondering, why exactly did you run? If you're innocent, why didn't you go to the police? Why didn't you go to the FBI? Why didn't you go to any of the authorities and explain to them what you'd done if it was really in self-defense and not to cover up a larger crime?"

My anger was rising, but I continued to hold my tongue.

"No, instead you didn't just flee the scene of a crime—the site of a major terrorist attack— oh no, you actually fled the country," the prince continued. "Using a false passport. Using fake credit cards. Using an alias, no less. Where does an innocent man get such things? And then you wind up in Baghdad on the very day—indeed, the very moment—of a coordinated prison break during which Abu Khalif escapes. You come back to Jordan and all hell breaks loose. Yet again, miraculously, you escape unharmed, or nearly so. You see where this is heading, Mr. Collins? You see why people are growing deeply concerned that maybe you're not covering this story—maybe you're causing it?"

I couldn't believe how quickly things were going south. I felt completely blindsided and disoriented, yet I realized there was no point answering the prince's accusations. I was, in essence, being accused of treason, and as Colonel Sharif had recently made clear to me, treason was a crime punishable by death.

"I want to meet with the American ambassador," I said as calmly as I could.

"No," the prince said.

"I insist."

"I'm afraid that's impossible."

"Why?" I asked.

"Because he's dead."

It was as if the wind had been knocked out of me. I suddenly remembered seeing the U.S. ambassador to Jordan in the audience at the summit, sitting with several dozen other ambassadors, most of whom had probably also been killed in the attacks.

"I'm very sorry to hear that," I replied. "Then I would like to speak to the attorney for the *Times*."

"All in due time," said the prince. "I have a few more questions I'd like answers to first."

"These aren't questions," I responded. "This is an interrogation. I'm an American citizen, and I'm entitled to legal counsel before I say anything else."

"You're certain of that, Mr. Collins?" he asked.

"Quite," I said.

"Very well, then; when this whole episode with the president is resolved, we'll see if we can't get the attorney for the *New York Times* to come over to Amman so the two of you can have a chat."

With that, the prince instructed the MPs to handcuff me and take me immediately to the detention center. "Put him on level B, cell number three," he said.

Then he turned and walked away.

20

★ ★ ★

The door slammed and locked behind me.

I was alone.

Cell number three was a narrow, dark, damp cinder-block room containing only an army cot, a metal toilet without a seat, and a small metal sink that dispensed only cold water—very cold at that, and not much of it. The room was so narrow I could stretch out my arms and almost touch both walls at the same time, though not quite. Oddly, its ceiling was very high, perhaps five or six meters. There were no windows and thus no natural light, only a bare, dim bulb hanging by a thin cord from that high ceiling, far too high for me to reach.

There were no books or magazines or newspapers or reading materials of any kind. There was nothing on the walls—no signs, no markings, and certainly no mirror. Indeed, as I glanced about, the two most noticeable features of the cell were how barren it looked and how cold it felt. One thin green blanket was folded up at the end of the bed, but there were no sheets on the threadbare mattress, and the tiny pillow was made of plastic and had no pillowcase. Nevertheless, I lay down and stared up at the lightbulb and tried to settle my nerves and gather my thoughts.

I'd not been allowed to bring a notepad or pen or any other personal items into the cell. Everything had been removed by the guards when they first brought me into the detention center— everything except my grandfather's gold pocket watch. I'm not sure why they let me keep it. I guess they didn't fear I could use it either to escape or try to harm myself. So I pulled it out, wound it up, and took note of the time. It was just before eight o'clock on the morning of Monday, December 6. The ISIS deadline was just forty-six hours away, and in the midst of the most important story of my lifetime, I was now in prison.

The prince's last words to me rang in my ears. No one was coming to see me, much less get me out of here, until *after* the deadline was over and the president's fate had been decided one way or the other. What was I going to do? No one even knew where I was. Allen knew only that I was in a secure, undisclosed location somewhere near Amman. He didn't know exactly where, and he certainly didn't know I was now behind bars. No one did.

For the life of me, I couldn't even remember the name of the *Times'* law firm. I couldn't remember the name of a single attorney who worked there. And even if I could, how were any of them supposed to get to me? Amman's only international airport was closed indefinitely, a smoking wreckage, its employees murdered by ISIS in a brazen and despicable chemical weapons attack, its runways completely unusable, pockmarked with craters left by enemy mortars and artillery. And even if a sympathetic attorney could physically get not just to Amman but to Marka, to this base, to this makeshift prison, to this cell, why exactly would anyone take such a risk? The forces of the Islamic State were running rampant. People were being slaughtered in the streets of America's most faithful—and until now, most stable—Arab ally. The president of the United States had been captured by ISIS terrorists. What lawyer in his right mind would come here to bail me out?

Theoretically, much could be done by phone, but with whom would a lawyer working on my behalf speak? The king was busy. So were the prince and everyone else on the base. Jordan's minister of justice was on life support in a local hospital and not expected to make it. And even if the Jordanians assigned someone to discuss my case with my lawyers by phone, how likely was it that they were ever going to let me go? The prince was all but accusing me of espionage and treason, both capital crimes. I wasn't going to be released on my own recognizance. There was going to be no bail. With Jordan in flames, I'd be lucky if there was even a trial anytime soon. And what would be my defense?

Upon that thought, I was suddenly on my feet and trying to pace. There wasn't much room, but I certainly couldn't rest. I was utterly exhausted, but sleep was out of the question. I had to figure this out. Someone was guilty of the crimes Prince

Feisal had accused me of, and it definitely wasn't me. But who was it?

I decided to make a list of every possible suspect. From the Jordanians' perspective, clearly, I was at the top. Right beside me, apparently, was Yael Katzir. They didn't have her name yet. Or rather, they hadn't yet connected Yael Katzir, the Mossad agent who had just helped me save the lives of the royal family, with the "mysterious woman" in Istanbul they now considered the prime suspect in the car bombing that had killed my best friend in the world, Omar Fayez. But how much longer would that take?

If they suspected me, wouldn't they soon be suspecting Yael? Once they did, they would undoubtedly "rewind the clock" and play out their theory to its logical conclusion. They would send her photo to the authorities in Washington to see if Yael was in any way connected to the shootings at Union Station. She wasn't, of course, but then they would send her photo to the authorities in Istanbul and ask them to run her face against all surveillance videos of people coming in and out of the airport in the days surrounding the car bombing. Using state-of-the-art facial recognition software, how long would it be before they identified that Yael had in fact been there? A few seconds? A few minutes? Of course, when the Turks crosschecked Yael's face with all the passports processed during her arrival and departure, they wouldn't find one bearing the name Yael Katzir in their database, would they? No. They wouldn't. Why? Because Yael had been using a fake name and a false passport. Why? Because she was on a mission for a foreign intelligence agency. That would lead to even more suspicions by dragging the Israelis into the mix.

My heart was racing. My pulse was pounding. I splashed some water on my face, but it didn't help. I was in danger of hyperventilating. I'd never been claustrophobic in my life, but now I felt like a caged animal, and I was desperate to get out. I needed my freedom. I needed to clear my name, and Yael's, and get back to work.

For it suddenly dawned on me that whoever the mole really was, he—or she—was still on the loose, still at work. This person had already caused the deaths of thousands and could even now be getting ready to kill again.

21

* * *

I woke up in pitch darkness.

Groggy and confused, I had no idea where I was or what time it was. But as I came to, I breathed a great sigh of relief. Clearly, this had all been a terrible dream. I wasn't in Amman. I wasn't in prison. I wasn't facing the death penalty for treason against a king. I couldn't be.

Yet as I felt around, I soon realized that I was not home at my apartment in Arlington, Virginia. Nor in a hotel room in some European or even Middle Eastern capital. I could feel the chilly, damp cinder-block walls. I swung my unshod feet over the edge of the bed and set them down on the cold, dirty floor. I reached out and felt the metal of the sink. And though the bare bulb was not on and thus not visible, I knew it was hanging above me. This was no dream. This was a nightmare.

Lying back down and staring into the great void above me, I did not recall taking off my shoes and socks, much less falling asleep. The last thing I remembered was starting a list of people who might be responsible for this horrific cascade of events. Yael and I topped the list of suspects, but I knew we were innocent. So whom did that leave? It was time to go back to work.

The prince was probably right that some of the most obvious suspects—the most senior aides to President Taylor, Prime Minister Lavi, and President Mansour—could be ruled out since they were dead. It was possible one or more of them was complicit in some way, but it would be difficult if not impossible to prove. For now, I would have to focus on the living. So who had access to the private schedules of all four principals? Who knew the exact details of the summit, including the expected location and movements of the leaders and the precise nature of the security arrangements?

The first name to come to mind was Youssef Kuttab. At fifty-six, he was Palestinian president Salim Mansour's most senior and trusted advisor. Born and raised in Jenin in the West Bank, Youssef had been a longtime member of the PLO before becoming a military aide to Yasser Arafat and later a political aide to Mahmoud Abbas. I knew he was a political mastermind, orchestrating Mansour's stunning electoral victory after Abbas finally decided to step down, then working quietly behind the scenes with the Israelis on the peace deal of the century. He'd been at the summit, of course, at Mansour's side when I'd interviewed the Palestinian leader over breakfast on Sunday morning. Later he'd been in the dining room of the palace, whispering in Mansour's ear just before the comprehensive peace treaty was about to be ratified in front of hundreds of millions of people watching around the world.

Was it all an act? Was Youssef really a closet Islamic Radical, masquerading as a Reformer? I'd known him for years. I'd interviewed him countless times, sometimes on the record but mostly on background. I couldn't imagine he'd be complicit in anything like this, especially when the attack had effectively derailed the treaty he and his boss had worked on so hard for so long.

That said, he had been privy to all the details. He not only knew the summit was going to happen, but I'd been told by multiple sources that Youssef had personally worked in the shadows to persuade the Jordanians to host the summit in Amman, at the palace. Could he actually have been engineering the ISIS attack? Was it possible that rather than supporting the deal President Mansour was striking with the Israelis, Youssef secretly thought the treaty was a catastrophic capitulation, a sellout that betrayed the best interests of his people?

And what of the e-mail he'd sent me just days before the attack? The words now rang in my ears. *I thought you were coming to Ramallah. Things are getting complicated. We need to sit down in person. Where are you?* What, exactly, had been so complicated—a peace deal that might actually get signed, not rejected out of hand by an Israeli prime minister?

I didn't buy it. But I couldn't rule out any theory right now. Everything had to be considered, and anyone running the criminal investigation had to be giving Youssef Kuttab a very hard look.

Also on my list of suspects was Hassan Karbouli, the fifty-one-year-old Iraqi interior minister. Though I considered him a friend and trusted source as well, I was suddenly looking at him very differently. There were several reasons.

First was Hassan's timing. After avoiding me for weeks and ignoring my repeated e-mails and text messages requesting a face-to-face interview with Abu Khalif, Hassan had suddenly and inexplicably summoned me for an interview with the ISIS leader at the Abu Ghraib prison just days before the peace summit. At first Hassan had warned me to stay away from Khalif. But then he'd done a complete reversal, out of the blue. Not only did he offer me an exclusive interview, but he also offered to personally take me to see Khalif. I'd been ecstatic, as had my editors. Now, however, how could the timing not seem suspect? *I got you your interview,* he'd said in his last text to me. *Hope you know what you're doing.* Had he known the prison break was being planned for the exact moment of my interview? Indeed, could he have been involved? How many people besides the Iraqi minister of the interior even knew Abu Khalif was being held in that particular prison, on that floor, in that cell?

Second were Hassan's religion and his politics. He was one of only a handful of Sunni Muslims serving in the predominantly Shia government in Baghdad, and I knew he was increasingly outraged by the moves the Iraqi government was making against Sunnis in recent months. Could he have become not only frustrated but completely enraged? Could he have lost all faith in the concept of democracy in Iraq? Could he have decided to secretly pledge his allegiance to Abu Khalif? Wasn't it possible he could have helped the ISIS leader escape the prison and then get to Mosul? Hassan had been born and raised in Mosul, after all. Who knew the city better than he?

As I lay there in the darkness, I flashed back to my arrival at the airport in Baghdad just a few days before. I could still see Hassan nervously greeting me in his ill-fitting suit. Why exactly had he been so nervous? Why had he changed his plans at the last moment and not gone to the prison with me as I had expected he would? I could still see the anger mixed with fear in his eyes as he railed against his own government. *The Shias have really fouled things up,* he'd told me. *They have no idea how to run the country. . . . Sunnis all across the country are absolutely furious. . . . We have no say, no voice. . . . People are demanding change, and so far the prime minister and his people aren't listening.*

I had never seen Hassan Karbouli so upset. I had never thought him capable of violence. But now I wasn't so sure.

There was a third reason my suspicions were growing, and this one put Hassan in a category of his own: he had known the Israeli–Palestinian peace treaty was coming before anything had been reported in the press. Indeed, he had told me about it himself. He'd pressed me to tell him what I knew, what the precise details were. I'd thought it strange at the time. But even more unnerving was that he had known that the Jordanians were the architects of the whole thing.

"I've heard some rumors," I'd replied, treading carefully. *"I guess we'll just have to wait and see."*

"Perhaps" was all Hassan had said before bidding me farewell.

Had he known more than he was letting on? Was he already deeply involved in plotting against the Jordanians? Did he, like Abu Khalif and ISIS, consider the king and his court infidels, not fit to live or govern any longer?

22

* * *

I suddenly heard a sharp metallic scrape.

Startled, I sat bolt upright in the bed. A sliver of light was leaking in through an open slot at the bottom of the cell door. Someone was sliding in a plate of food and a plastic cup. I jumped to my feet, hoping to talk to whoever was out there, to get my bearings and maybe some news from the outside. But just as quickly as whoever it was had come, he was gone.

It was dark again. I could hear the *tick-tick-tick* of my pocket watch. But there was no point reaching for it. In such darkness, I'd never be able to read it. I was guessing it was around noon, but it was unsettling to say the least to have no idea when the lights were coming back on, when I was going to have contact with another human being, or when I was going to get out of this blasted cell.

My heart started racing again. The claustro-phobia was returning. I felt around and found the sink and splashed more cold water on my face and neck. It was no longer chilly in there. Someone had turned the heat on. It was now boiling, and I felt like I was going to suffocate. I pulled off my shirt. Then I rinsed my hands again and trickled some of the brisk water down my chest and back. That helped a bit, but not nearly enough.

My stomach growled. I thought perhaps some calories would clear my head and calm my nerves. Freaking out wasn't going to help me get through this, though I didn't have a clue what would. Feeling around on the floor in the darkness, I found the plastic plate filled with something warm, and the cup, which was empty. Setting the cup in the sink, I repositioned myself in the bed, my bare back against the wall. Steadying the plate with my left hand, I used my right index finger to poke at the food and try to figure out what it was without burning myself. There was about a cupful of steamed rice, what felt like some overcooked vegetables, and a protein bar of some kind.

Famished, I quickly scarfed it all down despite the bland taste. Then I rinsed off the plate in the sink, set it back on the floor by the door, gulped two cups of water, and lay on the bed again in the darkness.

How much time had gone by? What if it was only an hour or two? How was I going to live like this, in alternating heat and cold, in utter darkness, with no one to talk to and no sense of what the future held? I knew I couldn't let myself panic, but I wasn't sure I had a choice. One of the things I valued most in life was my freedom to move, to travel, to roam—around a room or around the world. I'd never been held captive. I didn't know if

I could take it. Mentally. Physically. Emotionally. I wanted to be out. I wanted to be free.

I concentrated on breathing slowly and steadily. I'd never thought of myself as a fearful person. But this was a nightmare, and I didn't know how to wake up. I'd known men who had been held as prisoners of war. I'd interviewed them, written stories about them. Most of them had cracked eventually, I knew, and I feared I might too.

Back to the list, I decided. I had to stay focused, stay sharp.

So who else was a suspect? Who else could be the mole?

I closed my eyes—at least I thought I did, though in utter darkness it was hard to know the difference—and a new face came to mind. Prince Marwan Talal. I tensed. It wasn't possible, was it?

The oldest member of the Hashemite royal family, Marwan was an uncle to King Abdullah II. He was also arguably His Majesty's most trusted advisor, having previously served as a counselor to the late King Hussein, Abdullah's father. I'd first met Marwan through former CIA director Robert Khachigian on a brief trip to London. Khachigian had called the man "a most faithful, stalwart ally in the fight against the extremists in the epicenter." Yet hadn't Khachigian also told me that Marwan was a man who "lives in the shadows"? Hadn't he explained that "few people outside His Majesty's inner circle even know his name"? Then he'd added, *"But he knows theirs. He knows where all the bodies are buried. And I mean that literally."*

Marwan was not just a royal, however. He was

a devout Muslim, a fervent Sunni, a true believer in every possible way. Indeed, on my last visit with him at his lovely, palatial home overlooking the seven hills of Amman, Marwan had actually tried to convert me. He was entering the sunset of his long and storied life, but he still had a fire in his spirit. He was still advancing his goals. Was it even remotely conceivable that his goals included the overthrow of the very monarchy he had helped build over much of the last century?

On the face of it, the very notion seemed preposterous. Yet what if Marwan Talal had come to the conclusion—however painful and however reluctantly—that his nephew was no longer fit for the throne? What if King Abdullah's unwillingness to embrace a purist, fundamentalist brand of Islam was undermining his uncle's devotion to him? What if the queen's refusal to wear a headscarf and her embrace of the most stylish Western fashions had become an odious offense to Marwan? What if the soul and spirit of this elderly prince, this deeply devoted Muslim, this descendant of the Prophet, had heard the call of the caliphate and could not turn away?

As much as I didn't want to believe it, or even consider it, I realized it wasn't out of the question. It had to be considered. *I* had to consider it.

Everything I knew about the man caused me to feel guilty for simply raising such a possibility, even in the privacy of my own heart, even here in the darkness of a Jordanian prison cell. Being a devoted Muslim wasn't a crime. I didn't share Marwan's religious beliefs, no matter how hard he might try to convince me. Yet his fervency didn't make him a member of ISIS, did it? Of course not. The very notion was ludicrous.

Yet it was also true that just because not all devoted Muslims were terrorists, that didn't mean none of them were.

The king viewed Abu Khalif as a man who was perverting Islam. But didn't Khalif see himself as a wholly committed Muslim? Of course he did. Didn't every member of ISIS see himself as committed to the teachings of the Prophet, following his model, rebuilding his kingdom? Without a doubt. And didn't they see the king and all his fellow Reformers as the ones who were perverting Islam, selling it out, undermining its very essence and potency? There was no question of this.

The issue for me wasn't who was right. I wasn't an Islamic theologian. I certainly wasn't the arbiter of what was the true path of Islam. I was merely a reporter. But I was also being accused of a crime I hadn't committed. The question I had to ask was who had the motive to betray the king and usher in the chaos and terror that ISIS had brought.

Viewed from this vantage point, Prince Marwan Talal had to be considered a prime suspect. Who knew more about the king's movements, the details of the summit, the security arrangements, the points of vulnerability than he did? Who likely knew even the names and families of the fighter pilots flying "protection" overhead more than the elder statesman of the royal family? Who could possibly be better positioned not only to pull off a coup but to help provide theological legitimacy for Abu Khalif when the black flags of ISIS were raised over Amman than a direct descendant of the prophet Muhammad himself? King Abdullah would never do such a thing. But was it possible that his dying uncle—approaching eternity, preparing to see Allah face-to-face, with nothing left to lose and paradise to gain—would?

I had to admit it was possible.

And then another thought hit me. Where exactly was Marwan Talal? Hadn't he helped the king craft the very treaty that was supposed to have been signed? Hadn't I been told that many of the secret negotiating sessions had taken place at Marwan's own home? Then why hadn't he been at the summit? Why had he mysteriously disappeared, just before the attacks, as if he knew they'd been coming all along?

23

★ ★ ★

Without warning, the cell door burst open.

"Who's there?" I asked, shielding my eyes as light flooded the cell.

"Dr. Hammami," came the reply.

But he was not alone. There were two MPs at his side.

"What time is it?" I asked, trying to get my bearings.

"Just after nine."

"In the morning?"

"No, at night."

"What day is it?"

"It's still Monday. Now sit up. I need to check your vitals."

I had a hard time processing that. "You're saying fifteen hours have gone by already?"

The doctor nodded and took my temperature.

"How is that possible?"

"I administered a sedative while you were sleeping," he replied, then shone a penlight in my eyes to check my pupils.

"You *drugged* me?"

"I medicated you, Mr. Collins—for your own good. I've been monitoring you. You were in danger of hyperventilating. And you needed the rest. You've been through a great deal in the last few days. You needed to take it easy. You still do."

Take it easy? Was this guy insane? The president of the United States was being held by ISIS and threatened with his life. There were only thirty-three more hours to go before the deadline, and I was helpless either to make a difference or to cover the unfolding drama. How exactly was I to take it easy? "I want to make a phone call," I said, fighting to stay focused.

"Out of the question," Hammami replied as he wrapped a cuff around my arm and began taking my blood pressure.

"I'm an American citizen. I deserve at least a phone call."

"This is not America, Mr. Collins. Now settle down so I can get your readings."

With that I was on my feet. "Forget my blood pressure. I want a phone call. I have rights."

"Sit down, Mr. Collins," the doctor said with a tone I'd neither heard nor expected from him.

"Not without a phone call."

The lightbulb overhead suddenly flicked on. The MPs moved toward me. I immediately thought better of escalating a confrontation. I sat back down and tried a different tack. "Fine, fine; I'm sorry. Look, I'm just not used to . . . I need to speak to Prince Feisal."

"Be quiet and let me take your pulse, please."

"I just need a moment with the prince."

"Your pulse, Mr. Collins."

I stopped talking and tried to settle my frayed nerves as Dr. Hammami checked my wound and changed my bandages. "That's healing nicely."

I was glad about that, but I could also see the doctor was about to leave.

"Please, Dr. Hammami," I said, looking the man in the eye. "You know I saved the king's life, and the queen's and the crown prince's. You know I'm not a conspirator. I'm not a traitor. I'm a reporter. I traffic in information, and there's a critical piece of information I need to tell Prince Feisal. Please. It's a matter of life and death."

"His or yours?" the doctor asked, putting two pills in my hand and not waiting for an answer. "Take this for the pain, and I'll see you in twelve hours."

I protested, but he didn't seem to care. He turned and left as quickly as he'd come. The door shut and locked behind him. A moment later, the slot at the bottom of the door opened and another plate of food was slid to me. Then the slot closed, the footsteps faded, and once again I was alone.

I couldn't believe it. I just stared at the plate of steamed rice and overcooked carrots and potatoes and tried to comprehend what was happening to me. Was there a way out? I couldn't think of one. Wasn't Allen suspicious that I was no longer in touch with him? Was he asking questions? Was he taking action? I very much doubted it. He had too much else happening. And he probably thought I'd check in when I could. Which, I had to admit, had been my modus operandi lately.

Again I stared down at the food. In the dim overhead light it looked singularly unappetizing. But it could have been a fine steak. It wouldn't have mattered. There was no way I could eat.

Instead, I paced about the cell. I felt my blood pressure spiking again. My face and neck were once again hot. I was perspiring all over. Finally I looked at the painkillers in my hand and took them both, washed them down with a cup of water, splashed some water on my face, and then slumped back on the bed. It was clear the prince wasn't coming. I wasn't going to have a chance to warn him about the suspects on my list. I doubted he would even listen if I could. Maybe the doctor was right. Maybe sleeping through this nightmare was my best option. Maybe it was my only option.

I lay back on the cot. As I stared up at the lightbulb and listened to the ticking of my pocket watch, I thought about my mom and Matt and Annie and my niece and nephew. Were they together now? Were they safe? I knew they were praying for me. They couldn't know exactly what I was going through, but I had no doubt they were praying. It was about the only thing I knew for certain. Even little Katie was praying. Though she had only just turned four, I knew she was praying every night for her uncle James—to be safe, to be happy, and to give my life to Jesus. The last time we'd talked, Matt had said they'd all been praying for me, and there was no reason to think Katie was going to give up on me now, even if I was beginning to give up on myself.

It was strange to think a little girl on the other

side of the planet was praying so faithfully for me. Was I praying for them? No—not beyond my awkward prayer last night. I wasn't even praying for myself. But why not? What was really so hard? Why couldn't I turn to God the way they did? I didn't know. And that bothered me.

I tried to remember the Bible verses Annie had asked me to read. I tried to remember the ones Matt had said Katie was memorizing at Sunday school. It was all a blank. And that bothered me too. I had a nearly photographic memory. Yet for the life of me I couldn't remember the Scriptures that had meant so much to them, the ones they'd so wanted me to know and consider.

What was so different between us? I wondered. Why had Matt and I grown so far apart? After Dad had left us when we were kids, we were raised in the same broken family by the same great mom in the same loser little town, in the same lame church. Yet Matt had become a man of true faith. I'd become a man of so many doubts. Why?

This wasn't helping, I decided. All this introspection was just making me feel worse. If God was really up there, if he was really listening to the prayers of my family, then great—I'd be out of here soon enough. But I had nothing to say to him right now—certainly nothing he didn't already know.

And that's when Yael's face came to mind.

24

* * *

When I woke up—groggy yet somehow content—the light was off.

I couldn't tell what time it was, but I didn't care. It was the pills. It had to be.

Somehow, despite my mental fog, I vaguely recalled I was being held on suspicion of treason against the king. But at that moment, nothing seemed to matter. I couldn't feel my arm. I was in no pain at all. I couldn't even remember being in pain.

But I did have an intense desire for a drink. Vodka. Bourbon. Rum. A beer. It didn't matter. Just something alcoholic.

Before I realized, I'd drifted off.

* * *

The light was still off when I rolled over and pulled the blanket over my head.

I knew I'd been sleeping again, but I had no idea how long. And still I didn't care. But something had changed. There was someone in the cell

with me. Even in the darkness I could see the face
of Yael Katzir.

I knew it was a hallucination, yet her presence
gave me great comfort. "Hello, Yael," I said to the
darkness.

"Mr. Collins, over here," she whispered. "My, my,
you're getting soaked. Please, won't you join me?"

It was what she'd said to me the first time we
met, back in Istanbul, in front of the Blue Mosque
at midnight. She'd been standing there, in the rain,
wearing a stylish trench coat and holding a polka-
dot umbrella. I could see it as clearly as if I were
there.

I remembered thinking she was lovely even
before knowing who she was. I also remembered
being suspicious. I'd been expecting to meet Ari
Shalit, the deputy director of the Mossad. Instead
I'd met this striking brunette who somehow knew
everything about me. She'd claimed Ari had sent
her, and eventually I had believed her. But it had
taken a while.

"Nice to meet you, Miss Katzir," I whispered
into the darkness.

"Likewise," she whispered back. "Now let's
start walking arm in arm, like true lovers."

We had walked together through the streets of
Istanbul, the ancient metropolis that once served
as the eastern capital of the Roman Empire, holding hands so it seemed natural for us to be out
together that late. When a pair of policemen had
taken an interest in us, I had impulsively leaned in
and kissed Yael. Anything to keep up appearances.

The kiss had been all too brief as the policemen soon turned their attention elsewhere.

Now, in my dark, lonely cell, I relived the kiss. In my semiconscious state, I could actually feel her lips on mine, sense her breathlessness as we pretended to be lovers.

I blinked, and the mirage evaporated in the darkness.

Where was Yael right now? I wondered. Was she thinking of me? Did she remember our first meeting as fondly as I did? Did it matter to her at all?

I doubted it. It might have mattered yesterday, when she'd agreed to have a late dinner with me after the summit, after she put her prime minister on the plane back to Tel Aviv.

Now everything had changed. Everything she'd tried to warn her bosses about—an imminent attack by ISIS, the use of chemical weapons—had been ignored. Yet her worst fears had all come to pass. She'd been right. The world had taken a very dark turn.

And now I feared I would never see her again.

25

★ ★ ★

The electronic locks released.

The door swung open, again flooding the cell with light. Then the lightbulb overhead turned on. Dr. Hammami and the two MPs at his side were back.

"Good morning, Mr. Collins."

"Is it morning?" I asked, certain I couldn't possibly have heard him correctly.

"It is indeed," he replied, pulling out his stethoscope and starting through his routine again. "It's just before 10 a.m.," he said.

"Ten o'clock *Tuesday* morning?" I clarified, still not seeing how this could be true.

"That's right, Mr. Collins—six minutes before ten on Tuesday morning, to be precise. So how are we feeling today? Did we get some rest? How's the arm?"

The patronizing tone alone made me want to strangle him.

"Fine, yes, better," I said, fighting the urge to go ballistic.

Wiping the sleep from my eyes, I did the math.

I'd been locked up for almost twenty-eight hours. That meant there were merely twenty hours left until the deadline. I had to get out, find a phone, let someone know what was happening to me. I feigned grogginess, but with a burst of adrenaline I was wide awake now—wide awake and trying to develop a plan to escape.

"Blood pressure's still a bit high," he said when he'd completed the exam.

It was all I could do not to let the sarcasm fly. The only thing that stopped me was the over-powering urge to break out of this cell. Yet I knew that even if I overpowered the doctor (not a prob-lem) and one of the MPs (not easy but doable), I was still going to have to get the jump on the other MP (which seemed close to impossible). And even if I did succeed, how exactly was I going to get out of the hallway? The doors at both ends were electronically locked, and there were surveil-lance cameras watching 24-7.

"Would you put on your socks and shoes, please, Mr. Collins?" the doctor asked.

"What for?"

"You have an appointment."

"Yeah, right."

"Come now. You don't want to be late. Best get moving."

"An appointment? With whom?"

"I'm not authorized to say."

"Why not?" I shot back, my discipline slipping.

"Let's just put on our shoes and socks, Mr. Collins, and be on our way, shall we?"

"Where are we going?"

"The clock is ticking, Mr. Collins. Let's pick up the pace."

Clearly this banter was going nowhere. He wasn't about to answer my questions, so there was no point continuing to ask. When I did as I was told, my hands and feet were promptly shackled, and I was led down several hallways, through a series of electronically locked doors, to a windowless little room. There I was told to sit on a metal stool on the far side of a rectangular metal table. Both the table and the stool were bolted to the floor, and I was too after the MPs fastened my shackles to steel hooks near my feet. I was reminded of my first meeting with Abu Khalif, which had taken place in a room not too dissimilar from this.

The doctor excused himself. Now it was just me and the two MPs, stone-faced and obviously prepared for any foolhardy escape plan I was idiotic enough to concoct.

The minutes ticked by, and as I waited, I pretended I was in Vegas. I laid down odds for who was going to walk through that door at the appointed hour.

At the top of my list was some Jordanian prosecutor or perhaps a state-appointed attorney charged with my defense. This was the most logical. But next on my list, with two-to-one odds, was Prince Feisal. I had asked for the meeting, after all, and there was an outside chance he would take a break from the hunt for the president and Abu Khalif to humor me. I was ready for him, prepared to give him my list of suspects and the pros and cons for each. Seeing Colonel Sharif seemed a long shot at best, so I put him at seven-to-one odds. The king was even less likely, certainly not in a room like this, so I put those odds at five hundred to one.

Toughest to calculate were the odds of seeing Allen MacDonald or a lawyer from the *Times*, or someone from the U.S. embassy coming to help me out of this mess. All three were in roughly the same category, though clearly an embassy official had a far better chance of reaching me than the other two. Still, that would require the king or the prince or someone else in that bunker reaching out to the embassy and informing them of the suspicions—if not the charges—against me. Were they ready to do that with everything else on their plate right now? Prince Feisal had assured me the answer was a definitive no. Why would he have changed his mind?

Complicating matters even further was this question: Was the American embassy in Amman even open at the moment? Much of the staff, including the ambassador, had been at the summit, helping coordinate the visit of the president, secretary of state, and other high-ranking officials from the White House, State, and Defense. The ambassador was dead. How many others had survived?

In the end, I decided it was no better than a thousand-to-one shot that I'd see Allen or a lawyer this fast, while someone from the embassy was about fifty to one—possible but unlikely.

But when the door opened and a man I actually recognized stepped into the room, it suddenly became clear that not only was I playing the wrong odds, I wasn't even in the right casino.

26

★ ★ ★

"Mr. Collins, we meet again; how nice."

To be clear, I recognized the face. But I couldn't remember his name from Adam. He was an American, in his midfifties, well built, like he'd once been a Marine, a tad over six feet, with a strong jaw and a buzz cut that seemed like a throwback to the days of black-and-white television. He wore a dark suit and a white shirt with a thick dark tie and black wingtip shoes. I knew we'd met in Istanbul, in the hospital, just after the car bombing that took the life of Omar Fayez. He worked for the FBI—that, too, I remembered, but still I couldn't place the name. It was unlike me, and I chalked it up to sedatives and stress.

"Not to worry, Mr. Collins," he said as he watched me racing through my mental Rolodex and coming up blank. "You meet a lot of people."

He handed me a business card and I suddenly had a déjà vu moment. We'd done this before. The card bore the bureau's logo, a local office address in Istanbul, an e-mail address, a phone number, and the words *Arthur M. Harris, Special Agent in Charge*.

"Mr. Harris," I said. "Thanks for stopping by."

Harris didn't smile, not that I'd expected him to. Nor was I really trying to be funny. He wasn't coming to set me free. He was coming to bury me.

Harris sat down on the other side of the table, set his briefcase on the floor next to him, opened it, pulled out a digital voice recorder, and placed it on the table and hit Record.

"Have you been informed of the charges against you, Mr. Collins?" he began.

"Not in so many words, no," I said cautiously.

"Well, I'm here to do that," he replied. "But first, let's review your rights. You don't have to speak to me, of course. You can ask for a lawyer. But I'm hoping you'll first shed some light on what exactly has just happened."

I tried to decide if I should ask for a lawyer—or rather when to ask for one. If I was really facing charges that could lead to the death penalty, I couldn't take any risk in saying something that could be used against me. At the same time, I knew asking for a lawyer would shut down the discussion before it had begun, and I wasn't ready to do that. At the moment, Agent Harris was my only contact with the outside world. To dismiss him because I didn't have a lawyer meant being sent back to solitary confinement while the clock ticked down to the execution of the president. Harris, therefore, was my only hope of gleaning information about what was happening in the hunt for the president and Abu Khalif. He was also my only hope of learning a bit of what was going on with Allen, with my family, perhaps even

Yael, as well as getting messages back to any or all of them.

"By the way, when I refer to charges, I should say 'charges pending' against you," Harris clarified. "No formal charges have been filed. Not yet. Too much is happening at the moment. But the Jordanian authorities have made it clear to the bureau they are building a very strong case against you."

"What case?" I asked. "I risked my life to save the king's and his family's. They're going to charge me for that?"

"They say the royal family survived in spite of your efforts, Mr. Collins. And I have to say, the evidence they've shown me is rather compelling."

"They think I'm conspiring with ISIS against the Hashemite Kingdom?"

"In a word, yes."

"They think the fact that I've interviewed Abu Khalif and Jamal Ramzy means I'm in collusion with them."

"They wonder how you got such 'exclusive interviews.' They wonder how you keep managing to live when everyone else around you dies. They wonder why you were allowed to leave Mosul and get back to Jordan just before the peace summit when no other foreigner has been to Abu Khalif's secret headquarters and come out alive."

I'd heard all this before from Prince Feisal, but the list was no less incredible now. "What do they say about the fact that I was the one who spotted the F-16 breaking off from his wingman, that I was the one who alerted the chief of security for the Royal Court that a kamikaze attack was under way?"

"Too little, too late, they say."

"But it wasn't too late, was it?" I protested. "That 'little' bit of warning saved the king's life, not to mention President Taylor's, Prime Minister Lavi's, and President Mansour's."

"Look, Mr. Collins, I'm not here on behalf of the Jordanian government," Harris replied, deftly changing lanes. "I'm not here investigating the attempted assassination of the king, per se. I'm here investigating the attempted assassination of the president of the United States, along with the murder of the secretary of state and eighty-two other American citizens."

"You can't possibly think I'm complicit in any of that."

"Like I said, Mr. Collins, on a short list of suspects, you're the only one with irrefutable contact with the enemy."

I took a deep breath and fought to keep my composure. "Is the FBI charging me with a crime?"

"Not yet."

"But you intend to?"

"That's not my call."

"Whose is it?"

"The attorney general's—he's in the process of convening a special grand jury."

"And I'm a target?"

"Clearly."

"What are the charges the Jordanians are preparing to make? You never said."

"Murder, attempted murder, aggravated murder, terrorism, and espionage."

I felt sick.

"At the top of the list is treason—'making an attempt on the life of the king, the queen, or the regent.'"

"This is a joke. The only attempt I made was to save the life of the king and queen. A successful attempt, I might add."

"Don't kid yourself, Mr. Collins; this is no joke, and I am told they intend to prosecute all of these crimes to the fullest extent of the law."

"Which is?"

"These are all capital crimes. They are punishable by death."

I knew from Colonel Sharif that Jordan still had a death penalty, but I was pretty sure they hadn't used it in years. Were they really threatening to execute me for crimes I hadn't even committed? "But Jordan doesn't execute criminals," I said hopefully.

"Not true," Harris replied. "There are currently 106 convicted criminals on death row here. And the Jordanian government executed several ISIS and al Qaeda conspirators earlier this year."

If I was going to ask for a lawyer, this was surely the time. Instead, I leaned forward and lowered my voice.

"Agent Harris, I had absolutely nothing to do with these crimes. I'm a reporter, not a terrorist. I've been doing everything I can to understand the enemy and warn my country and the world about their intentions. It was my story with Jamal

Ramzy that warned the president and his senior advisors that a major attack was coming. It was my reporting that made it clear that ISIS had captured chemical weapons. The president wasn't convinced ISIS really possessed them. CIA Director Vaughn told me personally he wasn't convinced ISIS had weapons of mass destruction. It was my reporting—not his or his team's intelligence gathering—that provided conclusive evidence that ISIS had sarin gas. Every step of the way, I have warned American and Jordanian leaders—in print and in person—of grave and imminent dangers to them. Dangers that proved to be true. Dangers that have nearly gotten me killed numerous times. Dangers that got me shot, that led to the deaths of my closest friends. In short, Mr. Harris, I'm not guilty of these horrific crimes. Abu Khalif is guilty. ISIS is guilty. And anyone in a position of authority who didn't listen to my repeated warnings and take appropriate action bears no small measure of responsibility as well."

"Very moving, Mr. Collins, but save it for your summation."

27

* * *

I was getting nowhere fast.

Harris wasn't buying my defense, so I decided to go on offense. It was a risk, especially with a running audio recording, but it was a calculated one, and at that moment I felt I had no choice.

"Look, Agent Harris, like you, like my Jordanian friends, I'm convinced there's a mole at a very high level, a mole that has been feeding information to ISIS," I said, making an enormous concession I was sure no lawyer would advise. "Someone with access to the details of the peace summit must have supplied those details to Abu Khalif and his men in an attempt to kill all four principals and take over the kingdom of Jordan. I categorically deny I am that mole or that I am involved in a criminal conspiracy in any way, shape, or form. But I have been thinking long and hard about this and I want you to consider three possible suspects."

"Shall we begin with Yael Katzir?" he asked, catching me off guard.

"What? Of course not," I said. "She had nothing to do with this."

"How do you know?"

"Because it's ridiculous. Why would you even ask such a thing?"

"That's not a compelling argument, Mr. Collins."

"Yael? You're serious?" I shot back. "She had every opportunity to kill every single principal in the king's palace, but she fought back against the terrorists instead. She could have easily killed the royal family while we were escaping the palace and racing them to the airport, but she risked her life to save them instead. She—"

I suddenly stopped midsentence. I was about to say, "She did everything she could to help me expose the fact that ISIS had captured chemical weapons, including giving me classified Israeli intelligence to help me with my story." But I couldn't burn her as a source. If I wasn't going to tell Allen MacDonald and my editors in New York who my confidential sources were, I certainly couldn't tell the FBI, much less on the record.

Then Harris stunned me by saying it for me.

"Because she was your source for the chemical weapons story, wasn't she?" he pressed. "That's what you were about to say, weren't you?"

"No, it's not," I lied.

"Should I pull out the polygraph and see how you hold up?"

"You know full well I can't talk about confidential sources. And even if she was one—and I'm not saying she was—I couldn't tell you."

"A grand jury could compel you."

"I'm protected by the First Amendment,

Agent Harris—freedom of the press, in case you'd forgotten."

"You think the First Amendment is going to protect you if the attorney general charges you with treason against the president of the United States?"

"The First Amendment, the Fifth, and others—absolutely," I replied. "But I just told you, my reporting was to warn the president and the American government, not to commit treason against them. Why don't you believe me?"

"Perhaps because you're a liar, Mr. Collins," Harris said flatly. "I know you're lying right now. I know Ms. Katzir was your source, or one of them. I know she was the woman in the café in Istanbul, the one who fled after the bombing. I know Robert Khachigian was another source. And I know you fled the scene of a crime when he and a group of federal agents were murdered in Union Station. I know you still haven't bothered to tell your side of the story to the bureau on why you fled, why you left the country, why you immediately went to go see Ms. Katzir. I know Ms. Katzir sent you a text message while you were meeting with King Abdullah, and I know what it said."

Harris reached down, pulled a single sheet of paper out of his briefcase, and slid it across the table. I looked down and read the message, though I already knew every word.

James—thank G-d you're safe! Thnx 4 the note. Have been worried sick. We need to talk. Dangerous new developments. Call me ASAP.—Y

"You see where this is heading, Mr. Collins?" Harris asked, echoing the question Prince Feisal had asked me. "You see how all this is going to look before a federal grand jury?"

The man had done his homework. He had the enormous resources of the American government behind him, and he seemed determined to crush me. It was time to launch a counterstrike.

"You're chasing the wrong car, Agent Harris. Your case is circumstantial at best, not to mention completely illogical. Worse, you're not looking at other, far more compelling suspects—men who had the motive, the means, and the opportunity to pull off these crimes. And the longer you try to railroad me, the longer the real conspirators are still out there, still plotting, still putting our country and our allies in grave danger. Now look, I'm not a Muslim. I'm certainly no ISIS supporter. I've got no religious motivation to be involved in these crimes. I've got no political motivation. I'm a lifelong registered Democrat, same as the president. I've got no financial or personal motive. Any reasonable jury of my peers is going to see that every so-called fact you say damns me is completely countered by verifiable actions I took to warn these leaders in order to save their lives. If I was hell-bent on killing them, I had an MP-5 in my hands and plenty of ammunition. So did Yael Katzir. We could have finished them off at any time. But we didn't. So you tell me how it's going to look to a federal grand jury."

To my surprise, he was quiet for a moment. It wasn't clear whether I was convincing him or whether he was simply waiting for me to say more that he could use to further incriminate me. But then he leaned back in his chair and raised his eyebrows, beckoning me to make my case.

So I did. For the next ten minutes, I outlined the case against Youssef Kuttab, Hassan Karbouli, and Prince Marwan Talal, saving the best for last.

But Harris wasn't buying it. "Talk about circumstantial. You're essentially accusing three Muslims for being Muslims."

"You don't think the mole is a Muslim?" I asked.

"Not necessarily, no," Harris replied.

"Someone willing to risk his or her life to help the Islamic State—you don't think religion is a major element of their motivation?"

"Not every Muslim is a terrorist, Mr. Collins."

"I'm not saying they are," I countered. "Don't put words in my mouth. I'm saying that everyone risking life and limb to build the caliphate for Abu Khalif and the Islamic State is motivated above all else by his or her belief in Islam and desire to see Islam spread across the globe."

"So now you're an expert in Islam?"

I felt as if we were playing a high-level chess match, alternately attacking and countering, each of us trying to see five and six moves ahead, trying to set ourselves up for the best possible combinations. "I'm an expert in terrorism. I've been covering it for the better part of my career."

"You've talked to a lot of terrorists."

"Of course."

"Met with them?"

"Yes."

"Traveled the world to find them and spend time with them?"

"It's my job."

"And that makes you an expert?"

"I'd say so, yes."

"I can't wait for the grand jury to hear this. *I'm an expert in terrorism.*'"

"Don't be ridiculous," I shot back. "You know exactly what I mean. You're twisting my words to try to make me look guilty. But you're ignoring perfectly credible suspects. You refuse to look at anyone else but me, refuse to do any digging, any investigating whatsoever. Is burying your head in the sand part of the job description of a special agent for the Federal Bureau of Investigation?"

Harris sat forward. "And you've done your homework, Mr. Collins? You've looked at all the facts? You've been digging, investigating, have you?"

"Well, that's been a little hard to do given that I've been locked away in solitary confinement for the last thirty hours."

"Fine," said Harris. "Of your three suspects, which one do you think is most likely to have done it, assuming for a moment that you're even in the ballpark?"

"You're really asking me?"

"I am."

"And you'll really take it seriously?"

"That's my job. You said so yourself."

The chess match had just gotten more interesting. "Well, then," I said, trying to decide whether he was playing games with me or being serious. "Mind you, this is just conjecture at this stage."

"Of course."

"These are theories—possible theories—not accusations."

"Right."

"All three of these are friends of mine. I hope to God none of them are involved."

"Got it," said Harris. "But if you had to choose one."

"I'm sure the list is longer than just these three."

"I understand—now pick one."

"The prince."

"Talal?"

"Yes."

"Marwan Talal?"

"Perhaps."

"You think the eldest uncle of the king of Jordan is involved in a conspiracy to kill him and everyone in his family and bring ISIS to power in Jordan?"

"It's possible," I said. "More possible than it is that I'm involved."

"No."

"What do you mean, no?"

"I mean it's not possible."

"It's not possible that Prince Marwan Talal is the mole?"

"No."

"Then why was he missing from the summit? Why wasn't he there when he was ostensibly so deeply involved in the crafting of the treaty? That doesn't seem suspicious to you?"

"No."

"Yet my behavior does?"

"Yes."

"Why?"

"Because I know where the prince was," said Harris. "I know why he wasn't at the summit."

"How?"

"Because I've been doing my homework. I've been digging. I've been investigating."

"So where was he?"

"Baghdad."

"Baghdad?"

"Yes."

"The prince was completely out of the country at the moment of Jordan's maximum danger. A little convenient, wouldn't you say?"

"No."

"No?"

"No."

"Because you know why he was there?"

"Yes."

"And why was that?"

"You really want to know?"

"Yes."

"Very well then. He went because the king asked him to go."

I had to think about that for a second. "Why would the king ask his uncle to go to Baghdad?"

"To lay the groundwork for the king's state visit."

"The visit scheduled for this weekend?"

"That's the one."

"You're sure about that? I mean, absolutely certain?"

"The king told me himself," Harris said. "The prince confirmed it. I talked to the Iraqi prime minister, as well. They all tell the same story."

I felt as if the wind had been knocked out of me.

Check . . . and mate.

28

★ ★ ★

It was quiet for several minutes.

I just sat there, not sure what to say. I'd not only made a foolish and serious error, impugning a member of the royal family without any proof whatsoever, but I'd done it in front of an FBI agent who was recording me.

The game wasn't really over. I knew that. But for the first time I really did feel scared. This wasn't a game, after all. This was a criminal investigation. I was accused of espionage, murder, terrorism, and treason. And my life hung in the balance.

"I'd like to speak to a lawyer," I said finally.

Harris turned off the digital recorder. "Not so fast, Mr. Collins," he replied. "You have other options."

"No, really—I don't want to say anything else without legal counsel present."

"Now hold on and listen to what I have to say."

"I'm done listening, Agent Harris. I'd like a lawyer. That's it."

But Harris wasn't done. He leaned close and

spoke so quietly that the guards in the room had no chance of hearing him.

"Listen carefully, Mr. Collins. You're in a heap of trouble. I think we've established that. The only question now is whether you want to be tried in an American court or here in Jordan. And I'd like to recommend you choose option A rather than option B."

"I'm listening," I whispered back.

"You'd rather come home to face the music than stay here?"

"Yes," I replied, oblivious now to the president's fate and completely consumed with my own. I was at that moment no longer a foreign correspondent for the *New York Times*. I was an accused traitor facing death by shooting or hanging in a foreign court system where I had no leverage whatsoever.

"Then I'd suggest you make a call."

"To whom?"

"Jack Vaughn."

"The director of the CIA?"

"Yes."

"Not the attorney general?"

"No."

"Why?"

"You know Jack, right?"

"Of course."

"You've been friends for ages, right?"

"Absolutely."

"You believe he can vouch for your integrity."

"I do."

"Then call him."

"How?"

"I have your iPhone."

I stared at Harris. It felt like the chess match had resumed, but I was no longer seeing five moves ahead. Now I was struggling just to figure out my next move. "And say what?" I finally asked.

"Make your case. Ask him to call the attorney general on your behalf. Tell him to have the AG call the king and make arrangements for me to bring you back to Washington in my custody."

"And why would the king agree?"

"He's the one who lost the president, Mr. Collins," Harris explained. "Right now I think he'd do just about anything the American government asked of him."

"I wouldn't be so sure of that."

"You'll never know unless you try."

He had a point there. "So what's in it for you?"

"Nothing."

"Then why do you care?"

"I don't, since you ask," Harris said. "But you're an American citizen. You're being held for crimes as much against our country as any. And you're being held in a nation that is undergoing a coup. I wouldn't wish that on anyone. If you're guilty, then it should be our government that proves it before an American court of law, period."

I leaned back. I thought about what he was saying and assessed my options. There were only two. Make the call or go back to solitary with no telling what might happen to me next. That was no choice at all. But there was something odd about the whole conversation.

"May I have my phone?" I asked, deciding not to overthink the moment.

"You may."

Harris reached back into his briefcase, pulled out my iPhone, and slid it across the table. For a moment, I just stared at it. I wanted to call my mom. I wanted to call Yael. I needed to call Allen. But apparently I was getting only one phone call today, and I figured I'd better make it count.

"What time is it?" I asked.

"It's twelve minutes after eleven," Harris said.

That meant it was only twelve minutes after four in the morning back in Washington. Twenty-nine hours into the ISIS ultimatum. Only nineteen hours left until the president's execution.

"Shouldn't we wait a few hours until Jack's up?" I asked.

I didn't really want to wait, of course. I wanted to get out of Amman as quickly as possible. But I also needed Jack Vaughn to be awake, alert, and in a good mood. Calling him in the middle of the night didn't exactly strike me as the best strategy.

"This is a onetime offer, Mr. Collins. It's now or never."

I picked up the phone, searched through my contacts, and found the home number for the Vaughn residence in Great Falls, Virginia. I pressed the call button and held my breath.

The phone rang repeatedly, but no one answered. I got voice mail but hung up without leaving a message.

"Try again," Harris said.

"He's not there."

"Just try again," he repeated.

I was in no mood to argue, so I hit Redial and waited. Finally, on the fifth ring, I heard a man's voice on the other end of the line.

"Jack Vaughn," he said, sounding as groggy as he did annoyed.

"Jack, hey, it's J. B. Collins," I began. "I'm so sorry to call you at home, especially at such an hour."

"Collins?"

"Yes, sir."

"Is this a joke?"

"No, sir."

"This is really J. B. Collins?"

"Yes, sir. Again, I'm so sorry to call you so early."

Vaughn sighed irritably. "Where are you?"

"I'm in Amman, sir."

"But you're alive."

"I am, and I need your help."

"Help? You've got to be kidding me. Do you even know how much trouble you're in? I hear the bureau's about to put a warrant out for your arrest."

He was waking up fast.

"That's why I'm calling, sir."

"Look, Collins, I shouldn't even be talking with you."

"Sir, please, you know I'm innocent."

"I do? I don't think so."

"Jack, come on—I did everything I could to warn you and the president about what ISIS was planning. I risked my life to save the president's and the king's. And now I need your help."

Just then I heard a woman's voice.

"Who's that?" she asked.

"Never mind," Vaughn said. "Just go back to bed."

Oh, great, I thought, *now I've woken up his wife.*

"Is that Collins?" she asked. "J. B. Collins?"

"Yes, yes, now just . . . Listen, Collins, I need to go."

"No, wait, sir," I pleaded. "I have one specific favor to ask you."

"Where is he?" I could hear his wife asking him.

"Shhh, I told you, just get back in bed—I'll be there in a minute," Vaughn told her. "So what is it, Collins? Make it fast."

"Jack, I'm innocent of all of this. The evidence will completely exonerate me. But I want to be tried in an American court. Not here. Not in Amman."

"That's out of my hands. Now unless you know where ISIS is holding the president, I can't talk to you any longer."

"Jack, please—I'm asking you to call the AG," I pressed, my tone becoming more urgent.

"The attorney general?" he replied, clearly bewildered. "What for?"

"I want you to ask him to call the king and request that I be extradited back to Washington with the FBI agent who's come to interrogate me. I'll come willingly. I just want my day in court—an American court."

"Where is he?" I overheard Vaughn's wife say again. "Is he still in Amman?"

Just then Harris slipped me a handwritten note.

Just got an e-mail. The king wants to
meet with you in fifteen minutes. Jack
needs to call the AG immediately.

"Jack, listen, the king wants to meet with me
in fifteen minutes. Please, I'm begging you, have
the AG call him. I'm pretty sure His Majesty will
accommodate any request the U.S. government
has for him right about now."

"The king wants to see you?"

"Apparently he does."

"Why?"

"I have no idea, Jack. But that's why I need
you to call the AG right now and have him take
custody of me and this case."

"You know what you're asking?"

"I know, Jack, and I'm sorry. But I'm an
American citizen. I shouldn't be tried in a foreign
court."

"So where are you right now?"

I heard more whispering but forced myself to
stay focused and answer his questions. "I'm on a
military base outside of Amman," I replied.

"Which one?"

"Marka."

"At the general headquarters?"

"Yes. I'm in the detention center, level B, cell
number three."

"That's too much. I don't need all that. I just
want to make sure the AG understands which base

you're at. Who's the agent from the bureau there with you now?"

"Art Harris—do you want to talk to him?"

"No, no, I'm just trying to establish the facts. Are you calling me on a landline?"

"No, it's my mobile."

"What's the number?"

I gave it to him.

"And I can get back to you on this?"

"Hold on a moment," I said. "Let me check."

I turned to Harris and whispered the question to him.

He nodded, so I told Jack, "Yes."

"Fine," Vaughn said. "I need to go. I'll see what I can do."

With that, the call was over.

"And?" Harris asked when I set down the phone.

"And what?"

"Did he say yes? Is he going to get you transferred back to Washington?"

"I'm not sure."

"Did he say yes?"

"Not exactly."

"But he didn't say no?"

"Not exactly."

"So what did he say?" Harris pressed.

"He said he would see what he could do."

"You think he'll at least call the AG?"

"I don't know. I hope so."

"Okay, then," Harris said.

"So now we wait?" I asked.

"No, now we go see the king," Harris replied.

I had already forgotten about his note. "Why do you think he wants to meet with me?" I was certain I was still in great danger and not sure I wanted to look the monarch in the eye just then.

"Don't know," Harris said. "But we'd better not keep him waiting."

29

★ ★ ★

Harris stood and informed the guards we were going out.

Then he asked me for my phone back.

"But I thought you just said Jack and the AG could call me."

"They can, but I'm going to forward your calls to my phone," Harris explained.

"Why can't I keep the phone with me?" I asked.

"Because as far as the king and Prince Feisal are concerned, you're their prisoner. They ordered the phone removed from you, and I don't want to do anything to challenge their authority."

I nodded and Harris proceeded to fiddle with my iPhone to transfer all incoming calls to his phone. I was disappointed. I wanted to scroll through my messages. I wanted to see if Yael had written to me, wanted to send notes to her and to my family letting them know what was happening. But Harris was right. I was in too precarious a position to take unnecessary risks. So I steeled myself for what was ahead as he put my phone in his briefcase, set the briefcase on the table, and pointed me toward the door.

"Aren't you going to take that?" I asked Harris as I got up to follow him.

"Why?" he asked. "There's no point bringing it over to the bunker. The security guys won't let me take it in there. It'll be safe here. I'll get it when we're done."

"Fair enough," I said as the guards came over and released my leg shackles and prepared to escort me upstairs.

Just then, Harris's phone buzzed. I wondered whether it was my phone forwarding a call to his or whether he was receiving a call directly. Either way, when he looked at the screen, the expression on his face completely changed. He excused himself and stepped out into the hallway, and suddenly I was alone again. Unfortunately, that gave me more time to worry about this meeting with the king. How much had Feisal already told him about the case against me? Had they even had time for detailed conversations? On one hand, it seemed unlikely given everything else on His Majesty's plate. On the other hand, the mole hunt was critical to his own survival. I'd personally heard the king ask his younger brother for an update, and how could the two of them not make it a top priority in light of the damage this traitor or traitors had done already?

The minutes ticked by. Harris didn't return. And the longer he didn't walk through that door, the more my anxieties increased. Whom was he talking to, and what was taking so long? Had Jack

Vaughn called him to ream him out for letting me—someone under suspicion of espionage and treason against a foreign government—make contact with the director of the Central Intelligence Agency? Or was it the attorney general on the line, ripping Harris for getting him involved during what was arguably the most sensitive espionage investigation in the history of the bureau?

I glanced at Harris's briefcase. It was sitting there on the table. Was it locked? What else was in it besides my phone? Were there details about my case? I can't tell you how tempted I was to open it and riffle through his papers, even just for a few minutes. My guards had stepped out with Harris. I really was alone. But then I glanced up and noticed a small surveillance camera mounted on the wall, up in the corner, near the door, and I wondered if this was a trap. Were Harris and the Jordanians trying to set me up, trying to lure me into doing something incriminating, only to capture it all on video and hang me for it—perhaps literally?

Louis Brandeis, the renowned Supreme Court justice, used to say, "Sunlight is said to be the best of disinfectants." That surveillance camera was the sunshine, purifying me from all temptation. I had to watch my step, I reminded myself. I had to walk the line. Too much was at stake. Then I started to wonder: was Harris really on a call? Or was he in the control room, watching me on closed-circuit TV, waiting for me to seal my fate?

Almost twenty minutes later, Harris came back into the room. He apologized and told me to follow him, but his demeanor had changed. Why? Was he sorry I hadn't taken the bait? Or had there really been a call? And if so, who had called, and why did the news seem so bad? Every instinct in me wanted to ask him questions. It's what I did for a living, after all—ask people questions, ply them for information. I couldn't help it. It was instinct. But in this case I forced myself to keep my mouth shut. If Harris had something to say, he would say it. But I couldn't let myself be lulled into the notion that he was my friend or ally. He wasn't. He was my adversary. Sure, he wanted the king to hand me over so I could be tried in an American court. But he was still there to bury me, and I couldn't afford to forget it.

We took a right down the corridor and headed through another series of locked doors and maze-like hallways until eventually we were standing outside. Finally I was breathing fresh air. Cold air too. After a gorgeous and warm October with temperatures averaging in the seventies and eighties and a stormy but mild November with temperatures in the sixties, the first few days of December felt unseasonably cold. I hadn't seen a thermometer or heard a weather report in days, but it couldn't have been more than fifty degrees, possibly a good deal less. The patches of blue and rays of sun I'd seen the last time I'd crossed this tarmac were gone. Now the skies were dark and threatening. I tried to remember when I'd last worn my leather jacket. I could have used it just then.

Still, it felt good to be out of doors, even if my hands were still cuffed, even if there were three armed guards watching my every move, even if I was about to see a king and his senior advisors, who believed I had plotted to kill them all. It was strange to think how radically the past thirty hours or so had changed my perspective. No longer was I thinking about my next exclusive story for the *Times*. Now I just wanted to stand here, outside this detention center, and savor every moment out of that cell.

There were no F-15s or F-16s taking off or landing this morning. There were no troop transport planes arriving or departing either. I saw a Black Hawk helicopter powering up over by the main complex of buildings, where the bunker was located, and there was a small Learjet being refueled and serviced. But overall, it seemed awfully quiet for a base operating as central command in a winner-take-all battle to recapture the country from the forces of the Islamic State.

"Come on," Harris said. "We'd better get moving."

"Hang on a second," I said. "I want to ask you something first."

"Ask me while we're walking."

"No, this is important," I said. "Did the king or his people give you access to Jamal Ramzy's phone?"

"What phone?" he replied. "What do you mean?"

"When Yael—Ms. Katzir—and I killed Jamal Ramzy . . ." My voice trailed off. I paused a moment, then looked the agent in the eye. "Did you even know we did that—that we killed ISIS members, including the organization's second-highest-ranking leader?"

"Yes, I knew."

"And it doesn't mean anything to you that I was killing ISIS leaders rather than conspiring with them?"

"It's in the file," he said without tipping his hand.

That didn't give me much comfort, but it was something I'd have to take up with my own lawyers, not with the FBI. "But does it also say in the file that I pried a mobile phone out of Ramzy's bloody hands?"

"No," he said.

"Does it say that when Yael and I got the king and his family safely to the airport and under the protection of his own soldiers, I gave him the phone?"

"No," he said again. "No one's mentioned it."

"Well, you should ask about it," I said. "I gave Ramzy's phone to the king so they could analyze it—calls received and sent, to what numbers, in what countries, what cities and neighborhoods. I suspect there's a treasure trove of information in that phone, information that might even lead you to the president."

"Okay," Harris said quietly. "I'll be sure to ask about Ramzy's phone. Now let's go, or we're going to be late."

We started heading across the tarmac, walking briskly to make up for lost time. Just then I heard a buzzing in the sky off to our right. It was faint, and I barely noticed it at first. But it was getting louder. It sounded like a small plane—a prop plane, maybe a crop duster—not a jet. That was odd because this wasn't a civilian airport. There weren't any crop dusters or Piper Cubs or small prop planes of any kind anywhere near here. But there it was, getting louder and louder. It was coming from the east.

We kept walking, faster now but distracted by the sound. Harris and the guards heard it too, and then one of the guards said it sounded to him like a drone.

That's when we saw a flash in the eastern sky. It was a drone, and it had just fired a missile. I saw the contrail. We hit the deck just as the missile streaked over our heads.

The explosion must have been heard for miles. Burning debris was suddenly raining down on us. I wanted to cover my head, but my hands were still shackled. I turned my head and looked behind me. All I could see was a blazing fire and a smoking crater. The detention center was gone.

And then we heard another missile go slicing past us.

30

The second missile slammed into the central administrative complex.

This was the very building to which Harris and I had been heading, the very building that housed the command center from which the king was prosecuting the fight to regain control of his kingdom. This explosion was even more deafening than the first. A ball of fire soared into the air as the upper stories began collapsing and the main edifice of the structure imploded before our eyes.

"Come on; let's go," one of the guards shouted over the roar of the flames. *"We can't stay here. We need to move."*

He grabbed me and hauled me to my feet. The other two guards and Harris were scrambling to their feet as well, and we sprinted across the tarmac for the nearest hangar. There were no planes or helicopters parked inside, and I guessed this was why the guards were headed there. It was not likely a target and might give us some initial protection from the flames and flying debris. As we ran, I could hear the sound of antiaircraft batteries erupting behind and ahead of me, and moments later I could hear the sounds of sirens. Fire trucks and ambulances were streaming in from all directions, as were armored personnel carriers, military police vehicles, and probably even battle tanks. Moments earlier, the base had seemed so quiet, almost a ghost town. Now it was about to be swarming with soldiers and first responders.

As we reached the hangar, we were rocked by a series of secondary explosions as fuel tankers and other vehicles parked near the sites that had just been attacked erupted in succession. The guards ordered me into a corner. Then they chained me to the side of a tow truck.

Guns drawn, they then set up a perimeter and ordered Harris to hand over his weapon. Harris started to protest but quickly thought better of it. Slowly, carefully, he drew his .45, set it on the pavement, and kicked it gently over to one of the guards.

"Can I make a call?" he asked the lead guard. "I need to reach my superiors in Washington."

"Of course," the MP replied. "You're not under any suspicion, Agent Harris. We just have a protocol we have to follow."

"I understand, gentlemen," Harris said. "I know you're just doing your jobs."

With me chained down and Harris disarmed, the guards turned their attention from us to the possibility that anyone might be trying to help me escape. To me, of course, the very notion seemed ridiculous. This wasn't a breakout. This was simply the forces of ISIS bringing the fight to the vortex of the king's command-and-control operations. Abu Khalif had vowed to behead not only the president of the United States but the monarch of Jordan as well. That meant ISIS jihadists were likely attacking the Jordanian soldiers guarding the base. Would they break through? Would they actually make it here, to where we were now? What then? The only thing I feared more than being tried by the Jordanians was being captured by ISIS. There had been a time when I was useful to Abu Khalif. No longer. I had no doubt the ISIS emir would love watching me die a slow death.

"Op Center Alpha, this is Special Agent Arthur Harris with an emergency override. . . . Yes, sir—my access code is X-ray-Niner-Foxtrot-Three-Seven-Four-Three-Tango-Bravo. . . . Yes, sir. . . . Voice ID: 'Kensington Station.' . . . Yes, sir. . . . I am inputting that number now."

I couldn't imagine how Harris could hear over the triple-A fire, the sirens, and the raging fires. Yet before I could ask him what he was doing, he was dialing another number and talking to someone else. A few moments later, he handed the phone to the lead MP, who nodded a few times, asked a couple of questions, nodded some more, then passed the phone to his two colleagues. When the last one hung up the phone, he handed it back to the leader, who returned it to Harris. After they conferred among themselves, one of them made a phone call of his own. When that call was done, suddenly they were unlocking me from the wall and removing my handcuffs.

"*Follow me,*" the head guard shouted.

I had no idea what was happening, but Harris motioned for me to do what the man said and promised to be right behind me. We started walking briskly, then began running. Soon we were climbing into the back of a Black Hawk helicopter that was already powered up and ready to go.

Harris shouted at me to put on my seat belt and hold on tight. Then we lifted off and shot into the stormy morning sky, rapidly gaining altitude and leaving the chaos behind us. As we banked to our left and took a north-by-northeast heading, I felt numb, staring out the window at the leaping flames and billowing smoke and terrible destruction below. One thing I didn't see, however, was any sign that ISIS forces were striking the Jordanian troops holding the perimeter of the base, which only confused me all the more.

"What in the world is going on?" I shouted at Harris over the roar of the rotors as we reached a reasonably safe altitude and distanced ourselves from Amman. "Shouldn't we be trying to rescue the king and the prince and the others? We can't just leave."

"Don't worry," Harris shouted back. "They're not there."

"What do you mean they're not there?"

"The king and his team left the base yesterday."

"Why?"

"To avoid something just like that."

"Where are they?"

"I don't know."

"What do you mean you don't know?"

"They haven't told me," said Harris. "It's classified."

"But you said we were going to see the king."

"We are."

"I don't understand."

"We weren't heading for the bunker," Harris explained. "We were heading for this chopper. It's taking us to the king, wherever he is."

None of this was making any sense. "I'm not following," I told him. "Why did they remove my handcuffs? It's like they're letting me go."

"That's simple," Harris replied. "You're no longer a suspect."

"What are you talking about?"

"You're no longer a suspect, Mr. Collins—you've been cleared."

"I don't understand," I said again.

"You've been part of a sting operation—an operation that, I'm afraid, just went terribly wrong."

31

As we shot over the eastern desert, Harris told me a story I could hardly believe.

"You were never really a suspect," he began.

Try as I might, I couldn't process what he was saying.

"Our investigation, and that of the Jordanians, ruled you out almost immediately," Harris explained, "for all the reasons you spent the morning enumerating. We were also able to rule out fairly quickly the people you suggested could be suspects, though we looked at them all."

"Including Prince Marwan Talal," I said, more as a statement than as a question.

"He was actually the easiest to clear," Harris replied. "As I said, he was in Baghdad at the king's request at the time of the attacks."

I felt terrible. "So you know who's responsible?"

"Yes, and even as we speak, agents are arresting three suspects."

"Who?"

"This all has to be completely off the record, Mr. Collins."

"Of course."

"No, really. I'll tell you because you've been cleared. But there is still a significant amount of work left to do in this investigation. It's under way on three continents, in six different countries. And I believe there are many more arrests still to be made."

"But you've got the mole?" I pressed, dying to know who it was.

Harris glanced at his phone and silently read a text message. "We do, and two of his coconspirators. They were literally just taken into custody."

"So who is it?"

"You're sure we're off the record?"

"Absolutely."

"Because you're involved in this case, you can't write about it at all. I'm sure the *Times* will cover the story. I'm sure the bureau will work with other reporters from the *Times*. But eventually you're going to have to testify in this case, and we can't have you writing about it. Conflict of interest and all."

"I understand. You have my word."

"Can I have that in writing?" he asked, pulling a sheet of paper out of his breast pocket and handing it to me.

"You're kidding."

"I'm not."

I looked at the crumpled piece of paper on FBI letterhead. It was a nondisclosure form, but this was no boilerplate version. It contained detailed legalese written specifically for this case and specifically for me.

I laughed. "You don't actually expect me to sign this without a written guarantee the FBI isn't going to charge me with crimes against the United States or any other government, do you?"

"You're kidding," Harris said.

"I'm not."

He stared at me for a moment, then took the paper and scrawled out such a promise and handed it back to me.

"Now sign it," I said.

And he did.

"And date it."

He dated it.

"And I'm going to need a copy of this before the sun goes down."

"Right."

"I have your word?"

"Yes. Can we get on with it?"

"Fine," I said. "Can I borrow your pen?"

Harris handed me his pen, and I signed. When I was finished, I returned the pen and kept the form.

"When you show me a copier, I'll be happy to give it back to you," I said.

Harris wasn't happy. But to my relief, he didn't protest.

"So, you ready?" he asked.

Honestly, I wasn't sure, but I said yes anyway.

"The mole is Jack Vaughn."

I thought he was kidding. But Harris didn't smile. Harris never smiled.

"Jack Vaughn?" I asked in disbelief.

Harris nodded.

"Jack Vaughn at CIA."

Again Harris nodded.

"I don't . . . I can't . . ."

"Let me be clear," Harris said. "There is no evidence as of yet that Mr. Vaughn intended to betray his country or set into motion such a deadly chain of events. But the evidence is conclusive: he is the mole."

"That doesn't make sense."

"Mr. Vaughn is having an affair," Harris explained. "He and Mrs. Vaughn have been planning to buy a new house, waterfront property on the Potomac River, the Virginia side, a place where they would retire when he steps down from the agency. But along the way, the woman who was their real estate agent began meeting with Mr. Vaughn separately. She would show him various properties while Mrs. Vaughn was out of town. It all seemed harmless enough, but we now know the real estate agent seduced him and they began sleeping together at these various properties while Mr. Vaughn's security detail waited outside."

I still couldn't believe it. "How long has this been going on?"

"Several months," Harris said. "But what the director didn't know was that this wasn't just an 'innocent affair,' if any affair can be called that. It was a honey trap."

"A setup?"

"I'm afraid so," said Harris. "The woman is an American citizen. Her father is American. But her mother is from Qatar. The woman herself was brought up Sunni. For years she raised money in the U.S. for Hamas. But recently she began working for ISIS."

"You're sure?"

"We are. For the last two years, she's been receiving monthly wire transfers from the Gulf through a series of banks in Europe and the Caribbean. But that's not important. What you need to know is she has been buying and selling homes to military officials at the Pentagon, members of the House and Senate, and all kinds of other officials in northern Virginia. She's been using her access to these people's homes to gain classified information and feed it back to her superiors. Six months ago she received an order to approach Claire Vaughn and offer to help her and her husband find a retirement home. She came well recommended by friends in the area, so Mrs. Vaughn agreed. But the woman quickly bypassed Mrs. Vaughn and focused her attention on Mr. Vaughn. And once they started sleeping together, she began learning little tidbits of valuable information."

"Like details of the peace negotiations?"

"Exactly."

"And details of the summit?"

"Unfortunately, yes."

"And she was feeding everything she learned back to ISIS?"

"Yes."

"But you just said something about this being a sting operation that went awry," I noted. "What does that mean?"

"The bureau caught wind of Vaughn's affair a few weeks ago," Harris said. "It wasn't really our place to interfere in a personal matter, but the more we learned about the woman, the more concerned we became. Still, her tradecraft was too good. We were sure she was getting information out of Vaughn, but we couldn't get a judge to give us a warrant to bug his house or the houses where they would have their, you know, liaisons. What's more, we were having trouble finding out how she was getting her information back to ISIS, and without that we felt we couldn't execute an arrest warrant. In short, we hadn't yet built a case that would hold up in court."

"And then came the attack on the summit?"

"Right. At that point, Mr. Vaughn and his mistress were the prime suspects. But we still didn't have conclusive proof. I briefed the king on this, privately—as you can imagine, this is all extremely sensitive. I didn't even tell Prince Feisal. I couldn't. Only the king. I told him our suspicions, and then I told him our plan. What if he arrested you? What if I interrogated you? And what if I persuaded you to call the director and plead with him to help you—at a time where his mistress might be able to overhear the conversation or get the details out of him? My team and I felt certain that if this woman learned where you were and where the king was, she would find a way to feed that information back to ISIS. Once she did, we'd have her red-handed. And that's exactly what happened. Mrs. Vaughn is out of town. The woman was at the Vaughn home tonight. That's the voice you heard talking to him. Just minutes after you got off the phone with the director, my team recorded her making a phone call to a source and telling that source these details. Our theory had worked. What we didn't expect was that this would trigger a drone attack on the base."

"You could have gotten me killed."

"I'm sorry. We didn't anticipate that."

"But why did they hit the detention center?" I asked. "I mean, the main building I get. But the detention center? It doesn't make sense."

"There's only one explanation," Harris said. "They weren't just trying to get the king. They were trying to get you, too. Apparently you've become a bigger target than we realized."

"And they were tracking my phone," I said, suddenly realizing how close I'd come—again—to losing my life.

Harris nodded. "Again, I'm sorry. But thank God you weren't carrying the phone when the missile was fired."

"Or that you weren't."

"Right," he said, staring out the window of the Black Hawk at the vast stretches of desert below us.

"So who was the woman's contact?" I asked, trying to get my mind off my own mortality.

"Her son," Harris said.

"Did you suspect him?"

"No, actually."

"Why not?"

"He served in the U.S. Army, worked for several years at the Defense Intelligence Agency, now works for the NSA at Fort Meade," Harris explained. "I can't say she used him every time. My team is working on that right now. But he's the one she called today, and whomever he called, they obviously moved pretty fast to organize this strike."

My mind was reeling. Then we started experiencing violent turbulence. Hail began pelting the chopper. Lightning flashed all around us. We began descending, but not nearly fast enough for me.

"Do you think Jack knew who the woman was?" I asked. "I mean, do you think he was actively working against the president, working to kill him, to kill the king?"

"No, I don't," Harris replied. "As I said, the investigation is ongoing. But when it's all said and done, I think we're going to find out he was guilty of adultery, not treason."

"So where does that leave me?" I asked Harris, who was suddenly looking for an airsickness bag and not seeing one anywhere.

"You're in the clear," he replied, looking green and holding his stomach.

"And the king knows all this?"

"Most of it, but I'll need to fill him in on the latest."

"So why does he want to see me? Why isn't he sending me home?"

"Honestly, I have no idea," Harris admitted. "But I guess we're about to find out."

PART
THREE

32

★ ★ ★

AZRAQ, JORDAN

Jack Vaughn.

I still couldn't believe it. I'd known the man and his family for ages. I'd never have suspected him in a million years. Betraying his wife? Betraying his family? And in the end betraying his country? I felt as sick as Harris now looked.

I pulled out my pocket watch—it was almost twelve thirty on Tuesday afternoon. Just seventeen and a half hours to go before ISIS executed the president.

A brutal winter storm had descended upon the country. Driving rains and hail the size of marbles blown by whipping winds from the northeast buffeted the chopper as we came in on final approach. Sizzling sticks of lightning could be seen on the horizon. Great booms of thunder rocked the craft even more.

I turned to Harris to ask where we were. But he was white as a sheet. "You okay?" I asked.

But it was too late. Harris started heaving his guts out all over the chopper's floor. The stench was overpowering. I turned back to the window. We certainly weren't in Amman anymore.

As the pilot and copilot fought to maintain control, one of the MPs explained that we were arriving at a top-secret facility known as the Muwaffaq Salti Air Base in the Zarqa Governorate, in the desert east of Amman. I'd heard of this place. The base was built in 1976 near a landing strip once used by Lawrence of Arabia during World War I. The modern base was completed in 1980 and named after a Jordanian pilot who was killed in battle with the Israelis.

The first thing that struck me as we got closer—other than the fact that Harris was still puking his guts out—was how crowded the airfield was. Despite the brutal conditions and limited visibility, there were dozens of Jordanian F-16s taking off and landing, no doubt conducting sorties over the capital and some of the outlying towns and villages where ISIS had been making gains. But what really caught my eye was the number of American, Egyptian, and Saudi fighter jets, long-range bombers, attack helicopters, and special operations aircraft—dozens and dozens, perhaps well over a hundred, including a handful of American B-2 stealth bombers—being amassed at a base very few people had ever even heard of. Something was brewing, something big, and I wanted to know what.

The moment we touched down—hard but safe—near one of the hangars and exited the chopper, Colonel Sharif pulled up in an armored personnel carrier. He waved us over.

I turned to Harris. "You all right?"

"I'll be fine," he said, wiping his mouth and his brow.

I handed him a bottle of water. He took several sips.

"Just give me a moment with Sharif," he said. "I need to let him know what's happening with you."

I nodded and waited while Harris briefed the colonel on the latest developments with me and the case against Vaughn. I could see Sharif's eyes grow wide. The man was as stunned as I had been. But time was fleeting. The king was waiting.

"Welcome to Azraq, Mr. Collins," Sharif shouted over the storms and the Black Hawk's rotors. "Thanks be to Allah that you're safe—and innocent."

"Thanks, Colonel," I replied. "You're telling me."

"I'm afraid we can't linger," Sharif said. "Something urgent has come up. We need to go." The colonel asked me to get into the APC. By the time he got in beside me, we were both soaked to the bone and freezing cold.

I looked back and noticed an MP guiding Harris into another vehicle.

"Where's he going?" I asked. "Isn't he coming with us?"

"No," Sharif replied. "He's heading to the infirmary first and then to one of the administrative buildings. He's got a case to manage, and a fast-moving one at that."

Our driver took us around the hangar and across the air base to a nondescript strip of garages

housing various tow trucks and other service
vehicles. He pulled into an empty stall, parked,
and turned off the engine. "We're here," he said,
checking his watch, jumping out of the APC, and
motioning for us to disembark as well. "There are
dry clothes for both of you—fatigues, I'm afraid;
that's all they have here. Find whatever fits. There
are clean socks and boots of various sizes too. But
make it quick."

We did as he suggested, and soon I found
myself wearing a private's uniform. I also found
a towel and dried off my face and bald head. The
colonel changed as well, and then the MP who
had driven us here punched a code into a keypad
on the only door inside the garage. When the electronic lock released, he led the two of us down a
stairwell.

We descended several levels, then reached a
security checkpoint manned not by MPs but by
elite members of Jordan's special forces. The colonel showed his photo ID and was cleared, but
all of my personal possessions were taken from
me, including my grandfather's watch. Then we
stepped through an X-ray machine and were patted down and carefully examined by a team of
heavily armed soldiers before being allowed to
proceed.

After being cleared, we headed down a long,
poorly lit concrete tunnel and passed through two
more checkpoints, each manned by a half-dozen
soldiers, all of them toting machine guns, before
we finally reached a small waiting area with four
more soldiers guarding the vaultlike door to the

inner sanctum. A captain checked our IDs again and told us to take a seat.

We did as we were told and for a few minutes said nothing to each other. There was a coffee table but no coffee, and there were no magazines or newspapers, nothing to do but awkwardly avoid eye contact.

Eventually I leaned back and closed my eyes. My hands were shaking. My heart was still pounding. I still couldn't believe how close I'd come to dying in that drone strike. And I still couldn't shake the sick feeling from the reality that Jack Vaughn was responsible for all that had happened. What would have possessed him to have an affair in the first place? And how could he really not have known whom he was shacking up with? The man was the director of the CIA, for crying out loud. Then again, I couldn't for one second believe he had known that his mistress was working for ISIS. A philanderer? Maybe. A traitor? I couldn't get there.

I couldn't bear to think about it anymore. It was all too ugly. So I turned my thoughts to Yael. What was she doing just then? Was the gash on her forehead healing? What about the blows she'd taken to the face? Had the doctors at Hadassah insisted that she stay for several days so they could treat her wounds and so she could get some rest? Then again, hopefully her injuries weren't that bad. Maybe Ari had thanked her for her heroic service in saving the life of the prime minister and the king and given her the week off. I hoped so. She deserved it.

Thinking about Yael made me wonder how her people were responding to this geopolitical earthquake. The Israelis had to be terrified, I imagined. Jordan was a friend, a tacit ally. And now this? A solid, stable, quiet, calm Hashemite Kingdom was the essential cornerstone of the security architecture for this entire corridor, from Jaffa to Jerusalem to Jordan. Now what? Surely the Israeli Defense Forces had mobilized their military after the attacks on the summit. It was now very possible, even probable, that ISIS was going to launch chemical attacks against Israeli population centers at any moment.

Were the Israelis also planning offensive actions against ISIS? They had to be inclined to, and what fair-minded person could blame them? Abu Khalif had just tried to assassinate their prime minister. In the process he had succeeded in killing dozens of Israeli members of parliament and security personnel. But Israeli offensive operations inside Jordan, not to mention in Syria or Iraq, would play right into the hands of ISIS, I worried. Such operations could very well provide the immediate "justification" the ISIS leaders wanted to declare total jihad against the "Zionist enemy."

The vault door opened. The colonel was asked by a young military aide to come inside. I was asked to wait. Ten minutes later, the vault door opened again. This time the colonel beckoned me to join him. I took a deep breath, stood up straight, and followed him inside. I had no idea what to expect. But there was no turning back now.

33

★ ★ ★

I entered the war room.

It was buzzing with activity. At the far end, at the head of the table, was King Abdullah himself. At his right hand was Prince Feisal. Both were talking on separate phones. To the king's left were Lieutenant General Abdul Jum'a and Major General Ibrahim al-Mufti, huddled in conversation as they pored over a map with great concern.

None of them looked up. They neither noticed us nor seemed to care that we had entered. They certainly didn't welcome us, but unlike back in Marka, they weren't the only ones in the room. The colonel whispered that he had just briefed the king and Prince Feisal on the latest developments with me, Vaughn, and the criminal investigation Agent Harris was spearheading. Then he introduced me to General Amr El-Badawy, explaining that he was the commander of Egyptian special forces. After this, he quickly introduced me to Lieutenant General Marco Ramirez, though Ramirez I already knew. He was the commander of Delta Force and a legend in the SOF community back in the States. I'd interviewed him numerous times in Afghanistan and Iraq and once in Tampa, at CENTCOM. Finally, Sharif had me say a quick hello to a Saudi general as well as one from the United Arab Emirates. Then he had me take a seat with him, not at the main conference table but in the back, by the vault door, in a row of seats he said was reserved for aides to the military leaders, though there was only one in the room at the moment, and he was Jordanian.

"Most of these guys just arrived," Sharif whispered, handing me a pad and pen.

"How long ago?" I asked, trying to get my bearings.

"A few minutes ago. I was told the prince is about to give a briefing. That's why we were trying to get you here before it started."

"I don't understand," I whispered back. "I get why General Ramirez is here. But why the guys from Egypt, Saudi, and the Gulf?"

"Your guess is as good as mine," said Sharif. "I suppose we're about to find out."

Prince Feisal asked for quiet. Those on landlines—no cell phones were permitted in this bunker—put them down. The generals who'd just arrived took their seats. The vault door closed and locked behind us. The meeting was under way.

"Good afternoon, gentlemen. Thank you for joining His Majesty and me on such short notice," the prince began. "We will get into the assault planning in a moment. But first I want to bring you up to speed on several important new developments. I wanted you to be among the first to know that CIA director Jack Vaughn has been arrested at his home in Washington by the FBI. I am told by the attorney general that Vaughn will be charged with espionage and possibly with treason."

There were audible gasps around the table.

"While I don't have all the details, I can tell you that Mr. Vaughn was arrested with a mistress who was also at his home—indeed, apparently in his bed," the prince continued. "Allegedly, he told her various classified details about the peace summit as well as about the location of His Majesty and other principals in recent days. What's not clear at this hour is whether Mr. Vaughn knew this woman—of Qatari descent—was working for ISIS."

The men around the table were as stunned as I'd been, and it took a moment for the prince to quiet the room and continue his briefing.

"Furthermore, the FBI has just arrested a suspect at the NSA's headquarters at Fort Meade in connection to this case," Feisal explained. "I'm told this suspect is the son of Mr. Vaughn's mistress. Apparently he was providing the information gleaned from Vaughn back to ISIS, ironically through secure American channels."

"You're absolutely certain of this?" asked the Saudi general, visibly shaken.

"This is what we have been told," the prince said. "Obviously the investigation is ongoing."

At this, the prince glanced at me. But he did not seem angry. Nor did he mention to the others that I had been considered, for a time, a suspect. Apparently I had been fully cleared. Why else would they allow me to be in this of all rooms, with the king of Jordan, no less?

"I've known Jack Vaughn for a quarter of a century," the Saudi general continued. "I cannot imagine him as a mole."

"None of us can," the prince replied. "I'm sure we'll learn more details—including motives—in due course. For now, I'm afraid that's all I have."

"So three arrests thus far?" the UAE general asked.

"Yes—Mr. Vaughn, the mistress, and the son. That's all we've heard about for now."

"But is that it? Is the situation contained, or are the Americans saying more arrests are coming?" the UAE general asked.

"I really couldn't say," the prince said.

Clearly this didn't satisfy the group.

"Wait a minute, wait a minute—you're saying ISIS has penetrated the highest levels of the CIA and the NSA?" asked General El-Badawy from Egypt.

"That would appear to be the case."

"All to trigger an attack on four world leaders, including Your Majesty?" He nodded at the king.

"I'm afraid so."

"I highly doubt it's limited to three people," El-Badawy noted.

"I hesitate to speculate," the prince said.

"Fair enough, but this is an unprecedented penetration of American intelligence. Can we safely assume every member of the conspiracy has been identified and arrested? That seems highly unlikely, does it not?"

No one said a word. I glanced at General Ramirez. He hadn't yet said anything, but I guessed the conversation was about to shift to him.

"Look, this story is going to break to the public in the United States in a few hours," the prince said. "Obviously, as I said, there's still a great deal that we don't know. As we get more information, I will certainly pass it on to you all. For now, however, I suggest we shift to finalizing our war plans. I don't have to remind you that time is not on our side."

"Not so fast, Your Highness," El-Badawy protested. "With all due respect, we can't just shift topics. Clearly there has been a serious breach at the CIA and NSA. Maybe it's been contained, but maybe not. Maybe the FBI has captured everyone involved; maybe not. Either way, as I see it, this raises two immediate and very serious challenges. First, how reliable and secure is any intelligence coming from the U.S. right now? And second, what is Abu Khalif's endgame?"

"What do you mean?" the Saudi general asked. "Haven't the ISIS forces caused enough damage? What more could they possibly want?"

"Are you kidding?" El-Badawy asked. "Abu Khalif wants Mecca. He wants Medina. He wants Cairo. He still wants Amman. And that's just for starters."

A hush fell over the room. The king sat back and, for the moment, remained silent. His expression was inscrutable. I was taking notes as fast as I could. No one had laid down any ground rules, but I assumed we were operating by the same guidelines the king had previously established. Everything had to run through Colonel Sharif. But if he cleared it, I could write it. I knew I couldn't write anything about the FBI sting operation against Vaughn. But what I was watching had little to do with a crime story and everything to do with the rise of ISIS and the collapse of American credibility in the region.

Ramirez cleared his throat. "May I, Your Majesty?" he asked, directly addressing the king.

Abdullah nodded.

"Gentlemen, I understand your concerns, and I share many of them," the American general began. "But we don't have time to get sidetracked. I received this news moments before arriving here. I realize it raises profound and disturbing questions, as many for me as for any of you. But we need to stay focused. The president of the United States is being held by ISIS. By my count, we have only seventeen hours to rescue him before he is executed on YouTube, for all the world to see, if he hasn't been beheaded or burned alive already. I'm not interested in the long-term goals of Abu Khalif right now. I have one mission: get my president back. You all promised to help me. That's why we're here, and for no other reason. Now, are you going to help me or not?"

34

✦ ✦ ✦

The men all nodded to Ramirez.

Then they quickly returned to the urgent business at hand.

Ramirez began walking the group through the latest U.S. intelligence and analysis. "We believe we've identified the most probable location of the president," he said, "and all signs point to Dabiq."

My ears perked up at the mention of Dabiq. That was the place Abu Khalif had mentioned in his video, the site of the apocalyptic End of Days battle that he and the other ISIS leaders were hoping to trigger, according to General al-Mufti. Clearly the president's captors would have had time to transport him there by now. Was it possible that's where he was being held?

The Jordanian military aide sitting behind Ramirez pulled up a map of the region on the large flat-screen monitor behind the general and marked Dabiq, a tiny city—more of a village, really—in the northwest section of Syria, not far from the border of Turkey.

"Typically, there would be nothing to draw our

attention there," the general continued. "Dabiq is a town ordinarily populated by fewer than four thousand people, but in recent months it's become an ISIS stronghold. We estimate they have amassed about twenty thousand jihadists there, at least half of whom are foreign fighters. They've murdered most of the local men under the age of sixty. They've taken the young girls as sex slaves and murdered most of their mothers. The rest of the able-bodied women are serving the ISIS forces in various capacities—cooking, cleaning, laundry, and the like. But more importantly, many of the heavy artillery, tanks, and other advanced weaponry ISIS has captured from Assad's forces have been brought to Dabiq. They seem to be digging in for a major battle."

The aide now displayed a series of American spy satellite photos showing the buildup of forces over the past several weeks.

"General, do you have actual proof the president is there, or is this a working theory?" El-Badawy asked.

"I think it's fair to say we have very compelling evidence, but I wouldn't call it definitive proof— not yet," Ramirez replied. "Let me explain."

The Delta commander told the generals about the tracking device in the president's Jorg Gray 6500 Chronograph wristwatch. "Our satellites lost the signal coming from the transponder shortly after the president disappeared. But a few hours ago, we started picking it up again. Our tracking indicates it's coming from an elementary school in Dabiq."

"But this isn't necessarily proof of the president's location?" the Saudi general asked.

"No. It's possible the watch could have been removed by ISIS forces and taken to Dabiq, while the president could have been taken someplace else."

"Would ISIS forces know how to disable the tracking device and then reengage it a few hours ago?" asked El-Badawy.

"We don't think so," Ramirez said, "though we can't be certain. Still, there is a growing body of additional evidence that points to Dabiq."

He explained that a mobile phone belonging to Jamal Ramzy, the ISIS commander in Syria, had been taken from Ramzy's dead body during the firefight at the Al-Hummar Palace on Sunday. He didn't mention me. It wasn't clear he even knew I'd been involved in recovering the phone. He did, however, thank the king for making the phone and all its data available to the U.S. government.

"The very fact that the Syrian commander of ISIS was involved in a coup attempt here in Jordan is noteworthy, I think. But it's more than that. Jordanian intelligence experts and our top guys at the NSA have examined the phone thoroughly. It took us a while to get through the phone's encryption. But we now know that the call log indicates a total of nine outbound calls were made from the phone, and three calls were received. Of those, Ramzy—or someone else using the phone—made three outgoing calls to Dabiq and received one call from Dabiq. Not surprisingly, no one is currently answering at any of these numbers. But we have learned that the one call to Ramzy from Dabiq was placed from an apartment building less than six blocks from the school where the tracking signal is now being picked up."

Next, Ramirez shared some good news.

"Mr. Collins, you'll be glad to know that the Secret Service agent you found and rescued at the SADAFCO warehouse is going to live. He's making a solid recovery, and he's talking. As a sharpshooter, he'd been taking out ISIS forces as they converged on the president's position. Unfortunately, he was shot when the enemy swarmed the building he was in. They thought he was already dead, so they left him alone. But in that time, he overheard several of the terrorists talking about Dabiq and the battle that was coming. In fact, he told me that talk of Dabiq was the last thing he remembers hearing before he blacked out."

Then there was the video released by Abu Khalif, Ramirez added, noting that the ISIS leader had said specifically, "We are waiting for you in Dabiq."

"What's more," Ramirez continued, "Khalif denounced the president as 'the dog of Rome.' These, I'm told, are references to some sort of apocalyptic theology held by the ISIS leaders that the last battle in history—sort of their version of Armageddon—will happen in Dabiq. That's when, supposedly, the infidel forces of Rome will be defeated on the plains near this town. Does this ring true to any of you?"

"Of course it does," the Saudi general said. "It all comes from one of the hadiths. The Prophet— peace be upon him—said the Last Hour would not come until the Romans landed at Dabiq. An army of the best soldiers of the people of the earth will come from Medina to confront them, to fight them. This is a very well-known passage among Sunni true believers."

"Now, look, I confess, much of this is new to me," Ramirez conceded—much to my relief because it was completely new to me except for what had been discussed in the bunker the day before, however briefly. "When you say 'the forces of Rome,' does that mean the Italians, or is the language symbolic?"

General El-Badawy stepped in and took that one. "That question is oft debated among Sunni scholars," the Egyptian said. "Some say it's literal. Others say it refers more to the Vatican and the Christian forces of the West rather than to the Roman Empire or to modern-day Italians themselves. Still others say it might metaphorically refer to America, since your country has become known as the world's most powerful Christian nation."

"Clearly Khalif sees the U.S. as Rome," noted the general from the UAE, nodding to Ramirez. "As you pointed out, that's why he described your president as the 'dog of Rome' in the video."

"Indeed," El-Badawy said. "Not all Sunnis share this eschatology, mind you. Or if they do, most don't take action based on their beliefs. But Khalif is convinced that the End of Days has come, that the Mahdi is about to arrive on earth and establish his kingdom of justice and peace and unity under Sharia law. That's what's driving him and his forces. They believe the Romans will be led by the Dajjal, a figure of extreme evil. Some scholars believe this is a specific person. Others believe this represents the forces of the Western powers. It's possible Khalif believes your president is the Dajjal."

"So what exactly is supposed to happen in this apocalyptic battle?" Ramirez asked.

The Saudi answered this. "The hadiths tell us that one-third of the Muslim forces will flee and will never be forgiven by Allah for abandoning the battle. The text says another third of the Muslim forces will die in the battle as 'excellent martyrs.' The final third of the Muslim forces will fight the Romans, win, and conquer Constantinople—which might literally mean modern Istanbul but is more likely code for the West. Before the Muslims win, however, they will turn to Allah in devoted prayer. As they pray, Isa will come to pray with them and then fight with them. The text says Isa will 'break the cross' and 'kill the swine.' Then he will lead the Muslims to victory at Dabiq, then to complete victory over Rome, and then the Mahdi will establish his global caliphate." ·

I was writing furiously, trying to get it all down, but at this point I leaned over and whispered to Colonel Sharif, "Who is this 'Isa'?"

His answer floored me.

"Jesus."

35

★   ★   ★

"What do you mean, Jesus?" I whispered back.

"Isa is Jesus," Sharif repeated. "The ancient prophecies say he's coming back."

"To where?"

"To earth."

"Why?"

"To establish a global kingdom, the full caliphate."

"Muslims believe Jesus is coming back to earth?"

"Of course."

"To rule the world?"

"No, no," Sharif said. "He won't rule the world. He comes before the Mahdi and helps establish the conditions for the Mahdi to rule the world."

"The Mahdi being . . . ?"

"Our savior, our king."

"Jesus isn't the Mahdi?"

"No. He comes—well, you heard the general— he comes to conquer Dajjal, defeat the armies of Rome at Dabiq, and help the Mahdi establish the final caliphate."

I had no idea what the colonel was talking about. I'd never heard any of this before. I was jotting it all down, but I suddenly felt like I was talking to my brother, Matt. We'd had this exact conversation just a few days earlier, but in reverse. Matt had tried to convince me that a bunch of old Bible prophecies indicated that a terrible, cataclysmic judgment was coming upon Jordan and the neighboring nations. Matt said these judgments would fall at the end of history, and then Jesus would come and set up his Kingdom. It had all been new to me. Now these men were saying something so similar, yet so radically different.

". . . and one last thing," Ramirez was saying, wrapping up his presentation. "My team found a sermon by Abu Musab al-Zarqawi, who as we all know was the leader of the Islamic State's predecessor, al Qaeda in Iraq. Zarqawi said of his terror campaign inside Iraq just after the liberation in 2003, 'The spark has been lit here in Iraq, and its heat will continue to intensify until it burns the crusader armies in Dabiq.' Now, as we've just noted, Abu Khalif, Zarqawi's successor, is essentially saying the same thing. So the U.S. is training all our intelligence-gathering assets on Dabiq. We're doing everything we can to confirm that the president is there and that he is alive, and of course we're developing a battle plan to get him out. And that's why I've come here to meet with you all. We could do this alone, but we believe it's better if we work together. We believe it's better if the world sees this as a joint American–Arab operation, and not only to rescue the president but also to capture or kill Abu Khalif. Can we count on your support?"

El-Badawy had a question. "Where did the other calls on Jamal Ramzy's phone lead?" the Egyptian general asked.

"Excuse me?" Ramirez said.

"You said three of the calls on Mr. Ramzy's phone were made to Dabiq," El-Badawy said. "Where did the other calls lead?"

"Uh, well, I believe five outgoing calls were to the city of Homs, which is also in Syria, of course."

"To the same number?"

"Yes."

"And what was the number?"

"It turned out to be a switching station," Ramirez answered.

"The calls were transferred elsewhere?"

"Correct."

"To where?"

"We haven't been able to ascertain that yet."

"Did they go to Dabiq as well?"

"They may have, but I'm not sure."

"Why not?"

"The NSA is working on that, but they don't have an answer for me yet."

"Was this person who was just arrested at Fort Meade involved in this case?"

"I don't know."

"Is it possible?"

"I doubt it."

"But you're not sure."

"No, I'm not."

"Well, why should it be so difficult to know

where the calls were transferred to?" El-Badawy pressed. "If your government has confirmed the number is a switching station, surely they can determine to where the calls were switched."

"I'm sorry; I don't know," Ramirez said, looking through a briefing book full of notes but apparently not finding the answer. "I will check on that and get back to you."

"Is it possible the president is being held in Homs?" the Saudi asked.

"We don't think so," Ramirez said.

"Why not?"

"For all the reasons I just explained."

"Because all roads seem to lead to Dabiq?"

"Now that our satellites have reacquired the tracking signal from the president's watch, yes, we think so."

"But a moment ago you said you couldn't be sure."

"I said we had strong evidence pointing to Dabiq, not proof," said Ramirez. "I will stick to that assessment."

"But it is possible—just possible—that the watch was removed from the president and taken to Dabiq to throw us off the scent, right?" the general from the Emirates asked.

"Possible? Sure. Probable? I don't think so."

"Actually, there may be a reasonably strong case that the president *is* in Homs," I said, catching everyone off guard and getting quite a few looks from those who thought I should be seen and not heard.

"I'm sorry, J. B., but the floor is not really

open," Ramirez said. "You're a friend. We've known each other a long time. But we were all told explicitly that you're here as an observer, not a participant."

"I understand, General, and I promise I'll be brief," I said, plunging forward. "I'm just saying I've been to Homs. I've been to Jamal Ramzy's base camp. I've seen it, and it's an ideal safe house. It's underground. It's well protected. It's the perfect place to hide the president and Khalif, and I think it's a serious mistake to rule it out, especially if you have so many phone calls from Ramzy going to Homs."

"Wait a minute; I thought you saw Khalif in Mosul," said the Saudi.

"I did," I replied. "But I first met Ramzy in Homs."

Colonel Sharif leaned over and whispered to me to knock it off, that I was overstepping my bounds.

But El-Badawy wanted to hear more. "Could you find your way back to Ramzy's lair?" he asked.

"Of course not," General Ramirez shot back before I could answer. "J. B. was blindfolded going in and coming out. I read your article."

"Is that true?" the Egyptian asked.

"It is," I said, "but General Ramirez is forgetting one important thing."

"What's that?"

"I might not have known how to get there, but I knew where I was."

"What is that supposed to mean?"

"It means I was told by my contact to meet at

the Khaled bin Walid Mosque," I explained. "It was in a neighborhood of Homs called al-Khalidiyah. My colleagues—God rest their souls—snuck into Homs with me. We linked up with Ramzy's men. They took us to that specific neighborhood and that specific mosque, and from there I was taken through underground tunnels to the meeting with Ramzy. So, no, I couldn't find it wandering around that Dante's inferno of a city. But how hard would it really be for you all to find that mosque with satellites and drones and figure out what kind of activity is under way there right now?"

"And you think ISIS could be holding the president there?" El-Badawy pressed.

"I can't say that definitively, General," I replied. "All I'm saying is that you should take a careful look. I'm not saying it would have been easy for Khalif to get there or for ISIS to have gotten the president there without being noticed. But remember, Jamal Ramzy got himself from Homs to Amman without being noticed. Obviously they've figured out a way to transit back and forth. So we know it can be done. I'm not saying the president is not in Dabiq. Maybe he is. I'm just saying, isn't it a bit foolish to kidnap the leader of the free world and bring him to a town of four thousand people and then tell the world you have him there?"

"Maybe," Ramirez said, "unless you're trying to trigger a battle you believe will bring about the end of the world."

36

Prince Feisal suddenly leaned over and whispered something to the king.

Then he turned to the group and apologized. He explained that the vice president of the United States was on the line and that His Majesty needed to take the call in his private chambers. As the king excused himself and took a guard with him through a door at the other end of the room, the prince asked General Ramirez to walk through his plan to invade Dabiq and explain what role he expected each coalition partner to play in the attack. I was yet to be convinced the president was actually there but was eager to hear Ramirez's plan of attack.

Over the years, I had become deeply impressed with the intellect and courage of this three-star general. Ramirez was the eldest son of Cuban refugees and grew up in south Florida in a family of nine kids. He graduated first in his class from West Point and was recruited by Delta Force early in his Army career. He was one of the first American special operators sent into Afghanistan to fight al Qaeda and the Taliban after 9/11. Later, he was an instrumental player in hunting down and killing Osama bin Laden in Pakistan. He was one of the chief architects of the surprisingly successful "surge" strategy in Iraq, before political leaders far above his pay grade unraveled America's hard-fought gains by precipitously withdrawing all U.S. forces from Iraq in December 2011.

Rumor had it that he and his men were actually responsible for the capture of Abu Khalif several years earlier, though he had adamantly and repeatedly denied that U.S. forces had been involved in that operation at all. It made perfect sense to me that Ramirez and his Delta Force operators were being tasked with the rescue of the president and the recapture (or killing) of Khalif. Few knew the region better—indeed, few knew al Qaeda and ISIS better—than this six-foot-five, 230-pound former defensive tackle whom his colleagues had nicknamed "the Cuban missile." The stakes, of course, could not have been higher. As far as I was aware, this would be the first time in history that U.S. forces would fight on Syrian soil. The very president they were hoping to rescue had repeatedly vowed never to put American "boots on the ground" in Syria. Yet if there was anyone who could pull it off, I had to believe it was Marco Ramirez.

However, just as the general began handing out briefing books and explaining his approach, the colonel nudged me and insisted I follow him out of the war room and back into the waiting area. I assumed this had something to do with my speaking up in the meeting, which to be honest kind of ticked me off. Still, I had no choice. If I was going to get back in that room, it wasn't going to be by making a scene. So I stepped out with Sharif, pulse racing, and prepared to defend myself.

Before I could say a word, however, the colonel led me through a door I'd previously not noticed, down a narrow hallway, and past several more soldiers, where he knocked twice on a closed door, then entered a nine-digit code into a keypad and waved me through.

We were now in the king's spacious private office in what appeared to be the deepest recesses of the bunker complex. His Majesty was sitting behind his desk under a large portrait of his father, a Jordanian flag on a stand by his side. He was already on the phone but nodded to the colonel and me and motioned us to take a seat on the couch. Sharif whispered to me that I should pick up the phone on the end table to my right. Then he reached for a similar handset on the end table to our left and instructed me to select line two and hit the Mute button. I did and watched him do the same.

"Your Majesty, thank you for waiting," an older woman's voice said on the other end of the line. "Vice President Holbrooke will be right with you."

I pulled out my notebook and a pen and tried to calm down and shift gears. I'd been bracing for a fight, sure I was being thrown out of the Ramirez briefing for speaking out of turn. But I'd been dead wrong. I hadn't been thrown out at all. Instead, I'd been invited into the inner sanctum.

My mind raced with questions I wanted to ask Martin Holbrooke. The gray, grizzled, and somewhat-cantankerous seventy-seven-year-old VP was now in an extremely precarious position, and the nation—along with the entire world—was watching his every move.

I'd known Holbrooke for years, but he was a shrewd political operator and Washington insider long before I came on the scene. He'd first been elected to Congress from a district in northeastern Ohio back in the late 1960s. Later he'd won a Senate seat, played his cards carefully, and risen to become chairman of the powerful Armed Services Committee. By the time I met him, he'd become a heavyweight in the Democratic Party, raising enormous sums for his political action committee, investing in up-and-coming progressive candidates, making allies, earning chits, and laying the groundwork for a run for the Democratic nomination for president.

Holbrooke was also an early backer of Harrison Taylor and helped get the software CEO elected first to the Senate, and then, after only one term, elected governor of North Carolina. Along the way, Holbrooke had seen Taylor's popularity rising slowly but surely, both in the local grass roots of the party and nationally. And when the day came for Holbrooke to announce his candidacy for the presidency, he instead stunned everyone by using his announcement speech to become the first U.S. senator to endorse Taylor for president.

The effect was transformative. Taylor, a note-worthy voice on the center-left of the party, suddenly had the full backing of one of the country's most hard-core liberals for one reason and one reason only: Holbrooke was convinced Taylor was the only Democrat who could actually win, and he'd been right. Taylor went on to clinch the nomination and asked Holbrooke to be his running mate. The two won a brutally close race that fall, 50.3 percent to 49.7 percent.

I'd covered Holbrooke when I was a young correspondent for the *New York Daily News* and had interviewed him from time to time throughout my career. He'd always been generous with his time—and his liquor—and could be counted on for newsworthy quotes (as well as spicy off-the-record gossip about his colleagues on the Hill). I'd always found him a compelling, complicated, and often-conniving member of the U.S. Senate; he could write legislation and craft amendments and build unlikely coalitions—and simultaneously yet subtly sabotage his personal and political enemies better than anyone I'd ever seen. But I'd never really been convinced by him as vice president of the United States. The role was, in far too many ways, a complete mismatch of his skill sets. He was a particularly gifted and clever orator, yet his job now was basically to travel the country and B-level world capitals and give banal speeches that purposefully made no news. He was a master in the art of the deal, yet he was no longer tasked with any deals to cut.

And if that weren't bad enough, he absolutely hated to fly. For decades he had insisted on driving himself from his home near Cleveland to

Washington and back, had run his Senate campaigns from an RV traveling back and forth across the Ohio Turnpike, and had complained endlessly when having to travel abroad (which might be why he drank so much with the press when he'd reach his foreign destinations). Yet now he was in sole possession of Air Force Two and had racked up more frequent flyer miles than any other VP in the history of the country.

What concerned me most right now, however, was that he'd undergone triple bypass surgery less than six months earlier. He'd been on bed rest for several months and had only recently gotten back on the road. What's more, his wife, Frieda—his third in as many decades and almost thirty years his junior—had just been diagnosed with breast cancer and was now at the Mayo Clinic going through chemotherapy. Was Holbrooke up for this crisis? Physically? Emotionally? Mentally? He'd never served in the military. He'd never served in an executive capacity. Was he ready to be commander in chief?

37

★ ★ ★

Despite all my questions, I knew the best thing was to simply listen.

I was treading on thin ice as it was, or so I believed, and if this were true, then there was no point risking my position with the king any further. And truth be told, I suspected the VP might be less than candid with His Majesty if he knew I was listening in on their conversation. So I readied my pen and waited quietly until the VP came on the line.

"Abdullah, it's Martin; has General Ramirez briefed you?" Holbrooke asked straightaway, skipping any pleasantries and getting down to business.

"He has," the king replied. "You all believe the president is in Dabiq."

"We do, and the general seems to have developed a pretty solid plan for getting him back."

"He's just about to go through that with us," the king said, glancing at me. "But I have to say, Martin, my team and I are not completely convinced the president is actually in Dabiq."

"And why is that?" the VP asked, sounding

as exhausted as I'd ever heard him. "Our satellites have picked up his signal. We've got the calls from Ramzy's phone to Dabiq. We've got the testimony of the Secret Service agent. We have Khalif's own words in the video. It all points to Dabiq, Abdullah."

"You're not concerned your systems have been, perhaps, affected?" the king asked, raising as delicately as possible the emerging scandal at the highest levels of the U.S. intelligence community.

"Affected?" the VP asked.

"Compromised?"

"You mean this nonsense with Jack?"

"It sounds quite serious."

"It's a distraction. Our intel is solid. Believe me."

"But surely there's a risk that—"

"No," the VP interjected, cutting him off. "I'm telling you, this whole thing with Jack is an isolated incident. It's a nuisance, to be sure, but I have no doubt it will sort itself out in due time. But we can't let that sidetrack us from what we know—that all indicators are pointing to Dabiq."

"Martin, look, you may be right. But your own government has just arrested the director of the CIA. You've arrested a senior analyst at the NSA. Your intelligence systems have been penetrated by ISIS. And who knows who else is involved and where else this leads? These perpetrators have already used American intelligence to launch assassination attempts against President Taylor, Prime Minister Lavi, President Mansour, and myself. They're in the process of trying to overthrow my government and destabilize yours. Don't we have to consider the possibility that whoever is plotting against us is manipulating the very intelligence you're looking at to make critical decisions?"

"What are you saying, Abdullah?" the VP asked, sounding agitated and defensive. "That I can't trust the intel on my desk? Those phone intercepts that are pointing us to Dabiq came from a phone you gave us. The president's tracking signal is coming from Dabiq. Khalif said, 'We are waiting for you in Dabiq.' Those aren't my words—or Jack's—but his. I'm not saying this mess at Langley isn't a problem. Of course it is. But we've got to be able to sift this all through and take an objective read on the data we're seeing. And I'm telling you my guys say all the data is pointing to Dabiq. What more do you want?"

"More," the king said. "I don't have to tell you that if we all move on Dabiq and we're wrong, Khalif is going to behead the president on worldwide television, and all hell will break loose in this region. We will have just handed ISIS the most powerful propaganda tool we could possibly imagine. People will flock to join the caliphate. ISIS will have more money than they'll know what to do with. They could become unstoppable, Martin. The region will become completely destabilized."

"No one understands the stakes better than me, Abdullah. But we're running out of time. If we're going to move, we need to move soon. My guys are worried it may already be too late, that the president may already be dead. I can't operate that way. I'm going to trust that he's still alive until the deadline. But we're running out of daylight."

"I agree," the king said. "But first we've got to be certain we're not being set up."

"The evidence for Dabiq is overwhelming."

"It looks that way. But it all seems a bit too easy to me."

"You think ISIS is baiting us?"

"That's exactly what I'm afraid of. Look, we know Khalif wants to wage the final battle in Dabiq. He and his men have been planning it. They've been prepping for it. They've got an arsenal of chemical weapons that could turn the whole thing into a bloodbath. We have to seriously consider the possibility that this is a trap."

"I grant you Khalif had some chemical weapons. But he's used them already—at your airport. There's no evidence to suggest he has more. We can't let ourselves be paralyzed by Khalif's genocidal rhetoric, not when the president's life is on the line."

The king looked at me. I shook my head, though almost imperceptibly. We absolutely had evidence that ISIS had enormous stockpiles of sarin gas—far more than could have been used at the airport. I'd personally seen a warehouse full of warheads that Abu Khalif and Jamal Ramzy had told me were filled with sarin gas, and I'd seen it tested on Iraqi prisoners. I'd reported as much in my story in the *Times*. The king had read it. Certainly the VP had too. So why was Holbrooke downplaying the threat now?

"Martin, as you know, the *New York Times* reported that Khalif captured a warehouse full of sarin gas," the king said respectfully but without hesitation. "Based on what I saw at the airport in Amman, I think we have to believe not only that Khalif has much more, but that he's ready to use it—and where better than in Dabiq, where ISIS intends to make their final stand?"

There was a pause. "You could be right," the VP said finally. "But my guys say they're ready for anything. We can deal with poison gas. What we can't deal with is sitting on our hands doing nothing while time runs out. I don't have to tell you I'm under tremendous pressure here. This isn't just the president; this is my friend we're talking about."

"He's my friend too," the king said.

"I know, but for me he's not just a friend," Holbrooke added. "He's the constitutional leader of my country. And if you're watching the American press at all, you can see there's already a steady and almost-deafening drumbeat for the attorney general to declare that Harrison is no longer president and to have me sworn in immediately to replace him. That puts me in a very dicey place. I don't want to even consider stepping into the presidency unless I've done absolutely everything I possibly could to get Harrison back safely to his family and to the country."

As the two men kept talking, I could see the strain in the king's face and shoulders. This wasn't some run-of-the-mill Middle Eastern hostage situation. It was, back in the U.S. at least, fast becoming a constitutional crisis.

The VP's comments underscored how cut off I was from all news coming out of the States. I needed access to the Internet. I needed to get up to speed on the political and geopolitical nuances of this fast-moving story. I knew, at least in general terms, that Article II, Section 1 of the Constitution stated that "in case of the removal of the president from office, or of his death, resignation, or inability to discharge the powers and duties of the said office, the same shall devolve on the vice president." I also knew that the Twenty-Fifth Amendment to the Constitution stated plainly that "in case of the removal of the president from office or of his death or resignation, the vice president shall become president." The question was whether the capture of the president by foreign military forces fit the definition of the president's inability to discharge his powers and duties. Did the current crisis warrant removal of the president from office?

It seemed to, on the face of it. But America had never faced such a situation before. Four American chief executives had been assassinated in office since the nation's founding—Lincoln, Garfield, McKinley, and Kennedy. Four more American leaders had died in office of natural causes—William Henry Harrison, Zachary Taylor, Warren Harding, and Franklin Delano Roosevelt. Nixon had resigned the office under the shadow of the Watergate allegations and the prospect of impeachment. But what was unfolding now was completely unprecedented in the annals of American history.

This, of course, was why Section 4 of the Twenty-Fifth Amendment had been written—to cover all potential ambiguities. I couldn't remember the text precisely, but it essentially explained various scenarios under which the vice president could become acting president temporarily and then, with the authorization of the cabinet and Congress, reinstate the president to his full powers once the situation was resolved and he was capable of serving again, or else permanently remove the president from power and give full authority to the acting president until an election could be held.

As far as I was concerned, it didn't take a constitutional scholar to determine that Taylor, even if he was alive, was not currently capable of functioning as president. Thus Holbrooke was for all intents and purposes operating as acting president at the moment. But even from half a world away, I could picture the political weight on Holbrooke's shoulders. He didn't want to trigger Section 4, a provision that had never been invoked before. He didn't want to act—or be seen as acting—precipitously. The nation was operating in treacherous and uncharted waters. Holbrooke, uncharacteristically, seemed to be resisting his standard political instincts of advancing his own interests. He seemed to feel—or at least wanted to be perceived as feeling—a deep sense of responsibility to act carefully, deliberately, and without haste.

Nevertheless, fateful decisions had to be made, and made quickly. The vice president was the only person back in Washington with the constitutional authority to send American military forces into battle, and it was clear he was getting ready to act on that authority.

"Martin, please hear me," the king was saying.

"The president may very well be in Dabiq. I'm not saying he isn't. I'm just saying we need to do everything we possibly can to confirm it beyond the shadow of a doubt and do our best to rule out any other possible scenario. History will never forgive us if we make a mistake."

"I hear that, Abdullah, and as always, I appreciate your concern and your wise counsel," the VP said. "I'll do everything I can to push my team to cross every t and dot every i over the next few hours. I assure you of that. But it's already afternoon over there. It's winter. The sun goes down in a few hours. If we're going to make a move, General Ramirez is strongly recommending we move just after night falls. That means he and his men—and your men and all those who have gathered with you—need to finalize a plan, make sure everything is coordinated, and be prepared to move out in five or six hours, at the latest. That's not a lot of time to make sure everything is done right. It's no time at all."

"No, it's not," said the king. "But we'll be ready. I promise you that. You and I go way back. And I want you to know that above all, I'm with you. My people are with you. The kingdom of Jordan has no better friend in the world than the American people and your government. We will do everything in our power to get the president back safe and sound and to bring these evildoers to justice, come what may. On this, you have my word."

38

★ ★ ★

"You're quite the diplomat," I said as the call ended.

"Why do you say that?" the king asked, pressing a button on his desk and summoning a steward.

"I mean, you're not convinced the president is being held in Dabiq."

"Nor are you."

"I'm not the one trying to convince the vice president to tread carefully."

There was a knock on the door, and a steward entered with a fresh pot of tea. He promptly served us all, beginning with His Majesty, and then stepped out.

"You're worried this thing with Jack Vaughn goes deeper than maybe anyone yet realizes," I said when the king, the colonel, and I were alone again.

"I hope not," the king replied. "But it's too soon to rule anything out."

"Because it's possible the intel being shown to the VP could be compromised."

"Perhaps."

"Which could mean someone is trying to lure

us into a fight in Dabiq when the president is elsewhere."

"And Khalif."

"But what if you're wrong?" I countered. "What if they really are in Dabiq?"

"You just heard me. My men are ready to go into Dabiq if that's where the evidence leads."

"And if it's ambiguous and you're out of time and you have to make a decision?"

"We'll follow the vice president's lead."

"Even if he's wrong."

"Yes."

"Why?"

"Because that's what friends do."

"Stand with each other in a fight."

"Absolutely," said the king. "As I said, Martin and I go way back."

"Back to his first Senate campaign, as I recall."

"Longer."

"Really—how long?"

"He and his first wife came on a codel when he was a freshman in Congress," the king said, using insider slang for a congressional delegation. "They came to meet my father. I happened to be home from boarding school for spring break. I was just a kid, but my father insisted that I join the group for dinner."

"When was this?"

"I don't remember exactly, but it was after the '67 war. Things were tense. The Holbrookes were very pro-Israel. But they'd heard good things about my father. They wanted to take his measure, to see if there was a way to deescalate tensions, maybe even to make peace."

"Did you ever think he'd one day be the VP?"

"Off the record?"

"Sure."

"Then no. He was a bright guy—don't get me wrong. One of the smartest men I'd seen enter Congress. But to be honest, he seemed to be more of a businessman than a politician. Very practical. Very pragmatic. A real can-do attitude. I thought he'd never make it in Washington. But what did I know? I was just a kid."

"Of course, you didn't think you'd one day sit on the throne either, did you?" I probed.

He shook his head and stared at the steam rising off the cup of tea in his hands. "Never. Never wanted it. Never sought it. Never even bothered to think it was something I needed to worry about."

"Worry?"

"'Uneasy lies the head . . . ,'" he said.

His voice trailed off, but there was no reason to finish. I got the allusion. He was referencing the title of his father's memoirs, written in 1962. The title was a line from Shakespeare's *Henry IV, Part 2*. I'd discovered the play and fallen in love with it in high school. I'd played the lead in college and still remembered every line.

The king sipped his tea. I sipped mine. Sharif said nothing. I held my tongue. If for only a moment, His Majesty was lost in thought and it was not my place to disturb him.

I thought about the significance of that line from *Henry IV, Part 2*: "Uneasy lies the head that wears a crown." Vice President Holbrooke didn't wear a crown, of course, but he was finding out just how uneasy—and how uncertain—a position of power could be. I hoped for all our sakes he would make the correct decisions in the hours ahead.

"My father watched his own grandfather, my namesake, be assassinated in Jerusalem—watched it happen with his own eyes," the king said eventually, though not so much to me or to the colonel as to himself as he reflected on the almost-unbearable challenges of the dynasty into which he was born. "I grew up seeing one palace intrigue after another, things young boys should never have to see. And now my children are watching it happen all over again. Will such curses never end?"

It was a quiet for a bit. Then I asked him if the queen and his children were safe. He said they were. A moment later, he added that he had sent them out of the country. I asked where. He would not say. I suspected they were now in the States, but it did not seem appropriate to pry any further, so I let it go. Almost.

"And the crown prince?" I asked of his eldest son. "Where is he?"

"In there," he replied, nodding to the door to his left.

"Getting some rest?"

"Well deserved," he said.

"Much needed," I added.

"Indeed."

"May I change the subject?" I asked.

"Please."

"The Egyptians," I said, nodding in the other direction, back to the war room beside us.

"A wonderful people," said the king.

"And the Saudis," I added, "and the Emirates . . ."

"Family."

"And yet the world is not used to seeing you all work together on military matters."

"Or any matters."

"Or any matters—that's true," I agreed. "You have all had many difficulties with each other over the years."

The king nodded.

"Pan-Arab unity was more of a dream than a reality?"

"Unfortunately. But things are changing."

"How so?"

"For one, new leaders with new outlooks have emerged," said the monarch. "For another, we find ourselves facing common enemies."

"ISIS?"

"Of course, but not ISIS alone."

"Iran."

"That is a very sensitive subject," he replied. "We are doing our best to maintain open and cordial relations with Tehran."

"But it's no secret that the Sunni Arab world feels the Shias of Persia could soon pose an existential threat."

"Many believe this, yes."

"Don't you?"

"The Arabs face many challenges on many fronts."

"You don't want me to quote you directly about the Iran threat."

"No."

"Then off the record."

He smiled grimly. "We face many challenges on many fronts."

Given how much access he and his team were giving me, I was intrigued by how guarded the king was in his comments to me. I had earned a degree of trust, and that trust was growing, to be sure, but clearly there were limits; there were red lines beyond which I could not go. Not now. Probably not ever. I wasn't a Muslim. I wasn't an Arab. I wasn't family. I was still an outsider, and a journalist at that. Monarchs didn't typically get close to reporters, no matter from what part of the world they hailed.

"Is it fair to say that Israel is no longer considered the prime and central threat to the Sunni Arab community?" I asked.

"Off the record, that's probably a fair statement—as I said, things are changing. As new and very serious and immediate threats grow, people's perspectives on past problems and conflicts tend to shift."

"There appears to be a widespread reevaluation of Israel's role in the region taking place among the Arabs—at least among Arab leaders, though perhaps not entirely among the people," I said.

"I don't think that's the right way to put it," the king said. "I think it's more a matter of priorities. A leader only has so many hours in the day. What is he going to focus on? Defending himself and his people from attack, from genocide, annihilation, subjugation at the hands of mortal enemies? Or planning to proactively, preemptively attack another nation that is here to stay, that isn't going anywhere? We face many challenges in our region. Poverty. Illiteracy. Economic inequalities. Tribal animosities. A lack of robust manufacturing. A lack of enough advanced, high-tech industries. I could go on, but you know the list. And the so-called Arab Spring was, I believe, a wake-up call for many leaders in this region. The people want us to focus on making their lives better. If we don't, they may turn to revolution. They may turn to dark forces. So no one in this region has the time or energy or resources to wage an unwinnable war in an effort to remove an entire nation and people from the map. Only the extremists want this. The rest of us want to find ways to create peace and prosperity and opportunity for all the people of the region."

"I hear you've become quite close to Wahid Mahfouz," I said, referring to the new Egyptian president.

"We speak often," he said. "We've spoken twice today."

"You went to visit him in January."

"And he came to visit me in June."

"And . . . ?"

"And we are finding common ground."

"You're working closely together?"

"On many fronts."

"Like what?"

That grim smile again. "Many fronts."

I noticed the king glancing at the clock. I wasn't going to have his attention much longer, and no matter what I tried, he remained so guarded.

"I hear Mahfouz is quite close to Daniel Lavi as well," I added, wanting to see if I could get the king to give me some insight into rumors that the Egyptians were developing a close strategic relationship with the Israeli prime minister and his unity government.

"You'll have to talk to Daniel about that," he demurred.

"I hope to—as soon as he recovers," I said. "But something has happened in the last few years. You and the Egyptians and the Saudis and the Emirates seem to be working quite closely together against ISIS, against Iran, and—less noticed by most people—with the Israelis."

"This is a very sensitive subject."

"But I'm not wrong."

"The Egyptians have a treaty with Israel. So do we. You would expect us to be working closely together."

"Not this closely."

"Maybe not in the past, but new breezes are blowing."

"The Egyptians have had a treaty with the Israelis since '79, but after Sadat's assassination, it was always a cold peace."

"Certainly under Hosni this was the case," the king said, referring to former Egyptian president Hosni Mubarak.

"Then came the rise of the Brotherhood in Egypt."

"A very dark time."

"But now that the Brotherhood has been removed . . ."

"That's a question for Wahid," the king said diplomatically. "It's an interesting story. But it's not one for me to tell."

"I understand," I said, disappointed but not surprised.

I didn't really need the king to confirm to me the significance of what I saw happening in the next room. A historic, extraordinary Sunni Arab alliance was emerging. The Jordanians, Egyptians, Saudis, and Emiratis were working together toward common goals and objectives. They were working with the Americans to launch a major military operation to attack ISIS, a Sunni Arab group, in the territory of Syria, an Arab neighbor, to rescue an ally, the president of the United States, who had just tried to complete a peace treaty between the Palestinian Sunni Arabs and the Jews of Israel. And behind it all—arguably driving or at least accelerating this historic move toward unity—was the specter of an even larger threat looming over the entire region: the prospect that the Shia Muslim Persians of Iran might be about to build nuclear weapons.

"Of course, you can't write about any of this," the king said out of the blue.

"Any of what?" I asked.

"The call with the vice president. The players you see in the room next door. The operation being planned for later tonight. These are all extremely sensitive."

"Isn't this why you brought me here?" I responded. "To tell these stories?"

"Not yet, not now," the monarch said. "In a book, perhaps, years from now. I realize this is history and eventually it does have to be told, and I believe you will do a fair and honest job, Mr. Collins. But like a fine wine, it takes many years before it is ready to be sold and sipped and savored, does it not? Or so I'm told."

It was an interesting analogy for a Muslim who wasn't supposed to drink wine, but I think I got his point. Still, I needed a story. I needed to file something, and soon, and I said so.

"I'm not saying you can't write anything," the king clarified. "I'm just saying some things are particularly sensitive."

I needed His Majesty to clarify what he meant, but just then the door to the war room opened. Prince Feisal stepped in, apologized for interrupting, and whispered something to the king, who immediately rose.

"Forgive me, Mr. Collins; something has come up," he said with a new sense of urgency, and suddenly he was gone.

39

* * *

I glanced at the clock on the king's desk.

It was now just after two o'clock on Tuesday afternoon. Sixteen hours until the deadline. Less than three hours until the sun went down.

"What's going on?" I asked.

"I can't say," said Colonel Sharif, reading an e-mail or a text on his phone, though from my angle it wasn't clear which.

"Why not?"

"I really can't say," Sharif repeated. "We'd better go."

"Where?"

"Upstairs," he said. "I'm supposed to give you a tour of the base."

"I don't want a tour," I said. "I need to go back in there."

"Not right now."

"Why not?"

"If I could tell you, I would. But I can't. So let's go upstairs, and we'll come back when I get the all clear."

"No, Yusef, this is completely unacceptable.

This is precisely why the king brought me here, to cover this whole crisis from beginning to end."

"I understand, Mr. Collins. But there's been a development."

"And you can't talk about it."

"I'm afraid not."

"So where does that leave me?"

"Taking a tour of the base."

"No," I said again. "There's no point and no time. If I can't go back into the war room yet, then I need a phone and a computer and access to the Internet."

"What for?"

I just looked at him for a moment, wondering if he could possibly be serious. "To do my job," I said.

"Let's go upstairs," Sharif replied. "I'll see what I can do."

But I wasn't about to take no for an answer.

"Yusef—Colonel—listen to me. Please. You don't seem to understand. I've been as patient as anyone could expect. I've been arrested, imprisoned, and put in solitary confinement. I've been used to do a sting operation against the director of the CIA. I've had my phone taken away. I've had my computer taken away. I've been made to sign nondisclosure papers preventing me from writing about the biggest story of my lifetime. I've been brought to a top secret military base to sit in on high-level meetings with the military leaders of five countries but prevented from talking to my editors or even to my family. I get the sensitivities of the moment. And I get that you have a job to do. But so do I—and I *have* to be in touch with my editors. I *have* to know what other people are reporting. And I *have* to file a story soon. Which means you have to help me—or let me go."

"I understand how you feel, Mr. Collins."

"But you're not going to help me."

"I'm going to help you as best I can. But there will not be any communications off of this base until this operation to rescue the president is planned and executed. Period. Please understand—I'm not trying to be rude. But the fate of our kingdom is on the line here, and I have my orders. Now, if you'll follow me upstairs, I'd be quite grateful."

The next thing I knew, we were riding the king's private elevator back up to the ground floor. We rode in silence. I was livid but determined not to say anything stupid. There had to be something I could offer Sharif to get him to change his mind. But what? I had no ideas and no leverage.

When the elevator doors opened, we were met by the two MPs who'd brought us here in the first place. They asked us to step inside an armored personnel carrier that was idling in the garage, and soon we were heading back out into the storm, which had not let up one bit. If anything, it had intensified. The clouds were thicker, the sky darker, and the booms of thunder far louder than when we'd first headed down to the bunker. The base was no longer being pelted by hail, but the winter rains were coming down in buckets. Even with our high beams on and the windshield wipers going at full speed, visibility was limited at best, and I couldn't help but wonder how this was going to impact the operation the king and the generals were planning down below.

"How long is it supposed to go on like this?" I asked our driver.

"They're saying most of the night, sir."

"Like this, or is it supposed to let up a bit?"

"Actually, they're saying it's going to get a lot worse."

"How's that possible?"

"I have no idea, sir. But that's what they're saying."

"Is anyone still flying?"

"Not many. Last sorties went out about thirty minutes ago. Should be back soon. But we hear everything else is being grounded."

This didn't bode well for the president, I thought, but decided against stating the obvious. Instead, I changed the subject. "Any word on Agent Harris?" I asked.

Just then the colonel's phone rang.

"Still in the infirmary, sir," the MP in the front passenger seat said as Sharif took the call.

"Is he okay?" I asked.

"Sorry, sir. We haven't heard."

"Could we take a few minutes and go see him?"

The driver shrugged. "I guess, if you'd like."

"I would, very much," I said.

Admittedly, my motives were less than humanitarian. Aside from General Ramirez and myself, Agent Harris was the only other American on the base. If it came time to bail out of the Jordanian orbit—which I increasingly felt was the case—

Harris would be the key. I was fairly certain that if I asked him, he'd be willing to let me accompany him back to Washington. The Jordanians certainly couldn't force me to stay on the base, operating under their rules of military censorship. And as intrigued as I was with watching all this unfold from the inside, if I couldn't report any of it in real time—and had to wait several years until I could even write a book about it all—then there was no point staying.

But I wasn't sure I wanted to head all the way back to D.C. The more I thought about it, the more it seemed to make sense to head to Tel Aviv instead. I very much wanted to see Yael for personal reasons, but I also thought I might have a better shot at being able to cover the unfolding saga in the region using my sources in Israeli intelligence and the IDF than I would by returning to the States. Of course, it now seemed unlikely that Harris and I could even get off the base before daybreak at the earliest. But hopefully we could be on the first flight out of Jordan once conditions permitted.

What's more, I thought, Harris had a phone and thus access to the outside world. Perhaps he'd let me use it to call Allen and touch base with my family and catch up on the headlines.

Brilliant flashes of lightning repeatedly illuminated the desert skies. With each bolt, I saw more of the base and the tanks and APCs blocking every entrance and providing perimeter security. I felt bad for the soldiers standing guard in such terrible conditions but at the same time was grateful they were out there. This base was one of the largest in Jordan, but we weren't that far now from the Syrian border and the genocidal conditions that had emerged within. Nor were we so far from the border with Iraq and the murderous rampage ISIS was perpetrating there as well.

When the colonel finished his call, our driver glanced in his rearview mirror and asked if it was okay to head to the infirmary. But to everyone's surprise, Sharif said no.

40

"Take us to ISR," the colonel ordered our driver.

I had no idea what that meant, but suddenly we were doing a U-turn, then turning onto a service road not far from a row of barracks and pulling up to a long, squat, unmarked, and otherwise-nondescript administrative building. The front door opened and two MPs carrying large umbrellas dashed out to our vehicle, opened the rear passenger door, and rushed us inside. Once we cleared security, Sharif introduced me to the two-star general who ran the facility. The general put us on an elevator, punched a security code, and took us down several floors to meet the rest of his team.

He explained that I was now in the nerve center of the Jordanian air force's ISR command. ISR stood for intelligence, surveillance, and reconnaissance, and it was here, the general told me, that all of Jordan's air operations were planned. At the moment, several dozen staff on the floor just below the main level were planning and analyzing all the air strikes against ISIS targets in the capital, particularly at or near the Al-Hummar Palace.

One floor below them, other staff were designing sorties against ISIS targets in other cities and towns throughout Jordan, particularly in Irbid in the north, which I now learned for the first time had come under heavy assault by forces of the Islamic State.

However, we didn't stop on either floor. When the elevator finally did stop, I could no longer hear the thunder or the rain or wind or any other element of the storm outside. Indeed, one of the first things that struck me as we exited the elevator was the unusual quiet. The overhead lighting was dim, and the staff—all of them young and sharp and serious—worked in small offices and tiny cubicles in front of banks of flat-screen computer monitors and wore big headphones and spoke in hushed voices.

"This is where the general and his team are doing the legwork for tonight's raid on Dabiq," Colonel Sharif explained. "And that's why the king called me and wanted us to come over here. He's got a new crisis he's dealing with at the moment, but he wanted you to see this."

"Why?" I asked, fearing this was part of a tour I had no interest in being on. I didn't care about all this high-tech wizardry. I didn't have time to hang out with a bunch of young air force officers in their twenties and thirties, no matter how important their work might be. It was clear I wasn't going to be allowed to write about any of this anyway, which was why all I wanted at that moment was to reconnect with Agent Harris and nail down a plan to get off this base as quickly as humanly possible.

"The king wants you to start looking at Homs," the colonel replied.

"Homs?" I asked, not sure I'd heard him correctly.

"Yes."

"What for?"

"To see if he's missing something," said Sharif. "Everything seems to be pointing toward Dabiq. But if the president is being held in Homs, the king needs to know, and he needs to know fast."

The colonel then explained the situation to the two-star. We needed an intel suite, his most proficient analyst, real-time feeds of all the satellite and drone coverage he had of Homs, a fresh pot of coffee, and anything else we asked for. The general readily agreed and led us to his cramped office, where he picked up a phone and asked one of his aides to join us immediately. A moment later the aide ushered Colonel Sharif and me into an adjoining room that was about the size of the bedroom I'd had growing up in Maine but looked like a broadcast news control room. The far wall was covered with seven flat-screen monitors, a large center screen with three others above it and three below it. In front of that was a long console that at first looked like an audio mixing board but upon closer examination turned out to be an integrated series of laptop computers, radar displays, and a bank of phones.

There was a quick knock at the door, and the aide introduced us to Zoona, a young lieutenant—couldn't have been older than thirty—wearing glasses and a light-blue headscarf.

The colonel quickly explained the situation. Zoona, in turn, explained that she had been working for the past several hours on analyzing the intel on Dabiq.

"Are you convinced the president is there?" Sharif asked.

"I wouldn't say convinced," she replied. "But it's compelling."

"Maybe you could take a moment and show us why," I said. "Then we can compare it with whatever we see in Homs."

She agreed, and her fingers went to work. She pulled up a range of images and maps and status reports on the six smaller screens, then put a live satellite feed of Dabiq on the main monitor, zooming down from space as if we were using a commercial application of Google Earth.

"Okay, this is the elementary school where we're picking up the tracking signal," Zoona said. "As you can see, it's a fairly simple three-level structure built in a horseshoe configuration. There's the playground on the north side of the compound, and you can see the parking area there on the south side."

"What are those?" I asked, pointing to several large, blocklike images in the parking lot.

"Those are our problem—they're SAMs," she explained, zooming in farther and changing the angle somewhat so I could see the surface-to-air missile batteries more clearly. "Those five are SA-6 units, a mobile model, each with support vehicles and cranes to load more missiles as needed. And that's not all. There are four more batteries in other parts of the compound—three sixes and an eleven—there, there, there, and . . . there."

"That's a lot of firepower for a school."

"Tell me about it," she said. "Each missile fired by an SA-6 can reach a top speed of Mach 2.8 and can hit almost any aircraft up to forty-five thousand feet at a range of up to fifteen miles."

"What about the SA-11?"

"Bigger, farther, faster—let's just say a single missile has a 90 to 95 percent probability of destroying its intended target."

As if this weren't bad enough, she then explained that there were numerous triple-A or antiaircraft artillery batteries in and around the school and the entire village.

"But at least you know where they are, right?" I said. "I mean, you could take all these out with air strikes before they even knew what was coming, couldn't you?"

"Not exactly." Zoona zoomed out a bit and pointed to nine more SAM batteries in a several-block radius around the school, all positioned close to houses, shops, and even a nearby hospital. Her meaning was clear. Any effort to take out the SAMs by air strike would likely cause enormous collateral damage.

"Are people living and working in each of those buildings?" I asked.

"Quite a few."

"Tell me they're all terrorists working on those batteries and guarding that school."

"Some, sure, but we've got video images of women and children living there too."

"How many?"

"Several hundred at least."

"The kids are using the playground?"

"Every day," she said. "From noon to one and then again from three in the afternoon until sundown."

"How come there aren't any there now?"

"For the same reason you're not outside right now," she said. "This storm is hitting the whole region pretty hard right now, Dabiq included. Everyone's inside."

"Can you go back in on the school?"

"Of course."

Using what looked like a video-game controller, Zoona zoomed in again on the three-level structure and then on a particular window in the northwestern corner. I could see the faint outline of a person inside, apparently looking out the window.

"Can you enhance that?" I asked.

Zoona nodded and soon the image came into focus. To my astonishment, looking at a real-time feed from a billion-dollar American KH-12 Key Hole spy satellite operating two hundred miles above the planet, I was staring at the face of a little Syrian boy, no more than five or six years old. He was holding his mother's hand and staring out at the storm that was making it impossible for him to play on the swing sets and jungle gym just a few meters away.

"The tracking signal is coming from the basement of the school," Zoona explained. "And for the last several nights, the kids have been sleeping in the school."

"That's not normal?"

"No."

"What about their parents?"

"Several women are staying at the school each night with them. We assume they are mothers and grandmothers. There are a lot of men in the building as well. Some are probably fathers. But we've also counted at least sixty armed terrorists there."

"Phone calls?"

"We're monitoring everything, but no—no calls in or out over the past few days."

"But the cell towers are working?"

"They are."

"What about e-mail traffic?"

"Minimal and nothing of particular value."

"But you think they're hiding something there," I said.

"Or someone," Zoona concurred. "And they expect we're coming."

41

"What about chemical weapons?" I asked.

"They've got artillery batteries and mortar cannons strategically positioned all over the village," Zoona answered. "So far we can't say whether the shells are filled with sarin gas. But the command has come down from the top that we should assume that's what they've got."

"And prisoners?"

"What do you mean?"

"Are they holding prisoners in the basement of the school or anywhere else?"

"Besides the president?" she asked.

"If he's even there," I said. "But all this is circumstantial evidence at the moment. The tracking signal is the most compelling piece, I grant you, but the watch could have been removed from the president when he was captured or anytime afterward."

"Then, no—there's no sign of other prisoners being held at the school, unless you count the children and their parents."

"And it's not an ISIS command-and-control center?"

"If it is, they're not talking to anyone. No cell calls. Minimal radio chatter. Minimal Internet traffic. Everything's hot; everything's working; there's just no evidence they're talking to each other via electronic means—not much, anyway."

"And the calls to and from Jamal Ramzy's phone?"

"Actually, we just heard from the NSA on that last night. Two of the calls did go to a cell phone at the school. Several others were relayed there from other switching stations. But beyond that, as I said, there's been very little phone traffic not just to the school but to any of the homes within a five-block radius."

"Doesn't that seem odd?"

"It does."

"What do you make of it?"

"I don't know. There's not enough data to support a conclusion."

"Are there any other buildings with this kind of profile in Dabiq?" I asked.

"You mean surrounded by SAMs and triple-A batteries?"

"Right."

"None," Zoona said. "The school has become the security vortex of the entire town. Everything ISIS has done appears designed to protect the school and those inside it from a foreign attack."

"Ground or air?" I pressed.

"Both," she said. "The main roads into the town are blocked by cars, buses, nails, booby traps, IEDs, you name it. And it's not just the main roads. Every street that could possibly be used by ground forces to get to the school is blocked and booby-trapped." She redirected the satellite to show me several examples.

I looked at Colonel Sharif and asked what he thought.

"I'd say she's right," he replied. "It's pretty compelling."

"Okay, can we look at Homs now?" I asked.

"Of course," Zoona said, wiping all the screens clear and reloading them with satellite and drone images of the city that was once Syria's third largest but was now nearly a ghost town. "What specifically are we looking for?"

"The Khaled bin Walid Mosque," I said.

"What part of the city?"

"From the center, it's due east, in a neighborhood called al-Khalidiyah, not far from the M5 highway."

Zoona began typing coordinates into her laptop. Soon she put up on the main screen the live feed from a surveillance drone. I'd never seen the city from the air, so at first nothing seemed familiar. But after a few moments something caught my eye.

"Wait—there, in the upper left," I said, pointing to the monitor.

"What, the playground?" she asked.

"Exactly. Can you zoom in on that?"

"I can, but there aren't any mosques in that neighborhood."

"I know, but I—"

And then there it was. It looked different from the sky, but I was suddenly looking down on the large field Omar, Abdel, and I had crossed to get into Homs. There were the towering yet abandoned apartment buildings ringing the field. There was the old VW van. There was the broken-down school bus and the deserted playground and the burnt-out Russian battle tank.

And then I spotted something else and every muscle in my body tensed. Even from miles over-head, I could actually see the small crater in the ground and the charred grass and soil, the very place where Abdel had stepped on a land mine, the very place where he had—

The horrific images flooded back. I could see the look of stark terror on his face, the panic in his eyes, just before he stepped off the mine. Just before—

The colonel asked me what was wrong, but I couldn't speak. Zoona asked if she should keep searching, but I couldn't reply. I could barely breathe. I felt like I was suffocating, drowning in my own guilt.

Finally I asked for a glass of water. Zoona went to fetch one. While she was gone, I forced myself to look away from the monitor. But all I could think about was that Abdel was only the first of so many colleagues and friends who had died since I'd started to pursue this story about ISIS and chemi-cal weapons. And the deaths just kept piling up by the hundreds and perhaps soon by the thousands.

When Zoona returned, I drank the entire glass of water in mere seconds. Then I asked her to keep searching for the mosque. I knew it was close, but I had no desire to explain to her—to either of them—what I'd seen or what I'd remembered. I felt cold and tired and completely disinterested in what we were doing.

As Zoona kept looking, images of schools and churches and restaurants and shops blown to smithereens or burned to the ground flew by on the monitor. I could see shuttered supermarkets and bodegas. I could see the twisted wreckage of cars and trucks and motorcycles and roads riddled with the craters of bombs and mortars of all kinds. What I didn't see were people. No soldiers. No civilians. No one. Some six hundred thousand people had once lived in Homs. Where were they all now?

"Okay, there's Clock Square," Zoona said. From there, she directed the drone eastward down a boulevard named Fares Al-Khouri, and a moment later there it was. We could see the large green spaces all around the mosque. We could see the two minarets out in front, though only one was still intact. The other had been hit by some sort of bomb and was only half there.

"You're sure that's where you were?" Sharif asked me.

"That's it," I said.

"And that's where Jamal Ramzy was?"

"Not exactly, but he was close," I said.

I explained to the two of them that my colleagues and I hadn't actually walked directly to the mosque. Rather, we'd each been captured by ISIS rebels, drugged, stripped almost naked, and blindfolded before being brought to the mosque. We'd each been grabbed by different teams and likely each taken to the mosque by different routes.

"How did they get you there?" the colonel asked.

"I don't know."

"So how do you know that's really where you were?"

"I had no idea how long I'd been unconscious," I explained. "But I woke up with a bag over my head and tied around my neck. I was freezing. My clothes were gone. My hands and feet were tied, and I was sitting on a cold concrete floor. There was a huge thunderstorm bearing down on the city—not so different from tonight. When someone finally ripped the bag off my head, three armed men covered in black hoods dragged me down a bunch of flights of stairs to the ground level. That's when I realized we were in what was left of the Khaled bin Walid Mosque. It had been shelled and shot up pretty good, but everything about the architecture made it clear it was a mosque. When we reached the ground floor, we stepped into another stairwell and descended to the basement, where we walked down a series of dripping hallways until we reached a mechanical room of some kind."

"What happened then?" the colonel asked.

"One of them shoved the barrel of a machine gun into my back. They forced me to go through an opening in the wall into a makeshift tunnel that had been dug under the city. I remember thinking it was strange because even though most of Homs was blacked out, the tunnel had power and was reasonably well lit. It was no more than five and a half feet high and at best four feet wide, but it was long. It seemed to go on forever. But eventually we wound up under another building. We climbed up a ladder and they sat me down in front of Jamal Ramzy."

Zoona positioned the drone over the mosque and moved it around, and we examined the structure from every angle. It was immediately clear that there were no ISIS forces guarding its entrances. There certainly were no SAM or triple-A batteries anywhere to be seen. In fact, there was no one there. Not a soul. The building had clearly been further damaged since I'd been there last. Upon closer examination, it looked like the south side of the structure had collapsed entirely. It seemed unlikely in the extreme that the president or any other high-value prisoner was being held there.

So we broadened our search. We went building by building, street by street, block by block, looking for any signs of heightened ISIS activity or any activity at all. But we found nothing. Zoona then brought up ten days' worth of archived Key Hole spy satellite images of the mosque and its neighborhood and the adjacent neighborhoods spanning twenty blocks. But there were absolutely no signs of an ISIS safe house to be found. Just utter, catastrophic destruction.

We had come to a dead end. And had wasted almost two hours in the process.

I felt sick to my stomach.

42

* * *

It was now 4:17 p.m.

Less than fourteen hours until the deadline was up.

Not even a half hour until the sun went down.

The colonel and I were silent on the elevator ride back up to the main floor, where the ISR command's meteorologists worked, along with most of the administrative staff and technical support team. When the doors opened, the MPs were waiting to take us back to the armored personnel carrier. But as we headed toward them, I noticed a group of young officers clustered together around a TV set. Curious at what they were watching, I peeked over someone's shoulder and found them absorbed by a report on Al Arabiya.

Israeli prime minister Daniel Lavi had just passed away.

I couldn't believe what I was seeing. The anchor repeated several times that the information was still unconfirmed, but he referenced two separate reports—one from the BBC and one from Agence France-Presse—citing unnamed doctors at

Hadassah Medical Center and a senior officer in the IDF, all of whom wished to remain anonymous since they were not authorized to discuss the prime minister's condition.

I couldn't breathe. It wasn't possible. I stopped and leaned in, hoping to learn more, but the rest was just a discussion between the anchor and two political analysts via satellite—one from Cairo and one from Dubai—discussing the possible implications of Lavi's death, "if it is proven true."

I turned to Sharif and told him what had happened. He, too, could hardly believe it and came over to hear more. It was amazing to see how hard the news was hitting each of these young Jordanian military officers and support staff. I'm not saying they had suddenly become Zionists or that they had a deep love for Lavi or his unity government. But they were deeply traumatized by the events that had transpired in their own capital in recent days. They were heavily engaged in fighting to protect their country from the forces of the Islamic State. They knew all too well the pain that they and their people were suffering, and they seemed to identify with the trauma the Israelis were now suffering as well.

"Please, Yusef, I need to be in touch with my office and my family," I whispered to the colonel after he'd had a few moments to absorb the shock of the discussions.

I prepared myself for resistance, for an argument, but to my relief he said, "Of course; I understand. Come with me. Let's find someplace quiet."

Sharif motioned to the MPs that we were going

to be a few minutes; then he led me down the hall and around the corner to a small kitchenette. There he pulled out his smartphone and entered his passcode.

"I'm still under strict orders not to let you call off this base," he said. "But if you want to dictate notes to a few people, I'm happy to send them myself and let your people know they can reach you through me."

It wasn't quite what I was hoping for. I wanted real contact. I needed real conversations, not a few impersonal e-mails. But with zero hour fast approaching, I realized this was the best I was going to get, and I intended to take full advantage of it.

I asked that the first text messages be sent to my mom and brother and gave Sharif their phone numbers. I explained that I was still in Jordan, but safe. I told them that my phone and computer had been destroyed in the attacks but that I had only minor injuries, certainly nothing life-threatening, and that they shouldn't worry. There was no point in telling them I'd been shot. Or imprisoned. Or that I'd killed anyone. Or experienced a sarin gas attack. It was only going to freak them out. There was nothing they could do about any of it, so I figured they didn't need to know. Instead, I told them I was covering the latest developments but had very limited access to the outside world, and I apologized for not being in touch sooner. Finally I told them that I loved them and that I couldn't wait to see them again, and to please keep praying for me and not to let up for a moment.

Sharif typed the message, then showed it to me to make sure he'd gotten it right. I reread that last line asking them for prayer. I wondered if that might give them the idea I was still in harm's way or going back into it. But then again, wasn't that the truth? I was in a forward operating base in the midst of the worst military crisis in Jordan in decades. The fact that I'd narrowly escaped death numerous times in recent days was, I was beginning to think, potentially related to how much my family was praying for me. Regardless of how unclear I was about God and Jesus and my own eternity, I figured I'd be an idiot not to ask for prayer. It was working. They were willing. Why not?

I thanked Sharif and he hit Send.

Then I asked him to send a quick message to Allen MacDonald back at the *Times* D.C. bureau. The colonel agreed but said I couldn't say anything newsworthy or substantive, only that my phone and computer had been destroyed but that I was alive and safe and still on the story—essentially the same as I'd told my family, without the reference to prayer.

"Can I ask if this story about Lavi is true?" I inquired.

"No."

"Can I ask what he's heard about Jack Vaughn being arrested?"

"Absolutely not."

"So that's all I get?"

"Was there someone else you wanted to write to?" he asked.

"Many."

"One more."

"Why just one?"

"Because I just got a text message from the war room," he said. "They want us to come back immediately. We need to move fast. So is there someone else—your wife, perhaps? Laura, right?"

I looked at him sharply. That was not a name I ever expected to hear again—not this far from Washington—and I was completely caught off guard not only by the suggestion but by the fact that a Jordanian colonel whom I had only just met somehow knew so much about me. Did they have a dossier on me? What else did they know? And what gave him the right to bring Laura up at such a time as this?

"Ex-wife," I said coldly.

"Right," said Sharif. "I'm sorry."

"Don't be."

"Should I send her a note, tell her you're okay?"

"No," I replied.

"Then is there someone else? We only have a moment."

There was, of course—Yael Katzir. But I didn't dare say it. Not the name of an Israeli Mossad agent. Not her personal mobile number. Not in such a sensitive moment in relations between Jordan and Israel. Not with Agent Harris on the same base, just a few buildings away, still wanting to talk to her about why she'd fled the scene of the car bombing in Istanbul.

Yet Yael was the one I wanted to reach out to, the one I found myself thinking about in every spare moment I had. I was worried about her, especially after the death of her prime minister.

But that wasn't the only reason I wanted to reconnect. The truth was I missed her. It embarrassed me to think it. But I missed her. I wanted nothing more than to sit with her and have coffee and listen to her talk and pry her for more stories and get to know her better. It wasn't simply a physical attraction, though it was certainly that. There was just something about her that fascinated me, intrigued me, drew me to her, and I wanted to find out what it was. But now wasn't the time or the place.

"No," I said at last. "We'd better go."

The king was waiting for us, though I had no idea why.

43

* * *

"I'm divorced too," Sharif said as we drove back to the war room.

"Sorry to hear that," I said, not exactly in the mood for small talk, if that's what this was supposed to be, and certainly in no mood for baring my soul or having the colonel bare his.

"It's the girls I miss the most," he continued somewhat wistfully as the storm raged around us. "Amira is my oldest. Just turned five."

"That's a lovely name."

"It means 'princess.'"

"You must be very proud."

"You have no idea. And then there's the three-year-old, Maysam, which means 'my beautiful one.'"

For the first time since we'd met, he actually handed me his phone. But it was not to make a call or read the latest headlines. He wanted me to see some digital pictures of his girls, taken at the younger one's most recent birthday party.

"Adorable, both of them," I said, doing my best to be polite. "Congratulations."

I forced myself to hand the phone back to

him. I could see Sharif wasn't smiling. He was just staring at the pictures and his eyes were growing moist.

"How often do you see them?" I asked.

"Never," he said. "Well, it seems like never. Once a month. Maybe twice. They live with their mother in Aqaba. It's hard for me to get down there."

"I'm sure. That's quite a drive from Amman. How long does it take?"

"Four hours."

"But you have the whole weekend with your girls?"

"No, just an hour," he said, choking back his emotions. "I leave before sunrise on a Friday. We have an hour for lunch. I'm back by dinnertime. But after all this? I have no idea when I will see them again."

Just then lightning struck a nearby electrical transformer, creating a small explosion, sparks spraying everywhere. At almost the exact same moment, multiple booms of thunder rocked our vehicle. The storm was directly upon us now, and even though the sun had not technically set, it was eerie how dark the skies had become.

I felt bad for Sharif. He was a reserved and quiet soul, fiercely loyal to the king, proficient at his job, and overall had been quite decent to me. But for the first time I realized his mind was far away. Here we were at a secret base in the northeastern part of the country, and his heart was nearly four hundred kilometers away in Jordan's southernmost port city. I had no idea what the circumstances were that led to his divorce and ripped him away from the two little girls he clearly loved most in the world. Certainly it was not my place to ask, and it wouldn't have been right to anyway. All the deep and hurtful wounds that he typically kept in check in order to perform his official duties were presently forcing their way to the surface, and I genuinely wished there were something I could do to comfort him.

Yet what advice could I possibly give him? I'd completely failed as a husband. Laura and I had been married for only five years. It had started as a torrid love story. We'd met as interns in Robert Khachigian's Senate office, and I'd fallen for her immediately. We dated all summer, got married that Christmas, and everything had seemed like an intoxicating dream . . . until it didn't anymore. Suddenly she was as cold as ice. Then she announced she wanted some "time away" to figure things out. And the next thing I knew, she was moving in with some hotshot lawyer she'd met at the New York firm where she'd just been hired and was filing for divorce. The whole thing completely blindsided me. I never saw it coming. I still didn't know what I'd done wrong. And ever since, I'd avoided thinking about it, and certainly talking about it, like the plague.

The only sliver of grace in the entire emotional train wreck was that we hadn't had kids. I'd wanted to. Lots. Right from the start. She didn't. Not till she was done with law school. Not till she was with the right firm. Not till she was a partner. If I was being honest, I'd have to admit I resented her for that—and for a million other things—but I had to be grateful we hadn't brought some adorable little souls into this world only to drag them through our selfish, twisted, mixed-up lives.

All that had been a long time ago, of course. Almost twenty years. But my wounds had never fully healed. I couldn't imagine how much worse it would have been with little children caught in the middle.

We pulled into the garage over the main bunker, the door lowered behind us, and the colonel and I were soon on our way back down to the war room. Neither of us said anything, both lost in other thoughts, other troubles, far from this war. But just as the elevator doors reopened, Sharif handed me his phone.

I really didn't want to see more pictures of his children, but nor did I want to compound his pain. So I took the phone and looked at the screen.

There were no pictures of children. Instead there was a text message from my brother.

> **J.B.—Thank God you're okay—we've been worried sick.**
>
> **When are you coming home?**
>
> **We're back in Bar Harbor and staying at Mom's. She sends her love. So do Annie and the kids. We're all praying for you.**
>
> **Please call ASAP. Something urgent I need to discuss with you. Can't wait. Time sensitive.**
>
> **Love, Matt**

P.S.—Here are the verses the kids are
memorizing this week. Thought you might
find them encouraging too. "Come to Me, all
who are weary and heavy-laden, and I will
give you rest. Take My yoke upon you and
learn from Me, for I am gentle and humble
in heart, and you will find rest for your
souls" (Matthew 11:28-29).

I read the message twice, then handed the phone
back to Sharif and stepped off the elevator. Rather
than taking me into the king's private office, however, Sharif led me down the narrow, dimly lit corridor to the waiting area outside the war room. As
we walked, I wasn't thinking about the discussion
that was coming with the generals. My thoughts
were back in Bar Harbor. All I wanted to do at
that moment was see my mom and make sure she
was okay, catch up with Matt and Annie, hug their
kids, and have a home-cooked meal in that big old
drafty house, even if my whole family did want to
convert me. They'd been trying for years, and it
had annoyed me something fierce for as long as
I could remember. But I knew they didn't mean
any harm. They loved me. They believed Jesus was
the answer to my problems. They wanted me to
believe it too. I still wasn't sure. Religion wasn't my
thing. But I guess I'd finally become convinced my
family meant well. They weren't trying to bother
me. They were trying to help me. And the older I
got, the more help I realized I needed.

Seeing them all in person was not in the cards,
however. Not anytime soon. The best I could

hope for was a phone call with Matt. But even that would have to wait. An unprecedented coalition of Americans and Sunni Arab countries was going to war inside Syria, and I was about to get a front-row seat on the plan and—I hoped—a seat on one of the choppers going into battle as well.

44

"Yael?" I said in shock as I came around the corner.

To my astonishment, she was sitting in the waiting room. Beside her was her boss, the elusive Ari Shalit. They seemed to be making notes in a briefing book, but for the life of me I couldn't imagine why they were here.

"J. B.?" she replied, looking up, removing her reading glasses, seeing me in fatigues, and clearly as surprised to see me as I was to see her.

Before I could respond, she stood and gave me a hug, careful not to press the wound on my left arm, the wound she'd been the first to dress. Her dark-brown hair was wet from the rain, and several drops ran down the back of my neck, but I didn't care. She was warm to the touch and smelled great and looked incredible in a dark-gray suit with a two-button blazer, pleated slacks, an ivory silk camisole, and black flats.

"Wow—what are you doing here, both of you?" I asked, feeling self-conscious for holding Yael a bit too long and turning quickly to shake Ari's hand.

"You'll find out in a moment," Ari replied.

"Well, I'm–I'm glad to see you both," I stammered. "Ari, Yael, I'd like you to meet Colonel Yusef Sharif. He's the king's spokesman and handles all of his media affairs. He's been taking care of me. Colonel, this is Dr. Ari Shalit, deputy director of the Mossad, and his colleague, Dr. Yael Katzir, also with the Mossad, a WMD specialist."

"Pleasure to meet you both," the colonel said, shaking their hands.

"The pleasure is ours," said Ari.

"Dr. Katzir, though we have not had the pleasure of meeting before, I do, of course, know who you are," Sharif continued. "Her Majesty the queen has spoken very highly of you, as has His Majesty. The Jordanian people owe you a great debt for what you and Mr. Collins did to save His Majesty and his family."

"You don't owe us anything. We're friends— allies, even—but you're very kind to say so," Yael replied.

"Actually, we're very sorry to request to see you all with such little notice," said Ari. "As you know, my boss—the director—could not come."

"How is he?" Sharif asked.

"Not well."

"Cancer?"

"Yes, pancreatic," said Ari. "Stage IV, I'm afraid."

"I'm sorry."

"Thank you. And I suspect you've heard the news about the prime minister."

"We just heard some rumors on TV," I said. "Please tell us it's not true."

"I fear it is," Ari confirmed.

"I'm very sorry for that as well," Sharif said.

"All Israel is in shock," Ari said. "But of course Jordan has been suffering far worse in recent days. We are deeply sorry for all that has happened and for all that you and your people are going through right now."

"We are suffering, but we still have our king," Sharif replied. "Please accept my condolences for your terrible loss. Prime Minister Lavi was truly a man of peace and a good friend of His Majesty and the kingdom. He will be deeply missed."

"Thank you," Ari said. "That's very kind."

Ari and the colonel chatted quietly for another few minutes. Yael and I said nothing. But as we listened, I couldn't help but keep glancing at her. Her large, brown, beautiful eyes were tired and full of grief. And I realized that she was wearing makeup. She hadn't worn any in Turkey, and she wasn't wearing much now. It might not even have been apparent to anyone who didn't know her. But I noticed and then realized why. She was covering injuries she'd received during our escape from the palace—the two blows she'd taken to the face when fighting hand to hand with one of the jihadists and the gash she'd gotten on her forehead when our SUV smashed into a car outside the palace gates. I wanted to ask her about it, see how she was feeling, find out whether she'd sustained any other injuries.

But before I could, Ari took me aside. He asked me how I'd wound up here and what I was doing. I gave him a brief summary of what had happened until I realized that what he was really getting at was whether I was going to tell the world he and Yael were here. I assured him that Colonel Sharif was not allowing me to publish anything at the moment and that I would not do anything to burn him. He still didn't look comfortable at the prospect of having a reporter around, but just then the door to the war room opened behind us.

Prince Feisal came out and greeted us somberly, then asked us to step inside.

As we did, the king stood, came around the conference table, and embraced Ari as a brother. They said nothing. Nor did they need to. They were roughly the same age. Both in their midfifties. Both sons of the Holy Land. Both had bravely served their countries in the special forces. Once they'd been enemies. Now they were friends. One was a monarch. One was a spy. They knew the fates of their countries were both on the line, and they knew the price of victory.

When the king released Ari, he turned to Yael, took her hands in his, looked into her eyes, and both expressed his condolences and thanked her for all that she had done for him and the royal family. I found it hard to define the chemistry between them, but it was clear that Yael was deeply touched by the king's kind and gracious spirit. She and Ari had come as professionals. They had been welcomed as friends.

His Majesty asked the two to sit next to him at the head of the table and quickly introduced them to the rest of the assembled group. When he got to me, he repeated his assurances that everything said and done on the entire base was off the record and that no reports of any kind from these meetings would be published in the *Times* or anywhere else without his permission. I still wasn't sure that comforted everyone, but he was the king, and it was his room and his rules, so no one said a thing. At that point, he turned the floor over to Ari.

The colonel and I were sitting in the back of the room. Notebook in hand and ready to transcribe everything that was about to unfold, I was positioned directly behind the Egyptian general. Still, even from this less-than-ideal vantage point, I had a decent view of Ari—and more importantly, Yael.

"Thank you, Your Majesty," Ari began. "I apologize for the timing, but it could not be helped. And, gentlemen, I realize that this is a bit unorthodox, having Ms. Katzir and me here with you at such a critical moment. But the purpose of our visit is very simple. We know you believe President Taylor is in Dabiq. We understand the case. We've been studying the evidence. And we agree it's compelling. But in the end my colleagues and I don't believe he's there. We believe it's a trap. The president is not in Syria. He's in Iraq."

45

* * *

The room fell silent.

"We believe the president is being held in a small village known as Alqosh," Ari continued as Yael set up a PowerPoint presentation.

The first slide they posted was a map of northern Iraq and a red dot marked *Alqosh*, along with two variant spellings: *Al-Qosh* and *Elkosh*.

"Alqosh is an ancient Assyrian town," Ari went on. "Its history dates back before the time of the Babylonian Empire. As you can see on this map, it's located on the plains in the Iraqi province of Nineveh. It's about fifty kilometers north of Mosul, not far from Dohuk, right off Highway 2."

"But Alqosh is a Christian town, not Muslim, isn't it?" asked General El-Badawy.

"That's true, General," Ari replied. "Alqosh has been a Chaldean Christian community, a mixture of Orthodox and Catholic. It has been captured several times in recent years by ISIS, then liberated several times by the Iraqis, but finally retaken by ISIS forces about a year ago and has been held securely by ISIS since then. During these battles, most of the Christians fled. Those who didn't get out in time were crucified or beheaded. The population has plunged from more than three thousand to just a few hundred today, most of whom are ISIS leaders and their families."

"So why do you think the president is in Alqosh, of all places?" the Egyptian general pressed.

"Several reasons," Ari said. "First, let's look at the phone calls made to and from Jamal Ramzy's cell phone."

Ari nodded, and Yael posted the next slide, an infographic detailing the call log.

RAMZY PHONE LOG

Outgoing Calls:

1. Thursday, 25 November: Dabiq, Syria (9 seconds)

2. Sunday, 28 November: Dabiq, Syria (9 seconds)

3. Monday, 29 November: Homs, Syria (4:17 minutes)

4. Tuesday, 30 November: Dabiq, Syria (9 seconds)

5. Tuesday, 30 November: Homs, Syria (3:54 minutes)

6. Wednesday, 1 December: Homs, Syria (2 minutes)

7. Thursday, 2 December: Homs, Syria (4:36 minutes)

8. Friday, 3 December: Homs, Syria (6:13 minutes)

9. Friday, 3 December: Irbid, Jordan → Fairfax, Virginia (12:09 minutes)

Incoming Calls:

1. Tuesday, 30 November: Homs, Syria
   (2:29 minutes)
2. Saturday, 4 December: Homs, Syria
   (53 seconds)
3. Sunday, 5 December: Dabiq, Syria
   (9 seconds)

"As you can see, the log shows that nine out-bound calls were made from Ramzy's cell phone, and three inbound calls were received," Ari said. "Now, it's true that three of the outbound calls were made to a number in Dabiq, including two of the first three calls made. But our analysis shows that each of these calls lasted only nine seconds. It's possible, of course, that Ramzy—or whoever was using the phone—had a brief conversation with someone in Dabiq each time, passing along a small bit of information—a name, a phone number, a date and time, something along those lines. But how likely is it that his conversation lasted exactly nine seconds each time? Not very."

"He was entering a passcode," General al-Mufti said.

"Yes, General, that's what we believe," Ari concurred. "We can't prove it. And we don't know what the code was. But obviously the caller had some reason to dial that number in Dabiq and complete the same procedure each time, a pro-cedure that took exactly nine seconds. The only inbound call from Dabiq also lasted nine seconds. In this case, whatever procedure had been agreed upon in advance was being done in reverse."

Ari looked around the room and then back at the king to make sure everyone was following him. We were, and the king encouraged him to proceed.

"Of course, this doesn't prove the president is *not* in Dabiq," Ari readily conceded. "The phone records show Ramzy calling this number—and it's the same number every time—in Dabiq. Clearly there's a strong connection to Dabiq. But for my team and me, at least, it doesn't make sense that Ramzy was talking to Abu Khalif when he made those calls. Yet Ramzy was Khalif's deputy. They should have spoken several times during this period. At the very least Ramzy should have spoken to someone close to Khalif, someone who could have reliably passed information back and forth between the two. But clearly that didn't happen on any of the calls to or from Dabiq. That leads us to Homs, which I will get to in a moment. But before we do, let's take a look at the last outbound call."

Yael put up a new slide.

FINAL RAMZY
OUTGOING CALL

9. Friday, 3 December: Irbid, Jordan → Fairfax, Virginia (12:09 minutes)
    * Irbid → drugstore
    * Western Union office
    * Two money transfers

"This call is surely the oddest of them all," Ari said. "At precisely five o'clock on the afternoon of Friday, December 3, a call was made from Jamal Ramzy's phone to a number just outside of Washington, D.C. We've been able to determine that the cell tower the call originated from was located on the outskirts of the city of Irbid. So either Ramzy or someone on his team using this phone was operating inside the Hashemite Kingdom, whereas all the calls made or received before December 3 were transmitted from cell towers in various parts of Syria. Everyone still with me?"

We all were.

"Which means Ramzy or his team crossed the border from Syria into Jordan sometime between eleven o'clock on the night of Thursday, December 2, and 8:32 on the morning of Friday, December 3, when the second-to-last call is made from the phone," Ari continued. "What makes the call stand out, of course, is that it's the only call outside of the Middle East. It's the only call to the United States. And curiously, it's to a phone number for a drugstore in Fairfax, Virginia. Now, why is that significant?"

Ari had no takers, so he continued.

"The drugstore is located on Route 123, also known as Chain Bridge Road. Was it a mistake? Was it a wrong number?"

"No," General Jum'a said. "It's the longest call Ramzy made."

"Exactly, General," Ari said. "The call lasted more than twelve minutes. So we have to assume Ramzy, or the person using his phone, meant to call a drugstore in Fairfax. But why? He's not calling in a prescription. He's not checking if they have mouthwash or a certain brand of razor. Why is he calling this drugstore?"

"It's about the money," the Saudi general said, engaging the Israeli agent for the first time.

"Correct," Ari said. "It turns out there is a Western Union office at this drugstore, and when we investigated further, we found that two money transfers were made from overseas to that Western Union branch on that day. The first was for six hundred dollars. It was sent to a nineteen-year-old Indian student from Mumbai who is a sophomore at George Mason University. But the family seems to have no possible connection to terrorism, so we examined the second transfer. This one was for five thousand dollars. It was sent from Dubai to a thirty-four-year-old woman who works as a real estate agent in Vienna, Virginia."

"Real estate?" I asked.

Ari nodded.

"Let me guess," I said, stunned to see how this was unfolding. "This is the woman who was working for Jack and Claire Vaughn, the one having an affair with Jack."

"The very same," Ari said. "We passed this information along to the FBI as soon as we got it."

"Okay, this is all fascinating," Prince Feisal interjected, "but I hope I don't need to remind you we are fast approaching the launch of military operations into Dabiq. So far you haven't convinced us you have a better target."

46

*   *   *

"My apologies, Your Highness," Ari quickly replied. "I'll pick up the pace."

"Please do."

"This brings us to the calls to and from Homs," Ari continued. "They represent seven of the twelve calls sent or received and a total of twenty minutes of conversation. So putting together what we knew from J. B.'s articles—notably that Jamal Ramzy had a safe house in Homs—we began considering the possibility that Abu Khalif was in Homs and that perhaps the president had been taken there as well. But then our technical team made an important discovery. Yael, would you put up the next slide?"

RAMZY PHONE LOG

Outgoing Calls to Homs:

1. Monday, 29 November: Homs → Mosul
   (4:17 minutes)
2. Tuesday, 30 November: Homs → Mosul
   (3:54 minutes)

3. Wednesday, 1 December: Homs → Mosul
   (2 minutes)
4. Thursday, 2 December: Homs → Mosul
   (4:36 minutes)
5. Friday, 3 December: Homs → Mosul →
   Aleppo → Baghdad → AQ (6:13 minutes)

"What they discovered was that Homs wasn't a base of operations for ISIS," Ari noted. "It turned out the number in Homs was nothing more than a switching station, and all of the calls were being switched to a series of numbers in Mosul."

"A series of numbers?" the UAE general asked.

"Yes," Ari said. "To keep things simple, I didn't put all the data on the slide. But once the calls were routed from Homs to Mosul, they were rerouted again five, six, sometimes seven times before finally connecting. I'm afraid we weren't able to determine where the two inbound calls were coming from before they were routed to Ramzy's phone. But we were able to figure out where each of the outgoing calls was routed to, and the last call becomes the most important."

The next slide showed a blizzard of detailed technical data: certain phone numbers that were used to specific cell towers in Jordan, Syria, Iraq, Syria again, and Iraq again, and so forth. Given the constraints of time, Ari told us he would skip a thorough explanation and just cut to the chase.

"This last call was bounced around the most, a total of nineteen times through three different countries," he said. "In the end they weren't able to throw us off the scent. In fact, by taking such precautions, they revealed that of all twelve calls to and from Ramzy's phone, this was by far the most important. It wasn't as long as the call to the Western Union office in Virginia, but at six minutes and thirteen seconds it was the longest call in the region. It was clearly the call the ISIS team worked hardest to camouflage. Any guess where it went?"

"Alqosh," Al-Mufti said.

"Exactly," Ari confirmed. "Now, I wish I could tell you that we were able to intercept and record the actual call. I wish I could tell you we had Jamal Ramzy and Abu Khalif on tape plotting the assassination of our leaders and their plan to bring the president back to Alqosh. But I can't. Maybe NSA has it. But to be honest, given the high-level penetration of NSA this week, we didn't think discussing it with our friends in Fort Meade was the best move right now. But this is where my colleague Dr. Katzir enters the picture. With your permission, I'm going to hand things over to her now."

The king and prince both nodded, and Yael stood. She straightened her jacket and smoothed back her damp hair. She was moving slowly and seemed stiff.

"Thank you, Your Majesty and Your Highness, for allowing us to come over on such short notice," she began. "Dr. Shalit brought me here today because my specialty—first in the IDF and for the last several years with the Mossad—is weapons of mass destruction and particularly chemical weapons. I have a master's from UC Berkeley and a doctorate from MIT in chemical engineering.

My father was a chemist for Pfizer and now teaches chemistry at Tel Aviv University, which is how I developed my love for the subject. Anyway, a number of weeks ago, as you know from Mr. Collins's reporting, ISIS forces led by Jamal Ramzy's top deputy—a guy named Tariq Baqouba—attacked a Syrian military base near Aleppo. We don't think Baqouba knew at the time that it was a storage facility for chemical weapons. The U.N. had, after all, supposedly moved all of Syria's WMD out of the country. But the Assad regime was still secretly hoarding a great deal of chemical weapons. So when the fight was over and Baqouba and his men gained control of the base, they found—most likely to their surprise—stockpiles of sarin nerve gas and the bombs and artillery shells to deliver them."

I was disappointed that she'd called me "Mr. Collins" rather than "J. B." or "James." But other than that I was enjoying just being in the same room with her, having the chance to look at her for long stretches of time without it seeming odd, and getting to hear her speak with just a mesmerizing hint of an accent.

Ari now put up a series of photos of the Syrian base in question, taken from Israeli drones, but I never took my eyes off Yael.

"As you might imagine, we'd been using drones to monitor each of the sites where we believed the Assad regime had been making or keeping chemical weapons," she continued. "We'd also been monitoring all radio, phone, and e-mail traffic in the area around these bases. Bottom line, we watched Baqouba and his men cart away the sarin precursors, load them onto trucks, and drive away."

Ari now played a video clip showing drone footage of the ISIS convoy of five white box trucks driving away from the base.

"For the next five days, we tracked these five trucks as they drove through Syria, across the border into Iraq, and on to Mosul," Yael explained. "Unfortunately, our drone fleet was stretched thin at that time, and when the convoy got to Mosul, the drivers split off in five different directions. As a result, we lost four of them, but we did follow one, and it led us here."

For the first time, I forced myself to look away from Yael and toward the main monitor on the wall. A new video clip showed one of the trucks exiting a highway, driving down a long country road, entering a small village, and pulling into a heavily guarded compound on the edge of the village, just along a mountain ridge.

"Let me guess," General El-Badawy said. "That's Alqosh."

"It is," Yael confirmed. "Now, when we watched this whole thing begin to unfold, I had never heard of Alqosh. Nor had Dr. Shalit. But he tasked me with learning everything I possibly could about the town: who was there, why ISIS would park a truck filled with sarin gas there, and so forth. So I set up the same type of monitoring operation as I had at the Aleppo base. We started tracking phone calls, e-mails, text messages, anything we possibly could, and of course we kept a steady eye on the drone images. But we had gaps.

I wanted a second drone so we'd have nonstop coverage of the compound. Unfortunately, there weren't any others available. So we had to keep bringing the drone we were using back to Israel for refueling and maintenance. My team and I feared the weapons would be moved out of Alqosh and we'd miss it. Instead, we actually captured on video two more of the white box trucks arriving at the compound a few days after the first, amid numerous cars coming in and out at all hours of the day and night, and we began to consider the possibility that ISIS was actually storing the bulk of the chemical weapons they'd captured at this particular compound in Alqosh."

"This is all well and good, Dr. Katzir, but it doesn't put the president there," Prince Feisal protested.

"I realize that, Your Highness," she said calmly and without seeming to take offense. "I'm getting to that."

"With all due respect, you need to get there faster. The clock is ticking."

47

* * *

"Of course, Your Highness," Yael replied.

She leaned forward to pour herself a glass of water. I noticed she winced as she did so and held the glass with two hands. She was in more pain than she was letting on.

"Gentlemen, it's at this point that we intercepted a series of e-mails sent from inside the compound. Both were going to an e-mail address in Washington, D.C., an address belonging to one Allen MacDonald."

Stunned, I looked around the room and then back at Yael. No one else knew whom she was talking about, but I did, and I could hardly believe she was serious.

"Who's Allen MacDonald?" al-Mufti asked.

"He's Mr. Collins's editor at the *New York Times*," Yael explained. "We suddenly realized that Mr. Collins was at that location, writing two articles and sending them back to the foreign desk. When we read the articles, we realized what was happening. ISIS forces had just attacked the Abu Ghraib prison near Baghdad. In the process, they had liberated their spiritual leader, Abu Khalif. They had also captured Mr. Collins, who was writing about these events in great detail. What's more, he was writing about his exclusive interview with Khalif and the demonstration he witnessed of ISIS operatives testing sarin gas on several Iraqi prisoners."

Ari now stood. "I give tremendous credit to Dr. Katzir and her team," he said. "They not only tracked the movement of some of the most deadly weapons in the Syrian arsenal, but they also identified the location of one of the highest value targets on the Mossad's most-wanted list, not to mention each of your own. Because my own boss is so ill and I'm serving as acting director at the moment, I took this to the prime minister at once with a request that we take immediate action."

"What kind of action?" I asked, my heart racing.

"We wanted to neutralize the target," Ari replied.

"Neutralize?"

"Yes."

"You mean destroy?"

"Of course."

"With me inside the same compound?"

"Well, that did complicate the situation enormously."

"I guess so."

"So what did Danny do?" the king asked.

"He put two F-16s on strip alert, ready to hit the compound on his orders, but he also went straight to the security cabinet," Ari said. "They debated it for hours."

"*Hours?* What for?" El-Badawy pressed. "You

had the head of ISIS, likely his top deputies, and a cache of chemical weapons all within a couple hundred meters of each other. Why in the world didn't you take the shot?"

"General, this was exactly my position," Ari said. "The national security of the State of Israel was in grave peril. We didn't know, of course, what was about to happen in Amman. But we knew enough that in my judgment we had to act. And to be completely candid—and completely off the record—the majority of the security cabinet recommended the strike as well."

"But in the end, Danny called it off," said the king.

"Yes."

"And not taking out Abu Khalif when he had the chance cost him his life."

"I'm afraid so, Your Majesty."

I looked at Ari, then at Yael, then down at my notes. But there was one person I couldn't look at just then—the king. He and the Israeli prime minister—"Danny"—had been friends for years. They had also worked together for months on the peace treaty with the Palestinians they had all come so close to signing. And now Daniel Lavi was gone—because of me.

There could be no other reason Lavi had hesitated to attack Alqosh than to protect my life. Ari hadn't said it in so many words, but everyone in the room knew what he was saying. And now hundreds were dead. Many more were wounded. The Hashemite Kingdom was on the brink, and the president of the United States had been captured.

And yet again I had nearly died. When I'd been taken captive by Khalif and his jihadists, I was convinced I was going to be beheaded on YouTube for all the world to see. I never imagined two Israeli fighter jets were on standby, waiting for a single order to drop two five-thousand-pound bombs and kill me and everyone around me before any of us even realized what was happening.

I shuddered at the thought. How many times in recent weeks had I been so close to death, so close to slipping out of this world and into the next? More than I dared count, especially since I knew I wasn't ready to die. My brother was pleading with me to give my life to Christ. He kept telling me that receiving Christ was the only way to heaven. He kept telling me I was going to spend eternity in hell with no way of escape if I didn't. I used to be furious with him for saying things like that. But I no longer believed he was trying to be cruel. I was convinced now that Matt absolutely believed this in the core of his being. I knew he genuinely feared that I would be separated from God and from him and from the rest of our family forever. He loved me. He wanted the best for me. But I couldn't bring myself to do it.

I wasn't even sure that he was wrong. I was actually beginning to wonder if he might be right. But something in me couldn't say yes to Christ. I couldn't have explained why. I'm not even sure I knew. I just couldn't, and yet a fear was engulfing me like I'd never experienced before. My hands started trembling again. I set down my pad and pen on the conference table and put my hands in my lap. I was perspiring and my mouth was dry, but I didn't dare reach for the glass of water on the table before me. I was too afraid of spilling it.

A new video started playing on the main monitor. It was a night-vision shot showing a car and an SUV driving away from the compound.

"That night, we observed two vehicles leaving Alqosh in the middle of the night," Yael said, breaking the awkward silence. "Because we had only one drone operating over the site, we couldn't follow the car. We believed at the time that Abu Khalif was leaving. The problem was that the mandate of my unit was to track chemical weapons, not ISIS leaders per se. It was a brutal call to make. I was cursing my superiors for not giving me a second drone. But I had my orders. I couldn't disobey them. I had to stay with the compound."

"So you didn't know it was Mr. Collins who was being taken away from the town instead of Khalif?" Prince Feisal asked.

"No, Your Highness, I did not."

"Why not?"

"There were tarps over the driveway and carport in the compound, preventing us from seeing faces of people entering or exiting the vehicles inside. And the windows of the vehicle were tinted. Plus it was night. So it wasn't possible to make proper IDs, I'm afraid."

"But if you had known?" the Saudi asked.

"If I'd known what, General?"

"If you'd known Collins had left instead of Khalif, would you have hit the compound?"

"Well, of course, it wasn't my decision to make,"

Yael replied. "But yes, I would certainly have recommended an immediate strike. I know for a fact my superiors would have agreed and taken my recommendation directly to the PM. And I have no doubt that the PM and the security cabinet would have ordered a strike. As it was, we didn't know who had left the compound, so the PM ordered the F-16s to stand down."

"But even without Khalif there, you could have hit the compound anyway," the Saudi pressed. "I still don't understand why you didn't take the opportunity to destroy all those chemical weapons when you had the chance."

Yael said nothing but looked to Ari.

"I wanted to do just that," he replied. "But Dr. Katzir pleaded with me not to."

"Why not? It was a perfect opportunity."

"In some ways, yes," Ari agreed. "But Dr. Katzir argued it would have exposed our knowledge of the site. It would have destroyed all the highly valuable intelligence that was surely at the site. She strongly recommended, instead, that we find a way to send several operatives—"

"Spies?" the Saudi asked.

"Okay, yes, spies, to infiltrate the compound and find out who exactly was there and what their intentions were," Ari added.

"You couldn't have believed that would have really worked."

"It was a compelling case," Ari said.

"This wasn't about intelligence," El-Badawy interjected. "She was trying to protect Collins."

"We did have an innocent American citizen—

a highly respected and accomplished journalist—in the compound, yes," Ari concurred. "It's not our practice to kill innocent civilians, whatever the media in the region say about us."

"But there was a higher mission," El-Badawy insisted. "Wasn't it worth killing one man to save the lives of so many others?"

48

★ ★ ★

"In the end, I took Dr. Katzir's recommendation," Ari said.

"Just to save a reporter?" the Saudi asked, indignant.

"She was the lead analyst on this," Ari responded. "She had an impeccable service record. I've always trusted her judgment. I didn't necessarily agree with her. But I respect her, and at the time I couldn't say definitively that she was wrong."

"But she was."

I couldn't believe what I was hearing. My blood was boiling. The colonel could see it. He reached over and put his hand on my arm, a subtle reminder—perhaps a plea—not to say anything, to let this thing play out without jumping in. I looked at Yael. She was surprisingly calm. I didn't know how she did it. But I could see this was getting to Ari. His jaw was clenched as he carefully chose his next words.

"Dr. Katzir could not have possibly known what was coming, General," he finally replied. "Nor could I. Nor could our prime minister. Nor could any of you. Not that night. Not based on what we knew at that precise moment. We had a judgment call to make. Hindsight is twenty-twenty. But I believe we made the best decision we could, given the imperfect information we had at the time."

I was grateful for the answer. The Saudi general, however, wouldn't let it go.

"But in the end you cannot escape the brutal fact that you chose to risk the lives of thousands—thousands of Arabs, I might add; thousands of Muslims—to save the life of a single man, a single reporter."

"An American citizen," Ari added, "and a friend."

"Ah, and now we get to it," the general said, his face red as he leaned forward in his chair. "This was not just an American and not just a reporter; this was someone Miss Katzir knew personally."

"*Dr.* Katzir."

"Someone that *Dr.* Katzir knew personally."

"Yes."

"Someone she is friends with?"

"You could say that."

"Close friends?"

"Perhaps—they've certainly been through a great deal together."

"And perhaps more than friends?"

"What are you implying?"

"I'm not implying," the general said. "I'm merely asking."

"You're asking if there is some kind of inappropriate relationship going on here?" Ari asked, incredulous.

I glanced at Yael. She was mortified. Her face said it all. And she was growing angry. Her back stiffened. She leaned forward in her seat. For a second, I thought she might unleash on the general. But she was too much of a professional for that. She let Ari defend her, and Ari was doing a fine job. But I was livid, about to explode. Sharif tightened his grip on my arm, silently imploring me to stay calm and let others defend our honor.

"General, these are two people who risked their own lives to save the life of this fine and honorable king from these ISIS monsters," Ari responded. "Perhaps you're not aware that Dr. Katzir killed dozens of the jihadists, or that she was engaged in hand-to-hand combat with them. Perhaps you're not aware that she personally shot and killed Jamal Ramzy or that Mr. Collins was the one who had the wherewithal to recover Ramzy's phone, which has given us such critical intelligence. Or that he was shot and wounded protecting the lives of the royal family. Or that he drove the vehicle that whisked not only the king and his family to safety but also the Palestinian president and my prime minister. Rather than cowardly insinuations, I believe everyone in this room owes these two people a great debt."

The room was silent, but Ari wasn't finished.

"Furthermore, General, with all due respect, you are distracting this group from the real objective, which is to analyze the evidence we have brought you," he continued.

The general tried to speak, but Ari would not let him.

"No, I'm sorry; you can respond in a moment, but I haven't yet completed my presentation," he said as calmly as he could. "Look, all of us deeply regret not seeing these attacks against the summit coming. And we all regret not doing more to prevent them. Personally, if I could do it all over, would I have made different decisions? Of course. We've got three drones over Alqosh right now and, I might add, four over Dabiq. That's what we can do—make adjustments, course corrections, based on what we've all learned. But we cannot look back. We can't get bogged down in finger-pointing and recriminations. Not now. We do not have the luxury. As His Highness has reminded us several times, the clock is ticking. So this brings me to my last and final point. Aside from the vehicles that left the compound in Alqosh to take Mr. Collins to the Kurdish border, we had observed no other vehicles coming in or out of not just the compound but the entire village until around four o'clock this morning."

Yael took a deep breath and put a final video clip up on the main screen. It was more night-vision footage, this time of a convoy made up of three SUVs pulling off Highway 2, heading into Alqosh and right into the compound.

"We believe you are watching the president of the United States arriving at Abu Khalif's lair in the town of Alqosh on the Nineveh plains," Ari said.

The video now switched to thermal imaging of the three SUVs coming to a halt inside the walled compound under the tarps Yael had previously mentioned. So while we couldn't see faces, I counted nine men carrying weapons exiting the first and third vehicle. Then I watched as four more armed men got out of the middle vehicle. I could see them opening the trunk and pulling out a body. At first I thought they were handling a corpse, and my heart almost stopped. But then I saw movement. The person's hands and feet appeared to be bound. But whoever it was writhed and twitched and seemed determined not to go quietly. Was that really him? I wondered. Was that really President Taylor?

"Now, what was particularly curious to us was that within minutes of this particular convoy arriving, communications of every kind in the village shut down completely," Ari noted, and as he did, the video ended and the screen went black. "The lights in the village stayed on. They hadn't lost power. But the nearby cell tower was abruptly switched off. We're not sure how. All Wi-Fi services in the village went dead as well. Since 4:15 this morning, no calls, no e-mails, no text messages, nor any form of communication has come in or out of the entire village. But we did intercept the last text message sent by a mobile phone inside the main residence in the compound just before everything went dark."

"What did it say?" asked the Saudi.

"'The package has arrived.'"

49

★ ★ ★

It was now 5:57 p.m.

Just twelve hours until the deadline.

The sun had been down all across the Middle East for more than an hour.

And now the king asked Ari, Yael, the colonel, and me to step out of the room. They had heard the evidence. They had a decision to make and not much time to make it.

I didn't envy the position these men were in. I'd jotted down a list of questions on my notepad, each of which was as vexing as the next.

Were the Israelis right—were the president and Khalif in Alqosh?

Or was General Ramirez right about the evidence pointing to Dabiq?

I found myself leaning heavily toward the case Ari and Yael were making. Perhaps I was biased, but I was trying to analyze the evidence as objectively as possible. And when it came to Alqosh, the pieces fit.

Still, even if Ramirez and the others were persuaded by the Israelis' case, could the U.S. afford not to send forces to Dabiq, given that the tracking signal from the president's watch was unmistakably being picked up from there? What if Ramirez put all his chips on Alqosh and he was wrong—or vice versa?

Then again, did the coalition have enough forces to embark simultaneously on two rescue missions?

And if they did, with the raging storm bearing down on the region, could the coalition's forces get safely to either site and back?

As we stepped out of the war room and into the waiting area, I was eager to get the others' take on all these questions, and there were so many more.

If the storm was too intense to fly special forces teams to either or both sites, was there a realistic ground option that could be pulled off in the next twelve hours?

And if they decided to fly, what would they do if one or more of the choppers went down due to weather or mechanical failure or enemy fire?

What's more, if they could even get to either or both of the sites, how would coalition forces protect themselves against the possible use of chemical weapons?

Above all, what if they were all wrong? What if neither the president nor Abu Khalif was at either site? What if the president was already dead? What if another major attack was coming against Jordan, against Israel, or against the United States?

When we got out into the hallway, the colonel pulled me away from the others and showed me his phone. He now had five text messages and two missed calls from my brother, begging me to call him immediately.

In an instant, my entire perspective changed. "You need to let me call him," I told Sharif.

"I can't," he replied. "You know that."

"Then why show me all these messages?"

"I'm just trying to keep you informed."

"And I'm grateful," I said. "But you have to let me call him. Something's wrong. He's not like this. He never texts or calls this often."

"I wish I could, Mr. Collins. But I'm under strict orders not to let you—or anyone—communicate outside of this base. I've already bent those rules as far as I can. I can't do more."

"Colonel—Yusef—you have to."

"I'm sorry."

"But you don't understand," I pleaded. "Abu Khalif personally threatened my family. What if something's happened to them? Please, ask the king to make an exception."

"Absolutely not. You heard His Majesty. He and his war council are making their final plans. They cannot be distracted by civilian affairs."

"There's got to be something you can do."

"There isn't."

"Think, Colonel—I'm not a prisoner any-more. I'm not a hostage. You can't deny me access to my own family in an emergency."

"The needs of the kingdom rank higher than our own personal needs, Mr. Collins."

"For you, yes, but you're a subject of the kingdom—I'm not," I argued. "I'm an American citizen who has done everything I can to protect the king and his family, not out of obligation but because of the respect I have for them. Surely you can help me protect my family in a time like this."

"The king's command is sacrosanct, Mr. Collins. You may not speak to anyone off this base."

"That doesn't apply to you, though, does it?"

"Of course not."

"You've been in touch with foreign media and foreign officials in the last few days, right?"

"Yes, of course, but what's your point?"

"Call him for me."

"Your brother?"

"Yes, you can call him. Find out what's wrong. Maybe I can listen in but not say anything, or just hand you a note if there's something I need to tell him, and you can decide whether you can pass the message along or not."

Sharif didn't immediately say no. I had five more arguments to make, but I held my fire. I didn't want to push him. And in the end, I didn't have to.

"Okay."

"Really?"

"Yes."

"You'll call him?"

"Yes. Come with me."

Sharif excused himself from the Israelis, encouraged them to have a seat, and said we'd be right back. They were a bit surprised, to say the least, but the colonel didn't wait or discuss it with them. Instead, he led me down the hall to the security command post and into a break room typically filled with off-duty guards. Except that

314 ★ THE FIRST HOSTAGE

it was empty now. No one was off duty. Sharif pulled the door closed behind us, and we sat down on opposite sides of a small table covered in used coffee cups and napkins.

"Get out your notepad," he said as he found Matt's number and started the call.

"Why?" I asked.

"If there's something you want me to say, write it down and slide it over to me. Otherwise, you keep your mouth shut or I hang up immediately. Got it?"

"Yes."

"No exceptions."

"I understand."

With that, he hit the Speaker button and suddenly Annie's voice filled the room. "Hello?"

"Yes, hello, I'm looking for Dr. Matthew Collins. Do I have the right number?"

"Yes, this is his wife. May I ask who's calling?"

"Of course—I'm Colonel Yusef Sharif. I work for His Majesty King Abdullah. I'm returning a call from your husband. Is he there?"

"Yes, yes, he is," Annie replied. "Just a moment and I'll fetch him."

It was a joy to hear her voice. Her kids were fighting in the background over some toy, and one of them started to cry. Typically things like that annoyed me, but not anymore, or at least not today. Those were the sounds of home, and for perhaps the first time in my life I wanted to be with them instead of on the front lines of a major story.

Then, before I knew it, Matt came on the line. "Hello? This is Matt Collins. Who's this again?"

The colonel greeted him and explained who

he was. "Your brother is okay, Dr. Collins," he told Matt. "He's safe and covering this unfolding drama over here and doing an excellent job, I might add. But I'm afraid with all that's going on, there are restrictions on foreign nationals making calls outside the country, at least those foreign nationals who know where His Majesty is. I hope you'll understand."

"Well, I guess so," Matt said. "But it is really urgent that I talk with him."

"I realize that, and that's why I'm calling you back. Again, it's not that J. B. doesn't want to speak to you. To the contrary, he's dying to talk to you and to his mother, your mother. But for security reasons, no one but government officials are allowed to call out of the location we're currently in. But I can certainly pass along a message."

There was a pause. I could tell Matt was weighing his options. Whatever he had to tell me, it was clearly sensitive. I scribbled down a note and passed it to the colonel. He read it, then looked at me, then closed his eyes.

"Listen, I understand this isn't an ideal way for you two to communicate," Sharif told Matt. "But I'm afraid right now it's this or nothing. I'm not sure I'm allowed to tell you this, but I'm going to because your brother has been a true friend to the kingdom. You should know that your brother is sitting right here with me. He's listening to our conversation. He seems glad to hear your voice and your kids in the background. He's not allowed to speak to you, but I want to assure you that he's not going to miss anything you're saying."

"Really? J. B., can you hear me?"

Instinctively, I was about to respond, but Sharif held up his finger and cut me off. "Dr. Collins, like I said, he's right here, but he's not allowed to say anything. But you can speak to him if you'd like."

"How do I know he's really there?" asked Matt.

"What do you mean?"

"I mean, how do I know you are who you say you are and that he's really at your side?"

"I guess you'll just have to trust me."

"I'm afraid I can't do that, Mister—Colonel—whoever you are. For all I know, you work for ISIS."

50

* * *

"I don't work for ISIS," Sharif insisted. "I work for the king of Jordan."

"So you say."

"Dr. Collins, I realize you're under a lot of stress right now. But I'm in the middle of a war. I really don't have the time or interest to argue with you. Would you like to pass a message on to your brother or not? I'll remind you that you called me. I'm simply returning your call."

"Not exactly," my brother shot back. "You texted me first. You said my brother was passing along his greetings. But you offered no proof, and you still haven't."

That's my brother, I thought. For all his faults, the man was no fool.

Sharif checked his watch and took a deep breath. "Fair enough, Dr. Collins. Ask your brother a question to which only he would know the answer."

"Really?"

"Yes."

"Okay," Matt said. "What was it that we talked

about in the hallway just before we went in to see Annie and the kids?"

Sharif pushed my notebook back across the table. I wrote as quickly as I could and then slid the notebook back to him. He read the note and looked quizzically at me for a moment, but to his credit he read it to Matt anyway.

"You were explaining a bunch of prophecies from the Old Testament, from the book of Jeremiah."

"Go on," Matt said.

I grabbed the notebook and wrote more.

"They were prophecies about the End Times," Sharif told Matt. "You said that in the last days terrible judgments were coming on Jordan. You said you hoped what ISIS was doing wasn't the beginning of the fulfillment of those prophecies. You said you liked the king, that he seemed to be wise and wanted to keep the peace, that he's one of the good guys."

"Okay, fine, but that wasn't actually the last thing we spoke of," Matt replied. "There was something else."

Sharif slid the notebook back to me. This time, I wrote a note on a single sheet of paper and slid that across to him, rather than the whole notebook.

"He says he warned you to leave Amman immediately, that your life was in danger."

"Everybody knows I'm not in Amman any longer, Colonel. You'll have to do better. There was one more topic. The last thing we discussed before we entered the front door of my apartment."

I couldn't think. My mind went blank. Sharif again glanced at his watch. We were running out of time, and we hadn't even gotten to what Matt wanted to tell me yet. I closed my eyes and leaned back in my chair. What was he getting at?

Our conversation had been almost entirely theological, which was probably why I remembered as much as I did. It was so unlike any other conversation I'd ever had. I'd interviewed all kinds of people in my career—presidents and prime ministers, generals and jihadists, soldiers and spies—but I'd never known, much less interviewed, anyone like my brother. I never talked with people about the Bible. No one I knew talked about it. We certainly didn't talk about Bible prophecy or the End of Days. But Matt loved this stuff. He was, after all, a seminary professor, an Old Testament scholar, and the author of a textbook for Bible colleges and seminaries on how to study and teach biblical eschatology. I'd never read it. It had never seemed interesting in the slightest to me. In fact, if I was honest with him—which generally I had not been over the course of our strained and at times contentious relationship—I'd always found the whole subject a bit loony. I mean, really, how in the world could a dusty old book thousands of years old tell us what was going to happen in our times? The very notion seemed insane—except he explained it.

After all these years, Matt was starting to get my attention. I remembered being intrigued when he explained that thousands of years ago the biblical prophets foretold the rebirth of the State of

Israel, predicted that Jews would return in droves to the Holy Land after centuries of exile, and posited that with God's help the Jews would rebuild the ancient ruins and create an "exceedingly great army." Most people considered the idea lunacy for almost two thousand years, including many of the church fathers who thought such prophecies couldn't possibly be true—not literally, anyway. But Matt argued that May 14, 1948, changed everything. Suddenly the State of Israel *was* back in existence. Jews *were* returning. They *were* making the deserts bloom and constructing great cities and building a mighty army.

What could explain such dramatic, unexpected developments? I didn't have an answer. True, there were certain historical and sociological and geopolitical realities that made the rebirth of Israel as a modern nation more likely in the mid-twentieth century than ever before. The collapse of the Ottoman Empire, the Holocaust, the implosion of the British Empire, the rise of political Zionism, and the support of Christians for a Jewish state were all contributing factors. But it was still one of the most unlikely events to ever happen in the history of mankind. What other people group exiled from their homeland for two millennia had ever come back home and reclaimed not just their sovereignty but their nearly dead language? Maybe God did have something to do with it. Maybe there was something to all those old prophecies.

It was intriguing, I'd conceded. But it didn't prove Jesus was the Messiah. It certainly didn't prove that he was coming back to reign over the earth for a thousand years, let alone coming back soon, even in our lifetime. These were bridges I couldn't cross. But Matt really believed such things, and despite the fact that I'd mocked him for years, he wasn't an idiot. Though I was loath to admit it—to him or to others—he was a lot smarter than me. I'd been a decent student back in the day, earning my BA in political science from American University and an MA in journalism from Columbia, my grandfather's alma mater, though I'd partied far too much and almost certainly spent more on beer than books. Matt, by contrast, had five degrees. He'd earned a BA from Harvard, three master's degrees—one in theology, another in Hebrew, and a third in ancient Greek, each from Princeton's school of divinity—and had a PhD in theology from Gordon-Conwell, with an emphasis in Old Testament studies. What's more, he'd graduated at or near the top of his class each time. It made it hard to dismiss my older brother as completely as I'd wanted to for the last few decades.

So when we'd talked back in Amman last week, we'd talked theology. What else? He explained the prophecies about the future of Jordan. He'd said it was possible the prophecies might come to fulfillment sooner than anyone could imagine. It made me wonder what he thought of Khalif's eschatology. Did the Bible say anything about Dabiq? Did it give any clues about the rise of an Islamic caliphate? And what really was the difference between what the Qur'an had to say about the End of Days and what the Bible had to say? I had a feeling Matt knew a lot about this subject. It actually might make an interesting story for the *Times*, especially given Khalif's video message. But that would have to wait for another day.

"Are you still there, Colonel?" Matt asked.

"Yes, I'm still here," Sharif said. "I'm just waiting for your brother to reply. He doesn't seem to remember. And you've got to admit what he's said already could only have been known by him."

"No, he could have told you those things under duress," Matt said. "But I'll give you—or him—a hint."

"Okay."

"It was something Katie said."

I looked up and scribbled a note.

"She just turned four," Sharif said.

"Keep going."

I wrote another note.

"She's in a Sunday school class," Sharif told him. "She loves it. Can't wait to get there every week. And she loves memorizing the Bible. There's some sort of game if you memorize verses."

"What were the last verses she memorized?"

I scribbled down a single sentence—less than that, actually; just a phrase.

"Something from 1 John."

"What was it?"

I winced and shook my head.

"Come on, Dr. Collins, that's enough," Sharif said. "We're running out of time."

"The verse, Colonel," Matt pressed. "I want to hear him say it."

This time I closed my eyes and put my head

down on the table. But try as I might, I couldn't remember. Instead, the most horrific images from the last few weeks flashed through my brain.

Abdel and the mine in Homs.

Omar and the car bomb in Istanbul.

Khachigian in the café at Union Station.

The beheadings in Baghdad.

The sarin gas test in Mosul, which I now realized had actually happened in Alqosh.

The kamikaze in Amman.

And the children. All those precious children.

Suddenly I sat bolt upright. I reached for my notebook and wrote two sentences as fast as I could. My handwriting was so illegible I couldn't imagine how Sharif could decipher it. But he did, and he read it, and I was right.

"'And the testimony is this, that God has given us eternal life, and this life is in His Son. He who has the Son has the life; he who does not have the Son of God does not have the life.'"

51

★ ★ ★

"That's it," Matt exclaimed. *"That's my brother!"*

Just then there was a knock on the door. It was Ari Shalit.

"Colonel, His Majesty is asking for you," the Israeli said.

Sharif thanked him and said he'd be right there.

"It seems he needs you right away," Ari added. "It's fairly urgent."

Sharif nodded but turned back to the call.

"Dr. Collins, you've got one minute," he told Matt. "If you've got something to say to your brother, now's the time."

"One minute?"

"Fifty-four seconds."

I handed Ari a note explaining who was on the phone. He looked impatient but waited by the door.

"Okay, right, well, it's about the video," Matt stammered. "The video that Abu Khalif made, with the president in the cage—you know the one?"

"Of course," said Sharif. "What about it?"

"I know where it was shot."

"How?"

"I've been there."

"Where?"

"Nahum's tomb."

"Where?"

"They shot the video next to Nahum's tomb."

"Nahum who?" the colonel asked.

"You know, the Hebrew prophet, one of the minor prophets, wrote the book of Nahum in the Bible?"

"I guess," Sharif replied, not exactly tracking with Matt's train of thought and not exactly having the time to pursue it.

But Matt kept going. "Okay, well, Nahum was a minor prophet only in the sense that his contribution to the Scriptures was small. His book isn't very long. But it was enormously consequential because he prophesied the coming judgment of the city of Nineveh."

"Nineveh in Iraq?"

"Yes, precisely," Matt said. "You see, God told Nahum to warn the people that their wicked city would be utterly destroyed, but tragically they refused to listen. They didn't repent. And Nahum's prophecies of cataclysmic destruction all came to pass in 612 BC."

"So where is Nahum buried?"

"In a little town, a village really, in northern Iraq, on the plains of Nineveh," Matt explained. "It's a place called Elkosh. Have you ever heard of it?"

I looked at the colonel and then at Ari. They were as stunned as I was.

"Alqosh, you say?" Sharif clarified.

"Yes—have you heard of it?

"We've heard of it," Sharif said. "Tell me more—but make it fast."

"Well, Nahum was Jewish, but he was born and raised in exile, far from the land of Israel, in what was then the Assyrian Empire," Matt explained. "The Bible says Nahum was an 'Elkoshite.' He was born there, and he was buried there as well. There's a mausoleum at the site with Hebrew writing on the walls dating back twenty-five hundred years. I was there a number of years ago with some colleagues from my seminary."

"How long ago?"

"I don't remember exactly—five or six years, I guess—but I actually have pictures of me standing at the exact spot where Abu Khalif was standing, just a few feet to the right of the tomb."

"Can you send me those pictures?"

"Absolutely."

"Then text them right now, Dr. Collins. Please—time is of the essence. We have to go."

"Wait, Colonel; my mom wanted to say hello to—"

But suddenly he was gone. For a moment I thought the call had been dropped. But when the colonel jumped up, headed out the door, and told Ari to follow him, I realized that he'd actually hung up on him, and I was now sitting by myself. But at least I'd gotten to hear Matt's voice. He'd just come through for me in a huge way, and I was grateful.

What were the chances that my brother had

ever been in Alqosh? On the face of it, it seemed preposterous. But of course it wasn't. This was a guy who was in the middle of a yearlong sabbatical in the Hashemite Kingdom of Jordan studying the ancient prophecies of Ammon, Moab, Edom, Bozrah, Mount Seir, and who knew how many others. This was a guy who had taken his wife to Iraq—to the city of Babylon, to be precise—for their honeymoon back in the late 1980s, during the reign of Saddam Hussein, to visit the ancient ruins and see the beginnings of the rebuilding of Babylon—including the famed Ishtar Gate—that Saddam had ordered. It was nutty stuff like that that had caused the rift between us. Now it seemed my brother's nutty ideas were paying off big-time.

I just sat there, closed my eyes, and tried to catch my breath. I was exhausted and the pain in my left arm was growing. I pulled a bottle of pills from my pocket, the ones given to me by Dr. Hammami, and swallowed one without water.

As I worked the pill down my throat, my thoughts turned back to Alqosh. The evidence that Abu Khalif and the president had been there was now almost ironclad. The case that they were still there was intriguing yet merely circumstantial. What if Khalif and his men had taken the president from the compound after filming the video? Could they have slipped out of the village during a gap in the Israelis' drone coverage?

It was possible, I had to admit, but was it likely? And even if they'd managed to leave Alqosh, had they really gone all the way to Dabiq? Wasn't it more likely they were in Mosul, a city of more than a million and a half people, a city completely controlled by ISIS forces? The Iraqis and Americans had been talking about retaking it for months, but they still hadn't. If I were the head of the caliphate, wouldn't I be in Mosul? It was the wrong way to think, of course. I was thinking like a Westerner. Abu Khalif wasn't living in the twenty-first century. He was living in the seventh. He wasn't trying to protect himself. He was trying to follow the path of the Qur'an.

But did that make it more likely that his base camp was next to the tomb of Nahum in Alqosh than in Mosul? So far as I knew, Nahum wasn't a prophet mentioned in the Qur'an or typically recognized by Muslims. So where did that leave me? I had no idea.

"Hey, need some company?"

That was a voice I knew. I opened my eyes and found Yael peeking through the door with a somewhat-shy smile on her face.

"Absolutely," I said, standing. "You didn't go in with them?"

"I think my work in there is done."

Reaching behind her, I closed the door to the break room, and for the first time since Istanbul, we were alone.

"How're you doing?" I asked, standing only inches away from her.

She shrugged.

"Yeah, me too," I said.

We just stood there for a few moments, looking into each other's eyes, neither saying a word. It wasn't that we didn't have anything to say. It was because there was too much to say, and we had no idea where to start. That was my excuse, anyway. I couldn't really read her. I didn't know her well enough. Not yet.

"I'm sorry," I said finally.

"About what?" she asked.

"Danny . . . this . . . all of it."

She nodded and leaned toward me. I could feel her breath on my face, minty and sweet. My pulse quickened, as did my breathing. I can't tell you how much I wanted to kiss her right then. But I knew I shouldn't. It wasn't my place. She was wounded and vulnerable. She was as exhausted and in as much pain as I was. Maybe more. Probably more. I could see it in her eyes. And we hadn't talked, not really. She didn't know how I felt about her. I certainly didn't know how she felt about me. I thought I did. I hoped I did. But that wasn't the same as knowing for certain. The only way to know was to ask, and I didn't know how to ask right then. What if it was all wishful thinking on my part? What if none of it was real? What if it had all been an act? That was her job, wasn't it? To deceive people. To get things out of them. To get you to give her what she wanted and make it feel like you were doing it because you wanted to, not because she was manipulating you.

Yael Katzir was a spy. I was her mission, or part of it anyway. In Istanbul, she'd needed to get my attention and hold it and win my trust and get me to talk, and she'd done it beautifully. What a fool I'd be if I really fell for an act, no matter how convincing. What an idiot I'd feel like when I was rebuffed, as I surely expected to be.

And even if it was true—even if she really did have some feelings for me and I wasn't completely misreading the situation—then what? Ari and the colonel would be back any second. Did I really want them to burst in on us making out? Did I really intend to go back into the war room having discredited Yael in the eyes of everyone in there? It was one thing to contemplate chucking my career out the window to run away with this girl and start a new life. It was another thing to jeopardize everything she'd spent a lifetime working for.

So I stood there and stared into her eyes and forced myself not to kiss her. But then she surprised me by putting her arms around me and leaning her head against my chest. I didn't know what to say. So slowly, hesitantly, I put my arms around her, too, and closed my eyes again.

I forgot where I was, forgot who might be coming through the door at any moment. All the arguments swirling around in my head evaporated, and all I could think about was how warm her body felt against mine and how her hair smelled like strawberries.

I had a thousand questions and finally the privacy to ask them. But I kept quiet. I didn't want to ruin the moment. I just stood there in the break room under the harsh fluorescent lights and held this young woman I'd become so fond of. There was nothing romantic about the setting, nothing nostalgic, nothing personal. It wasn't how I'd imagined it.

But as I held her in the silence, she began to cry.

52

★ ★ ★

After a few minutes, she pulled away.

She said she was embarrassed. I told her not to be.

"This isn't like me," she said, fishing a tissue out of her purse and wiping away the tears. "I should know better."

"Your secret's safe with me."

She wasn't amused. Well, a little. But only a little. She took a small mirror from her purse and checked her makeup.

"You took a couple of nice shots," I said.

"You too."

"At least no one can see mine."

"That's true," she said. "I saw you noticing the makeup."

"Was I that obvious?"

"Uh, yeah."

"Sorry."

"It's okay."

"I'd never seen you wear makeup before."

"I usually don't."

"How bad is it?" I asked.

"The bruising?"

"Uh-huh."

"Could be worse." She shrugged. "You should see the other guy."

I smiled for the first time in days. "I did." A pause, then I asked, "You on meds?"

She nodded. "Are you?"

I nodded back.

"How bad is yours?" she asked.

"I'll live."

"Me too."

"Good," I said. "I hope so."

"Not all of us have been so lucky," she replied, a sadness coming over her again.

"Danny?"

She nodded and looked away.

"Unreal."

She walked to the other side of the room and stared out the little window in the door to the hallway.

"How's Miriam doing?" I asked of the prime minister's wife.

"She's a mess."

"I can't imagine."

"I was there," she said, "with her, at the hospital, when she got the news."

I said nothing.

"The shriek that came out of her mouth . . . the grief . . . the anguish . . . I'd never heard anything like it. Just total . . . total despair."

Then she said something that surprised me.

"And I knew just how she felt. . . ."

Her voice trailed off. I wanted to ask her what

she meant. But I held back. She wasn't really talking to me. She was talking to herself. I just happened to be in the room.

"The kids are worse," she said, staring at the crumpled tissue in her hands. "They're in shock, all of them . . . except little Avi."

"The two-year-old?" I asked.

She nodded. "He's oblivious," she said, her voice quiet and distant. "Doesn't understand what's happened, just playing with the nanny like he hasn't a care in the world. I mean, he knows Mommy is sad. He can see that. And he was so precious holding her hand and drawing little pictures for her. He just doesn't know what's happened. I'd like to be like that. . . ."

We were quiet for a while.

"Do you have kids, J. B.?" she asked, looking up, completely out of the blue.

The question startled me, but I shook my head. "No."

"Did you want them?"

"I did."

"And?"

The questions were suddenly so personal. But I didn't mind. "Laura didn't."

"Why not?"

I shrugged. What else could I do? I didn't know then. I certainly didn't know now. Not really. Not for certain.

"Do you regret it?" she asked.

"All of it."

"No, not the marriage. I mean . . ."

"I know," I said and looked down at the floor and thought about it more. "Yeah, I regret it."

"You'd have liked kids?"

I nodded but didn't say anything for almost a minute. I didn't know what to say. It seemed like an odd conversation to be having under the circumstances. Strange. Unexpectedly intimate. But surreal. We'd never really had time to talk personally. I realized I knew hardly anything about her.

"What about you?" I finally asked.

"What?"

"You want to be a mom someday?"

"More than anything," she said, still looking out the little window.

Again she'd surprised me. I'd thought of Yael Katzir as the consummate professional. She was completely immersed in her work. She'd labored incredibly hard to get to where she was. She was working among the most highly respected experts in the world in her field and was one of the few women to reach such heights in the Israeli intel community—or in any intelligence, especially since she was only thirty-four.

"Really?"

"Does that surprise you?"

"A little, yeah."

"Why? You don't think I'd be a good mom?"

"No, I'm sure you'd be great. I just . . ."

"Just what?"

"I don't know. You seemed like . . ."

"Too old?"

"No."

"Too self-centered?"

"No."

"Too married to my job?"

At that I hesitated. The last thing I wanted to do was offend her. "So, speaking of married, how come a pretty girl like you never got married?" I asked, almost wincing at how uncomfortable I felt asking such a stupid question and feeling like I'd crossed a line.

"Who said I've never been married?" she asked, raising her eyebrows and giving me a sly look.

"You were married?" I asked, trying not to sound as stunned as I felt.

"Right out of the army."

"How old were you?"

"Twenty, almost twenty-one."

"Oh . . . I had no idea."

"It's not the kind of thing that always comes up on a first date, is it?"

"Have we had a first date?"

"Excuse me, Mr. Collins," she said. "I seem to recall us making out in front of the Blue Mosque."

"I thought that was you being a spy," I said.

"It wasn't."

"No?"

"No."

"But I thought . . ."

"What?"

"I thought you said we had to seem like lovers or the police would think you were . . . you know . . . ?"

"A lady of the night?"

"Something like that."

"Did I say that?"

"Yeah, you did."

"Oh, well."

"What's that supposed to mean?"

She shrugged.

"Was it true?"

She shook her head and smiled again.

"It wasn't true?"

Again she shook her head. Now I was really confused.

"You made it all up? We didn't have to walk the streets like a couple?"

"Nope."

"Why not?"

"It was Istanbul, J. B., not Mecca," she replied. "It's a modern, Western, sophisticated city. They don't care whom you meet on the streets late at night—not if you're not Muslim, anyway."

"So why . . . ?"

"Why what?"

"Why'd you tell me to do it?"

She shrugged again. "Seemed like fun."

"Fun?"

"Wasn't it?"

"Well, yeah, but . . ."

"Come on, it was a rainy, foggy night in Istanbul, under the streetlights."

"Right out of the movies."

"Exactly. And I thought you were . . ."

"What?"

"You know."

"No."

"Adorable."

"Adorable?"

"Yeah, adorable."

"Me?"

"Yeah, you—and it worked, didn't it? The police didn't suspect a thing. Neither did you. So yes, I'd say that was our first date. And it was going rather nicely until . . ."

She caught herself, and it was quiet again. Neither one of us wanted to talk about the car bomb that had killed my friend Omar. I changed the subject.

"So you were married?"

"I was."

"And it didn't go well?"

"No, it went fabulously."

I guess I looked as startled as I felt.

"I was head over heels for him," Yael explained. "We met in the army on the first base I was assigned to, up north in a town called Yoqneam."

"And?"

"And we got married the day after I got out of the army."

"And?"

"And what? He got promoted, became an officer. We were just crazy for each other."

"What happened?"

"Hezbollah happened. Lebanon happened. He was on a patrol along the border, and one day someone fired an antitank missile at his jeep. His buddies survived. Uri did not."

"I'm so sorry."

"Yeah, well, what can you do?"

Her eyes began filling with tears again. I wanted to cross the room and hold her once more—not to kiss her, just to comfort her. But just then we heard footsteps coming down the hall. Then the door opened. It was Sharif.

"His Majesty would like to see you both."

Yael dabbed her eyes with a tissue, composed herself, and stepped out first. I followed close behind. But I had no idea what was awaiting us back in the war room.

53

* * *

Or rather *who* was awaiting us.

Prince Marwan Talal.

He was hunched over in his wheelchair, sitting beside His Majesty at the far end of the conference table, upon which sat a large reel-to-reel tape deck. Wearing his white robes but with a wool blanket wrapped around him to keep him warm, the man looked as bad as I'd ever seen him. His face was gaunt. His skin was sickly pale. Clearly his health had taken a turn for the worse in recent days, and I couldn't imagine the brutal conditions through which he had just returned from Baghdad. Had he actually flown through this treacherous weather, or had someone driven five-hundred-plus miles to get him here?

King Abdullah welcomed Yael and me back into the room, and we took a seat beside each other. Then the king recapped what his uncle and most senior advisor had been discussing with the group, namely that Iraqi intelligence had become convinced that President Taylor and Abu Khalif were now in Dabiq. His Majesty noted that Hassan Karbouli, the Iraqi interior minister, had played for Prince Marwan tape recordings of two intercepted phone calls between two senior ISIS commanders—one in Mosul and the other in Aleppo—discussing preparations to take "the jewels in the crown" to Dabiq. The two commanders had apparently discussed routes, accommodations, fueling stops, and security precautions, and one had insisted that "time is of the essence."

"We've been discussing the meaning of the tapes since you left," the king said, "and how best to move forward."

"And have you come to a conclusion?" I asked.

"We have. First, the group is agreed that our highest priority is to rescue the president. Capturing or killing Abu Khalif is an urgent task, but it must come second to the president's welfare. Second, the group is divided on what the evidence shows. We all now agree the data indicate both the president and Khalif were in Alqosh in recent days."

Then His Majesty addressed me directly. "Mr. Collins, Colonel Sharif shared with us the information provided by your brother, including pictures of him visiting Nahum's tomb."

The photos—which I had not yet seen—flashed on the screen, alongside still images from the latest ISIS video. There was no question both sets of images had been taken at the same place, and that place was the town of Alqosh on the plains of Nineveh.

"We all found your brother's photos conclusive proof the president *was* in Alqosh," the king continued. "Unfortunately, that doesn't prove the president is *still* in Alqosh. Some around this table are convinced the president has been moved to Dabiq. Others are equally convinced that he remains in Alqosh."

"So what are you going to do?" I asked.

"We've decided to launch simultaneous operations against both targets," the king replied. "General Ramirez will lead a force into Alqosh. General El-Badawy will lead the mission into Dabiq. If we can maintain the element of surprise—and synchronize the two assaults—we may just have a shot at success."

The analysis seemed solid. But it was a stunning change of plans. Ramirez had come to Jordan determined to take Dabiq. The vice president had been equally adamant. Now everything had changed.

The king then turned the presentation over to Ramirez.

"For the record," the American general began, "I still lean toward the president being in Dabiq, though I concede the data is not as conclusive as I'd come here believing. And I will be honest with you all that when I spoke to Vice President Holbrooke a few moments ago, I recommended sticking with our original game plan to have me lead the force into Dabiq. But the vice president has decided to accept the counsel of His Majesty, as well as President Mahfouz in Cairo, the king in Riyadh, and the emirs in Abu Dhabi. I know you all believe that if we Americans try to take Dabiq, we will be giving Khalif and his men exactly what they want—a reason to call even more Muslims into the jihad against the infidels of 'Rome.' So given this unanimous opinion that it would be more prudent to have a joint Sunni Arab Muslim force handle the attack on Dabiq, I can support this approach. Therefore, I'll lead a Delta strike on Alqosh. Let's just pray the president is still breathing and that one group or the other can find him and bring him back alive."

I glanced at Yael and at Ari, who was sitting to her left. Both seemed pleased with the decision, as was I, but Ramirez wasn't finished. He explained that the vice president was about to address the nation in a live televised broadcast from the White House Situation Room. The goal was to comfort a country rattled by the events of recent days and to explain the American government's intended course of action.

First, Holbrooke was going to explain his official role as acting president under the current circumstances.

Second, he was going to say that while he had no constitutional authority to require the American people to convert to Islam, he certainly personally had a great deal of respect for "this religion of peace."

Third, Holbrooke was going to say that his military advisors had examined options for trying to rescue the president but had ruled all of them out. He would say the Pentagon was not clear on where the president was being held at the moment and that weather conditions in the region prevented any serious effort to move forward with such a plan, even if one existed.

Fourth, he was going to explain that he was in the process of recalling Congress to pass emergency legislation that would authorize him to transfer several hundred billion dollars to the numbered account in Switzerland designated by the Islamic State. However, he would add that even if the legislation passed, he would not sign it in his role as acting president unless ISIS offered incontrovertible proof that President Taylor was still alive.

"It's all a ruse, of course," Ramirez said. "Under no circumstances is the vice president going to transfer more than $300 billion to a terrorist organization. Nor would Congress authorize such a transfer in the first place. But we've got to create the impression that he is open to capitulating to at least some of Khalif's demands. So members of the House and Senate will start flying back to Washington. The White House will whip up a media feeding frenzy over the possible imminent transfer of the funds. The VP will summon the Speaker of the House, the Senate majority leader, and the minority leaders of both houses of Congress to the White House within the hour. Drafts of the proposed legislation will be leaked. The treasury secretary will confer with the Fed chairman, and so forth—all to buy as much time as possible."

"I'm not convinced Khalif will fall for it," said Prince Marwan, his voice strained and hoarse. He was barely able to lift his head off his chest.

"I'm not sure there's another way," Prince Feisal weighed in, perhaps sparing the king from having to.

The Egyptian general then spoke. "We are presently about five hundred kilometers—more than three hundred miles—from Dabiq." El-Badawy clicked a button and brought up a map on the main screen over His Majesty's left shoulder as he spoke. "We're nearly eight hundred kilometers—some five hundred miles—from Alqosh. It would typically take about an hour's flying time to Dabiq, and about an hour and twenty minutes to Alqosh. The X factor right now is the weather. At the moment, the situation outside is so bad that neither General Ramirez nor I believe it is wise to put any planes or choppers in the air. But the meteorologists are telling us we should have a window where things are slightly improved in about four or five hours, and we expect to launch then. In the meantime, we'll work with our men, update them on the changes, brief them on the latest intel, and answer their questions. But first, are there questions from any of you?"

Four or five hours? I glanced at the clocks on the wall behind the king. It was already several minutes past seven in the evening. There were fewer than eleven hours until the deadline. With an hour to an hour-and-a-half flight—perhaps significantly longer because of the weather, even if things did improve slightly—El-Badawy was saying the strikes wouldn't even begin until two or two thirty in the morning. Wasn't that cutting things awfully close? Then again, what more could they do? If Mother Nature didn't cooperate, all these plans could be for naught.

"Seeing none, then I respectfully give the floor back to His Majesty and just want to say what an honor it will be for me to lead this joint Arab operation. May Allah grant us favor and a great and resounding victory."

At this, the king rose from his seat. We all followed suit, save Prince Marwan, of course, who appeared to me to be in great pain and in deep emotional anguish over everything that was happening to his country and to the region. I suddenly felt a renewed pang of guilt for ever having doubted his fealty to the king or the kingdom and hoped he never found out what I'd said to Agent Harris when my own loyalties were being attacked.

"Dr. Shalit and Dr. Katzir, I want to thank you and your government for your immense help," the king said. "The world may not know for many years—or perhaps ever—what a significant role you have played in helping your Sunni Arab neighbors and the Americans prepare for this moment. Especially because I have no intention of letting Mr. Collins go on either of these missions or write about any of these matters going forward. But *I* know. And each of the men in this room knows. And I think your involvement is a testament to the tremendous good that can be done when neighbors work together despite their real and deep and many differences. And I want to personally thank you, in the presence of all these gathered."

Ari and Yael bowed slightly to acknowledge the king's gracious words. But I was livid.

"Your Majesty, may I say something?" I asked, restraining myself as best I could.

"Not right now, Mr. Collins. We don't have time."

"But, Your Majesty, I really must insist you let me cover American forces going into battle to rescue an American president."

"Sorry, Mr. Collins," the king replied. "The answer is no."

"Why the sudden change?" I pressed. "You brought me here to make sure the world had an unbiased view of what was happening."

"The situation has changed."

"I don't see how it has."

"The unanimous view of every single person in this room says it has," the king replied slowly and firmly.

I was about to protest further, to insist they embed me with the Delta team, but as I scanned the faces around the table, I could see there was no point. There wasn't a sympathetic gaze in the bunch. I sensed that Ari was about to say something, but I was certain it was an intelligence matter, nothing to support my case.

But the king was not finished. "There is one piece of unfinished business to which I must attend," he said, turning his attention to Yael. "Dr. Katzir?"

"Yes, Your Majesty?"

"I have a favor to ask of you."

"I am at your service, Your Majesty," she replied.

"Is that a yes?"

"Of course."

"Very well," said the king. "I would like you to accompany General Ramirez and his forces to Alqosh."

348 ★ THE FIRST HOSTAGE

I did a double take.

"I beg your pardon?" Yael asked, her countenance betraying that she was as surprised by the king's request as I was.

"You know more about that town, that compound, and the chemical weapons that are stored there than any person in this room," the king explained. "I realize, of course, that it would be politically unwise to have an Israeli Mossad officer formally participating in the invasion of an Iraqi village, especially launching from Jordanian soil. But at my request, General Ramirez is prepared to make you an honorary American for the night. He will give you a uniform to wear and a weapon to fight with, and you'll be at his side for the entire operation."

My stomach clenched. I turned to Yael. The whole room was staring at her. The blood was draining from her face. I knew what she was thinking. She'd thought she was through with all this. She'd done her part; she was finished. She had no intention of going into battle. She just wanted to go back to Tel Aviv and take a nice hot bath and a long, well-deserved break. I could see it in her eyes, in the way her whole body tensed.

That's what I wanted for her too. At the very least, I wanted her at my side here in the war room as we tracked the latest developments in Alqosh and Dabiq. I was still hoping to write dispatches on the operations that were about to unfold, and who better than her to help me make sense of what exactly was happening and its significance? The thought of her going back into harm's way physically sickened me, as I'm sure it did her, especially after the conversation we'd just had, and I was proud of her for her ability to respectfully decline the king's invitation. She'd certainly earned her right to say, "No thank you."

But that's not what she said.

"I'd be honored to, Your Majesty," she said instead.

"Thank you," the king said. "Then it's settled."

"Not quite," Yael added.

"What do you mean?"

"I mean I would be honored to go, but only on one condition."

The room was dead silent. Ari turned and looked at her, as did we all. The king's poker face remained unruffled, but surely rare were the times the king's request for someone to go into battle was met with a condition.

"A condition, you say?"

"Yes, Your Majesty."

"And what would that be?"

"I will only go if Mr. Collins here is permitted to go as well."

PART
FOUR

54

★ ★ ★

EN ROUTE TO ALQOSH, IRAQ

"What if we're wrong?"

My question hung in the air. No one wanted to touch it. Not Yael. Not Colonel Sharif. Certainly not any of the Delta operators around us. And I have no idea why I asked it. Nerves, I guess. It was a pointless question, foolish to ask. If the president wasn't in Alqosh when we arrived, we could only hope he was in Dabiq. And if he wasn't in Dabiq either, then he was not long for this world.

The more important question, the one I should have been asking, was whether either team could get to its target in time. I pulled out my grandfather's pocket watch and wiped away the condensation on its face. It was now 5:02 a.m. The deadline was less than an hour away. The fate of the president hung in the balance, and even if by some miracle he was still alive, I didn't see how either team was ever going to reach him by six.

Nothing had been going according to the plan Generals Ramirez and El-Badawy had mapped out. Starting just after midnight, we'd sat at the end of runway 17R at the Muwaffaq Salti Air Base in Azraq, cooped up in a freezing-cold C-130 Hercules with four more troop transport planes lined up behind us, all battered by gale-force winds and hail the size of golf balls, all waiting for hours for clearance from the tower that I soon feared would never come. Finally, around three thirty, our captain came over the intercom and told us we had a narrow window. The hail had stopped. The winds had dipped somewhat. The meteorologists and the guys in the tower couldn't promise we'd make it to Alqosh. But they were unanimous: as bad as conditions were at that moment, they were as good as they were likely to get. If we didn't take off right then, we never would. So the pilots revved the plane's four turboprops to max power and we hurtled down the runway into the dark and cold of night.

Now we'd been in the air for just over ninety minutes, on a route typically flown by Royal Jordanian flight 822—usually an Airbus 320—from Amman to Erbil. By my calculations we were only a few minutes out, which meant the most terrifying moment of this operation—to me, at least—was coming up fast. We were about to do a HAHO jump into the storm.

HAHO was special ops talk for a high altitude, high opening parachute drop. In covering the American military over the years, I'd heard of them, of course. But I'd never expected to do one. I'd never jumped out of a plane at any altitude. Nor, frankly, had I ever even seriously considered it. When Yael got me into this operation and I'd signed six pages of legal waivers (three for the Americans and three for the Jordanians), no one had said anything about this. But Sharif had made my role clear.

"Mr. Collins, fate and Allah have brought us together for this moment, a moment much larger than any of us or our countries. We've said yes to you being an embedded reporter. You've done it lots of times before. You've got plenty of experience. But this isn't going to be like any of those other times. The good news is that when it's over, the king wants you to tell the world the truth. Exactly what happened. And exactly how. In the meantime, keep your head down and don't do anything stupid, like get yourself killed."

On the one hand, I was thrilled that the king had evidently changed his mind and was now going to let me do my job and not just observe but actually report on the things I was observing. On the other hand, I was starting to realize just how dangerous this mission really was.

Suddenly I felt the plane descending. I glanced at the altimeter strapped around my left wrist like a watch. It was dropping fast. A moment ago we'd been flying at 42,000 feet. Now we were at 34,000 and still descending.

Yael shouted something at me. But I could barely hear over the roar of the propellers and the intensity of the storm, which might have been another reason no one had answered my question a few minutes earlier. Maybe no one had even heard me.

We were all suited up for the jump, wearing

insulated jumpsuits, gloves, and boots to protect us from the subzero temperatures at this altitude. We were also, of course, wearing special helmets, goggles, and oxygen tanks in addition to the rest of our gear—from bulletproof vests to ammo belts and grenades—since there wasn't exactly a lot of air to breathe at such heights. The noise and the helmets and the cold and the constant shaking and rattling of the plane lumbering through the storm had made for a long and lonely journey. We'd said hardly a word to each other. We'd all been alone with our own thoughts and fears and questions, and now the moment of truth had finally arrived.

We were now at 31,000 feet.

30,000.

29.

28.

27.

Yael again shouted something at me, but I still couldn't hear her. We were all wearing comms gear but maintaining strict radio silence. Finally she stood and motioned for me to do so as well. I saw Colonel Sharif and the others getting up as well, so I followed suit. Then Yael motioned for me to turn around; when I did, she turned on my oxygen supply.

Ramirez moved to the back of the plane and held up two fingers. Two minutes to go. I was terrified. I hadn't admitted as much to anyone, of course, not even Yael when she'd finally told me how we'd be getting to our target. To begin with, I didn't think she'd believe me. I was sure she'd tell me the gun battle at the palace and the harrowing race to the airport had been much more dangerous. She'd also tell me I was far more likely to die in the imminent battle for Alqosh than by parachute failure. And I was sure she'd be right. But aside from claustrophobia, there was one primal terror I'd long and carefully avoided at all costs: heights.

The rear ramp of the plane began to open, and every muscle in my body tensed. One by one, the Delta operators gave a final check to their weapons and stepped into formation. Yael helped me put on my pack filled with almost fifty pounds of camera equipment, a chem-bio suit and related gear, bottles of water and PowerBars, and plenty more ammo to go with the MP5 strapped to my chest. I'd insisted I wasn't going to fight, of course. But Ramirez, who'd made it clear he didn't want me coming at all, had insisted that if I was going in with Delta, I had to be armed. In addition to the MP5, Ramirez had given me a .45-caliber Colt M1911A1 with a few extra seven-round magazines. When I protested that I was a journalist, not a combatant, the general had taken his case directly to the king, who in the end had sided with Ramirez, reminding me that I'd been armed at the palace, and that was likely the only reason—aside from the mercy of Allah—that I was still alive.

Sharif turned and attached his harness to mine. This was going to be a tandem jump. There'd been no time to train me. So we'd be strapped together on the way down. I'd be depending on his chute the whole way, though I had a reserve chute of my own—"just in case," as he put it. Not exactly the words I'd wanted to hear.

Ramirez held up one finger.

We were one minute out and stabilizing at 25,000 feet as the entire fuselage shuddered in the storm. The ramp in the back of the plane finished opening. I held the strap above me in a death grip and stared out into the utter darkness. I wondered what my mom was doing right then. Was she praying for me? Were Matt and Annie praying as well? I hoped so. I didn't know how to pray for myself. Part of me wanted to. After all, there was a very real chance I wasn't going to make it out of this thing alive. I knew that, and I was racked with fear over what would happen to me after I died. But I felt like a hypocrite. I hadn't "gotten right" with God. Matt had begged me to, but I couldn't. I just wasn't there. I didn't believe. Not like he did. Not yet. Maybe not ever. I still had too many questions, too many doubts. Yet as I stared into the void, five miles over northern Iraq, the last words Matt had said to me before I went into Iraq the last time rang in my ears.

"Are you ready, J. B.? Are you ready to die?"

The answer was still the same—no, I was not.

55

* * *

Ramirez jumped first.

Then one by one, his ODA—Operational Detachment Alpha—followed him off the ramp. That meant two teams of twelve men each, for a total of twenty-four Delta operators, plus three command-and-control men, a commander, a radio operator, and an Air Force CCT or combat controller. Yael followed them. And then it was just the colonel and me and the jumpmaster manning the controls by the ramp.

My heart was racing. My legs felt numb. My feet wouldn't move, so Sharif nudged me forward, closer and closer to the edge. There was no longer anything to hold on to. The wind was whipping around me. The rain had already soaked my jumpsuit, and though the plane was flying through thick, dark clouds, I could actually see flashes of light below me. At first, I wondered if the Air Force was dropping bombs. Then I realized it was lightning. The lightning was below us—and we were about to jump into it.

I held up my hand. I needed a moment to

gather my wits and reconcile myself with what was coming. This was now officially the craziest thing I'd ever considered doing, I decided, far worse than sneaking into Syria to find Jamal Ramzy. Sure, Yael had already jumped. But she'd been trained for it. For all I knew she loved jumping out of planes. Maybe she and her first love had done this on dates. But it was different for me. No matter what the stakes were. No matter what the story was. I was just a civilian. It wasn't the same for me. I just had to—

I never finished the thought. Before I realized what was happening, Sharif had kicked me in the back of the knees and launched us out of the plane. And then we were free-falling. Sharif was behind me, so I couldn't see the plane above us. I looked down but couldn't spot the Delta operators below us either. I couldn't see anything except the flashes of lightning. But I could feel the bone-chilling cold. I could hear the wind howling past my mask and helmet. I could feel my stomach in my throat and my heart pounding so hard in my chest I feared it was going to explode. It never occurred to me to check my altimeter and track my descent. It never occurred to me to check my watch and figure out when Sharif was going to pull the rip cord. My mind went totally blank. What few instructions Sharif and Yael had given me were completely gone.

Then my harness suddenly tightened around my armpits and crotch. My head snapped back. It felt like we were being jerked back into the sky above us. I craned my neck and caught a glimpse of the canopy above us. Sure enough, the chute had deployed. I'd never seen a more beautiful sight. We weren't free-falling anymore. We were still descending, of course, but not nearly so fast. Sharif was manipulating the cords to navigate our route and regulate our descent. As he did, my breathing began to slow a bit. So did my heart rate. I could think again.

I remembered what Sharif had told me—that we'd only be free-falling for ten to fifteen seconds. I remembered, too, what Ramirez had said about the whole point of the HAHO being to enter the airspace over Alqosh quickly, quietly, and covertly. With the odds stacked against us, our only chance of success—thirty-three men and one woman versus more than five hundred ISIS fighters—was to seize and maintain the element of surprise. We certainly couldn't afford to let the grumble of the C-130 tip off the jihadists who controlled the village. So we'd jumped almost forty miles out. By now, our plane had already turned back. There were choppers en route, about an hour behind us. They were coming for our exfiltration. There were fighter jets coming too, sooner than the choppers. But for the moment it wasn't safe for them to be anywhere near us. In that sense, the storm was actually helping us—at least we hoped it was—providing low cloud cover to obscure our arrival and plenty of thunder and rain to muffle what little sound we would inevitably make.

Our route hadn't taken us all the way to the Kurdish capital of Erbil, of course. Instead, we'd flown about twenty kilometers north of Dohuk, then essentially done a hook so we'd be headed southwest along a range of mountains that led straight to Alqosh when we jumped. The big problem at the moment was the crosswind, which was whipping us around like rag dolls and had the very real potential, I feared, of blowing us far off course.

Sharif, like the others, had a GPS device strapped to his right arm. He was constantly making course corrections, and I knew I could trust his years of experience in Jordanian special forces. But our drop zone was narrow—precisely 36.735 degrees latitude and 43.096 degrees longitude—and there was no margin for error. To veer even slightly off course could put us dozens of kilometers from our ideal landing site, all of which would have to be made up by walking—more likely running—or could drop us right in the middle of Alqosh and the ISIS forces that controlled it. I knew all too well the stories my grandfather had written when he'd covered D-day for the Associated Press, stories of drops gone badly and untold numbers of American and Allied paratroopers spread out far from each other, behind enemy lines, with little chance of survival much less the chance to link back up with their own. I desperately didn't want to become one of those stories.

For more than twenty-five minutes, Sharif battled the winds, the rain, the lightning, and the cold, zigzagging north, then south, then back north again, trying to keep us on track for our landing site. At precisely 5:36 local time, we slipped under the clouds for the first time. My altimeter showed us at 1,700 feet and coming in red-hot. There were only twenty-four minutes to the deadline.

Just then Sharif tapped me on the back and pointed to the left. In the distance, at about ten o'clock, I could see the lights of a village. There weren't many, and they were faint, but was that it? Was that Alqosh? I didn't have a GPS, so I couldn't be sure. But a minute later—we were now at only 900 feet—Sharif gave me a thumbs-up. Before I knew it, he was kicking my boots. I was confused. That was the sign he'd prepped me for that it was time to land. But at still so high, I thought maybe I'd misunderstood. Then he kicked me again, more urgently this time, and suddenly we were smashing into the side of a mountain.

I was caught unprepared; my feet weren't up when we hit, and I stumbled forward and hit the rocks face-first, pulling the colonel down on top of me. Fortunately, my helmet, goggles, and shin guards took the worst of the impact, but the real problem was that we weren't stopping. The winds were so fierce that we were being dragged along the ridge with no way to self-arrest. The rains were so intense that the granite was too slippery to gain a foothold, and what little topsoil there was so close to the summit had turned to mud. For several hundred yards, we bounced and crashed and scraped across the ridgeline, ripping gashes in my hands and face, tearing my jumpsuit, and slicing up my knees. Rain and blood were streaming down my face, and in the fog I could see almost nothing. I was in unbearable pain now and experiencing near vertigo as we blew and toppled forward like tumbleweeds. I had no idea what to do or how to stop. And then I saw the edge of a cliff surging toward us.

I remember this question flashing across my mind at that moment: *Can I grab something and hold on before we go plunging over the edge, or are we better off going over the edge anyway, since at least we have a parachute?* But no sooner had I thought it than we came skidding to an excruciating and abrupt stop, not thirty yards from the edge.

I lay there facedown in the mud and gravel, in searing pain but suddenly motionless and on solid ground after hours in the air. It took me a moment to catch my breath and look up. But when I finally did, I saw Sharif maybe five yards from the cliff edge, beginning to crawl back toward me. In his right hand he held a bowie knife that glinted in the intermittent flashes of lightning, and it dawned on me what had happened. He'd cut me loose from him, then cut himself loose from the parachute, and in so doing he had almost certainly saved both our lives.

"You okay?" he asked, putting the knife away and scrambling over to me.

"I think so," I lied.

"Nothing's broken?"

I moved my arms and legs, then my fingers and toes. Then I rolled over, sat up, and wiped the blood and mud from my goggles. To my surprise, despite the pain, I hadn't broken anything.

When I shook my head, Sharif grabbed my hand and pulled me to my feet. "That was a close one," he said with a smile, wiping blood and mud from his face and goggles as well.

"Certainly was."

"But you're sure you're okay."

"My arm's killing me."

"Which one?"

"Left."

"The gunshot?"

"Yeah."

"Here, I'll give you something for it." He pulled off his backpack and fished around a bit until he found a first aid kit. Then he gave me some painkillers and a bottle of water to wash them down. "What else?" he asked.

"My knees," I said.

We looked down and found my knee pads were gone. There were enormous tears in my fatigues on both my left and right knees, revealing bloody gashes smeared with pebbles and dirt. Sharif found some rubbing alcohol and tweezers in the first aid kit and did his best in the fog and rain to clean my wounds, apply some antibiotic cream to them, and then bind them up with gauze pads and duct tape. A moment later, he found another pair of knee pads in his pack and helped me put them on.

It was clear I needed stitches and just as clear it wasn't going to happen anytime soon.

56

"Gentlemen, we need to move."

I turned as General Ramirez and the rest of his men came up behind us, weapons at the ready. They didn't stop to chat. They were double-timing it to the peak of this ridge, about fifty or sixty yards away. Yael brought up the rear.

"You guys okay?" she asked.

"I'll be fine," Sharif said. "This guy got pretty banged up, but I think he'll pull through."

"You're a mess," she said to me.

I agreed but waved it off and asked if she was okay. She said she was fine, just a bit winded, and I was relieved to see she didn't look any worse for wear. As we scrambled together to the top, she explained that most of the group had landed quite a ways down the slope and had to hustle to regroup.

It was now 5:47. We had only thirteen minutes.

I was moving the slowest, but Yael and the colonel helped me to the top of the ridge, where we found the Delta team on their stomachs, peering down into the village below. Sharif turned on his night-vision goggles and pulled a pair of high-powered binoculars from his pack. A moment later, he handed them to Yael, who looked briefly and handed them to me.

Looking through the binoculars, I could see the compound on the north side of the village. It was no more than five hundred yards down the other side of this ridge. I could see the warehouse where the terrorists were storing the chemical weapons. And about 150 yards to the west, I could see the crumbling mausoleum built around Nahum's tomb. It all seemed so quiet and surreal, hardly noticeable and certainly not an obvious threat to the uninitiated like myself.

But then I spotted the cage. Beside it were a video camera on a tripod and several TV lights on stands. I saw twelve or fifteen armed men wearing black hoods milling about. The president was not in sight, but I feared he might be soon.

"Okay, men, turn on your comms," Ramirez whispered, and his men relayed the message up and down the line.

I fumbled a bit in the darkness to find the switch, but Yael helped me and made sure the volume was set correctly.

"We good? Everyone on?" Ramirez asked over his whisper mic.

"Five by five," came the unanimous reply.

"Cracker Jack, Lucky, you guys have a shot?" Ramirez asked his snipers.

Both men said yes, and Ramirez took another moment to size up the situation. Ramirez's second in command would lead the Red Team to the warehouse. Ramirez would lead the Blue Team to the compound. The colonel, Yael, and I had already been ordered to stick with the Blue Team and help guard their flanks.

"Okay, you know what you've got to do," the general said at last. "Let's move."

Before I'd even gotten to my feet, the two teams were on the move and racing down the southern slope with impressive agility. But soon I was up and moving too. Yael took point. I was in the middle. The colonel had our backs. My injured knees were on fire, but once we started down the mountain, there was no stopping.

The problem was, it was pitch-black. It's hard to describe just how dark it was. With thick cloud cover, there was no moonlight whatsoever. We still had maybe thirty or forty minutes until dawn began to break. There were no streetlights in the village below and no lights on yet in the main compound where we hoped the president was. Nor were there any lights on in the warehouse. This meant we all had our night-vision goggles on. But whereas everyone else was used to running with them on, I was not. As such, I was losing ground to Yael and stumbling often. Several times I tripped over rocks or slipped in the mud and came close to sliding down the mountain. But what worried me most was falling and accidentally making a sound that could draw attention to the team's approach. Fortunately, each time I stumbled, Sharif grabbed my arm and kept me from slipping. Pretty quickly he decided to stay by my side rather than behind to make sure I remained on my feet.

Ninety seconds later, Yael, the colonel, and I had made it down the slope. I was sucking air into my burning lungs as fast as I could, but I still had another two hundred yards across relatively flat ground before I reached the large stone wall on the north side of the compound and the iron gates that led into the driveway. The Blue Team was already there, and they weren't waiting for us. They were scaling the walls. Remarkably, they still hadn't been detected. By now I'd expected the shooting to begin. So far it had not. When I finally reached the wall and peered through the gates, I saw why. Ramirez's snipers had taken out four guards and hadn't made a sound.

There was no way I was going to make it over that wall. But Ramirez had already planned for that. He'd given Colonel Sharif plenty of Semtex and an order to blow the gates off their hinges at the first opportunity. Yael took one side of the gate. I took the other. Together we made sure no one could come around the corner and shoot us from behind. Then came the explosion that told the whole village we were here.

The force of the blast was deafening, and I could feel the heat scorching the back of my neck. I'd stood too close and was grateful I hadn't been hit by any of the shrapnel. For a moment my ears were ringing and I couldn't hear a thing. But then it was as if the volume had been turned back up and I heard automatic gunfire inside the main building. Soon it intensified and spread through two separate wings. And then, on cue, I could hear the high-pitched scream of an incoming missile.

"Hit the deck!" Yael shouted, but it was too late.

The second explosion—far more powerful than the first—lifted me off my feet and sent me hurtling through the air. I landed on my side, rolled for a bit, and couldn't have been more grateful when I not only was alive but still hadn't even broken anything.

I was in the thick of the action. And according to the wristwatch I'd been issued for the mission it was 5:58. The drone strike on the town's only cell tower, located just across the street, had come right on time, just like we'd been briefed back on the air base. The raid was unfolding like clockwork.

I dusted myself off, scooped up my MP5 again, and peered into the darkness. So far no one was coming my way. But I could hear people shouting. The voices were angry, confused, and all in Arabic. Down the driveway and toward the west side of town, lights were coming on in house after house, building after building. Then I heard Yael and the colonel calling for me to follow them. I made one last check of my sector, reported we were clear, and headed into the compound. The sounds of automatic gunfire filled the night.

As I raced through the smoking gates and across the muddy courtyard, I could see through several of the windows the brilliant flash of stun grenades going off, followed by more gunfire and the shrieks of dying men. And then I heard one of the Delta operators say something over the radio that chilled me to my core.

"POTUS isn't here."

57

"What do you mean he isn't here?" Ramirez shouted over the radio.

"We've cleared the north wing, sir," one of his commandos reported. "We've got nothing."

Ramirez then demanded a status check from the men clearing the south wing. He got the same reply. They'd checked every bedroom, every closet, every stairwell, every bathroom, every storage area and crawl space, and they hadn't found Taylor.

"What about Khalif?" Ramirez demanded.

One by one his men radioed back that there was no sign of him.

I heard the general order his men to keep looking as Yael and I burst through the front doors of the main house. Sharif was right behind us. Dead ISIS jihadists lay everywhere. Shards of glass littered the blood-soaked floor. The terrorists' weapons—Kalashnikovs, pistols of various types, and several RPGs, along with thousands of rounds of ammunition and rather sophisticated communications gear—had been stripped from them and were in a pile on the dining room table. Two

Delta operators had taken up defensive positions at the living room and dining room windows, all of which had been blown out in the attack. They occasionally fired into the night and fog, trying to keep the ISIS reinforcements at bay while their commander figured out our next move.

Ramirez was pacing in the kitchen and talking on a satellite phone. I could tell he was briefing the king and the commanders back in the war room on the latest developments, and I picked up bits and pieces of his side of the conversation. But the staccato bursts of gunfire made it difficult to catch much.

It wasn't just these operators near me who were shooting and being shot at, after all. Across the street I could still hear a ferocious gun battle going on at the warehouse. I'd heard no radio traffic from the Red Team yet. That could mean only one thing: they were still locked in a brutal fight for control of the chemical weapons. Was it possible the president was being held there? Could Khalif be there too?

When the general saw us enter, he signaled Sharif to take up a position at the front door and make sure no one we didn't know made it inside. Then he waved Yael and me to come to the kitchen. Stepping over the bodies and shards of glass, we made our way from the large entryway toward the kitchen. For such a small village, this was a rather sprawling villa; I wondered who had first built it and who owned it now. Each room was spacious—not palatial, but more than comfortable for even a large family. The chairs and sofas were old and worn. The carpets were not only threadbare but now freshly covered with muddy bootprints. The light fixtures were as dusty as they were outdated. A grand piano stood in one corner of the living room, but it looked like it hadn't been touched in ages.

We entered the large kitchen and found appliances and dishes that looked like they dated back to the seventies. It was clear that whoever owned the place had once had a great deal of money. Yet somewhere along the way that money had apparently dried up and the place was now a shadow of its former glorious existence. How recently had Khalif and his men seized it? I wondered. And had the owners surrendered it willingly, or had they been murdered?

Just then the radio crackled to life. I heard the voice of the Red Team leader. He said they were encountering much stiffer resistance than expected. They'd secured the perimeter of the warehouse along with the main floor. But they'd discovered that the facility had two lower levels, something the intel briefing hadn't revealed. The lower levels, he said, were accessible by one of two freight elevators. There were also two stairwells, one at each end of the building. But with four points of entry to cover with only a dozen men, plus the need to protect the main floor from ISIS reinforcements, they needed backup, and fast.

"They're on their way," the general radioed back. "Stand by one."

I fully expected Ramirez to send Yael, Sharif, and me, especially since Sharif was a full colonel with plenty of combat experience and Yael was the chemical weapons expert of the bunch. We all knew she was anxious to see exactly what Khalif had on location, how much, and whether the sarin gas precursors had already been mixed and loaded into mortars and artillery shells and were ready to be fired. But that would have violated the general's strict rule that we were to remain with him at all times. So he ordered the two commandos in the living and dining rooms to hightail it over to the warehouse and "get this thing locked down." Then he turned to Yael and me. "Get to those windows and shoot at anything that moves. Collins, you always wanted to be in the Army. Don't let us down."

My heart was pounding and my palms were sweaty as I moved to the dining room window. I couldn't dry them off on my pants because I was soaked to the bone. The winds were driving the rains inside the villa through the blown-out windows, and everything was soaked. Yael reminded me to put more resin on my hands to keep my weapon from slipping.

I grabbed some from my pocket and followed her advice—and just in time. The night lit up with a spray of gunfire. I ducked away from the window and pressed myself against the wall. When the shooting paused for a split second, I pivoted around the wall, aimed my MP5 into the darkness, and squeezed the trigger in three short bursts. Then I pulled back and waited for the return fire, which came an instant later. In fact, it sounded louder if that was possible. The jihadists were advancing.

Again I pivoted around the corner and fired three short bursts. Then I ducked back and tried to steady my breathing. I glanced at Yael. I saw her open fire again and then pause to reload. As she did, she motioned for me to put my night-vision goggles back on. They were affixed to my helmet, so I could flip them down into place or flip them up so I could see normally. I'd flipped them up upon entering the kitchen, since a small lamp was on and several candles were burning next to the stove, illuminating the general's laminated map of Alqosh and floor plans of the compound. I quickly flipped the goggles back in place and turned to fire again.

What I saw terrified me. At least four and possibly five armed men were climbing over the eastern security wall not fifty yards from me. When they dropped to the ground, they'd be coming right at me. To my right, at least as many terrorists were scaling the fence closer to Yael. Two were already firing at her. I could see the flashes pouring out of their barrels. There was nothing I could do to help her, so I aimed at the men in my sector, pulled the trigger, and shouted for Ramirez to come help. I felled one jihadist instantly. I downed a second but he wasn't dead. He screamed in pain and started crawling back to his weapon. So I pulled the trigger again, but this time nothing happened. My magazine was empty, and three more jihadists had just cleared the wall.

I ducked back out of the window and against the wall, ejected the spent magazine, and fumbled in the darkness to reload. As I did, Ramirez rushed to my side, his MK 17 SCAR assault rifle in hand. He opened up with four quick bursts. I finished reloading and pivoted back around the corner to help, but it was immediately apparent the general had finished off everyone in the yard, including several of the terrorists trying to charge Yael. Then he let go of his weapon, letting it dangle at his side, grabbed a grenade, pulled the pin, and threw it over the wall. The flash was blinding. The boom was deafening. But the effect was decisive. We heard screaming for a few moments, and then all was silent save the gun battle behind us in the warehouse.

Just then, six Delta operators converged in the living room and called for Ramirez's attention. One of them explained that they had left the rest of their men firing at ISIS forces from bedrooms in the north and south wings of the building. The general ordered three of them to replace Yael, Sharif, and me, and the other three to head up to the second floor and take defensive positions there. Then he motioned us to follow him down a dark hallway in the north wing. We did as we were told and quickly found ourselves in what looked like it had once been a master bedroom that had been converted into a communications center. There were no beds or dressers but rather tables lined with shortwave radio equipment, laptops, printers, satellite phones, and open cases of video cameras, lights, and sound gear. There were also three dead bodies on the floor and blood splattered everywhere.

"When you and your team were surveilling

this compound, did you see ISIS forces moving back and forth between here and the warehouse?" Ramirez asked Yael.

"No, not really," she said. "Why?"

"Doesn't that seem odd?"

"What do you mean?"

"This was clearly the headquarters," Ramirez said. "I suspect Khalif spent most of his time in here and in the adjoining room over there."

He led us through a bathroom to another room, which no doubt had also once been a bedroom. It, too, had been cleared of beds and anything else domestic. Instead, there were several card tables set up, a half-dozen wooden chairs and stools, three additional laptops, a printer, a television set, a large map of Amman on one wall, and a blown-up satellite photograph of Dabiq on another wall. The second map had several buildings marked, including the elementary school. There were also two dead bodies on the floor, clearly recent casualties of the Delta raid.

"Doesn't it seem odd to you that Khalif and his closest advisors never went over to the warehouse, never checked on the progress of the weapons?" he asked. "Never? Not at all?"

"I guess so, yeah," Yael replied.

"Unless we're missing something," Ramirez said.

"Like what?" Colonel Sharif asked.

And then I got it.

"A tunnel."

58

★ ★ ★

Ramirez raced for the main stairwell with Yael, Sharif, and me right on his heels.

We headed to the basement, weapons drawn. My heart was racing. But my hopes were fading fast. The longer the president wasn't found, the more likely it was that he was dead or in the process of being killed, or at least being dragged away to another building by forces tipped off by the initial shooting and explosions—if he was here at all. And we still didn't know.

At this point, the only possible clue was the armed men in black hoods who had been gathered around the cage and video camera and lights at Nahum's tomb, just down the road, a few hundred meters from where we were now. Had they been preparing for the president? Or had they simply been planning to kill other hostages they captured and post the footage on YouTube?

Ramirez took point, gun at the ready, and motioned for us to check the rooms behind him on each side of the hallway. Yael took the rooms on the left. I was to search those on the right. Sharif kept our backs.

As I entered the first room, a small bedroom, the MP5 in my hands was shaking. It seemed unlikely to the point of being impossible that the Delta team—with all their training and experience—could have missed any terrorists who were hiding down here, much less the president. But could it be possible that in the darkness and the rush of battle the general's men had missed the entrance to some kind of makeshift tunnel leading to the warehouse across the street or anywhere else? Probably not. In any other circumstances I would have bet everything I had against it. But the truth was, we were down here because their boss thought it very well might be possible after all. So, night-vision goggles on, I was now looking under the beds, behind dressers, under carpets, and in the backs of closets.

I found nothing in the first room, so I moved into the hall and into the room next door and repeated the process. As I did, I couldn't decide whether I wanted Ramirez to be right or not. If he was right, we might find the president after all. But we might also stumble across one or more jihadists ready to shoot or butcher us.

"Clear," I heard Yael shout from across the hallway.

"Clear," I shouted back, referring to the first room, and a few moments later I repeated it to account for the second room.

The next room on my side of the hallway was a rather large but absolutely filthy bathroom. To the right there was a bulky wooden vanity containing two dust-covered porcelain sink bowls along with two sets of rusty faucets. To the left was a shower stall overflowing with bags of trash and a separate bathtub filled with tools and building supplies. I saw bags of cement, boxes of nails, hammers, and numerous other things I didn't have time to identify. Straight ahead but in a small nook off to the right, I spotted a smashed porcelain toilet and a rusty bidet, neither of which had clearly been used in quite some time. The floor tiles were chipped and broken, and the room was cluttered with all kinds of odds and ends, from an old bicycle to mildewed wooden crates containing empty glass bottles to soiled clothes and other random items—everything, that is, except an opening to a tunnel.

"*Clear,*" I yelled again, coming back into the hallway and hearing Yael shout the same.

Sharif was still in the hallway, watching our backs. But Ramirez wasn't. Instead, he had just finished clearing the last bedroom on Yael's side—a rather generous room with three rows of dilapidated bunk beds on one side and two more on the other. Now he was meticulously scouring a storage area on my side of the hallway. His night-vision goggles were off, and he was using a flashlight. Yael came alongside me as I watched the general getting more and more frustrated. He was yelling. He was still quite controlled, but his body language made it clear he was growing angry and perhaps not a little bit frantic.

"No luck?" I asked, turning to Yael.

She shook her head. "Same with you?"

"Yeah—what are we missing?"

"I don't know."

The gun battle at street level was intensifying. The sounds were muffled, but I could tell things were heating up. And it wasn't hard to figure out why. Dawn was about to break over the plains of Nineveh. The storm was dissipating. The winds were beginning to push the system off to our east. The sky was starting to brighten ever so slightly. And every minute that passed made our situation more precarious. The entire village now knew the Americans had arrived, and they knew precisely where we were. Any fighter who had been asleep ten minutes earlier was now awake, dressed, armed, and heading our way. What wasn't clear yet—but would be soon—was whether any calls or other communications had gotten to ISIS forces in Mosul before the drone took out the cell tower. If so, thousands of fighters could be here in the next fifteen to twenty minutes.

A series of explosions shook the foundations of the house. It almost felt like an earthquake, but as I steadied myself against one wall and pieces of Sheetrock fell from the ceiling, Yael said that was the sound of the U.S. Air Force dropping their ordnance on ISIS reinforcements who apparently were getting too close for comfort.

Then Ramirez started cursing up a storm and stomped back into the hallway. He didn't say a word to us. Instead, he began personally rechecking each of the rooms we had just checked ourselves, starting with Yael's. His desperation was palpable and growing, and what little hope I had was draining away fast. Yael offered to stand guard, but I don't think Ramirez heard her. I saw Colonel Sharif step into the first bedroom I'd checked back at the other end of the hallway, and I decided I couldn't just stand there doing nothing. So I started rechecking the rooms I'd just been through. It seemed ridiculous. There was nothing new to find. These rooms had no windows. They had no other doors besides the ones to the hallway. Their closets were small. I'd checked under beds and behind dressers and in every other conceivable place. I was sure I hadn't overlooked anything, but then I stepped back into the bathroom.

And something wasn't right. It's hard to explain. It's not that I saw anything new, but I felt something different. Call it a sixth sense, call it what you will, but I took off my night-vision goggles and started using the flashlight from my belt. Inch by inch, section by section, I reexamined everything—the shower stall, the tub, the toilet, even the bidet. All of it was dirty and disgusting, and I soon began to realize it stank as well, though I couldn't quite place the source of the stench. This time through I noticed there were dead flies everywhere and various insects crawling about. But when I got back to the rusty, filthy double sink, I just stood there and stared. A layer of plaster dust covered everything, and there was more dust lingering in the air now that the fighter jets were dropping five-thousand-pound bombs on our next-door neighbors. But there was something else.

Slowly, carefully, thoroughly, I shone the flashlight over every centimeter of that vanity. I was racking my brain for what was bothering me, but I still couldn't place it. I could hear Ramirez tearing up the other rooms, convinced we were missing the obvious. And then the light caught something on the floor, at the base of the vanity. At first I thought it was just a few pieces of chipped tiles, but as I stooped down to examine it more closely—and poked a bit with my gloved left hand—it began to dawn on me that I was looking at drops of blood. They weren't fresh drops, as if they'd been left here a few minutes earlier. But the spots weren't completely dry either. They were tacky, sticky, like the blood I'd found in the hallway of that bombed-out apartment building back in Homs. These drops weren't more than a few hours old.

I examined the section of the floor in front of the vanity more closely. Everything looked different without the night-vision goggles on. What had previously appeared as streaks of mud I could now see were deep black scrapes in the tiles in two parallel lines, about a meter apart.

"Yael, come here," I whispered, not wanting to attract the general's attention yet.

"What is it?" she asked, coming to the door of the bathroom.

"I'm not sure, but would you hold this for a moment?" I asked as I handed her the flashlight.

"Sure. Why?"

I didn't reply. Not immediately. Instead, I moved my machine gun so it was hanging down my back and wasn't in my way. Then I had Yael shine the flashlight at the base of the large vanity, pulled my gloves on a little tighter, and reached out and grabbed both sides of the wooden base of the sink. Then slowly, cautiously, and as quietly as I could, I started to pull. To my astonishment, it wasn't heavy or difficult. To the contrary, the entire sink pulled away from the wall rather easily. I expected the pipes connected to the back wall of the bathroom to stop my progress any moment. But the pipes weren't connected at all. And when I'd pulled the whole thing completely away from its base and pushed it over beside the shower stall, Yael and I found ourselves staring at a hole in the floor roughly four feet by two or three feet, with a wooden ladder going down at least twenty feet.

59

★ ★ ★

I was about to call to the general when a voice crackled over the radio.

"We have a man down. I repeat, we have a man down."

It wasn't immediately apparent to me who was speaking. I didn't know each of these men well enough to recognize their voices. But I could hear the stress in this voice, whoever it was, and the cacophony of gunfire and grenades going off non-stop was clearly audible over the radio. From this I deduced the transmission was coming from the warehouse.

Whoever it was gave no other details—no name, no rank, no description of how serious the injuries were or whether they were life-threatening. But before Ramirez or anyone else could ask, the same voice came over the radio with an update.

"Cancel that. We have a KIA on level two of the warehouse. I repeat, we have our first KIA. Request more backup if at all possible."

I couldn't believe it. I heard the words but couldn't process them. The heaviness in the voice sucked the wind out of me. A moment earlier I'd been so excited to find this tunnel. Now the angel of death had struck this little team for the first time, and I couldn't imagine how this death would be the last.

I heard the general racing down the hall and bounding up the stairs. At the same time he was asking for a status report on the battle inside the warehouse. I turned to Yael, but she shook her head, pointed back at the hole, immediately clicked off the flashlight, and put on her night-vision goggles. I did the same, then squatted and aimed my MP5 down the shaft. She didn't say it, but I knew she was telling me not to take my eyes off the hole under any circumstances. We had clearly found something we weren't supposed to find, and there was no telling who or what was down there. She slowly lowered herself into a crouch and positioned herself directly behind my right ear.

"I'm going to radio this in and get the colonel to cover us," she whispered. "And then I'm going in."

"Shouldn't we wait for backup?" I whispered.

I highly doubted she had experience in tunnel warfare. I certainly didn't. And Sharif—a trained commando who had served faithfully at King Abdullah's side for years—was in his forties, which was why he was now a spokesman. Surely there were two dozen men more qualified to do this than any of us.

But Yael was adamant. "There is no backup," she said without any trace of emotion.

"What are you talking about? There's got to be—"

But she quickly cut me off.

"Trust me, J. B.," she whispered with a level of intensity in her voice I'd never heard before. "The fight up top is getting worse. They can't spare anyone. We're it. Now make a space. I'm going in."

"Wait a moment," Sharif said from behind us. "I'll go."

I hadn't even heard him enter the bathroom.

"No, you stay here and stand guard," Yael said.

"You have no training for this," the colonel insisted. "I do."

"What, twenty years ago? Twenty-five? I appreciate it, Colonel—really, I do—but we don't have time to argue."

"You're right; we don't," he said. "So step aside. It's a dangerous job. A soldier's job. A man's job. You're brave, Dr. Katzir. But this is something I must do myself."

"Forget it," she shot back, though careful to keep her voice low. "I'm the smallest, and I'm the closest, and I'm going in. Now watch my six."

Before either of us could say another word, Yael slung her machine gun over her shoulder, took out an automatic pistol from the holster on her hip, and disappeared down the ladder even as she radioed the general and gave him a brief description of what we'd found and what she was doing.

I was impressed with her courage, and I could see from the look on Sharif's face he was too. But I was scared for her. Brave was one thing. Crazy was another. And I still thought it was crazy for her to do a job the Delta guys were eminently more qualified for.

Still, I couldn't argue with her logic. With the first of our team killed in action and the general calling in close air strikes, it was becoming clear to me we were in real danger of being overrun. If anyone could hold ISIS back, it was Delta, not Yael, Sharif, and myself. But that meant it fell to us to head into this tunnel and find out what was there.

I looked down the shaft and saw Yael position herself flat on her stomach, pistol out in front of her. She said nothing for a full minute. Then she looked up at me. "We're clear."

"There's no one there?"

"Not that I can see."

"Good, then get back up here."

"No," she said. "The tunnel curves to the left about twenty meters ahead. I need to go see what's up there. I'm going to scootch forward. You come down behind me."

"What?"

"You heard me. I need you."

"For what?"

"Backup. Now get down here, and bring your pistol."

So I pulled out the .45 Ramirez had given me, stepped around the vanity, and made my way down the ladder, heart pounding, sweat pouring down my forehead. I had no idea who or what I was about to find, and my claustrophobia was going crazy, especially when I reached the bottom. Sure enough, the tunnel ran in the direction of the warehouse. However, unlike smuggling tunnels I'd seen on the U.S.–Mexican border, or the ones in Homs, or the one I'd once been to under the DMZ on the thirty-eighth parallel between North and South Korea, all of which had been significantly wider, able to handle several people astride for hundreds of meters, this one was low and narrow in the extreme. At over six feet tall, there was no way I was going to be able to walk erect. Indeed, I gauged the height of the tunnel at no more than three or four feet, which meant I was actually going to have to crawl on my injured knees, and only a few feet wide, which meant I was already feeling cramped. That said, it had clearly been built by people who knew what they were doing. This wasn't a mine shaft from the California gold-rush era with dirt walls and wooden supports. This was made of concrete and actually had a lamp hanging on steel supports in the wall every fifteen or twenty feet, providing plenty of lighting.

I got down on my hands and knees and tried to steady my breathing, tried not to hyperventilate, tried to ignore the pain. I couldn't wait for long. Yael was already crawling forward, and I needed to follow. Every ten yards or so, we would stop, lie flat on our stomachs, weapons ready, catch our breath, and look again for signs of movement. But continuing to see none, we kept moving.

We made the first left and found that the tunnel did not exactly continue in a straight line. It zigzagged a bit, and at each turn I feared what we would find. But turn after turn, we found nothing. No terrorists. No president. No clues.

After six or seven minutes, we were surprised to come upon a T intersection. In front of us was a much larger tunnel, at least eight feet high, and significantly wider. It, too, was carefully constructed of steel and concrete, but unlike the narrower tunnel we'd just come through, this one had metal tracks, like railroad tracks, running down its center. They appeared to be tracks for mine carts, though I didn't see any at the moment. Then again, looking to my right, it was pitch-black. To my left, the new tunnel was much better lit than the tunnel we'd just come out of.

My grip on my pistol tightened. Claustrophobia was no longer the issue. I realized now that there was a very good chance we were going to encounter the enemy, and soon.

60

Yael put away her pistol.

Then she took off her night-vision goggles and used the scope of her MP5 to look down the well-lit portion of the tunnel. There wasn't anyone immediately apparent, but here again the tracks curved to the right and we had no idea what was around the bend. As she radioed a status report back to Ramirez, Sharif, and the others, I put away my .45, put my night-vision goggles on, and aimed my MP5 into the darkness behind us.

"Carts," I whispered when Yael had finished transmitting.

"What do you mean?" she said, her back still to me.

"Follow me," I said.

I began walking forward, my weapon at the ready, and the deeper I went into the darkness, the more mining carts I saw. Five, six, seven, ten, fifteen, twenty, thirty—in the end I counted fifty-one carts, leading all the way back to a cement wall, the end of the line. Moving cautiously toward the wall, fully expecting an ambush, I ducked behind the last cart and gave a quick glance inside. To my relief no one was there. Instead, I found at least a hundred artillery shells. I motioned for Yael to move up one side of the tracks. I took the other, each of us checking every other cart. When we came to the front of the line again, we examined the cargo in the first cart. Like each of the others, it contained a pile of shells, but as I looked more closely, I found that they were all marked with skulls and crossbones and the word *warning* in Arabic.

"These are M687s," Yael said.

"What's that?" I asked.

"It's a chemical weapon, a nerve agent," she said. "The M687 is an American design—a 155mm artillery shell with two canisters inside. The first contains one of the liquid precursors for sarin gas. The other canister holds the second. Between them is what's called a rupture disk. When the shell is fired at the enemy, the disk is breached and the two chemicals are mixed in flight. Then when the shell lands: *boom*, death—a very, very painful death for a whole lot of people."

"Did the U.S. ever use them?" I asked.

"Tested them but never used them in combat," she said. "They were eventually banned by the CWC—the Chemical Weapons Convention—and your government destroyed your stores. But the design has been knocked off by lots of different countries—and now by ISIS."

"They've got over five thousand of them here," I said, trying to imagine how many people ISIS could kill if they had the chance to actually use these weapons.

"They're stockpiling," Yael said.

"Why?"

"I don't know," she said. "Maybe to use. Maybe to sell. But either way . . ."

Yael didn't finish the sentence. She didn't have to. I realized both of us had left our backpacks containing our chem-bio suits back in the villa, in the living room. Yael radioed Ramirez to let him know what we'd found. Then she turned and continued toward the light. I followed.

We moved forward, Yael still on one side of the tracks and me on the other, and I suddenly noticed how eerily quiet it was. After the chaos on the surface, we were now at least twenty if not thirty feet belowground, and we could only barely hear the fight above us. Every now and then we'd get an update over our radios, but the bursts of information were few and far between and often in a military jargon that was lost on me. The only thing coming through loud and clear was that the team holding the villa was starting to worry about their supply of ammo, while the team assaulting the warehouse already had one KIA, three men injured, and no reinforcements on the way.

Just before we reached the bend in the track, Yael signaled for me to step behind her. As I did, we got the report that there'd been another KIA in the warehouse and two more injuries.

Yael pressed her back against the wall of the tunnel's right side. I was less than a yard behind her. As she inched forward, so did I. She shot a quick peek around the corner and then pulled back. She said nothing, but all the color was gone from her face.

"What is it?" I asked. "What's there?"

I waited a moment, but she couldn't respond. I asked her again, but she just shook her head. Her hands were quivering. She was taking deep breaths. I'd never seen her react this way, even in circumstances far more dangerous than this.

Slowly, cautiously, I moved around her, took a deep breath, then pivoted around the corner, ready to shoot. But now it was I who could not speak. I felt the blood instantly drain from my face as well, and my hands too began to shake.

There were no ISIS members waiting for us. There was no ambush. We were in no immediate mortal danger. But never in my life had I seen anything like this.

Partially decomposed bodies were hanging from the ceiling on each side of the tracks, their necks wrapped tightly in chains. I counted nineteen men and nineteen women, all of whom I guessed were in their forties and fifties, and twenty-seven children, both boys and girls, ranging in ages from maybe eleven or twelve up to perhaps eighteen or nineteen. But that wasn't the worst of it. Parked on the tracks were a dozen mine carts, and all of them were filled to overflowing with human heads.

For a moment I just stood there and stared, too stunned to think, too paralyzed to move. Then suddenly I turned and vomited all over the tracks near me, again and again until there was nothing left in my system. When my dry heaves finally ended and I had steadied myself against one of the walls, Yael handed me a bottle of water. I took some, swished it around in my mouth, and spit it back out. Then I took some more and swallowed and felt it burn the whole way down my throat. Only then did I notice that Yael had just finished vomiting too.

Wiping my mouth, I gripped my weapon and forced myself to keep moving. Yael started moving as well. Once again, she stayed on the right side of the tracks with me on the left. She picked up the pace, eager to get out of this house of horrors as quickly as possible, but I lagged behind. I tried not to look at the dangling corpses above us or the bulging eyes and gaping mouths of the heads stacked in the carts. As I kept my head down and eyes averted, I couldn't help but notice piles of debris running along each wall. Curious, I finally stopped and took a more careful look, and then I realized these weren't heaps of garbage. These were crosses and icons and Communion cups and Bibles and other holy books. And then I knew who these people were and why they had died such grisly and horrible deaths.

Shaken like I'd never been in my life, I, too, picked up the pace and caught up to Yael just as she was pivoting around another bend in the tracks. There were no bodies this time, nor even any carts. Nor were there any signs of ISIS fighters. But here the tracks and the tunnel began to tilt upward, and we started climbing back toward the surface.

Eventually we came to another bend in the tunnel, and again no one was immediately visible.

But there was something I hadn't expected: a large retractable steel door—almost like a garage door or a blast door—coming down from the ceiling and completely blocking our path. At the base of the door were two rectangular notches about three and a half feet apart that accommodated the rails. As we got closer, I noticed that there was also a smaller door built into the larger one that would permit a person to pass through while the larger door still blocked passage of the mine carts in either direction. Yael motioned for me to move to the right side of the smaller door. She moved to the left. Then she silently counted down from three with her fingers, turned the handle, and cautiously stepped through, her MP5 leading the way. I followed immediately and shut the door behind us.

We were now standing in the pitch dark. I quickly switched back to night-vision goggles, and when I did, I was aghast at what I saw. For here, against each wall—both on the left and right sides of the tracks—were metal cages. Inside each cage was either a young boy or young girl, ranging in age from maybe eight to no more than ten or eleven years old. They were naked, gaunt, and shivering. And now that they knew someone had just entered their hell, they were awake, wide-eyed, backing away, and cowering in fear.

They couldn't see us or each other in the blackness, of course, but they must have been awakened by hearing us open the door, and they had surely seen the light spilling in from the other side as we had entered. Perhaps they had seen our silhouettes as well. None of them dared to say anything. No one called out and asked who we were. But neither did we call out. I didn't dare. I knew they were hostages. They were captives. They were slaves. But they weren't here to work—they were far too young. Which meant they were being held here for only one purpose: to be sex slaves to—and likely to be brutally raped by—their ISIS masters.

An involuntary shudder rippled through my body. I'd rarely experienced the presence—the physical presence—of evil before. But I did now. I'd heard rumors of ISIS members engaging in sexual slavery. I'd seen some unsourced reporting. But I'd never taken it very seriously. I'd certainly never believed any of it. All the allegations and insinuations seemed so outlandish, so far beyond the pale, as to be unworthy of serious attention. This was the twenty-first century, I'd told myself. No one was savage enough to be engaged in such barbaric behavior, I'd convinced myself.

But what else were these children doing here, naked and alone, at such tender young ages?

61

* * *

The stench in the place was overwhelming.

The children were living in their own filth. But it was the horror in the eyes of these kids—staring out through the darkness, trembling in terror, unable to see us but knowing we were there—that haunted me most.

The monstrosity of it struck me hard. I grabbed Yael's arm and tried to pantomime what I was thinking, that we should let them out and lead them back through the tunnels. But Yael shook her head, put her finger over her lips, and then pointed forward. We had a mission. We had to stay with it. And of course she was right. These children weren't going to be any safer in the tunnels behind us or up in the villa than they were right now. Their only hope was for us to clear these tunnels of the enemy, link back up with the Delta Force teams, and hold our own until the choppers came to rescue us. Then, just maybe, hopefully, we could get these children not just out of the cages but out of Iraq to somewhere clean, somewhere safe. Until then, they had to remain where they were. And quiet.

So we kept moving. Carefully. Stealthily. My heart was alternating between compassion and rage. But in the end I chose rage. It seemed the only possible choice.

Turning forward, we could see that there was another large steel door, similar to the one we had just passed through, about thirty meters ahead. It too had a smaller door built into it. As we approached, we could hear the sounds of a gun battle growing louder and louder. The good news was that the racket masked what little noise we were making. The bad news was that I suddenly realized we were coming up on the back side of the battle the Delta Force team had been engaged in for the last forty minutes. On the other side of this steel divide was the third and lowest level of the warehouse. This was where several dozen ISIS fighters were holding their own against America's finest. What chance did we have? Going through that door might very well be suicide.

Yael was going anyway, I had no doubt. I saw her back stiffen and her stride quicken as she headed for the small door. I raced to catch up with her and grabbed her by the arm again just before she turned the handle. I shook my head. I couldn't let her go through that door. There had to be another way. We could radio back to Ramirez. We could explain the situation to him. He could send some of his men through the tunnels to link up with us. They could help do the job their colleagues couldn't get done on their own. And we could stay to protect the children.

The only problem was that I couldn't say any

of this. I didn't dare do anything that might alert the jihadists to our presence. We had one ace up our sleeve, and only one, and that was the element of surprise.

But just as I was about to let go of Yael's arm, I looked over her shoulder at the cage not five feet behind her. I had thought it was empty, which seemed odd since it was the only one of sixteen cages that wasn't filled. But at that moment I thought I saw movement. I pivoted her around and aimed my weapon into the cage. Then I saw it again. Something or someone was in there, hiding under a blanket. Yael saw it too, and it momentarily stopped her from going through the doorway. Whatever it was, it seemed too large to be another child. Perhaps it was an animal, maybe a dog of some kind. But then it moved again and I saw a foot slide out from under the blanket—only for a second, and then it disappeared again. But it was definitely a foot. A human foot. A man's foot. A bloody foot.

I moved toward the cage, aiming my MP5 at the center of the mass. Yael didn't stop me. I didn't want to take any unnecessary chances. I handed her my machine gun. Then I handed her my .45. I was going into this cage one way or the other, but I didn't dare run the risk that an ISIS fighter trying to take a nap—or God forbid, having his way with one of these children—might grab one of my weapons and kill me and Yael with it.

Wiping my sweaty hands on my rain-drenched fatigues, more out of instinct than because it dried them off, I reached for the door of the cage. It was cold to the touch. Only then did I notice the padlock. There was no way I was getting this door open without the key. So I started looking around. Maybe it was hanging on a hook somewhere. Yael searched as well. But we found nothing. And when our search was over, we found ourselves standing in front of the cage again. I wasn't going in. That much was clear. Not without killing whoever had the key. So Yael handed my weapons back to me, and I began to back away toward the door, toward the inevitable. We were going through it, come hell or high water. We were going to take ISIS on from behind.

And then, just as I was about to turn toward the doorway, the figure under the blanket rolled over in his sleep. For a moment, the blanket slipped away from his face. Only for an instant, for he shifted again and pulled the blanket back over his face. But that instant was all we needed. It was unmistakable. It was Harrison Taylor.

62

★ ★ ★

I stood there in the darkness and couldn't believe it.

Had we really just found the president?

I turned to Yael, and she nodded slowly. She'd recognized him too.

But now what? We were no more able to get him out of that cage than any of these children, and even if we could, we had no place to take him. Seething with rage, I moved to the small door within the larger doorway and motioned for Yael to follow me. There was no point in delaying the inevitable. The only way we were getting out and getting the president and all those children out and going home was by going through that door and killing everything that wore a hood and moved.

Again Yael didn't stop me. So I took a deep breath, put my finger on the trigger, and turned the handle.

The first thing that happened was that I was temporarily blinded. The room on the other side was fully lit, and it felt like my night-vision goggles had just burned holes in my retinas. Yael saw me turn away in pain and quickly removed her goggles and scrambled into position behind me to assess the situation. Fortunately, the gunfire was so intense it masked any sounds we were making.

As I recovered, it was clear we had indeed made it to the bottom level of the warehouse. Through a smoky haze I could see no fewer than nine ISIS fighters. One was close, maybe five yards away. Others were spread out in a row. The farthest was about fifteen yards away. They were all hiding behind mine carts, overturned metal tables, and pallets stacked with steel boxes of some kind and piles of unused artillery shells they'd apparently been filling with sarin precursors before the Delta offensive began. And they were all firing in the direction of exit doors and elevators on the far side of this lower level of the warehouse.

I aimed at the closest fighter, pulled the trigger, and put four bullets in his back. Blood darkened his shirt, and soon he stopped screaming and twitching and fell to the floor, dead. Without waiting, I pivoted slightly to the right, fired another burst at the next closest fighter, and felled him instantly. Yael, meanwhile, fired at the terrorist farthest away and began working back across the room from right to left.

The effect was to create chaos in the warehouse. We had completely caught the ISIS fighters off guard, but we'd blindsided the Delta team, too. They had no idea who we were or where we were coming from or that we were allies. Bullets were flying everywhere. The jihadists were scrambling in all directions. Yael was radioing the general what was happening, but I can't imagine he or anyone else on the comms could hear over the battle.

Several of the black hoods now turned toward us and began firing back. Instinctively, I pulled Yael back through the doorway and slammed the door shut. I could hear a barrage of bullets hitting the door, but none of them could penetrate.

"Red Team Leader, Red Team Leader, this is Katzir and Collins!" Yael shouted over the radio as both of us reloaded. "We've found a way into the warehouse—lower level—from the back. That's us doing the shooting. Over."

"That's you, Katzir?" came the reply.

"That's affirm—press the offensive."

"Roger that. Do you have grenades?"

However hot the firefight had been sixty seconds earlier, it had just gotten exponentially hotter.

"Say again," Yael shouted into the radio. "I repeat, say again."

The terrorists seemed to be unloading everything they had against the smaller of the two doors. And then I realized there was no lock. The bullets were breaking through the steel. But if any of the fighters still alive on the other side decided to open the door, we had no way to stop them except to shoot them point-blank.

"Grenades, Katzir. Do you have grenades?"

"Yes, I have two," Yael replied.

"Get them ready," said the Red Team leader.

"Okay, hold on," she said, then turned to me and told me to back up, aim for the door, and not let anyone past, no matter what. She pulled out a flare, set it off nearby to give us a little light to operate since there was no way we could keep switching to night vision and back again. Then I watched as she pulled two grenades out of her vest.

The children were screaming now. I didn't blame them. But then I heard Taylor's voice, trembling and in shock. "Collins? Collins, is that you?"

"It is, Mr. President. Just hold on."

"How did you find me? And who's this with you?"

"We came with the Delta Force, Mr. President. They're here to rescue you. But I can't explain any further. Not right now. Just move to the back. Stay against the wall."

I saw the president comply as Yael moved to the door.

"J. B., come here," Yael shouted.

Immediately I moved to her side.

"Set your gun down."

"You're sure?"

She nodded. "Set it down."

I did.

"Now hold the handle and when I say go, open it just a crack—just enough so I can toss these through. Got it?"

"Yes," I said and grabbed the handle.

"Okay, I'm ready," Yael shouted over the radio.

At that point I noticed that bullets were no longing pummeling the steel door. I wasn't sure why, but I took it as a positive sign.

"Okay, good; we've drawn their fire back to us," came the response from the Red Team leader. "Now you're going to toss them both through— one to the center, one to the left, on my mark."

"Your left or mine?"

"Mine. Your right."

"So center and my right."

"Yes."

"Ready."

"Good. On my count—one, two, three, go—now-now-now!"

I yanked the door open about half a foot. Yael pulled pin one and tossed the grenade to the right. Then she pulled pin two and tossed it to the center, just as she'd been told. She yanked her hand back and I slammed the door shut. We both reached for our weapons as we heard the explosions go off. And then all was silent.

63

★ ★ ★

We waited for a moment, just to be sure.

Then the Red Team leader said the words we both wanted to hear. *"We're clear."*

For the first time in several minutes, it seemed, I finally started to breathe again. I turned to Yael, but she was already moving back to the door. She readied her weapon just in case and radioed ahead that she was coming in. Then she slowly turned the handle and pulled the door open. Instantly she was hit in the face by a wave of black smoke. She immediately shut the door again but the damage had been done. Thick, acrid smoke poured in, and I smelled the ghastly odor of burnt flesh. I turned away and covered my nose and mouth, but it wasn't enough. My eyes started watering. My throat was burning. I heard the president and the children choking and gagging behind me.

"Mr. President, are you okay?" I asked, moving toward his cage.

"I think so," he sputtered, trying to clear his throat and catch his breath. "Is it over?"

"Yes, Mr. President, for the moment," I said.

"But we still need to get you and all these children out of here. American rescue choppers are inbound. We need to get you aboveground and fast."

"Start with them," he said between coughs. "They've been living a nightmare."

"Of course, Mr. President," I replied. "Let me just tell the others that we've got you."

I radioed to the general and the rest of the Delta team that Yael and I had found the president. He was safe. But we needed medical and logistical help immediately. Then, as Yael lit several more flares to provide some desperately needed light, I explained the situation as we'd found it—the cages, the locks, and the children. Ramirez immediately ordered the Red Team leader to take charge of freeing the president and the children while the rest of Red Team moved back upstairs to the ground floor to aid the men fighting to keep the ISIS forces at bay.

"The choppers are twenty minutes out," Ramirez told us. "Everybody stay focused. Keep fighting. But don't lose heart. The cavalry is almost here."

I didn't find myself rejoicing, however. The strain in Ramirez's voice was clear. The intensity of the gunfire around him was clear as well. A moment later we heard him make a satellite call back to CENTCOM in Tampa and call in the most devastating series of close air strikes so far. *"They're everywhere,"* we heard him say. *"I don't know if we can hold them back much longer."* Then someone next to him told him he was still on comms, and he fumbled to shut off his mic.

A chill ran down my spine. We weren't out

of the woods yet, and twenty minutes suddenly seemed like an eternity.

Just then someone started pounding on the door.

"Katzir, Collins, it's me," shouted the Red Team leader. *"I'm coming in."*

Yael opened the door and let him through, and more billows of smoke poured in with him. She closed the door again immediately and then turned a flashlight on President Taylor. I did the same.

"Mr. President, we're here to take you home," the Delta leader said. "How are you feeling?"

"I'm fine; I'm fine," he insisted. "Just take care of the kids."

"Dr. Katzir and Mr. Collins will do that," he replied. "My job is to take care of you. Now stand back as I get this door open."

"Did you find the keys?" I asked.

"No—I'm afraid they were blown to kingdom come with everything else on the other side of that door."

"Then how are you getting in?"

"Semtex—now stand back."

He pulled out a small piece of the puttylike plastic explosive, attached it to the padlock, and told us all to cover our ears. Then he triggered the detonator. After a small, measured explosion, it was over. The padlock blew apart. The chains fell off. The door swung open. The president was free.

The team leader then handed a small case of the explosives and detonating cords to Yael, who proceeded to blow the locks off all the cage doors.

Meanwhile, I rushed into the president's cage and helped the Delta leader get Taylor to his feet.

"When was the last time you had something to eat, Mr. President?"

"A few days ago, I'm afraid," he said, standing now in the orange jumpsuit we'd seen him in on the video, his legs wobbly and his hands quivering.

"And to drink?"

"Yesterday, a little—or maybe it was the day before," he said. "I'm sorry. The days are running together."

"That's okay," the leader said, handing him a small bottle of orange Gatorade. "Take a little of this, in small amounts. But don't worry. We'll get you back up to speed."

"Thank you, all of you. I can't tell you how grateful I am to see your faces. I never thought I'd see a friendly face again."

"We're glad to see you, too, sir. Can you walk?"

"I think so," Taylor said.

"Good; then I need you to come with me. We're going to get you out of here. Okay?"

"Thank you—thank you so much. I couldn't be more grateful."

The smoke was clearing now, apparently being sucked out by an exhaust system neither Yael nor I had noticed. But the president was still coughing and wheezing. He was also getting emotional. His eyes were welling with tears, and it wasn't simply from the soot or the stench. He had several days of growth on his face. His gray hair was unwashed and askew. And his mouth and lips were trembling. I was sure he was going to break down and start sobbing any moment. I'm sure I would have done the same.

Seeing how fragile the president was physically and emotionally, Yael insisted I accompany him and the team leader back through the tunnels to the villa.

"Forget it, Yael; I'm staying with you and the children," I said.

"J. B., the president needs you," she shot back more forcefully than I'd expected. "You know the way. And I'll be fine with these kids. Don't worry. We'll be right behind you. But move. You don't have much time."

I could see she wasn't going to take no for an answer. So I slung the MP5 over my shoulder and took Taylor's right arm while the team leader took his left, and we started moving.

"Thank you, gentlemen," the president said, still on the verge of succumbing to shock and relief.

"It's an honor, sir," I said as we began walking.

"I guess I owe you an apology," the president said as he limped forward.

"No, sir," I said. "Not at all."

"Of course I do, Collins," he said. "I didn't see it. I didn't see what was coming or how fast. You did. I should have listened, and I'm sorry."

"Thank you, Mr. President," I replied. "I appreciate that. Can I get that on the record?"

"Don't push it, Collins."

"Fair enough, sir. May I ask you a question?"

"Of course."

"Abu Khalif—do you know where he is?"

"I wish," he said. "Last time I saw him was

when they made the video. But we'd better catch him. When we do, I want to personally flip the switch on him."

"Wait till you see what's ahead," I said.

But first, the Red Team leader pulled out a satellite phone and hit speed dial.

"White House Situation Room," said the watch officer who picked up the call.

The Delta team leader identified himself and asked to be patched through immediately to Holbrooke. When the watch officer said the VP was busy, the team leader handed the phone to Taylor.

"This is the president of the United States—put me on with the vice president—*now*."

64

* * *

News of the president's rescue was relayed back to King Abdullah.

The monarch ordered Jordanian and Egyptian forces to stop their ground operation in Dabiq and to withdraw immediately. Soon we learned that the operation there had been messy, to say the least. Coalition casualties were high, and there was apparently a brutal firefight under way. I had no doubt the king was right to order a retreat. If the president was in Iraq, what was the point in losing the lives of any more coalition soldiers in Syria? The final battle of Dabiq would have to wait.

It quickly became clear the president was badly wounded and suffering from dehydration. For most of the way back to the villa, one of us had to support the president with his arm over our shoulders. He explained that he'd been tortured extensively, beaten on the back, stomach, legs, and feet—anywhere that couldn't be noticed on camera. The hardest part was getting him through the low tunnel. He was simply in too much pain to crawl and probably wouldn't have had the strength anyway. So we ultimately resorted to wrapping him in his blanket, putting my bulletproof vest on him, tying the straps from our machine guns to the vest, and pulling him through the tunnel.

It was 7:13 when we finally got the president back to the villa. Sharif was waiting for us and helped us get him out of the shaft and onto a stretcher. A Delta medic was also waiting for us and immediately began administering first aid, including putting Taylor on an IV to rehydrate him and pump some desperately needed painkillers into his system. Ramirez rushed down to the basement to greet the president and take a few quick pictures he could transmit back to CENTCOM, the National Military Command Center at the Pentagon, and the White House Situation Room. These were the "proof of life" pictures everyone in the chain of command had been waiting for.

Ramirez wanted to put the president on the phone with the chairman of the Joint Chiefs. But Taylor was exhausted and the general thought better of it. Besides, we were by no means out of danger yet. So Ramirez left us with the medical team and raced back upstairs to keep fighting with his men, ordering Sharif to come with him as they hadn't a soldier to spare.

I could hear the roar of fighter jets streaking over us, and I could feel the building being rocked by the almost-nonstop explosions of American smart bombs taking out approaching ISIS forces.

Part of me wanted to join the general and Sharif and defend our location against the attackers. We had the president. He was in good hands. He was resting. He had a medic. And he certainly didn't need me.

But just then, Yael arrived with the children. I helped her get them up the ladder one by one, then down to a working bathroom. There Yael and I gave them each a quick sponge bath, dried them off, and wrapped them in sheets I ripped off the cleanest beds I could find. It wasn't much, but it was all we had.

I scrounged up as many PowerBars and bottles of water and Gatorade as I could and brought them to the bunk room, where we had decided to keep all the kids for the moment. They were trembling, all of them, terrified by the bombs and the automatic gunfire. We held them and rocked them and told them that it was going to be okay. Neither Yael nor I could be sure it was true, and it was clear none of the kids believed us—if they even understood us. But there was nothing else to be done. The choppers were still several minutes out, we were told, hampered by weather and anti-aircraft fire.

The medic soon came to check on the kids, and when he did, Yael leaned over and whispered in my ear.

"Go," she said.

"Where?" I asked.

"Upstairs to fight."

"No, I'm staying with you," I said. "You need me, and so do the kids."

"They need you more," she said. "And we'll be fine. The choppers will be here soon."

"You're sure?"

"Absolutely; go—and don't do anything stupid."

"Like get killed?"

"Exactly."

"Okay," I said, grabbing my MP5 and giving her a kiss on the forehead. "I'll be back for you soon. I love you."

Then I left.

As I raced up the stairs, I realized what I'd just said. I hadn't planned to say it. It had just come out. And then I'd bolted. I couldn't believe what I'd done or imagine what she was thinking. But I didn't have time to worry about it.

When I reached the main floor, I learned that three more of Ramirez's men were dead. One was critically wounded. All were nearly out of ammunition. They were using the AK-47s stripped off the dead ISIS fighters, but even the ammo in those guns was running low.

"*Six minutes,*" Ramirez shouted. "*The choppers will be here in six. We need to hang on till then.*"

I found my backpack and pulled out five full mags. "Here, General. This is all I have, plus the one in my weapon."

"Then keep two and get upstairs," he said, taking the other three off my hands. "Take the bedroom in the southwest corner. Kill anything that moves, but don't waste a shot. We've still got to get up that mountain."

"What mountain?"

"The one we landed on."

"That's where they're picking us up?"

"Yeah. Now move."

"Why not here?" I asked.

"Too dangerous," he said. "Blue Team will take the president and the kids out first. The rest of us will follow. Now get going. We've got men down up there, and more bad guys are coming up that road all the time."

I did as I was told and raced up to the second floor. I found the bedroom to which I'd been assigned at the end of the hall. And inside I found the body of a Delta member on the floor, shot just minutes before. He looked merely wounded, but I checked. He had no pulse. He was definitely dead. But his body was still warm and being pelted by the driving, freezing winter rain that was pouring through both sets of windows, the one facing south and the others facing west.

Perhaps the storm had let up enough to bring the choppers in, but one could hardly tell. The wind seemed as fierce as the last time I'd been aboveground. The rain hadn't abated at all, and the temperature was dropping fast.

The room was a disaster. I couldn't even begin to count all the bullet holes in the walls, door, and ceiling, and the furniture had all been ripped to shreds. But as I moved to the smashed-out windows on the west side, I was even more stunned by the vast destruction of this small village. It seemed every house was ablaze or a smoking crater. What few nearby buildings were undamaged were filled with snipers. I could see the flash of their muzzles and hear bullets whizzing past my head. I took one more glance and then pulled back from the window, images of dead ISIS fighters fresh in my mind's eye. There were bodies and body parts everywhere, hundreds of them, bullet-ridden, bloody, rain-soaked. And yet the fight was so far from over. More fighters were coming from every direction.

65

I opened fire on a group of five coming over the wall.

In three quick bursts, I killed two and wounded two more. But one got past me. I fired again and again but missed every time and now he was inside the building. Panicked, I shouted to my colleagues over the radio only to hear a burst of gunfire directly below me and confirmation from two Delta operatives that the enemy was down.

Two more fighters now sprinted out the front door of a blazing house. I shot them both before they crossed the street. But up the road to my right, about two hundred yards out, I spotted a white pickup truck filled with jihadists racing toward me. I aimed at them, waiting for them to come within range, but they never got to me. Instead, the entire truck, its driver, and all its passengers erupted in a massive ball of fire, and then an Apache helicopter gunship came roaring past.

More frightened than relieved at that moment,

I just stared at the new flaming crater in the road, only to be startled by another burst of gunfire coming from my right. Too close for comfort. I dove for cover as bullets and shrapnel filled the bedroom. When the shooting paused for a few seconds, I scrambled back to my feet, pivoted to the west window, and saw a band of three hooded men huddled behind what was left of a stone wall. I didn't have a clean shot at any of them and didn't dare waste any rounds. Still, they were too close not to engage them.

That's when I remembered the grenades. I drew back against the wall, away from the window, and pulled off my backpack. It was mostly filled with a chem-bio suit and related gear. But there were three grenades at the bottom. I grabbed one and took a quick glance to make sure the three terrorists were still behind the wall. They were, but four more had just joined them. I pulled the pin the way I'd seen Yael do it, then threw a fastball across the courtyard, aiming for the wall so as not to overshoot. It hit just a few feet shy but rolled close enough and detonated an instant later. When I looked again, that section of the wall was gone, and all that remained were charred body parts.

I ducked back to reload the MP5 and heard three shots from a second-floor window across the street. *Crack, crack, crack.*

This time I could feel the rounds passing by my head. If I hadn't ducked when I did, I knew I'd be dead. There was a sniper out there that had a bead on me. He was expecting me to pop back up any moment, but I wasn't going to give him an easy target. I got down on my belly and crawled along the floor, across the glass and the blood and the spent rounds, over to the south-facing window. Then I ejected the spent mag, popped in a new one, steadied my breathing the best I could, jumped out, and aimed for the second-floor window across the street. Two shots. Then I paused. Another shot. Then I paused again and forced myself to wait four seconds. *Beat. Beat. Beat. Beat.* I saw the barrel of his rifle coming back out the window and I let loose. Three bursts at the base of the window and then a fourth, and suddenly the rifle dropped out the window to the ground below.

I started breathing again. But as I pulled back inside for cover, I noticed in my peripheral vision a white blur to my left and the sound of someone gunning an engine. At once curious and worried, I got down low and crawled on my hands and knees away from my post, out the door, into the hallway, and to another bedroom on that side. Here I found another dead body, this time an ISIS fighter, not a Delta operative, and by the looks of him he'd been dead from the moment we'd arrived, almost ninety minutes earlier. But that wasn't what I was looking for. Instead, I raced to the window, popped my head up just for a moment, and was aghast at what I saw.

Three white vans were tearing out of the compound. I watched them clear the front gate and race up a dirt road on the mountain. They had to be going seventy or eighty miles an hour. Then I

looked toward the summit where they were heading and saw three Black Hawk helicopters coming
into view. The cavalry had arrived. The president
and the kids were being whisked to safety, which
meant Yael had to be with them. And I had been
left behind.

"General, this is Collins; do you copy? Over,"
I shouted into my headset.

There was no reply.

"General, I repeat: this is Collins; do you copy?
Over."

Again there was nothing.

It made sense to me that the general would be
in the van transporting the president to safety. But
if the rest of us were going to be next, why wasn't
anyone communicating over the radio?

I knew I had to get back to my post, so I
ducked down and raced back across the hallway just in time to see bullets flying everywhere.
Facedown on the floor, I kept calling out over
the radio, trying to get the general, one of the
team leaders, the medic, or anyone from Delta to
respond. But nobody did. Why not? Was everyone dead? Or was everyone in those vans racing
up the mountain?

I had to buy more time to figure out what
was happening. I jumped up, glanced out the
window, and focused on three more ISIS fighters
running toward the villa from the south. I didn't
hit any of them when I opened fire, but they
did scatter and take cover behind the burning wreckage of a van and an SUV. Then they
started returning fire. I waited until they paused

to reload, then pivoted back to the window and fired two more bursts, one at each vehicle. But before I could duck for cover, I heard two shots from my left side. Then I found myself snapping back and smashing to the ground.

66

I landed on my back.

I'd been hit just below my right shoulder. It was impossible to describe the pain. It was a searing, blinding, excruciating sensation like someone had just taken a red-hot poker and driven it into my chest. I instantly dropped my weapon, and the MP5 went skittering across the floor.

I didn't scream. I wanted to, but I didn't dare let the thugs down below know they'd hit me. Instead, I gritted my teeth and fought to stay conscious. If I blacked out now, I knew, no one was going to find me. For all I knew there was no one left in the building. But I had to alert my team that I was in trouble—if any of them were left. I couldn't just lie there alone and bleed to death. I needed to press the wrist-mounted button to activate my microphone, but it was attached to my right wrist, and the burning sensation was rapidly spreading from my chest down my right arm. It would likely be numb in a few seconds, and there was no way I could make my right hand push the button in any case.

Finally, groaning from the pain, I reached over and pressed it with my left hand.

"Man down, man down. I've been hit. Over."

But again, no one responded.

"This is Collins. I need a medic. Over."

Still nothing, and now I began to panic.

"This is J. B. Collins. I'm in the southwest bedroom on the second floor. I've just been shot. I'm bleeding badly—in need of immediate assistance. Is anybody out there? Does anybody hear me?"

My arm was going numb. Inch by inch, it was shutting down, and with it my ability to shoot and my ability to reload—not that it mattered, as I realized I had only half a mag left.

Suddenly the room erupted again in a hail of gunfire. I covered my face with my left arm and rolled over on my stomach. When there was a brief pause, I slid my MP5 across the floor, through the doorway and into the hallway. Then I began pulling myself across the floor after it. If there was anyone left in the villa, I had to find them. Otherwise I was going to bleed out.

I heard a metallic clunk and something bumping across the floor. I turned and saw a live grenade rolling toward me. Instinctively I swatted at it and pushed it away, sending it into the far corner of the room. Then it detonated and everything went black.

★ ★ ★

When I came to, General Ramirez was dumping a bucket of water on me.

"Where have you been?" he screamed at me. "I've been calling and calling you on the radio. You never answered."

"Where am I?" I asked, wiping the water from my eyes and hearing gunfire downstairs and bombs dropping and buildings exploding outside, closer than ever.

"Still in the villa," he replied, pulling me into the hallway. "Now sit tight."

He had a needle in his hand. He was filling it with something and jabbing it in my arm. I winced in anticipation but didn't feel a thing.

"What happened?"

"You got shot and then nearly killed by a grenade, but you did a heck of a job, soldier."

He helped me sit up and drove another needle into my leg. As he did, I looked at myself in horror. My right shoulder was wrapped in a blood-soaked bedsheet. The right side of my uniform was covered in blood, as was much of the room. The other side of my uniform—what was left of it—was scorched, shredded, and smoking.

"I'm not a soldier," I groaned, trying to make sense of it all.

"Yeah, yeah, you're a reporter—whatever. Look, you took out a lot of bad guys from this room and bought us the time we needed."

"Where's the president?" I asked, trying to get up. "Is he safe?"

"He's safe. That's what I'm talking about. You bought us the time to get him out. He's on a chopper with my guys, and he'll be fine."

"And the kids?"

"They're on another chopper, right behind the president."

"What about Yael?"

"Downstairs with three others, holding down the fort."

"She didn't go with the children?"

"I told her to, but she wouldn't go," he said.

"What are you talking about?" I felt like I couldn't completely understand what he was saying. I heard his words but couldn't process them.

"Said she wanted to fight with us. Now look, can you get up?"

"I'm not sure—but why didn't she go with the kids?"

When another bomb exploded nearby, rocking the building, Ramirez ignored my question. He grabbed my MP5 and asked if there was any ammo left in it, and when I told him that there was, he went back to the two windows and fired several bursts. I could hear the screams of the dying, and I knew how they felt.

When he was finished shooting, Ramirez came back, knelt at my side, checked my radio, and cursed. "It's shorted out," he said. Then he grabbed me by the collar, pulled me out into the hallway, and hoisted me to my feet.

"Come on; let's move," he said.

I knew I should be in agony but felt curiously numb. "Why is Yael still here?"

Again he ignored me. I couldn't feel my right arm at all. The left side of my face and body had severe burns, but I couldn't feel them either. The general dragged me downstairs. I could see three of his men firing out three different windows, and then, as Ramirez helped me around a corner, I saw Yael firing out the front door.

"He's alive," Ramirez told her.

She finished a burst, ducked back inside, turned toward me, and gasped. *"Oh, look at you!"* she yelled and rushed to my side.

Ramirez moved to the doorway and kept shooting.

"I'm fine," I lied.

"Oh no, you're not. General, we need to get him out now."

"We don't have another bird."

"What are you talking about?" she shot back. "You said the next one would be here in a few minutes."

"I know. I just got the call," he said.

"What do you mean?" she asked. "What's wrong?"

"The chopper that was coming for us was just shot down."

"Where?"

"About two klicks from here."

"How?"

"RPG—it was coming in low."

"So now what?"

"They're sending another—from Azraq."

"How far out?" she pressed.

"Twelve minutes."

"General, we don't have twelve more minutes."

"I know."

"We're out of ammo, sir. We're being overrun."

Then she turned to look at me. She was bloody

and sweaty and a total mess. She didn't say anything, but I could see in her eyes that she was worried about me. She wasn't sure I was going to make it. She looked back at Ramirez, but he had nothing to say. He killed another few terrorists racing into the courtyard, and then his gun stopped firing. He was out of ammunition and had no more mags. I watched him pull out his pistol and brace for the inevitable.

"There's got to be a way, General," she yelled. "There's got to be a way out of here."

"There isn't."

"There has to be."

I couldn't believe it. This couldn't be the end. We'd come too far. We'd rescued the president. We'd gotten him to safety, and now we were going to be captured and shot—if we were lucky. Or more likely, slaughtered like cattle.

It wasn't possible. It couldn't end like this. Yet the look in Yael's eyes and the tone in the general's voice and the silence from the others and the fact that all but one of them was reduced to firing with pistols made it clear. We were all going to die. And soon. It was not a matter of if, nor even of when, only how.

67

★ ★ ★

"I'm out!" shouted one of the general's men.

I watched as he tossed his pistol aside.

"Here!" I shouted back. "Use mine." I struggled to pull it out of its holster but couldn't manage it, so Yael helped me and tossed it across the room. The commando caught it, and just in time. He fired twice and killed a terrorist rushing across the yard.

"Okay, this is it; I have to make a call," Ramirez said. "We either let ourselves be overrun, or I call in an air strike and end it now."

He fired at two more jihadists trying to penetrate the courtyard, then turned and took a vote. All three Delta operatives voted for the Air Force to go ahead and drop its ordnance on us and finish us off and the attacking ISIS fighters along with us. Reluctantly, Yael did as well.

"Okay—then it's settled," Ramirez said.

"Whoa, whoa, wait a minute," I said. "I didn't vote."

"You want ISIS to cut your head off?" Ramirez asked.

"Of course not," I said.

"Then you just voted."

"No, wait. I have an idea."

"We don't have time, Collins," Ramirez said, firing again and trying to keep three hooded men at bay. "I have to call it in now. I only have two rounds left."

"Wait, wait, listen to me," I said.

"I can't, Collins; I'm sorry. We're out of time and out of options."

Ramirez called Yael over to guard the door. She propped me up against the stairs, then rushed to his side and took his .45 while he pulled out his satphone and speed-dialed CENTCOM.

"General, listen to me. I think there's another way."

"Forget it, Collins. I know you don't want to die. None of us do. But it happens to everyone. The only question is whether we die with honor or are butchered by cowards."

"No, stop—you're not listening," I yelled, unbelievably intense pain shooting through every part of my body.

"CENTCOM, this is General Ramirez, requesting an air strike on my location. Repeat, I'm requesting an immediate air strike on my location."

There was a pause. The soldiers around me were firing their last rounds.

"Yes, sir, I know what I'm asking," Ramirez continued to the CENTCOM commander in Tampa.

There was another pause.

"You can see it on your screen. We're being

overrun. It's over. Take us out, and everyone around us. . . . Yes, I understand. . . . Thank you, sir. It's been an honor. . . . God bless us all, sir, and God bless the United States of America. Over and out."

Ramirez hung up the phone and the room began to spin. I couldn't believe what he'd just done. But I didn't have the energy to stop him. I was getting woozy. I heard myself mumbling, but I knew I was passing out. I saw my mom. I saw Matt and Annie and Katie and Josh. I tried to remember the verses. I tried to remember what Matt had told me, what he'd begged me to accept, but everything was going dark. I couldn't think straight. I was fading. . . .

"What? What are you saying? J. B.—wake up. What did you just say?"

I was looking at Yael's face. I couldn't tell if it was a dream or if it was real. But she was shaking me, hard, and demanding that I tell her what I'd just said.

"I don't remember," I said and closed my eyes again.

"*You do,*" she yelled, shaking me again. "Come on, J. B.—stay with me. What did you say?"

"The war . . . ," I mumbled.

"The war? What war? This war?"

"No, the ware . . ."

"The where? I don't understand."

"The warehouse . . ."

"The warehouse?"

"Yeah."

"What about it?"

"Hit it."

"What do you mean?" she screamed, shaking me even harder.

"The warehouse," I said again, barely able to keep my eyes open. "Hit it."

"Hit the warehouse?"

"Not us."

"Why, J. B.—why?"

"The sheh . . ."

"What?"

"The shells."

"What about them?" Yael asked, pleading with me to stay with her.

I heard Ramirez telling her to let it go. "He's delirious, Katzir. Let him be. It'll all be over in a moment. The F-16s are inbound as we speak."

"No," she shot back. "He's trying to tell us something."

Then she turned back to me, took my face in her hands, and looked me straight in the eye. "What about the shells, J. B.?"

"The M-six . . ."

"M687s?"

"Right."

"What about them?"

"They'll go off."

"If we bomb the warehouse?"

"Right."

"They might, but why? We'll all die if they go off."

"No, just them."

"Who?"

"The bad guys."

"Just the bad guys will die?" she asked.

"Right."

"No, J. B., that's not how it works," she replied, pity in her voice. "The sarin will kill us all—and believe me, that'll be far worse than being bombed or beheaded."

"No, no," I said. "We have the s . . ."

"The what?"

"The su . . ."

"I can't hear you, J. B.—talk to me."

"Suits," I sputtered. "We have the suits."

Then suddenly she got it.

"What is it?" Ramirez asked as understanding dawned on Yael's face.

"We have the chem-bio suits—all of us," she yelled. "Call them back. Redirect the air strike. Have them hit the warehouse. The chemical weapons will detonate. The gas will be released. There's more than five thousand shells down there, and hundreds more on the upper floors. The gas will spread through the entire village. It'll kill everyone. And we just might survive."

"Might?"

"It's worth a shot, General—it's worth a shot. But you've got to call them now."

I saw Ramirez look at me. He hesitated, but only for a moment. Then he hit speed dial and got CENTCOM back on the phone and started barking authentication codes and orders. In the meantime, Yael raced to get her backpack and returned to my side. Then she and Ramirez helped me upstairs and propped me up against another wall while the others grabbed their backpacks and raced upstairs with us.

And soon the bombs started dropping.

Boom. Boom. Ba-boom.

The ground shook like nothing I'd ever experienced before.

"*The warehouse,*" someone yelled, though I couldn't see who. "*They just hit the warehouse.*"

He'd done it, I realized. Ramirez had made the call. And the Air Force had responded already. There was just one problem. We weren't ready yet.

An immense burst of adrenaline shot through my system. I was still in enormous pain, but my heart was racing. I was breathing more deeply now. I was starting to refocus, to see and hear more clearly. Ramirez and two of his colleagues took up positions to guard the stairs while I struggled to get my suit on. I can't explain it. Maybe it was the prospect of my imminent death. Maybe it was the prayers of my family. I don't know for sure, but I felt a wave of energy surging over me. I wasn't better. I wasn't healed. But I did suddenly have the will to live and to fight.

Still, with my right hand numb and much of my body badly burned, I couldn't fasten my helmet. Yael tried to help me, but time was running out. If the warehouse had already been hit, then the gas was already spreading. It would be here any moment. She had to move faster or she'd be dead.

"*Forget about me,*" I yelled. "*Get your own suit on—now!*"

68

★ ★ ★

But Yael wouldn't quit.

As bombs exploded all around us, closer and closer every second, I pushed her away and screamed at her to save herself. But she wouldn't do it. She got my helmet attached, turned on my air tank, and checked to see it was operating properly. Finally she started putting her own suit on.

The deafening, crushing sound of the explosions seemed to bring me to my senses. I forgot about my injuries. I forgot about my pain. I turned and noticed that some of the others were struggling to get their suits on. The general had found a large tear in his. One of his colleagues had a hole in his air hose. Both handed Yael and me their pistols and the last of their ammo and ran off to find other backpacks, other suits, ones left by commandos who'd already been killed.

Time was running out. But there was nothing we could do to help them except make sure not a single ISIS fighter got up those stairs.

I watched down the stairwell as one jihadist after another stormed the first floor. I saw them desperately searching for us. Then one of them spotted the stairs and gave a shout. The moment his foot hit the first step, I started shooting. When his colleagues joined him, Yael opened fire as well. She killed three with six shots. I killed one and severely wounded two, but suddenly I was out of bullets. Yael kept shooting, but there were too many of them. They were coming too fast.

I yelled for help, but no one could hear me. Then I saw that one of our guys was severely wounded. He'd been hit by a round coming up the stairs or through a window. Someone had pulled him down the hallway and gotten him into his suit and leaned him up against a wall. But he was holding his side and doubled over in pain. I also noticed that he had four grenades on his lap, and now he rolled one to me. I grabbed it, pulled the pin, and tossed it down into the living room as fast as I could. The explosion took out six or seven terrorists. But still they kept coming. I looked back down the hallway and my wounded comrade tossed me another grenade. Again I pulled the pin. Again I hurled it into the living room. This explosion took out five or six more. We did this two more times, and then the grenades were gone, and Yael was out of bullets.

That was it, I thought. We'd done as much as we could. And now it was over. I could see no more ISIS fighters from my angle. Not yet. The vestibule and living room were a sea of blood and body parts, and for a moment the hordes stopped advancing. Maybe no one else was down there. Maybe they were down there but thought we had an endless supply of grenades. Either way, we had a respite, though I knew it wouldn't last. They were coming. Soon. And there was nothing we could do.

But now a new barrage of bombs and missiles came raining down on us, and not just on the warehouse and the houses and buildings nearby but on the courtyard and the backyard and even on the north wing of the villa. One after another, the bombs kept falling and exploding and raining down death on everyone coming to kill us. They were dropping closer and closer and becoming louder and more violent, though I could no longer tell the difference. The villa wasn't going to be able to take much more. The structure was shaking and heaving. Walls were cracking. Beams were splintering. And then the section of roof directly above us gave way, bringing with it a fiery downpour. Burning timbers and tiles came crashing down on top of us.

I grabbed Yael and covered her with my body. I might have been yelling. She might have been too. But I couldn't hear a thing. I could barely see, either. The air was filled with smoke and dust. But was it also filled with gas—*sarin* gas? Had it come? Was it here? I had no idea. It was colorless. It was odorless. How would we know?

I could no longer see the two soldiers down the hallway to the north, including the one who'd given me the last of his grenades. I turned to look behind me and saw Ramirez dragging one of his men down the hall in the other direction, toward the south end of the building. I nudged Yael and pointed toward the general, urging her to follow. But she didn't respond. I shook her, but to no avail.

I started to panic. I wasn't sure if she was dead or just unconscious, but I scrambled forward and began dragging her with me. I could use only my left arm. My right arm was completely paralyzed by this point. But as more and more of the roof collapsed, I had no choice. I couldn't wait for Ramirez to come back for us. I had to get Yael to safety.

Screaming at the top of my lungs and straining every fiber of every muscle in my body, I pulled and pulled, desperate to get her through the burning wreckage. And then the floor collapsed as well.

69

★ ★ ★

We landed hard.

Then what was left of the blazing roof came down on top of us—and not just on the two of us, but on all the bodies littered across the living and dining rooms.

My suit caught fire. I furiously rolled and twisted to put it out, then stumbled over all the burning debris to reach Yael. She wasn't moving. Her helmet was cracked, though it didn't appear to have busted open completely. If she hadn't been dead a moment ago, I feared she was now or would be soon. Still, I couldn't leave her there.

I kicked away the burning timbers and used my left arm to pull her through the living room, through the dining room, and down the hallway toward a bathroom I'd seen earlier. It took several wrenching, deafening, terrifying minutes, but I finally got her there, pulled her inside with me, and shut and locked the door. Then I covered her again with my body and prepared to ride out the attack or die trying.

And then suddenly it was quiet. Not completely quiet but eerily so.

I could still hear the raging fires. But the gunfire had stopped. The bombing had stopped. The explosions had stopped. I no longer heard fighter jets overhead. I no longer heard men shouting in Arabic—or in English. I didn't know why. Was I dead? Was it all over? I couldn't see a thing. Everything was black—so black I couldn't tell if my eyes were open or shut. I tried to move my right arm, but nothing happened. I tried to move my feet and toes and my left hand and arm. All of them worked. I wasn't dead, just severely wounded. Trapped, but alive. Hiding from terrorists in a house that was burning down around me. But I wasn't finished yet. There was still time.

I shifted off Yael and tried to turn her over. I still couldn't see. But now I knew it was because the bathroom had filled with smoke. I couldn't smell it through my chem-bio suit filters. But we had to get out of there fast.

I groped around in the darkness and felt Yael's back. I slid my hand up higher and sat quietly for a moment. I could feel her body rising and falling ever so slightly. She was breathing, which meant she was alive. But now what?

I sat there in the darkness, trying to decide what to do. I was still a bit foggy but dramatically better than I'd been a few minutes earlier.

Why had the bombs stopped dropping? The generals at CENTCOM and back in Azraq were surely watching by satellite and with drones. They could see whether the ISIS forces were still swarming all around us. Was it possible the danger had passed?

I moved to the door and decided to peek out. But when I did, I found that several burning timbers had fallen directly in front of the doorway, blocking our escape. There was no way forward, and now more smoke was filling the bathroom. I closed the door and made a decision. I moved around Yael and felt in the darkness for the window above the toilet. I found a latch and tried to open it, but it wouldn't budge. No matter what I did, nothing worked. I heard a beeping in my helmet. It was an alert from my air tank telling me I had less than five minutes of oxygen. We couldn't stay here. We had to get out now. I stood on the toilet, braced myself against both walls and smashed the window with my boot. It occurred to me that I might be making a dangerous blunder, making so much noise and thus giving away our position. But I didn't see I had a choice, and anyway, what was done was done. So I cleared the rest of the glass away with my boot as well.

Very quickly the smoke in the bathroom dissipated. I could see again. I could see and hear the rain pouring down on the courtyard outside. I could also see at least a dozen hooded men twitching and convulsing and writhing in pain and dozens more lying all across the field, lifeless and still.

The air strikes had worked. I could hardly believe it. The gas had been released. The battlefield had been cleared.

Turning to Yael, I knelt down and, using only my left hand, pulled her onto my back. I grabbed the side of the tub to steady myself, then lifted with my legs and got to a standing position. Then I stood on the toilet again, leaned toward the back wall, and rolled Yael out through the window. She landed with a crunch on the broken glass below, but that was the least of my worries. I climbed out the window myself, jumped to the ground, and checked to see if she was still breathing. She was, but her tank, like mine, had less than four minutes of oxygen to spare.

I reached down, picked her up the best I could, and pulled her over my good shoulder in a fireman's carry. Then I started moving through the courtyard, away from the blazing wreckage that had once been a beautiful villa. I decided my only hope was to get to the top of the mountain, away from the sarin gas, away from the flames and any ISIS forces that remained standing. But as I climbed over bodies and twisted, molten pieces of metal—the remains of the missiles and bombs that had, so far, saved our lives—I collapsed. I scanned the horizon for anyone who could help Yael. But all I saw was death in every direction. Those who had been overtaken by the sarin gas released by the air strikes were twitching and convulsing and foaming at the mouth. They were dying a slow and painful and grisly death. But they were dying. They couldn't kill me. And for the moment, to be honest, that's all I cared about.

I struggled to my feet, the excruciating pain

once again spreading across my body. I had no idea how I was going to get Yael up that mountain.

Suddenly someone grabbed me and spun me around hard. I balled up my fist, prepared to strike, but found myself looking into the mask of General Ramirez. We just stared at each other for a few seconds, and finally I started to breathe again. My heart—temporarily frozen in terror—resumed beating.

Ramirez was saying something, but it was muffled at best. But then he took Yael, hoisted her up on his shoulders, and motioned for me to follow him up the mountain.

But he wasn't walking. He was running flat out. I couldn't keep up. My legs and lungs were burning. My head was pounding. Sweat was pouring down every part of my body. Finally, several hundred meters up, I saw Ramirez stop abruptly and set Yael down. When I reached them, he took off her mask and then his own. At first I looked at him like he was crazy. Did he want to die? Was he trying to commit suicide and take Yael with him? But then I heard another beeping sound in my helmet. I had only thirty seconds of oxygen left. It hadn't been five minutes yet, I thought. It couldn't have been. But I checked the meter and realized I'd nearly sucked the tank dry. And if I didn't get this thing off fast, I was going to suffocate. With the general's help, I quickly removed my helmet, tossed it aside, and breathed in the bitter cold air as the rains drenched me anew.

"What about the gas?" I asked, fearing each breath.

"It can't hurt you up here," Ramirez said.

"What do you mean?" I replied.

"Sarin is heavier than air," he explained as he knelt down and checked Yael's pulse and breathing. "Stays low to the ground. We're already almost five hundred feet above the village. We should be fine."

Should be wasn't exactly what I wanted to hear, but we had no choice.

I turned to Yael. "How is she?"

"I don't know," he said bluntly. "We need to keep moving."

Ramirez picked her up again and started for the summit. I followed as best I could, and before long we were at the top amid the whipping winds. The first thing I saw was pieces of two corpses scattered over the top of the ridge. They were the remains of the two Delta snipers who had been laying down covering fire for us. They had apparently been hit with an artillery round or two. I could barely believe my eyes. I wasn't sure how much more carnage I could take.

Ramirez said nothing. His eyes were hard and his jaw was set. He laid Yael down on the north slope, trying to shelter her a bit from the direct force of the wind.

"Where's the rest of your team?" I asked as I sat down beside her.

But the general shook his head and looked away.

"None of them survived?" I asked in disbelief.

"No," he said quietly.

"What about Colonel Sharif?"

Again he shook his head.

"It's just us?" I asked.

"I'm afraid so," the general replied.

I didn't know what to say. The cost of what we'd just done was growing by the minute.

Turning now, I looked down at the unbelievable devastation in the valley. It was like a scene out of the Apocalypse. The town of Alqosh was gone. All of it. Not a single building remained standing, except one, and barely, at that—the mausoleum around Nahum's tomb.

Then I saw a group of five men emerging from the flames of the compound. They were heading our way, running at full speed. They had chem-bio suits on, but a wave of fear washed over me. Could some of the ISIS forces have stripped our guys of their suits and put them on? We had no weapons. We had no way to defend ourselves. But as they approached us, they took off their helmets. They were Delta. Ramirez rushed over and embraced them, amazed and thankful that anyone else had made it out alive.

I greeted them too, grateful beyond words. One of the men was a medic. He and Ramirez and I carefully removed Yael's chem-bio suit, and the medic examined her injuries. She had a major gash on the back of her head, and her left arm was broken. It was bloody and swollen and part of the bone was actually visible. But for the moment there was nothing we could do. We had no first aid kit, no medical equipment, no drugs, just a satellite phone, which Ramirez used to call CENTCOM. He gave them our status and position and requested an extraction.

Meanwhile, I just sat beside this incredible, mysterious woman, held her hand, stroked her hair, and begged God to have mercy on her, whatever it took. I couldn't bear any more loss.

70

A few minutes later, a Black Hawk roared into view.

Before I knew it, a team of American special operations forces was fast-roping down to us, as there was no place for the chopper to land on the summit. They put Yael on a stretcher and hoisted her back up to the chopper. I was next. Then Ramirez and his team were brought up.

On board, a doctor and a nurse immediately began working on Yael. They strapped me down on a stretcher right beside her. A young African American Army medic, probably in her early thirties, began assessing my injuries. By the time we lifted off, she had put me on an IV and was giving me several units of blood. I tried to ask questions, but the woman attending to me wouldn't allow it. It wasn't my problems I wanted to know about, I told her. It was Yael's. But she insisted that I settle back and rest during the flight, and she promised me it wouldn't be long.

"Where are we going?" I asked.

"You really need to stop talking, Mr. Collins."

"Please," I said. "I just want to know if we're heading back to Amman."

"We're not."

"Then where?"

"You don't take no for an answer."

"No, I don't—are we heading back to Azraq?"

"No," she said as she started cleaning the severe burns I had over much of my body.

"Then where?" I asked. "Because I need to talk to the king."

"That'll have to wait, Mr. Collins."

"Why?"

"We're not going to Jordan."

"Then where?"

"We're heading to EIA."

"Where?"

"Erbīl International Airport."

"Erbīl?"

"Yes."

"The Kurdish capital?"

"Yes, sir."

"But why?"

"I don't give the orders, Mr. Collins. I just follow them. Except to you. I do give you orders, and right now you need to rest."

"But I need to get back to Azraq. It's urgent."

"Then I'm afraid you just got on the wrong flight."

I turned to General Ramirez. A nurse was working on him, too, and only then did I realize that he had been shot as well.

"What happened to you?" I asked.

"Nothing," he said. "I'll be fine."

"But you . . . I didn't . . ."

"Don't worry. I'll be fine," he said again, and he sounded like he meant it.

"You're sure?" I pressed.

"Believe me, Collins, I've been through much worse."

On that, it was hard to doubt him.

"Can you make them tell me about Yael?" I asked.

"They'll tell us when they know something," Ramirez said.

"What's that supposed to mean?"

"It means she's not out of danger yet, Collins. So just stay quiet, let the docs do their job, and we'll all know soon enough."

The satellite phone rang. Ramirez was getting stitches and refusing additional anesthesia, but he still took the call.

"Yes, sir. . . . Right now. We're en route. . . . I don't know—maybe six minutes, maybe eight. . . . Got it. . . . No, sir, we did not. . . . It's possible, but I couldn't say for sure. . . . No. . . . No. . . . I appreciate that, but with all due respect, sir, I need to go back. . . . I understand. . . . Yes, we need to secure it, but my men are back there. We need to get their bodies and get them home to their families for a proper burial. Can you put that together? . . . I'd be grateful. . . . Okay, that's—sir, what's that? . . . Yeah, he's right here with me. . . . No, I think he's going to be fine. . . . Yeah, she's here too. . . . I don't know. Too soon to say. . . . Okay, out."

"Who was that?" I asked.

"CENTCOM," the general replied.

"And?"

"They want to know where Abu Khalif is."

"And?"

"I have no idea."

"Could he have gotten away?"

"He could be a pile of ashes right now for all I know," the general said. "Who knows? We need to put boots on the ground, secure that site, and go over it inch by inch. There may not be much left down there. But we've got to try."

"And get your men back too."

Ramirez nodded. "And get my men back."

There was quiet for a bit, and then I asked him for an update on Dabiq, wincing as the medic cut away more scorched sections of my uniform to treat the burns on my legs.

"Don't go there, Collins."

"Why not?"

"Dabiq is a mess."

"What do you mean?"

"You should rest."

"That bad?"

"Really, Collins, you should rest."

"Just tell me what happened."

"Off the record?"

"Of course," I said.

"I have your word?"

"You do," I assured him, but he didn't seem convinced. "Look, the *Times* will have plenty of coverage of that fight, but I promise none of it will come from me."

Ramirez sighed. "It was ten times worse than this," he said.

"You're kidding," I replied, not sure that was possible.

"I'm not," Ramirez said. "The guys at CENTCOM didn't have time to go into a lot of detail, but they told me ISIS was waiting for our friends. They launched chemical weapons almost the moment the Jordanians, the Egyptians, and the Saudis got there. Our friends fought well, I'm told, but they took heavy casualties."

"How heavy?"

"You have to remember they went in with a much bigger force than we did."

"How heavy, General?"

"It was a bloodbath."

"How many dead?" I asked.

"At least two hundred dead."

I didn't respond. I had no words.

"In the end, it may be more," he said. "The fighting is still under way."

"I thought the king ordered his forces to withdraw once we found and secured the president."

"He did," Ramirez confirmed, "but the bulk of the assault force was already on the ground and moving into the school when the retreat order was given. The men got caught in a wicked cross fire. It seems most of the forces who went in were lost. The rest are fighting their way out, but it doesn't look promising at this point. At least six coalition helicopters were shot down trying to get the men out. And then there's the collateral damage."

"How bad?"

"You don't want to know," Ramirez said.

"Yes, I do."

Ramirez shook his head as the chopper shot across the plains of Nineveh. "First reports indicate all or most of the buildings around the school were filled with civilians, primarily women and children, just like the school itself," he said. "Once ISIS started using the sarin gas, everyone in the neighborhood was doomed. CENTCOM is saying the civilian body count could top fifteen hundred by day's end, maybe more. It's . . . I don't know; it's just . . ." The general's voice trailed off.

"A mess," I said.

"Yeah," he said. "A total mess."

I lay back against the pillow. The scope of the carnage just kept getting worse. The magnitude of the Islamic State's evil was like nothing I had ever seen or heard of. I would have thought by this point in my career I had seen it all. But clearly I had not. Where was it all leading? What was coming next? How would it end? I had no idea.

Suddenly the face of Colonel Sharif came to my mind. I couldn't believe he was dead. I thought of his kids. I wondered who would tell them and when. I wondered how they were going to bear the loss. They'd already been through so much.

The medic leaned over to me and whispered again that I should close my eyes and let myself fall asleep. But how could I? Every bone in my body was in pain. Most of my flesh was burning. I knew I was in good hands. I knew I wasn't going to die. Not in the air over Iraq. Not in the capital of Kurdistan. Not today. But I was still in enormous pain.

And Yael? She was a different story altogether. I still had no idea what was going to happen to her, and that hurt all the more.

71

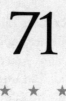

A few minutes later, we touched down next to a hangar.

Then the side doors opened and a team of Air Force doctors met us. They got a quick briefing from the medics who had cared for us and took Yael and me off the chopper on our stretchers. I was about to insist that I could walk well enough on my own, but the African American medic shot me a look that told me I'd better not dare cross her now. So I kept my mouth shut, and as they wheeled us both across the tarmac and put us in a waiting ambulance, I suddenly saw something I would never have expected to see—not today, not in the middle of Iraqi Kurdistan.

Air Force One was waiting for us. The president's gleaming blue-and-white 747 was refueled and ready to go. It was surrounded by dozens of tanks, armored personnel carriers, heavily armed American soldiers and Secret Service agents, and a detachment of the Peshmerga, the Kurdish military force. It was also surrounded by a squadron of American fighter jets.

"I'm afraid this is where I say good-bye, my friend," General Ramirez said just before the EMTs shut the ambulance doors. "It was an honor to fight with you, Collins. You did a heck of a job."

"Thanks, General. Can I quote you on that?"

"You can indeed," he said, though the smile I was hoping to get did not come. There was too much pain and too much loss for both of us. "Don't be a stranger. You're part of the family now. Come see us anytime."

"I'd like that, sir," I said, having to make do by shaking with my left hand. "Take care."

"You, too, Collins. Bye."

He shut the doors, tapped them twice, and the ambulance headed across the airfield. When we got to Air Force One, Yael's stretcher was wheeled onto a lift device, elevated, and brought into the back of the plane. My stretcher followed close behind. I'd only been on Air Force One once in my life, but I couldn't help but notice that the press section in the back where I'd sat had been completely reconfigured. It was now a mobile hospital, and several of the Iraqi children who had been rescued from the tunnels were lying on portable stretchers, receiving, no doubt, the best medical care they had ever gotten.

The first person I recognized was Special Agent Art Harris.

"Mr. Collins, thank God—you made it," he said, rushing over to me immediately.

"You, too," I said. "I was getting worried about you."

"Thanks," he said. "But I'm feeling much better."

"Someone poison you?" I quipped, only half-kidding.

"Nothing so exciting," he replied. "Just airsickness. But what about you? You look terrible. You going to be all right?"

"We'll see," I said, not wanting to talk about myself. "Any news on Jack Vaughn?"

"He was arraigned in federal court a few hours ago."

"How'd he plead?" I asked, trying to picture the scene of a CIA director being arraigned on charges of treason and espionage, for starters.

"Not guilty on all counts," Harris replied.

"And the woman and her son?"

"They'll be arraigned later today."

"Okay. Keep me posted," I said.

"Will do," Harris replied. "You take care of yourself."

"I'll try."

Just then an Air Force officer walked by and insisted Agent Harris take his seat immediately. The crew was kind and couldn't have been more professional, but it was clear they were feeling harried. They were rushing to get Air Force One off Iraqi soil as quickly as possible, and our arrival had obviously slowed them down and complicated matters. Two nurses locked Yael's stretcher into place. Mine was locked in right next to her. We were both strapped in tightly and before I knew it, we began hurtling down the runway.

No one said a word. Even the children were quiet, though it occurred to me that they might have been sedated. I'd overheard a Secret Service agent tell one of his colleagues as we were boarding that ISIS forces were now just a few kilometers from the airport. Tensions were high, as none of us knew what ISIS had planned next.

As we lifted off, I reminded myself that the presidential plane had the world's most advanced countermeasures to defeat ground-to-air missiles. It had also been retrofitted with engines nearly as powerful as those of a spacecraft. Thus, we were now rocketing almost straight up into the sky to get out of missile range as rapidly as possible. The g-forces were making the plane shake something fierce. I wasn't far from several windows, but I couldn't watch. My eyes were shut. My fists were clenched. I knew a dozen U.S. Navy fighter jets were flanking us. They were all from the USS *George H.W. Bush*, the Nimitz-class supercarrier operating as part of Carrier Strike Group Two somewhere out in the Med. They were there to get us out alive and well. But I still couldn't watch.

A few minutes later, we reached our cruising altitude of 41,000 feet. Not long after that, the pilot came over the intercom and informed us that we were now out of Iraqi airspace. I opened my eyes and breathed a sigh of relief as the entire plane erupted in cheers.

Suddenly I heard a familiar voice coming down the aisle. The next thing I knew, President Harrison Taylor was standing beside me, flanked by several bodyguards. "Mr. Collins, how are you?" he asked.

"Mr. President," I said, startled to see him at all, much less on his feet. "I'm fine, sir—how are you?"

"You don't exactly look fine, Collins," he said.

"Neither do you, sir," I replied.

"No, I guess I don't," he conceded. "But they say I'm going to make it."

"Glad to hear it, sir."

"Me too," he said. "And you?"

"We'll see."

Taylor nodded. He wasn't smiling. He'd been through too much, and I could see the pain and exhaustion in his eyes. He looked around the makeshift medical bay and asked if they were taking good care of me. When I assured him that they were, he asked if there was anything I needed. I said no. I saw him glance at the Iraqi children. He thanked the medical crew standing around us for "caring for these kids who really need our love and attention right now." Then he took a few moments to shake hands with each doctor and each nurse and thank them personally for all they'd done for him and his team and these children.

Then the president looked down at Yael. "How is she?" he asked.

"I don't know," I said. "They won't tell me."

The president turned to the lead physician.

"Miss Katzir is stable for now, sir," the doctor replied. "We'll know more in a few hours, but we're going to run a series of tests on her right away."

Taylor nodded and squeezed Yael's hand. I could see him fighting back his emotions, and he was not a man known for having much of an emotional side.

"Take care of these two," he told the medical staff, nodding toward Yael and me. "I owe them my life." Then he turned to me again. "Thank you, James," he said softly.

"Don't mention it, Mr. President," I replied, surprised to hear him call me by my first name.

"No, really," he said, looking me in the eye. "You were right about ISIS, about the summit, about the chemical weapons, about all of it. I should have listened to you. I'm sorry."

"It's okay, Mr. President."

"No," he said, "it's not. A lot of people are dead because I . . ."

He didn't finish the sentence. There was an awkward silence. Then he spoke again.

"Perhaps if I'd listened . . . maybe . . . just maybe all of this could have been avoided."

I didn't know what to say. He was right, but I was stunned to hear him admit it. Thousands of people were dead because he'd failed to take ISIS seriously and deal with them earlier on. I had questions I wanted him to answer on the record, and not just for the American people but for me. But now didn't seem the right time or place—not here on Air Force One, in front of his staff.

Still, I did want to ask him one question: what was he going to do next? ISIS had taken him hostage and broadcast the images of his captivity to the entire world. They had almost beheaded him. They had slaughtered nearly an entire Delta team. They had murdered dozens of American soldiers, not to mention hundreds of Jordanian, Egyptian, Saudi, and Gulf forces in Dabiq. And this was only the beginning. ISIS had scored a propaganda coup of unbelievable proportions. Money and recruits were going to flow in as never before. What's more, Abu Khalif was still at large. So what was the president going to do now? How was he going to learn from his failure to deal with ISIS sooner?

But the moment was interrupted. One of the Secret Service agents got a call on his satellite phone and handed the phone to the president.

"Yeah, it's me," Taylor said. "Okay, put him on. . . . Hey, Marty—what have you got?"

There was a long silence.

"I—that's not possible," he said, and there was another long silence. "What did it say? . . . No, no—not yet. Not till I get back. . . . Okay, let me know. . . . I will. Bye."

He hung up and handed the phone back to the agent. His face was ashen. I couldn't imagine what he'd just learned, and I hoped he didn't tell me. I couldn't take more bad news.

"That was the vice president," he said, looking back at me but saying nothing else.

I nodded but didn't reply. I guess I hoped if I stayed quiet, the president wouldn't tell me whatever he'd just heard. Maybe it was classified. Maybe it was personal. Regardless, he just stood there quietly for a few moments, looking away. Then he patted me on the shoulder and turned to leave.

I started to breathe again. But then he stopped and turned back to me. Every muscle in my body tensed.

"They just heard from the prison where they're holding Jack Vaughn," the president explained, looking down at the floor. "They found Jack's body."

"What?" I exclaimed.

"Apparently he hanged himself with a bedsheet in his cell. He's dead. Just like that. He's dead."

No one said a word. I could see the shock in everyone's eyes. Surely the word had spread through the staff earlier about Vaughn's arrest. I doubted the president even knew about my involvement in the sting operation that had cemented Vaughn's guilt, but clearly the notion of the CIA director being involved in a conspiracy to kill the president had rattled everyone on board. And now this news compounded everything.

"He left a note," the president said, a vacant look in his eyes. "Don't ask me how . . ." His voice trailed off.

"What did it say, Mr. President?" I asked after we had waited nearly a minute.

"The note simply read, 'I'm sorry. Just tell him I'm sorry. I never imagined . . .' And that was it."

What did that mean? I wondered. Tell who? The president? Someone else? Why hadn't Vaughn referred to Claire? Or his children? And "I never imagined"? What was that supposed to mean? That he didn't know his mistress was working for ISIS? That he didn't know he'd be caught?

A hundred more questions came rushing to mind, but the president just turned and walked away.

72

As soon as the president left, the doctors wheeled Yael away as well.

They said they were taking her for tests. I lay there in pain, staring at the ceiling, reeling from all that had just happened, with no way to move and no one to talk to. Rarely had I ever felt so alone.

I closed my eyes but couldn't sleep. All I could see was Jack Vaughn's body hanging, dangling, twisting. I opened my eyes and glanced at the Iraqi children, all of whom were now sedated and sleeping, but all I could see were images of them in those hideous cages. I turned and stared at the ceiling, but all I could see was Yael and Sharif fighting for their lives in that compound in Alqosh—fighting and, in Sharif's case, losing.

An Air Force nurse soon came by to check my IV and vital signs. "How are you holding up, Mr. Collins?" she asked. "Is everything okay?"

Are you kidding? I wanted to scream. *Do you have any idea what we've all been through?* But I just bit my tongue and nodded.

"Blood pressure's a little high," she said, putting

a note in my chart. "Are you comfortable? Can I get you anything?"

I gritted my teeth. Was there anything I wanted? *Of course there is, lady. How about ironclad proof Yael is going to be okay? How about my friends back from the grave? How about the last few days to have never happened? How about a phone to call home, a computer to write the story, and the Wi-Fi to transmit it back to my boss?* But I just shook my head and stared at the space where Yael's stretcher had been. I imagined the doctors working on her, hooking her up to all kinds of hoses and tubes and monitors, and I was scared for her.

"I'm fine," I lied. "But what about my friend— is she going to be okay?"

"We'll know soon enough," she said.

"She took a terrible blow to the head back there," I said.

"Yes, I know," the nurse replied.

"And her arm is broken," I added.

"We're on it," she insisted.

"And she's got severe burns all over her body," I noted.

"Don't worry, Mr. Collins; we're doing everything we can to take care of her," she assured me. "And when we touch down, we'll get her straight to Walter Reed. We've already alerted them. They're going to be standing by with a first-class team when we get there. Believe me, she's in good hands."

I nodded with gratitude, then wondered if I'd heard her right. "Did you say Walter Reed?"

"Yes, sir."

"The medical center?"

"Yes, sir."

"In Washington?"

"Well, Bethesda, but yes."

"We're not going to Tel Aviv?" I asked, somewhat perplexed.

"No, sir," she said. "Why would you think that?"

"Well, I just thought . . . I mean . . . Yael's Israeli, so, you know, I thought we'd be—"

"What, dropping her off?" she asked.

"Yeah, I guess so."

"Sir, this plane is carrying the president of the United States. We've got one priority, and that's to get the commander in chief back to D.C., back to the White House, as quickly and as safely as possible. That's it. That's our mission. Everything else will have to wait."

"Of course," I said. "Thanks."

"My pleasure, sir. Now you get some rest. We've got a long flight ahead of us."

"I can't sleep."

"Do you want me to give you something?"

"No, no, it's not that; it's just . . ."

"I know. You're worried about Miss Katzir. But I'm sure she'll be fine, Mr. Collins. And I suspect she'll be awake in a few hours. Why don't you get some rest? And when she stirs, I'll be sure to wake you."

"You'd do that?"

"Of course, sir. It would be my pleasure."

"Well, thank you," I said, choking up. "I'm sorry. I'm just . . ."

"It's okay, Mr. Collins. You need to rest. That's it. Just lie there and rest. You're safe with us now."

The funny thing, given the circumstances, was that I actually believed her. As I leaned back on the pillow and stared up at the ceiling, I realized I couldn't remember the last time I'd felt safe. But I did now. Sad, but safe. Mourning and hollow and racked with grief . . . but safe. And it was odd. Good, but odd.

Soon my breathing began to slow. My eyes started getting heavy. And for the first time in what seemed like forever, I began to relax. We'd rescued the president. He was safe. We'd rescued all these children, and they were safe too. Yael was getting the best care she possibly could, and so was I. There was nothing else I could do, nothing but rest and resist the temptation to slide headlong into a depression that would just make everything worse.

For a moment, I craved a drink, but I forced myself to think about something else—something, anything—and fast. I began to think about the story I was going to write. I tried to imagine what I was going to tell Allen first, the moment they let me use a phone. I tried to organize my thoughts and imagine how I was going to capture all that I'd been through and communicate it to a world that wasn't going to hear it any other way. This wasn't just a series of articles. This was a book. And I was no longer going to be under a military censor. My thoughts raced.

Soon the cabin lights were dimmed. Conversations turned to a whisper and then quieted completely. The people on this plane were as spent as I was, and everyone began to settle in for the twelve-hour flight. I glanced up the hallway and noticed a young Air Force officer pulling down all the window shades. Before she got to us, I looked out the window nearest to me and noticed that we had started banking west. It took me a moment to realize exactly where we were, but then I saw the Jordan River. I saw the barrenness of the Judean wilderness below us. I knew then that we were clearing the airspace of the Hashemite Kingdom. We were heading into Israel, toward the Mediterranean, and then home.

And then, as we began to level out, I could see the brave young men flying those Navy fighter jets, our escorts. One of the jets was so close I could have waved to the pilot if I'd wanted to.

Then the young officer arrived, and just before she closed the window shade, she turned to that pilot and caught his eye, and she saluted him. And the pilot saluted back.

And when he did, I broke. My eyes welled up with tears. I got a lump in my throat. I tried to hold back the emotions. They embarrassed me. But I couldn't help it. As the officer closed the last of the window shades and darkness settled on the medical bay, I closed my eyes again and began to shake, began to weep. Quietly. Not so anyone could hear me. I was simply overcome with relief and gratitude beyond measure.

And then, though it felt far from familiar, I quietly said a prayer. I thanked God for rescuing me, for giving me another chance. I asked him to take care of Yael, to bring her back to me safely.

And then I wiped my eyes and closed them and thought about those fighter jets at our side, keeping us safe.

I reached over and inched up the shade. Just a crack. Just to be sure.

The fighter escort was still there.

And no sight had ever looked as good.

TURN THE PAGE

for an excerpt from the next thrilling novel by

JOEL C. ROSENBERG

New York Times bestselling author

★ ★ ★ THE ★ ★ ★
KREMLIN
CONSPIRACY

A gripping tale ripped from future headlines!

PREORDER NOW!

Available in stores and online March 6, 2018.

JOIN THE CONVERSATION AT

www.tyndalefiction.com   CP1292

MOSCOW, RUSSIA

Louisa Sherbatov had just turned six, but she would never turn seven.

The whirling dervish had finally fallen asleep on the couch just before midnight, crashed from a sugar high, still wearing her new magenta dress and matching ribbon in her blonde tresses. Snuggled up on her father's lap, she looked so peaceful, so content as she hugged her favorite stuffed bear and lay surrounded by the dolls and books and sweaters and other gifts she'd received from all her aunts and uncles and grandparents and cousins as well as her friends from the elementary school just down the block at the end of Guryanova Street.

Strewn about her were string and tape and wads of brightly colored wrapping paper. The kitchen sink was stacked high with dirty plates and cups and silverware. The dining room table was still littered with empty bottles of wine and vodka and scraps of leftover birthday pie—strawberry, Louisa's favorite.

The flat was a mess. But the guests were gone and it was Thursday night and the weekend was upon them and honestly, her parents, Feodor and Irina, couldn't have cared less. Their little girl, the only child they had been able to bear after more than a decade and two heartbreaking miscarriages, was happy. Her friends were happy. Their parents were happy. They were happy. Everything else could wait.

Feodor stared down at the two precious women in his life and longed to stay. He had loved planning the party with them both, had loved helping shop for the food, loved helping Irina and her mother make all the preparations, loved seeing the sheer delight on Louisa's face when he'd given her a shiny blue bicycle, her first. But business was business. If he was going to make his flight to Tashkent, he had to leave quickly. So he gently kissed mother and daughter on their foreheads, picked up his suitcase, and slipped out as quietly as he could.

As he stepped out the front door of the apartment building, he was relieved to see the cab he'd ordered waiting for him as planned. He moved briskly to the car, shook hands with the driver, and gave the man his bag. The night air was crisp and fresh. The moon was full, and leaves were beginning to fall and swirl in the light breeze coming from the west. Summer was finally over, thought Feodor as he climbed into the backseat, and not a moment too soon. The sweltering heat. The stifling humidity. The gnawing guilt of not being able to afford even a simple air conditioner, much less a little dacha out in the country where he and Irina and Louisa and maybe his parents or hers could retreat now and again, somewhere in a forest with lots of shade and a sparkling lake for swimming or fishing.

"Thank God, autumn has arrived," he half mumbled to himself as the driver slammed the trunk shut and got back behind the wheel. Growing up, Feodor had always loved the cooler weather. The shorter days. Going back to school. Making new friends. Meeting new teachers. Taking new classes. Fall meant change, and change had always been good to him. Perhaps one day, if he continued to work very hard, he could save enough money to move his family away from 19 Guryanova Street, away from this noisy, dirty, run-down, depressing hovel on the south side of the capital and find some place really lovely and quaint and quiet. Some place worthy of raising a family. Some place with a bit of grass, maybe even a garden where he could till the soil with his own hands and grow his own vegetables.

As the cab began to pull away from the curb, Feodor leaned back in his seat. He closed his eyes and folded his hands on his chest. Yes, autumn had always been a time of new beginnings, and he wondered what this one might bring. He was not rich. He was not successful. But he was content, even hopeful, perhaps for the first time in his life.

He found himself reminiscing about the first time he'd laid eyes on Irina—the first day of middle school, twenty-two years ago. He was so caught up in his memories that he did not notice the car parked just down the street, a white Lada with its headlights off but its engine running. He didn't notice that the front license plate was covered with some sort of masking tape, revealing only the numbers 6 and 2. Nor did he notice the car's driver, nervously smoking a cigarette and tapping on the dashboard, or the two burly men, dressed in black leather jackets and black leather gloves, emerging from the basement of his own building. When the police would later ask about the men and the car, Feodor would be unable to provide any description at all.

What he did remember—what he could never possibly forget—was the deafening explosion behind him. He remembered the searing fireball. He remembered the taxi driver losing control and crashing into a lamppost not fifty meters up the street, and he remembered smashing his head against the plastic screen dividing the front seat from the back. He remembered the ghastly sensation of kicking open the back door of the cab, jumping out into the pavement, blood streaming down his face, heart pounding furiously, and looking up just in time to see his home, the twelve-story apartment building at 19 Guryanova Street, collapse in a blinding flash of fire and ash.

ACKNOWLEDGMENTS
★ ★ ★

Over the years, I've been incredibly fortunate to work with an amazing team for whom I could not be more grateful. They are consummate professionals, love what they do, and approach every detail with creativity and excellence.

Scott Miller, my literary agent, and his team at Trident Media Group are the best in the business.

Mark Taylor, Jeff Johnson, Ron Beers, and Karen Watson at Tyndale House Publishers are a great team, and it has been a true pleasure to work with them over the years. They truly get what I'm trying to do and are always helping me do it better. Their colleagues are absolutely outstanding: Jan Stob, Cheryl Kerwin, Todd Starowitz, Dean Renninger, the entire sales forces, and all the others that make the Tyndale engine hum. And I don't know what I'd do without Jeremy Taylor, my editor extraordinaire.

June Meyers and Nancy Pierce on my November Communications, Inc. team always give 100 percent, and I'm so grateful for their hard work, attention to detail, kind and gentle spirits, and faithfulness in prayer.

I'm so deeply blessed by my family. They have all been so encouraging, patient, and helpful on this adventure from the beginning, and I would never want to do it without them.

Thanks so much to:

My wife, Lynn, with whom I just celebrated twenty-five amazing years of marriage and can't wait for a million more!

Our four wonderful sons—Caleb, Jacob, Jonah, and Noah—who are true gifts from our Father in heaven to Lynn and me, and whom we cherish more than they will ever know.

My parents, Len and Mary Rosenberg, who have encouraged me as a writer since I was just eight years old and haven't given up on me yet. They just celebrated their fiftieth wedding anniversary in the summer of 2015 and have set a great example for our whole family of a marriage rooted in Christ.

The Meyers, Rebeiz, Scoma, and Rosenberg families, who fill our lives with so much love and laughter.

Lastly, but most importantly, I want to say thank you to the fans of these books in the U.S., in Israel, and all over the world. I am so grateful for your e-mails, Facebook messages, tweets, and letters. I only wish I could write these books as fast as you all read them. Thank you so much. I just hope *The First Hostage* manages to live up to your incredibly high (and growing) expectations.

ABOUT THE AUTHOR

★ ★ ★

Joel C. Rosenberg is a *New York Times* bestselling author with more than three million copies sold among his twelve novels (including *The Last Jihad*, *Damascus Countdown*, and *The Auschwitz Escape*), four nonfiction books (including *Epicenter* and *Inside the Revolution*), and a digital short (*Israel at War*). A front-page Sunday *New York Times* profile called him a "force in the capital." He has also been profiled by the *Washington Times* and the *Jerusalem Post* and has been interviewed on ABC's *Nightline*, CNN *Headline News*, FOX News Channel, The History Channel, MSNBC, *The Rush Limbaugh Show*, and *The Sean Hannity Show*.

You can follow him at www.joelrosenberg. com or on Twitter @joelcrosenberg and Facebook: www.facebook.com/JoelCRosenberg.

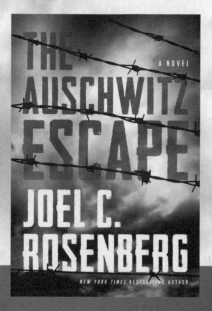